TRAPPED
IN EAST GERMANY

OTHER BOOKS AND AUDIO BOOKS
BY CAROLYN TWEDE FRANK

The Hitler Dilemma

TRAPPED
IN EAST GERMANY

a novel

CAROLYN TWEDE FRANK

Covenant Communications, Inc.

Cover image: *Little Girl Lost* © Catherine Lane; *Set of Keyholes, Keys and Locks Icons* © Gil-Design, courtesy of istockphoto.com; *Russia / Germany: 57,000 surrendered German troops, now prisoners of war, marched through Moscow, 17 July 1944 (b/w photo)* / Pictures from History / Bridgeman Images

Cover design copyright © 2016 by Covenant Communications, Inc.

Published by Covenant Communications, Inc.
American Fork, Utah

Printed in the United States of America
First Printing: July 2016

22 21 20 19 18 17 16   10 9 8 7 6 5 4 3 2 1

ISBN 978-1-52440-053-8

For Karin Graeber Adam, who passed away on October 23, 2015, shortly before the release of this book. I am so sad you were unable to see your amazing life's story in print, but in the pages that follow, may it live on to inspire all those who read it as it has inspired me.

CHAPTER 1

Lockwitz, East Germany, 1953

"I THINK WE SHOULD LEAVE." Karin's heart beat faster than she'd ever remembered. "*Mutti*, I'm willing to go," she petitioned her mother in a tone soft and low but filled with desire. She liked the idea, had even dreamed of it before.

But it scared Karin too. Perhaps part of the fear came from hearing her mother propose escape—Mutti had always obeyed the law.

Mutti glanced across the kitchen table at Karin and gave a nod in response. Mutti then returned her attention to Aunt Anna, who had stopped by their small apartment for a visit and to share a bit of bad news. Mutti reached out, gathering Aunt Anna's hands into hers. "Dear sister, we've weighed your other options. They're all grim."

"I know, Ida, I know!" Aunt Anna said to Mutti. "I'm afraid I'll be a drain on the republic wherever I go." She winced her eyes shut, wetting her lashes with tears. "I'm truly fearful of what this new government will do with old people like me."

"I'm concerned too." Mutti added, "Though I'm not surprised in the least. I don't doubt for a moment the government is capable of seeing that old people 'disappear' when they can no longer contribute to society."

Karin couldn't bear the idea of Aunt Anna being put down like an old plow horse that could no longer work the fields. But her aunt was old and often fell ill. Karin, too, didn't doubt it could happen, that Aunt Anna would just "disappear," as her doctor had warned.

"So we're going to do it?" Karin asked. Apprehension, excitement, and fear bombarded her insides. "We're going to escape from East Germany?"

Aunt Anna let go of Mutti's hands and reached across the table. She gave a gentle pat to Karin's arm. "Dear, it's not that easy to leave. And it is I who is old and in peril, not you. You're only thirteen."

"I'm fourteen next month," Karin said with emphasis.

"Still, I could never expect you," she glanced at Mutti, "or any of your family to come with me."

Mutti looked at Aunt Anna, her eyes heavy with concern. "But you're not well enough to go on your own. If you go, we're coming with you." She skirted her gaze to the apartment's south window, its lace curtains drawn for the evening, their hems folding at angles as they rested atop the singed fabric of the old blue couch. Her expression hardened, and Karin knew what she was thinking: "If that's what we decide to do. This is a decision that cannot be taken lightly. It will require a good amount of time on our knees because it won't be easy."

When had anything in Karin's life been easy? Difficulties only made her more determined not to let the enemy win—whoever they might be this time. She'd felt this way as long as she could remember. Scary things had happened early in her life. Even if she didn't like them, she was used to them.

Karin picked up a salt shaker from the table, letting her fingers glide over the glass, up and down one of their few keepsakes from better days. Her mind reached back, searching for good memories, searching for possible reasons for staying here. It managed to latch on to some happy moments. She felt a smile form on her lips as she remembered the times *Pappa* came home on leave from the army; how he would play with her and toss her in the air. The smile drooped into a frown as she remembered the days he had to make his way back to the war.

Her bottom lip then slipped between her teeth as she remembered the war coming to her. That's when it started, her determination not to let the enemy take the happiness from her life.

She was only five years old when the Allies bombed Berlin. It may as well have been yesterday, not nine years ago, the way the images and explosions still replayed in her mind . . .

Berlin, March 1944

Buckets of sand drew Karin's attention. Someone had left them on the landing of the stairs in their apartment building. She dug her fingers into a bucket and raked them in a circle, making a design in the sand.

"Stop that! That's not to play with." Christine grabbed Karin by the hand and dragged her down the stairs.

Karin wiggled her hand free from her older sister's. "Then why is the sand here?"

"In case of a bomb." Christine motioned for Karin to hurry down the stairs. "If you insist on walking me to the corner, quit asking questions I'm not supposed to answer."

Everyone knew what bombs were. Karin could hear them explode in the distance almost every night. So Christine shouldn't worry about Mutti being upset with her for telling about the sand. Karin just didn't understand what the sand had to do with bombs. But then, she didn't understand a lot of things. The older she got the more things in Berlin changed. They passed another bucket of sand on the bottom landing. Karin couldn't keep back the question. "But how can sand protect us?"

"I don't know." Christine's voice rose. "I really don't this time. I just know that *Herr* Warner is doing everything he can to help make our building safe. I'm sure he's got a good reason for the sand. Now come on, and stop asking questions." She grabbed Karin by the wrist and pulled her out the front door.

The breeze caught Karin's hair and blew it into her face. She pulled the strands of blonde out of her eyes so she could look around at the familiar trees and buildings that made her love the street she lived on. Her home was four stories tall, five if you counted the tiny attic apartment of Herr Warner's, the building supervisor. The ornately carved stone under the eaves and the vibrant red brick made it the prettiest of all the apartment buildings lining both sides of the street as far as she could see.

"Good morning." Christine waved to Herr Warner. He stood over a shrub in the yard, struggling with pruning shears, his hands twisted with age.

"Good morning, my lovely little ladies." Herr Warner removed his hat, displaying his bald head.

Christine giggled. Karin too.

As they walked away, Karin had another question. "Why are all the men old?"

"Pappa's not."

"I mean all the men around here?" Karin held out her hands and twirled around in a circle, indicating their neighborhood.

"Race you to the corner," Christine responded, as if she hadn't heard Karin.

Karin forgot her question and bolted down the sidewalk, determined to beat her ten-year-old sister. Christine's longer legs shot her ahead, arriving at the corner one stride before Karin's. "You win," Karin said, panting. She would like to have won; she'd never won against Christine. But it didn't matter. The best part of the race was just being included in her sister's ideas.

As soon as Karin got back from walking Christine partway to school, Mutti took Karin and dropped her off at the home of Sister Klein, the old lady Mutti knew from church. Mutti did this every day so she could go to work at the family store. After lunch, buttered bread and pickles, Karin weaseled in between the old lady's lace curtains and the window sill. She wanted a better view of the street now that the late-morning rainstorm had passed. It looked so different gazing out onto the street from the old lady's first-floor view rather than the fourth floor she looked out from at home a few blocks down. Not to mention the apartment building across the street was so much more pretty to look at than the old brown one across from Karin's apartment. The building had cream-colored walls with red tiles on the roof and red shutters at each window, giving it a cheerful feel.

Karin stared down the road in the direction of the market that housed the family store. Mutti always called it a store, but it was more like a stall displaying lots of household items. Next to it, a big-nosed lady sold fabric. The old man across the aisle sold leather handbags and *Ranzen*, just like Christine used to carry her books to school.

Puddles pocked the street, and Karin couldn't resist pushing the window up slightly, letting in the fresh scent of rain. When would Mutti get here? Today had been a long day. With the rain, there'd been no going outside to play with other children. Mutti's church friend, who was at least as old as Herr Warner, seemed too busy to play, or talk, or even listen to Karin's questions. And her apartment smelled of cooked cabbage.

Mutti's brown coat came into view. "I see her!" Karin slipped out of the curtains, careful not to hurt them—or let the old lady see that she'd played in them. She ran into the kitchen. "My *Mutter*'s on her way."

"Very well, child." The old lady helped Karin put on her coat. She had her standing by the door as soon as Mutti arrived. Karin grabbed hold of her mother's hand the moment they were outside. She swung their arms back and forth as they strolled down the sidewalk, listening to the birds chirp and the budding leaves flutter in the spring breeze.

Then the drone of a siren sliced into the early evening and erased all pleasant thoughts.

Mutti grasped Karin's hand and squeezed like it was a dish rag that needed to be wrung dry. "This time of day?" she muttered and pulled Karin into a sprint.

"What about Christine?" Karin's legs ached from running so fast.

"Let us hope she's home and not at one of her friends'," Mutti yelled, the blare of the siren smothering her voice to where Karin could barely hear it.

Karin knew Mutti wanted to be all together during an air raid. Karin did too. Sometimes they were stuck down in the cellar a long time before the safe signal was given and they could come out. Christine's company helped the time pass with fun. Mutti only fretted, never saying much. She just hugged Karin and Christine till it almost hurt, like they were rag dolls or something. Karin wished they could just stay in their apartment, in bed. Nothing ever happened during an air raid, just lots of noise. She wanted to ask if she could slow down and then hide under the blankets of her bed in their apartment instead of the cellar. But she kept running.

Bombs sounded in the distance. And then one exploded much closer. Karin stumbled, startled by the blast, her ears ringing. Mutti scooped Karin into her arms and ran faster.

By the time she and Mutti scurried down the narrow stairs into the darkness of the cellar, bombs were exploding every other second it seemed. Dusk's fading light filtered in through a small window. It spread across the cramped room. It revealed the colorless faces of her neighbors. Mostly women and children. They were packed together like sticks of chalk in a box.

"I don't see Christine." Mutti kept hold of Karin's hand and pulled her through the sea of bodies. "I don't see her. Look for her, Karin. Look for her!"

Karin could see nothing now, only bellies and backsides of neighbors.

Mutti's hand squeezed hers extra tight. "I see her! Christine!" Mutti called out.

They maneuvered through the crowd. Karin spotted her sister. She ran and gave Christine a hug. Mutti wrapped her arms around both of them.

Boom!

The explosion sounded closer than the last one. They huddled together and lowered themselves to the hard-packed dirt floor.

Boom! Boom, boom!

"They sound different this time," a voice said between explosions.

Karin couldn't tell who said it. She didn't care. She hugged Mutti tighter.

"They're coming closer." It was Herr Warner's voice, only a little higher pitched than usual.

Boom, boom, boom!

From all sides, Karin felt the mass of bodies press harder, more frantic. A salty, sickening odor of sweat overwhelmed her nose. Or was that what fear smelled like?

Boom! Boom!

"Lord, help us," a woman cried out. Sobs, some muffled, some flowing freely, filled the room like the dust that now made it hard to breathe.

It felt like time never moved as Karin sat there on the dirt floor. The cold penetrated her stockings, adding to the chill of the horrifying sounds. The small window offered little light with evening settling in. Dust from the shaking building above danced in swirls in the setting sun. The corner where Karin huddled with her family remained mostly in shadows. It grew darker. She wanted to turn on the switch to light the single bulb hanging from the ceiling, but she knew that was against the rules during a bombing.

Karin felt herself nodding off to sleep. Many a night she had fallen asleep down here in Mutti's arms.

CRASH!

Karin's eyes popped open. Her body tensed. The walls and ground shook, and she was sure everything was going to explode.

"That one hit us!" screamed a woman's voice

"Stay calm." Herr Warner leaped to his feet. "I don't think it's exploded yet. Everyone out! If it goes, it could take down the whole building."

CHAPTER 2

THE SAFE SIREN FINISHED ITS last drawn-out drone. The skies were finally quiet, but shouts and sobbing filled the streets. Karin huddled in the doorway of the apartment building with her family and neighbors.

Herr Warner emerged from the interior of the building. "Good news. We were hit, but the bomb did not explode. It started a fire, but the men and I put it out before much damage was done. You can return to your homes now." He paused and then softly, with obvious reluctance, said, "Most of you, that is." He stepped out of the doorway to allow passage to the women and children, all noticeably upset and shivering.

Karin clung to Mutti's hand; Christine grasped the other, and they pushed toward the door. Herr Warner latched onto Mutti's elbow and pulled her aside. Karin and Christine couldn't help but follow.

"I'm so sorry, *Frau* Graeber." Herr Warner's eyes appeared heavy with sadness.

"What?"

"You can't return to your apartment."

"Why not?" Mutti's voice projected strength, though Karin could see her mother was exhausted.

Herr Warner ran a hand down his face and clenched his chin. "It appears a fire bomb came through my wall and ended up lodged in your kitchen. As I'd thought, it didn't explode. But it started a fire. It damaged much of your apartment. We were able to put out the flames with the sand from the buckets, so it didn't spread. We can thank the Lord for that."

"Yes, we *can* thank the good Lord for that," Mutti said. "And thank Him it didn't explode and that we were all safe in the cellar. It could have been much worse."

"Is the bomb still in our kitchen?" Karin blurted out. Mutti gave her the mind-your-manners look. Karin didn't care. Fear had forced that question out, and it was still pounding inside her. She wanted to know.

"No." Herr Warner offered a weak smile. "We called the government, and they sent someone out to disarm it and take it away. His smile faded. "But I'm afraid your apartment is not fit to inhabit. The entire front room wall has been blown away. Do you have any family or friends you can stay with tonight?"

"We'll manage." Mutti hugged Karin and Christine close. "What about you, Herr Warner?"

"I have someone, thank you."

Mutti took Karin and Christine by the hands and descended the front steps. They walked slowly down the sidewalk, maneuvering around piles of rubble that had not been there before the air raid.

Karin wanted to ask where they were going. She hoped they would go stay with Liesel, even if it was all the way on the other side of the city. But how would her half-sister fit Karin, Christine, and Mutti into their tiny apartment? Maybe her new husband would be away again at the war. Karin knew that was not a nice thing to hope for. She bit her lip and let Mutti pull her down the street without a word.

Halfway down the block, Mutti spoke over the chaos filling the streets. Her voice was weak, not filled with the confidence Karin was accustomed to. "I hope Sister Klein won't mind if we drop in unannounced . . . at this ungodly hour and without so much as a threadbare blanket to offer."

Christine sniffed back tears. "What if her apartment's been destroyed too?"

"Then God will provide another place for us to go. Faith, Christine."

Karin stood in between Sister Klein's lace curtains and the window, watching Mutti and Christine walk away with boxes in hand. She wanted to stomp her foot and cry so she could go to their apartment too, but she knew it would do no good.

She looked instead out across the neighborhood. Tears moistened her eyes. The apartment building across the street no longer wore the color of fresh cream. Nor did red shutters frame each window. The top two floors were missing. The remaining two were singed black. Was that what her building looked like? Were all her toys burned down to nothing like a log in the stove? What about the green flowered wallpaper she loved?

"What happened?" Karin pointed across the street while gazing up into the face of her babysitter.

Sister Klein sat down beside Karin, draped a bony arm around her shoulder, and peered out the window. "The Americans bombed us. Or maybe it was the Russians. Heavens, I don't know anything anymore."

"Why'd they do that?" Karin gazed into the old lady's eyes, really wanting to know why someone would do something so horrible to someone else.

"Because they're our enemies."

"What are enemies?" Karin had heard the word before, but Mutti never wanted talk about it when Karin asked.

"Enemies? Well . . . how do I explain this to a child? They are mean people. People who hate Germans. People who want to make our lives miserable." She looked at Karin and said, "Miserable means bad, really bad." She returned her gaze to the window, scrunching her face and making it look like a prune. "They don't care if we die. In fact, they want us to die." Wiping her eyes, she abandoned Karin at the window and headed for the other room.

Karin surveyed the exposed fourth floor of the apartment across the street, thinking about the people who were so mean that they ruined not only Karin's home, but this family's too. Cupboards still hung from the wall above a sink; a kitchen table sat on what remained of the floor; even remnants of wallpaper could be seen peeling from the remaining wall, but blackened. With the front wall missing, the apartment reminded Karin of a doll house. But certainly not a doll house she cared to play with. Those people, those enemies as Sister Klein called them, must be really mean people.

Karin moved away from the window, unfamiliar feelings swelling up inside her. They were telling her to be scared. They were telling her to be mad. They were telling her to hate. She didn't like the feelings;

she didn't like to be told what to do. This was all those mean people's fault, and if they wanted her to be miserable, she wasn't going to do it! She forced her mouth into a shaky smile, telling herself she should be glad to stay behind while Mutti and Christine sifted through what remained of their home.

That evening Mutti and Christine returned with three boxes full of belongings. At bedtime as she and Christine lay on the floor, sharing a single blanket, she begged her sister, "Christine? What did it look like, our apartment? Was it all black, or was the wallpaper still green? Was it scary? Did it look like the building across the street?"

"I don't want to talk about it." Christine rolled onto her side and pretended to snore.

CHAPTER 3

KARIN STARED AT THE WALLPAPER in Sister Klein's kitchen. Its brown and orange stripes bored her. It was almost impossible to imagine images from its design like she'd done with the green flowery wallpaper in their kitchen. Giving up, she latched onto her doll, Hilda—the one toy Mutti and Christine had managed to retrieve from the rubble of their home.

She hugged the doll tightly. At least she had Hilda. At least they had Mutti's friend from church nearby, her floor to sleep on, and her roof to keep them warm from the early spring chill. And the old lady had one thing most homes didn't: a phone.

Mutti sat in a big armchair with the phone resting in her lap. Her face appeared more tense than normal. Karin could guess what Mutti was thinking. *How long does it take for Pappa to get a message and call us back?*

Karin brushed Hilda's fabric hand across the striped wallpaper. She danced her across Christine's open book on the table and then tucked her into bed in a make-believe cottage far away from the war. The ring of the phone awoke Hilda, but Hilda didn't mind. Neither did Karin.

Mutti jumped in her seat, sending the phone crashing to the ground. She hurried and picked it up. "Hello, Paul? Is that you?" Mutti's hand shook as she wrapped the cord around her finger. "I'm so glad they were able to locate you."

Pappa? Karin shuffled closer to Mutti.

"I don't know how to tell you this . . . our home was destroyed in the last air raid." Her voice cracked.

Karin planted her feet in front of Mutti, hoping she'd get to talk to Pappa too.

"Yes, the girls are just fine . . . Sister Klein's. But we can't stay here for long . . . Liesel has no room." Mutti turned a shoulder toward Karin as Pappa's voice crackled like static through the receiver.

Karin moved over to the couch. Her mother seemed upset. Something was wrong.

"Sell? But who would be able to buy a store the way things are in Berlin?" Mutti spoke louder than usual.

Karin's insides hurt—Mutti and Pappa had worked hard on that store. And now where would they get money for food?

"I guess I could take what we can use out of it first. But then what?"

Christine crept over from the table with book in hand and nestled next to Karin on the couch. "I'm scared," she muttered as she opened her book and stared at a page. Christine's feelings seemed to spread over to Karin, like a fever, making her sick too.

Mutti held the phone closer to her face. "We'll find another place. More and more people are fleeing Berlin." Her voice then raised in pitch with the words, "Totally away from Berlin?"

Christine's eyes widened. That made Karin even more uncomfortable.

After a long pause Mutti said, "Well, if you feel God is telling you this, then of course. How about Dresden? My sisters will have no room, but Richard's house is big. Maybe he can."

Christine slapped her book closed, glaring at Karin. "What about my friends?" She grabbed Karin's hand. "I don't want to move to Dresden."

It felt like an adventure—almost. Karin had never ridden in a truck before. She had rarely traveled into the countryside. The poorly maintained roads bounced her on Mutti's lap, making the experience even more fun. Christine sat in the middle, next to the old man who smelled of tobacco. Christine hadn't said a word since they had left Berlin. Karin wondered how her sister could be so quiet. Karin, herself, had a truck-bed full of questions.

"I thought you said those three boxes were all that was left of our stuff?" Karin turned and glanced through the back window at the beds, chest of drawers, and charred kitchen chairs.

Mutti patted Karin's hand. "Of the small, very valuable items, Karin. Christine and I couldn't very well have put a bed in one of those boxes, now could we?"

"I guess not."

Mutti made a quick glance through the rear window. "We are very fortunate to have been able to salvage what we did, however."

"Is he leaving Berlin too?" Karin pointed to the driver. "Did his house get hit with a bomb too? Is he moving to Dresden like us?"

"No, missy, your Mutter just hired my truck to help you move." The old man scratched his chin with one hand while the other remained clamped to the jiggling steering wheel. "Though I oft times wished I were leaving Berlin. It's not the place it used to be. But what's a poor person to do? I'm stuck."

"But aren't we poor?" Karin turned to give her mother a glance. "You're always telling us 'we barely scrape by.'"

"We have enough." Mutti gave her a firm look. "I was able to withdraw our small savings from the bank. We'll have that to live on until I can find work."

Christine spoke in a whisper, fading in and out. "Then why did we have to . . . ? If we had enough money, surely we could have found another place . . . in . . . Berlin."

Mutti gave Christine a stern look.

Christine quit talking and pinched her lips together.

"You'll make new friends," Karin assured her sister. "You're so good at that."

"Thanks." Christine straightened a lock of Hilda's yarn hair and gave the doll a half-hearted pat as it rested in Karin's lap.

After what felt like a long time, Karin wiggled out of her mother's lap, having grown tired of sitting there. She slid down and wedged herself between Christine and Mutti, making her sister scoot closer to the smelly man. The skyline of a city became visible in the distance. She turned to Mutti. "Are we going to live on the top floor, just like in Berlin? And can our home have red shutters?"

"Probably not, Karin." Mutti gave her a quick glance. "You have an uncle who owns a farm on the other side of Dresden; that's the city you can see. I'm hoping he will have some sort of work for me. Maybe even a place we can stay."

Christine's head jerked toward Mutti, eyes wide. "You don't know where we'll be living?"

"No." Mutti stared out the windshield as slushy flakes of snow began pelting the glass. "My brother's phone is not working. And there was not quite enough time to receive his response to my letter. But no matter; I've put my trust in the Lord. You girls must do the same."

"Oh." Christine bit her bottom lip. Fear shone in her eyes. "Okay."

Karin gazed at Mutti. If her mother trusted that God would help them find a place to live, then Karin would too. Mutti was good at talking to God.

Soon the tall buildings of the city towered above them as their driver maneuvered his truck through the snowy streets of Dresden. Karin crawled back onto Mutti's lap so she could get a better view of the beautiful building they passed. Was it round? No, more like square with a round dome on top and intricate stone spires topping each corner of the obviously very old building. "What's that?" Karin pointed out the window.

"It's a church," Mutti said.

"Is that where I'll go to Sunday School?" Karin bounced with excitement on Mutti's knee.

"Of course not." Christine stared out the same window but without even a shred of excitement.

"That's the Church of Our Lady, a Lutheran church," Mutti said.

"What about that one?" Karin pointed to a spire in the distance. "Is that a church too?"

"Yes, it is."

As the old man drove them closer, Karin could see more of the church. White stones, carved fancy and stacked in columns, reminded her of a picture of the Manti Temple she'd once seen. Except this building's single steeple almost looked like lace the way it reached into the sky, pillars upon pillars holding up intricately carved layers of stone.

"That's got to be our church, then." Karin opened her eyes extra wide as the magnificent building filled the window.

"No," Mutti said, "that's a Catholic cathedral."

"Why don't we get to go to church in pretty places like these?" Karin settled back into Mutti's lap, remembering the old furniture store they used to meet for church in Berlin.

"Because we're Mormons," Christine said. "Only Catholics and Lutherans have churches like that."

"Why?" Karin asked.

"Those churches have been around for centuries." Mutti leaned toward the window. "Our church is relatively new here. But what we lack in the way of buildings is more than made up for by everything else."

"Mormons, you say?" The truck driver squeezed the steering wheel. It was the first time he had said anything for hours. "Isn't that an American religion?" His voice sounded kind of mean and made Karin uncomfortable.

"Oh, no," Mutti said quickly. "It's not American. It's worldwide." Her legs stiffened, making it difficult for Karin to sit comfortably on her lap. "Be assured, it's one of the few religions Hitler still allows to meet together. The Fuehrer likes the Mormons—likes that we believe in being subject to kings, presidents, rulers, and magistrates, and obeying, sustaining, and upholding the law—that's one of our articles of faith."

Karin thought that was odd, since she knew Mutti and Pappa didn't really like the Fuehrer all that much. And they talked about going to America someday. She opened her mouth, "But—" Christine shot her a look. She closed it.

"We're very German." Mutti hugged Christine and Karin. "As I mentioned before, my husband is a soldier in the German Army."

"Sorry, Frau. I did not mean to accuse you of being pro-American. This ugly war just seems to put everybody on edge—always having to be so careful in what we say."

"It's okay." Mutti looked out the side window. "Girls. Quick . . . doesn't that look fun?" She pointed to children playing in the fresh snow, large flakes no longer adding to its depth. "It looks like they're going to build a snowman."

Karin made a point to look—Mutti never said anything appeared fun. She gazed out the window, only to see a couple of kids stomping a path to the street in the snow. Mutti stared at the children as if they were a picture to be framed.

The old man looked straight ahead, pulling a cigarette from his pocket. He slipped it between his lips and lit its end. Smoke soon filled the cabin. The smell made Karin pinch her nose. She turned on Mutti's lap and looked into her face. "I don't li—"

"Shhh." Mutti put a finger to Karin's lips.

After breathing the smoke of two cigarettes in a row, Mutti turned to the driver and pointed out the window. "That's the house, the white one with the big tree."

The driver pulled the truck to a stop in front of a house on the fringe of the city Karin presumed to be Dresden. With nighttime coming, the home looked gray, but Karin imagined it to be as white as fluffy clouds when the sun shone on it. A large willow tree drooped its snow-covered branches over the sidewalk leading to the front door. Karin couldn't wait to get out of the truck and walk through the crystal-like tunnel formed by the tree.

"Now, you girls be extra careful. The storm's made the walk slippery." Mutti opened the truck's door, lowered herself to the ground, and then helped the girls down. She clung to the opened door, hesitated, and stuck her head back in the truck. "Could you wait here for a minute, please?" After a grunt from the old man, she shut the door and treaded through the snow toward the front door. Christine followed Mutti, stepping carefully.

Karin brought up the rear, giving a little run and then a hop, gliding under the branches of the willow tree, smiling as she slid. The door was already open by the time she made it to the porch. Christine and Mutti blocked the doorway, just standing there talking to some lady with an unpleasant voice. Karin stepped inside and shut the door behind her.

"Yes, Richard got your letter, but . . . you're here sooner than we thought." The lady swept her arm into a room furnished with a long sofa, matching arm chairs, and multiple paintings hanging from the flowered wallpaper. Nothing else in the room seemed to belong. A mattress filled the middle of the room. Two half-naked toddlers jumped on it as a tired-looking woman tried to dress them for bed. A red-headed boy, about Christine's age, perched himself at the edge of the couch and glared at Karin. Karin diverted her gaze and stared at her wet feet.

". . . My sister and her family lost their home, too, from the air raids. Our daughter already shares her room with my Mutter, and . . . well . . ."

A door slammed in what sounded like a rush of wind. Boots clapped across the hard floor, and a tall man walked into the room from the kitchen.

"Uh . . . here's Richard. He'll tell you, too . . . there's no room or work for you here."

CHAPTER 4

WALKING UNDER THE SNOW-COVERED WILLOW tree was not as much fun the second time. Karin would have rather stayed and slept on the crowded floor, even if that red-headed boy continued to pull faces at her. She was tired. She forced her eyes open wide, not wanting Mutti to know and then feel bad. But she wanted, wanted, wanted to go to bed.

Mutti shuffled across the frozen sidewalk toward the idling truck with Karin and Christine in tow. She let go of their hands and opened the truck's door. "Sorry, we've still got a ways to go," she said to the driver. "My brother's got an old farmhouse ten kilometers from here in the village of Wittgensdorf. He'll lead the way." She pointed to the black car Uncle Richard was backing out of the driveway.

Christine climbed back in first, then Karin, then Mutti. The three of them huddled together on the truck's seat as the sun set, taking the daytime warmth with it.

"You realize, Frau, this will cost you extra." The old man pulled onto the road behind Uncle Richard's car.

Karin opened her eyes when the truck lurched to a stop. Mutti opened the door, and cold air rushed in, waking Karin further. The truck's headlights pierced the darkness, lighting the steps of a house with a wrap-around porch. A few lit windows indicated the house had two floors. Other than that, Karin had no clue of her surroundings.

Mutti walked ahead with Uncle Richard, suitcase in hand. "Are you sure that your tenants are willing to share? I mean, to give up three rooms they've grown accustomed to using would not be easy for anyone."

"Nothing is easy for anyone anymore." Uncle Richard inserted a key into the front door with one hand. His other hand held the suitcase Karin and Christine shared. "And don't you worry about my tenants, Ida. They had a choice: share the house with my sister, or move out."

"Oh, but Richard, you know I could never afford the rent they're paying. Not with Paul's paychecks not coming anymore."

"Hopefully that's just a governmental glitch and your money will be coming soon," Uncle Richard said. "For now, it's fortunate for everyone that these tenants decided to stay and share—they know they're lucky just to have a place away from the fighting." He pushed the door open. "They were supposed to have three rooms cleared out by tonight—I just got your letter yesterday. Let's hope they have."

They stepped into a sizeable square hallway with a flight of stairs running up one wall and doors on each of the other walls. Uncle Richard opened one of the doors. A foul stench of sewage wafted into the hall. "This is the toilet. You will have to share that with the Somers."

Before he closed the door, Karin could make out a wooden bench with a circular hole cut into it. It reminded her of the outhouses she'd used during her trip to Prague to visit Pappa at his army base last year. She wasn't thrilled; she preferred toilets that had tanks of water high up on the wall, ones where she could pull a chain and flush all the mess and smell out of sight.

"Your rooms are on the second floor." Uncle Richard headed up the stairs. A motion of his arm told them to follow. They ascended into a square hall similar to the one below, only in place of the front door there was a window. He pointed to one of three doors. "The two rooms behind this door are the Somers' as well." He stepped over to the next door. "This can serve as your kitchen. I realize it's small, but it does have a wood stove you can cook on and a sink with running water." He let them glance into the dark room and hurried to the final door on the wall opposite the stairwell. "The two rooms in here can be used for a bedroom and a living room." He opened the door and flipped on the light. "I'll go see if I can get Herr Somer and his son to help me and the old man bring in the rest of your things."

Karin huddled with Hilda and her favorite little blue patchwork quilt in a corner of the living room next to a stove. She kept hoping someone would build a fire inside its round black belly. Uncle Richard and the smelly old man came into the room. Maybe they would light a fire. Instead they hauled a mattress into the bedroom. Then a bed frame. Then a dresser. Every time they carried in something new, a wave of cold air gushed in from the hall.

She could hear them setting up the bed in the other room when the door opened again. In with the cold air shuffled an unshaven man wearing dirty overalls. He walked in backwards, struggling with one end of their couch. A young man with broad shoulders, and just as unshaven but not nearly so straggly-looking, hefted in the other end of the couch with seeming ease.

The man in overalls glared at Karin. "Where you want this blasted thing?"

An uncomfortable prickle spread down Karin's back. She hunched her shoulders in response.

The young man let his end drop, depositing the couch in the middle of the small living room. "Then how about right here?"

Karin hunched her shoulders again, staring at the young man's clothes.

He squinted at Karin. "What you looking at?"

"Where's your uniform?" She blurted out her thoughts.

"What?"

"Aren't you a soldier? I thought everyone your age was."

"Mind your own business, kid." The young man turned on his heel and headed to the door. "Pap, I'm through helping this lot." He stormed out.

"Ah, Fritz, ignore her; she's a stupid child." The man in overalls followed him into the hall.

Karin lay on the bare floor, huddling closer to Hilda, wishing those men had shut the door behind them—and had not even come at all.

The next morning Karin awoke to the soft folds of her favorite blue quilt wrapped around her. She sat up, looked around and pulled the quilt closer, tighter. Where was Mutti? Where was Christine? She recognized the bed she lay in as her parents'. The chest of drawers in the corner was her family's, but nothing else looked familiar, only scary. A single window lit the room with muted light; either it was early morning or stormy outside. The room held no other furniture—perhaps a good thing, as the room was fairly small. The walls appeared to have been papered once upon a time. Coats of paint now covered any designs, and only the seams could be detected. Karin couldn't decide if they had been painted gray or if the walls were once white and grime had faded their color.

She crawled out of the warmth of the bed to go and find Mutti or Christine. Wind howled through the room's lone window. It beckoned her to shut it. She shivered as she tried to pull the window tighter into the sill. It wouldn't budge. Outside snow danced around the glass, obscuring the ghostly forms of trees and an old barn. She scurried from the room, desperate to find Mutti—or at least Christine.

The living room offered no more warmth than the bedroom—and no signs of Mutti or Christine. Only their blue couch those two men had carried in last night. Its back and one of its arms was singed black—she hadn't noticed that before. There were a few boxes next to a small table and a lamp she didn't recognize. The stove still had no fire lit within. She opened the door and felt a rush of greater cold. Rubbing her arms for warmth, she stepped into the hall.

Which door led to the neighbor's rooms and which led to their kitchen? Mutti and Christine had to be there. She picked the door at the top of the stairs and opened it.

Two teenage girls stood in front a mirror, brushing their long brown hair. Boxes and clothing cluttered two single beds that had been pushed together in haphazard fashion. The youngest-looking girl caught sight of Karin in the mirror and swung around, glaring. "What are you doing in here, you little brat? Isn't enough you took my bedroom, now you want this room too?" She threw a brush across the room.

It hit Karin before she could shut the door. She hurried to the remaining door in the hall, knocked, and ran in.

Christine rummaged through a box of dishes. She glanced up. "You don't have to knock," she said in a quiet voice absent of feelings. She returned her attention to the box that sat on a green table with a black leg—Karin quickly recognized it as theirs from their old apartment, along with three of their four kitchen chairs.

Mutti stoked the fire in a small stove and then pulled a bag of oatmeal from another box. Karin remembered waiting in line with Mutti for hours to fill that box at the market yesterday just before they'd left Berlin.

"Are you hungry?" Mutti walked over to the sink next to the stove and stuck a pot under the tap.

"Yes, Mutti!" Karin felt her stomach growl in anticipation of the mush. She hadn't had a bite to eat since they'd left Berlin. "I'll help set the table." She smiled and scurried toward the table as Mutti poured in a small amount of oats and placed the pot on the stove.

Christine kept her eyes locked on the three bowls she'd pulled from the box. "Why are you so cheerful?"

"I'm not," Karin answered back. Not wanting Christine to disapprove of her actions, she let her smile fall. Though why her sister would chide her for smiling, Karin couldn't understand. She helped Christine place bowls in front of each of the chairs around the table and then watched Mutti at the stove. The speed with which the oatmeal cooked meant there wasn't much. Karin certainly didn't feel like smiling now. "That's not a lot of mush Mutti's making," she mumbled to Christine under her breath. "I'm really hungry."

"Me too," Christine whispered. "Shh."

After breakfast, Mutti cleared the table into the small sink and heated some water on the stove to do the dishes. "I can help." Karin grabbed a dish towel from the ones stacked neatly on a low shelf next to the sink.

"You go play." Mutti nodded toward the door. "Find Hilda. You'll have plenty of work to do before you grow up. Just because the Nazis are robbing you of your childhood doesn't mean I have to."

Karin wasn't exactly sure what Mutti meant, but if her mother wanted her to play with Hilda, then she'd make sure to do it. She slipped into the hall and then through the *correct* door to find her doll.

When she returned to the kitchen, Mutti was drying her hands on her apron. She stepped over to the window as she removed her apron and peered outside. "Christine, you keep an eye on Karin. The snow has stopped. I'm going out to look for work . . . and find out if there's anyone in the village who's Mormon."

"Okay," Christine said, though her sister's expression told Karin she didn't understand.

"Why?" Karin asked the question. "We have money, Mutti. You took some out of the bank before we left. I don't want you to go outside; it's too cold. And maybe the people that live below us are Mormons."

"Huh! I hardly think so," Mutti responded with a glare at the floor. She tightened her lips, pulled her coat from the hooks by the door, and slipped it on. "Karin, sometimes we need to take matters into our own hands rather than wait and hope others will do what they're supposed to. The only one you can trust in delivering what they say they will is the Lord. And that's why I'm looking for other Mormons. I want to see if we can ride with them to church tomorrow. I realize you two have to do without a lot of things right now. That's one thing I insist we will not do without—the Lord. We can't afford that," she said with emphasis and opened the door.

"Can't we just walk by ourselves?" Karin asked.

"Sure enough, if you don't mind a ten-kilometer hike in the snow." Mutti buttoned up her coat.

"Ten kilometers?" Christine pulled a face.

"Yes, the nearest branch meets in Dresden." Mutti wrapped a scarf around her head. "Now, I must be going. You girls take care. I have no idea how long this will take." She stepped into the upper hall and closed the door behind her.

"Now hurry and put on your shoes." Mutti glided over to the window and looked outside. The sun had barely risen, revealing a clear, blue sky. It was the first day the morning sun hadn't hidden behind clouds in the three weeks since they'd moved to Wittgensdorf. "Finally, some good weather," Mutti said. "Church starts at ten. I don't know how long it will take to walk there, so we'll need to get going as soon as I get our lunch packed."

"Lunch?" Karin had barely finished her small bowl of mush.

"It's too far to come home in between Sunday School and sacrament meeting." Mutti slipped three slices of brown bread into her bag. "We'll just stay all day and have a picnic." It looked like she forced a smile.

Karin sat on the floor next to the dying fire in the stove and struggled with her shoelaces. She wondered why Mutti would take them on a picnic in the middle of the winter. But if her mother wanted a picnic, so did Karin.

Christine knelt down at her side. "Here, let me help you." She guided Karin's fingers to make a bow. Leaning close to Karin's ear, she whispered, "Try and be tough today. If you get tired, don't complain. Mutti really wants to go to church."

Karin had tried not to complain lately, and it made her mad that Christine thought she would. "I can walk as far as you and Mutti," she spoke back to her sister in a voice nothing close to a whisper. "I want a picnic. And I want to go to church too." She jumped to her feet and put on her coat. "But why are we going now?"

"Because it will take several hours to get there," Mutti said while stepping out the door.

Christine ushered Karin into the hall behind their mother. "Shhh," she hissed behind a finger pressed to her lips. "It's early. You need to be more quiet."

Brunhilde, the youngest of the Somers' daughters, closed the door to the toilet as they came down the stairs. "My, my, aren't we up early on a Sunday morning?" Her long hair rested on her shoulders in tangles, and her face, as always, didn't appear the least bit excited to see Karin and her family.

"We're going to church," Karin said. "Would you like to come with us?" She wanted to tell Brunhilde that she might smile more often if she went to church, but Christine kicked her ankle before she could say anything else.

"Church?" Brunhilde's face contorted into a grimace. "Are you kidding me? Sunday is the only day I get to relax. Besides, religion is a waste of time. Tell me all your prayers are helping us. Go ahead; tell me they're helping Germany. Humph!" She cinched the sash of her thick robe tighter as she squeezed past them and trudged up the stairs.

"Come on." Mutti put an arm around Karin and guided her out the front door.

Sunshine peeked above the leafless trees in the distance. The early February air nipped at Karin's ears, and she buttoned up her coat. Karin and Christine strolled a pace behind Mutti down the lane that ran through the village of Wittgensdorf. Only cottages, and the occasional two-story stucco house like the one they shared with the Somers, lined the dirt road. "Where's the market and the shops?" she asked as her neck craned for her eyes to make a final scan.

"Mutti already told you last week; Wittgensdorf has no shops," Christine said like she was tired of telling that to Karin.

"Then where do we get our food?" Karin hadn't wanted to listen to Mutti. She wanted to believe Mutti was just too busy to go shopping— that's why there was no food in the house.

"Quit your gawking, and keep up." Christine motioned forward. "And quit expecting this place to be like home. This is *not* Berlin!"

Mutti glanced back over her shoulder. "What are you girls talking about?"

"Nothing important," Christine said.

Karin wondered why Christine would say such a thing. Food was important. Karin had really tried not to complain about the taste of the things Mutti had cooked since they came to Wittgensdorf. Taste wasn't that hard to go without. But not having anything to taste was.

By the time the skyline of Dresden came into view, Karin's toes were numb from the cold. Her feet hurt from walking, and her legs wanted to go to bed. The city was beautiful with its multiple church spires reaching above the tops of the trees. At the moment, she wanted to perch herself on the stone wall that ran along the road and stare at the church with the round roof and four steeples—and take off her shoes and rub her cold, tired feet.

She tried to ignore the pain and kept going.

It felt like a long, long time after she'd spotted the fancy church before they actually made it to where pastures slipped away and tall buildings consumed her view.

Mutti pulled a piece of paper from her handbag and studied the writing it held. She glanced up at a nearby street sign and then motioned with her hand. "This way."

Karin and Christine followed, weaving their way through pedestrians and busy streets. Christine finally wore a smile on her face.

"Do you miss living in a city?" Karin asked.

Christine's smile vanished. "Yes."

Karin didn't really care either way—as long as she had Mutti and Christine with her and knew Pappa could find them and come home to them after the war.

Mutti slowed her steps as she came to a corner bearing a streetcar sign. More people soon joined them on the sidewalk. After several minutes, a street car stopped, and everyone filed in. As the car clicked down its track, Karin leaned past Christine and stared out the window. "This city is prettier than Berlin."

Christine joined Karin in leaning and gazing out the window. "No, it's not," Christine said before she really took any time to look. She shifted her body back in place, tightened her lips, and stared straight ahead, looking like she was already in church listening to a talk. As the streetcar continued down its track, Christine glanced out the window here and there. The more she glanced, the lighter her eyes became, making Karin feel lighter as well—she didn't like it when her sister went silent and acted like a grownup.

A few blocks down the road when Christine sneaked a look out the window, her eyes lingered. Then she gasped and pointed. "Oh, look, Mutti, that apartment building. It looks almost just like ours back home." The four-story white building held a "for rent" sign in one of the bottom windows. "And it has an apartment for rent. Please, could we check it out on our way home from church?"

"No." Mutti folded her arms across her lap, giving the red brick apartments only a fleeting glance. "First, that is not an appropriate activity for a Sunday. Second, we have a place to live. I feel strongly that is where we need to be at the moment, and that is where we will be staying."

Christine quit looking out the window and stared at her feet this time instead of straight ahead.

Karin had to jab Christine with an elbow when Mutti stood to exit. They waited at the corner a few minutes before they caught another car. This time Christine glanced out the window even less. Just because Karin's sister didn't want to enjoy the view, it didn't mean Karin wanted to stare at the floor. She leaned over Christine's lap and gazed with wide eyes at the fancy carved stone trimming on building after building. Mutti, too, leaned toward the window but seemed intent on looking at street signs.

Mutti stood. "This is the street," she announced and motioned for Karin and Christine to stand. The street car stopped. They filed out the back exit and headed down a street that wasn't nearly as interesting as those Karin had seen from the street car. Buildings lined both sides of the road. Each blended into the other with identical window placement within the flat face of each structure. Only varying shades of brown and gray differentiated them. The only structure that warranted attention was a clock tower belonging to a building in the block beyond.

Karin wished she knew how to tell time. The little hand on the clock had moved past three numbers since they'd left home. Her tired toes wiggled inside her shoes, telling her it had been a long time.

Mutti pointed to a dark-brown building in the middle of the block with the number 135 formed out of gray metal and attached to the stucco above the door. "That's it," Mutti said. "And we've made it just in time."

Karin leaned her head back and examined the building from the roof to the street. The place in Berlin where they used to go to church was much nicer. With all the pretty places she'd seen in this city, why did their church have to be at this one? Unhappy feelings made her blurt out her thoughts. "This place looks ugly." She rushed her hand to her lips, stopping the rest of her words before she told all of what she felt. Mutti didn't like complaining. But it was more than that—Mutti didn't need to hear her complain. Karin could tell that from the way Mutti's eyes drooped. "But that's okay," Karin said a little faster than normal. "Maybe it's pretty inside." She grabbed Mutti's hand and Christine's hand and tugged them both toward the door. "Let's go find out."

Karin's Sunday School class got out a little early. She headed to the big room where everyone had met at the beginning of church. Mutti still sat in a row of folding chairs with the other adults at the front of the makeshift chapel. Karin climbed onto one of the folding chairs at the back of the long room along with some of the other children from her class and tried to wait quietly.

She heard a chair scuff against the hard wood floor and turned to see who was disturbing the chair next to her. Christine plopped onto the folding chair. After a moment or two of sitting quietly with her arms folded, she leaned toward Karin and whispered, "We learned about the children of Israel in our class. It kind of reminded me of us."

"I don't know that story," Karin said.

Christine stared at the ceiling as if trying to figure something out. "Funny thing, the teacher said she'd wanted to tell the story last week, but the Gestapo men were there—they used to visit our ward back in Berlin too. She said she couldn't tell us Old Testament stories if they were there. Why would the Gestapo want to go to church?" She shifted her gaze back to Karin. "Anyway, it's the story of Moses."

"Oh."

"Remember, Moses leads God's people out of Egypt, where they had lived forever, into the wilderness. And then they wandered around for forty years without a real home to call their own." Christine's hand moved to her stomach. "At least God gave them manna to eat every morning. I wish *we* had manna on our doorstep every morning."

Karin looked up at Christine, trying to understand why her sister would wish for such a thing. "I'd like some of that manna stuff too. But not on our doorstep. Brunhilde and Ella might step in it . . . or eat it up first." If she was going to wish for something, why not wish for it in the kitchen—and that the Somer sisters didn't have to share the top floor with them?

Christine rolled her eyes. She folded her arms and slouched in her chair. "Never mind. You're too young to understand."

"No, I'm not!" Karin stomped her foot. "I'm five."

CHAPTER 5

Wittgensdorf, 1945

KARIN DANCED HILDA ACROSS THE stove, imagining Pappa was home and they all lived in a faraway land where it was always warm and February rainstorms never made their house cold. They had lived in this house for almost a year now, and it was still cold even though Mutti had said, "Things will get better."

"Karin!" Christine called out. She was curled up on the couch with a quilt and a book. "Get away from there. You're going to burn your doll."

"No, I'm not! The fire's out." Karin didn't want to move away from the stove. It still held a bit of warmth from breakfast. "Why can't we burn some wood while Mutti's gone?"

"Because she said no."

"But there's still three logs left from what we gathered yesterday."

"Karin!" Christine furrowed her eyebrows.

A wave of cold air blew in from the shared hall and chilled Karin's back. She turned around to see Mutti scurrying into the kitchen.

"I've found a job!" Mutti wore a wide smile.

"That's wonderful." Christine clapped her hands together. "Where?"

"The farmer in the big white house down the lane said I could work for him. There won't be much for me to do until planting season, and then he can only pay me in produce."

"But at least it's a job," Christine said.

Karin wondered if produce was worth more than a *pfennig*. "Oh boy!" Karin added, not really caring. It meant there'd be more food to eat. Maybe they could buy some coal too.

Mutti rushed to the shelf above the sink and pulled down the loaf of bread she'd made yesterday. "He wants me to come this afternoon to clean out his packing shed. You girls hurry and have lunch so we can go."

"We?" Christine said.

"Yes, 'we.' He said I could bring you girls along to help me. Let's hurry now. I want to get started so we can finish before dark. There are no lights in his shed." Mutti cut two slices of bread, giving them to Karin and Christine.

"You forgot to cut you a piece." Karin pointed to the bread.

"I'm fine. I'm not that hungry."

How could Mutti not be hungry? It was so good. Karin chomped into her bread, taking huge bites, trying to hurry the salty-sweet mouthful into her stomach.

"But, Mutti, you're going to be working all day." Christine held her bread close to her mouth but had not yet taken a bite. Her lips curved down. "Won't you get hungry before supper?" She broke her bread in two and held a half toward Mutti. "Have some of mine."

"No, that's yours." Mutti waved a hand. She stared at the loaf, hesitated, and then sliced. "I *do* have a job now . . . after all." She picked up her thin slice and devoured it with the same big bites Karin had taken. Before she wrapped the bread back up in the towel, she quickly cut another slice, chopped it in two, and handed a half piece to Karin and Christine. "As soon as you finish eating, bundle up in your warmest clothes, and we'll get going."

Cold penetrated Karin's coat when she stepped onto the porch behind Mutti and Christine. She longed to be back in the kitchen—even without a fire in the stove. "I want to go back upstairs and play with Hilda," Karin said, jutting out her lower lip. She didn't want to be outside with the wind stirring the clouds like dark-gray cream in a churn.

Mutti shot her a tight-lipped glare.

Karin especially wanted to go back when she spotted Frau Somer walking toward them on the stone path that led to the porch steps. She rarely saw the tall, lanky woman who wore her graying hair pulled back so tight in a bun that it made her eyes look like narrow slits. Karin was fine with not seeing much of that woman. She figured Mutti was too. Although Mutti never said anything bad about Frau Somer, Karin noticed Mutti stiffen whenever she spoke to the woman or mentioned her in conversation.

"Good afternoon," Mutti said without emotion as Frau Somer approached them on the path.

"I suppose." Frau Somer cinched her coat tighter at her neck. "Where are you and your ducklings off to? It's not exactly picnic weather—at least not for the local folk."

"I'm going to work." Mutti squared her shoulders. "My employer said I could bring my children along today to help me."

"So you've finally found a job, have you?" Frau Somer slowed to a stop as she and Mutti met up.

"Yes, Frau," Mutti responded. "Herr Reinhart hired me to do odd jobs around his farm."

"Isn't that nice? I s'pose I don't need to tell you how lucky you are. With more and more of your kind flooding into the area, I'm amazed you found anything."

"And what exactly would that 'kind' be?" Mutti's voice took on the slow, stern tone it often did when Karin would try her mother's patience.

"Refugees, of course." Frau Somer glanced into the churning sky. "Thank God Dresden is a cultural center. It has no military value. The powers of heaven have seen fit to spare our city from the hell of an Allied attack." She returned her gaze to Mutti. "But all you damned outsiders are practically as bad as bombs. You're ruining the whole area around Dresden—crowding us locals out, eating our food, taking our jobs."

"Well, don't worry," Mutti said through stiffened lips. "I'm not taking a job from any in your family." She whisked Karin and Christine away and scurried down the path. Once on the lane, she muttered under her breath, "Especially not your grown son's. No, he can continue working at his Pappa's garage while my Paul labors at the front." She rushed her hand to her lips. Her eyes seemed to beg. "Sorry, children. Forgive me, please." She urged them onward, leading them briskly through the village.

The farmer's packing shed lay nestled in trees at the edge of Wittgensdorf. The long, narrow structure appeared to lean slightly to one side. Dingy white paint had flaked off its boards, making the shed appear more gray-brown than white.

When Karin stepped inside, the smell of mold and wet soil mixed with rotten fruit filled her nose. Round baskets of varying size lay strewn on tabletops and on the ground. Cobwebs clung to the rafters like a dusting of spun sugar. *Yum*, why did she have to think of sugar? Mutti hadn't bought any for such a long, long time. Karin forced her thoughts toward the broom Mutti held out.

Karin kept her coat on as Mutti set her to work sweeping the hard-packed dirt floor, the temperature inside the shed only slightly less cold than outside. Every time Christine opened the door to take out a load of baskets to knock the dirt from inside them, more cold air rushed in. She always seemed to spill a few rotten apples and dead leaves on the floor in the process. Karin's fingers grew numb. Her arms felt like they would fall off from all the sweeping. The delicious taste of Mutti's bread kept replaying in her mind, making her stomach wish for another slice.

After what seemed like fifty hours, the shed was clean enough to suit her mother. Mutti nodded and then said, "You girls wait here while I go get the farmer." She slipped out the door and returned with a gray-haired man in overalls. "Herr Reinhart," she said to the man, "I'd like you to meet my helpers. These are my daughters, Christine and Karin." Mutti pointed first to Christine then Karin.

Unlike most people Karin knew, Herr Reinhart's belly was round. He scanned the length of the building. "Ah, fine job," he said. "Unfortunately, I don't have much to give you in the way of fruits and vegetables at the moment. But your work certainly deserves payment." He pulled something from his pocket. He reached out to Mutti, dropping a few coins in her hand.

Mutti accepted the payment with a gracious smile. "Thank you," she said.

Karin watched Mutti slip the coins in her pocket. "What good will that money do us in Wittgensdorf?" Karin spoke up. "There are no shops. I'd rather have the fruit and vegetables."

"Shush," Christine said, and Mutti gave her a warning glance.

The farmer chuckled behind his big hand. He turned to Karin. "Hey, I've got something I think you'd enjoy. Would you like to come and see it?" He looked to Mutti. "Would that be all right?"

Mutti gave him a nod, and he led them outside.

Anxious to see, Karin ran alongside him as his wide steps led them through the orchard. When they neared the barn, smells Karin had never before experienced filled her nose. They stunk but smelled kind of enjoyable at the same time. Neighs and snorts of an animal sent happy goose bumps down her arms. "It's a horse, isn't it?" Karin ran ahead.

"Not just *a* horse." The farmer easily caught up with her.

"I don't get to see many horses." Karin's feet practically danced.

"As you've lived in the city most of your life, I guessed that would be the case," the farmer said. "Things are different out here, thank goodness." He unlatched the barn door and swung it open.

Its big, old hinges squeaked at the same time Karin squealed with delight. "Look at him, Christine; he's so pretty! And he's so, so big. Look, Mutti. His feet are as big as dinner plates."

"Those are called hooves, Karin. And I think it's a she, not a he." Mutti glanced at the farmer as they stepped inside the barn. "Isn't that right?"

The farmer nodded.

"What's her name?" Christine asked.

"Maria," the farmer said.

"Can I ride her?" Karin hopped on one leg then the other.

"Sorry, little Karin, she's a work horse—bred for plowing, not riding. Besides, she just gave birth a few weeks ago."

"There's a baby horse too?" Christine stretched her neck, looking around the big horse.

Karin's eyes immediately focused in on a dark patch she hadn't paid much notice until now. It nestled amongst the straw on the ground. "There!" She cried and pointed as the patch of color stirred in the straw. An adorable creature struggled up onto its legs. Its chestnut-colored hide glistened in the light that streamed through the barn's open door. Longer hair, the color of cream, flowed from the base of its spindly legs, mostly covering a set of hooves that looked too big for a baby. That same creamy white formed its mane and a sun-shaped patch above its big brown eyes.

"She's beautiful." Karin looked up at the farmer, wanting so very much to rush over and hug that baby horse. It was hard to keep her feet in place.

"This one's a he." The farmer pointed to the baby horse. "And he's old enough now that Maria here should let you touch him. Would you girls like that?"

Karin couldn't find her voice, so she nodded her head over and over again.

Christine clung to Mutti's side. "Are you sure its Mutter won't care?"

"I'll hold her bridle," the farmer said. "You'll be just fine."

Karin ran and wrapped her arms around the baby horse's neck.

Christine walked over slowly. She paused, lifted her hand, and petted the patch between his eyes. "He's so tall. I thought a colt would be much smaller."

"Like I said, these are work horses," the farmer said as he stroked the neck of the mother horse. "When that little fellow is full grown, he'll be almost half again as big as a regular horse. You'd need a ladder to mount him—if he'd even let you ride him. Probably wouldn't. He's not bred for that."

Karin switched places with Christine, reaching all the way up to stroke the white patch between his eyes while Christine hugged the baby horse's neck. "What's his name?" Karin glanced up to the farmer.

"Hasn't got one yet." The farmer looked over at Mutti, who seemed to be enjoying watching them fuss over the newborn horse. "I was thinking of naming him Adolf, you know, after the Fuehrer."

Mutti's face lost all expression.

"The Fuehrer ultimately, after all, was the one who gave this farm the mare, Maria. Also the Pappa—a fine stallion who's out grazing in the pasture right now. Since the war's made it impossible to keep my tractor in fuel, I petitioned the government for help, and I was given this little fellow's mother and father. I just thought Adolf might be fitting."

"But Adolf is such an old man's name," Karin said, not liking the name one bit. "It doesn't fit him at all."

"Karin!" Mutti's face took on an expression of fear.

The farmer studied the small horse, his head cocking to one side. "Perhaps you are right, child." He looked to Karin and Christine. "What would you girls suggest?"

The baby horse's soft nose nudged Karin's cheek as if he was encouraging her to come up with a better name. Giggling, she pulled away, her eyes catching sight of the cream-colored patch between his eyes. "*Sonnenschein*! That's what you should name him."

"But he's a boy," Christine said. "Sonnenschein sounds like a girl's name."

"But he has a patch like a sun," Karin stroked his forehead, "and he makes me feel happy like sunshine does."

"You're right." Christine resumed hugging. "He does."

"Sonnenschein it is." The farmer put his arms around Karin and Christine and pulled them away. "And right now, he needs his dinner."

Sonnenschein looked at Karin one last time with those big brown eyes and then wobbled over to his mother, nuzzled her udder, and began to nurse.

Karin could feel the smile on her face stretching her cheeks as wide as they could move. She skipped while everyone else walked out of the barn. Most of the clouds had cleared away. Karin's eyes wandered up. Pink and gold kissed remnants of clouds that framed the setting sun. Her gaze shifted to clear parts of the sky. What looked like a silhouette of an airplane moved across the beautiful scenery. Another joined. Then another, filling the gray-blue with black specks. The hum of engines followed. And then the cry of a siren.

The farmer looked up. "Hurry home!" He bolted toward the farmhouse. Over his shoulder he yelled, "It appears they're headed to Dresden, but you never know."

Mutti grabbed Karin's hand, and they ran.

All the way to the other side of the village.

When they veered from the lane onto the stone path to their house, Karin asked, panting hard, "Are we going to the cellar?"

"There is no cellar." Mutti pulled Karin and Christine up the porch steps.

"No cellar!" Christine screamed. "Then where do we go?" The roar of the airplanes in the distance hummed louder now.

Mutti threw open the front door and motioned to the stairs. "We'll just hunker down the best we can and pray those planes *are* headed to Dresden." She pushed Karin and Christine up from behind. Mutti guided them to the bedroom. As they crawled under the bed, Mutti gasped, "My Anna, my Sophronia, my Richard!" She sucked back a sob. "Dear God, please, please protect them too."

Karin knew her aunts and uncle lived in Dresden. She knew what happened in air raids. The urge to cry pushed hard from within. She couldn't hold back. The tears came.

CHAPTER 6

AFTER THE SIRENS STOPPED BLARING, Karin started to crawl out from underneath the bed. Mutti reached across Christine's belly and grabbed the sleeve of Karin's coat, pulling her back close. "No, wait a few minutes longer—to be sure no bombs are coming."

Karin waited for what felt like hours. Using her arm as a pillow, she tried to get comfortable on the hard floor. "I want to lie on top of the bed. Under the covers. Nothing's happening."

"Karin!" Christine elbowed her.

"But it's not." Karin elbowed her back.

"All right. I suppose it's safe now." Mutti gently nudged Christine and Karin. They crawled out from underneath the bed. After they stood, Mutti brushed off her dress. Karin didn't bother—Mutti kept everything so tidy. Even under the bed. "Let's get into the kitchen so I can build a fire and make supper," Mutti said.

Light filtered in through the hall window as Karin followed Mutti into the kitchen. The sun had already set. What was that eerie glow that lit up the outside? She crept toward the window.

Christine looked over at Karin just before stepping into the kitchen. "What are you doing?"

"It looks like fireworks." Karin pressed her nose against the cold glass, barely reaching to the bottom of the window. "Come see!"

"Where?" Christine's feet clapped across the hall floor. She stood next to Karin and stared out the window.

"There, beyond those hills." Karin pulled her nose away from the glass, pointing straight ahead. "See the sparkly lights falling from the sky. They're lighting up the night. Isn't it pretty?"

Christine pulled Karin's hand down. "I don't think those are fireworks."

"Of course they're fireworks," Karin said, certain her sister was wrong. She startled and jerked around.

Mutti approached. A worried look darkened her face. "*Ja*, they are fireworks. Come away from that window. Hurry! Your supper's ready." Mutti pulled Karin away and ushered her into the kitchen as if a big, hot meal awaited them.

After supper, Karin didn't want to go to bed. Mutti scooted her and Christine off to the bedroom like it was late and they needed to hurry and climb under the covers or they'd miss out on the entire night's sleep. Karin tried to look out the window as she was rushed through the hall. Were the fireworks still going? She couldn't see; Mutti was in the way.

After prayers and a story, Mutti kissed Karin and Christine on the forehead. "You girls go to sleep now. I'll be in after I finish up my work in the kitchen."

Karin sat up. "I can come help. I'm not tired."

"No." Mutti urged her back down into the bed the three of them shared. "You go to sleep." She hurried and turned off the lamp and shut the door.

Karin lay in bed, eyes wide open. Though the curtains in the bedroom were drawn, a hint of orange light seeped into the room. Now that there were no dishes making noises or people talking, she heard strange sounds pounding faintly at the walls. She crawled out of the covers, grabbing her robe at the foot of the bed. *Fireworks?*

"Karin, get back to bed," Christine said. "You heard Mutti."

Karin wanted to look out the hall window, toward the city. No one else seemed to be interested in the fireworks, even Christine. "I don't want to."

"Karin!"

"I . . . I've got to go to the toilet," Karin said, putting on her robe and proud of her good excuse.

"Then be quick and quiet so Mutti doesn't hear you."

"Okay." Karin slipped out into the hall.

The yellow-orange light glowed brighter from that window. Karin crept over and peered through the bottom of the glass. She pushed up the sash and heard thuds and pops accompany the faraway sounds that pounded at the night.

A door creaked.

Karin shut the window.

Footsteps clomped up the stairs. With only the light streaming in through the window, it was hard to see well, but Karin could make out Brunhilde emerging at the top of the steps. Her long brown hair was worked into two braids, one on each side of her face. Ella followed. They treaded over and stood behind Karin. Both of their jaws dropped as they gazed out the window. "Still going?" Brunhilde said.

"You like the fireworks too?" Karin asked.

"Little girl, those aren't fireworks!" Ella looked down her long nose at Karin through a pair of wire-framed glasses. A glow of orange reflected off the lenses. Her short, red hair seemed to come alive despite the dark hall.

"My name's Karin."

"Okay, *Karin*. Those aren't fireworks. They're bombs!" Ella clamped a hand onto Karin's shoulder as she leaned toward the window. "Actually, they're flares the planes drop first so they can see where to drop the bombs." Her grasp tightened, and her voice wavered. "And they're hitting Dresden good. All that light . . . the whole city must be on fire."

Karin gasped. "Maybe not the whole city."

"Let's hope not."

Brunhilde leaned over Karin's shoulder and peered intently through the window. "The Allies are such barbarians; they'll make sure they destroy every last church in Dresden. And person."

"Like the one with the lacy steeple?" Karin asked. It reminded her of the picture of the Manti Temple. Then she thought about her Aunt Anna, who lived in Dresden. Then about Aunt Sophronia and Uncle Richard, whom she didn't really know that well. "Those aren't bombs. They're fireworks! My *Mutti* said so."

"Well, she was wrong." Ella backed away from the window.

"Maybe they're special bombs—ones that don't hurt anything."

"Don't get your hopes up," Ella said.

Karin turned, intent on Ella's every word. "Why not?" She gazed at the grown girl, the orange glow from the window lighting the low-neck dress that showed the tops of her bosoms.

"Sorry, *Liebchen*, that's war." Ella patted Karin on the head. "And right now Germany's losing the war. All its good soldiers are either captured or dead."

"No!" Pappa couldn't be captured or dead. He just couldn't!

Brunhilde pulled away from the window and moved to her older sister's side. She hugged herself like she was scared. "Ella's right, little *von*-Karin. It's only boy soldiers fighting for us now."

Anger swelled inside Karin. It wasn't fair. "Fritz is big! Why isn't he fighting?"

"Because our Pappa is smart." Ella turned and motioned to Burnhilde to follow. "And knows the right people," she added, walking toward their door, her back to Karin.

The door to the kitchen swung open. Light from the lamp above the stove shot into the hall—along with Mutti. She halted when she spotted the Somer sisters. Her gaze moved to Karin, concern filling her eyes and pulling down her jaw. "Karin! Get to bed. Now!"

The Somer sisters slipped out of sight, and Karin ran back into the bedroom. Christine's slow, steady breaths told Karin her sister was asleep. She knelt beside the bed and offered an extra prayer for the night. "Heavenly Father, please let Pappa be alive. Please let him come home safe . . ."

The following night, as Mutti whisked her and Christine off to bed, Karin caught a glimpse of orange light in the hall window. She stayed put in bed with her pillow over her ears after Mutti's story and kiss. Ella and Brunhilde had destroyed Karin's desire to sneak out of bed and stare at the distant lights in the sky.

The next day Karin hugged Hilda tighter than ever as she curled up on a kitchen chair while Mutti made breakfast. There were no make-believe adventures to faraway lands or even dancing in warm, sunny places with lots of food awaiting them after their performance, only hugs and rocking back and forth, worrying more about Pappa than ever before. "When is Pappa going to send us a letter?" Karin asked.

Mutti set down her spoon and gazed at Karin with sad-looking eyes. "I don't know, Karin." She returned the spoon to the pot of porridge and stirred it like it was thick.

The mush didn't even taste that good. Karin ate it anyway. It would help keep her stomach from growling so much before supper—Mutti had told them there would be no more lunches until the farm started producing. She scraped her bowl clean and hopped down from the chair. Though the thudding sounds no longer pounded through the air when all was quiet, what if they returned? She tried not to think about it while carrying her dishes to the sink. As she headed to her coat and scarf by the door, she announced, "I want to go for a walk."

Mutti glanced at the window. Grey filled each pane, and wind howled through the crack. "Today? Why not stay inside and play with Hilda?"

"Because she wants to go for a walk too," Karin said. "Just a short one. Just down to Herr Schmitt's."

"Ah," Mutti responded like she understood. "No need to walk all the way down there in the cold. Perhaps he'll deliver the post today. Besides, what if there's still a chance an air—" Mutti rushed a finger to her mouth and chewed on a nail. She removed her finger and uttered softly, "Just stay inside today. Enough said."

That night there was no orange glow streaming in through the hall window. Mutti let Karin run over and peer out on her way to bed. Only darkness and the silhouette of trees touched by the moonlight could be seen.

The next day Mutti put on her coat and scarf after breakfast. "Christine, keep an eye on Karin. I've got to go speak with Herr Reinhart."

"Who?" Karin scrunched her forehead.

Christine looked up from the book she was reading. "Her boss, the farmer."

After Mutti left, Karin tried to play with Hilda, but she kept thinking about what Brunhilde had said. She needed to know Pappa was okay. The only way to know that was to get a letter. She tucked her doll into a box with an old dish towel for a quilt, stepped over to the door, and grabbed her coat. "Christine, let's go visit Herr Schmitt." She pulled Christine's coat from the hook and held it out.

"Mutti told you not to. You're to stay put." Christine took the coat and hung it back up.

"That was yesterday. She didn't say it today." Karin tugged at Christine's sleeve. "Please, come. If you don't, I'll sneak out and go anyway."

"Karin!" Christine shook Karin's hand loose. "Stop it."

"If you don't, Mutti will be mad at you for not watching me."

"Oh!" Christine reached for her coat. "All right!"

Karin stared at the hall window before she headed down the stairs. Only dark, billowing clouds could be seen. Not a hint of orange light. She scurried down the stairs in front of Christine.

"What's the hurry?" Christine caught up with her outside on the porch. "Herr Schmitt isn't going to have any mail for us. He never does."

"I still want to go. What if he does and he doesn't want to come out in the cold today?"

Christine rolled her eyes. She buttoned her coat at the neck as she walked down the stone path next to Karin.

The big pine tree in Herr Schmitt's yard swayed with the wind. Karin swung open the white picket gate and stopped. A rush of fear hit her—he was a big man . . . and not just the postman; he was the *Burgermeister*, a policeman, too. She wasn't used to talking to grown-ups without someone like Mutti next to her. Christine didn't count. Her sister rarely spoke to adults without being spoken to first.

"You want to go home?" Christine's scratchy voice sounded like she hoped that was the case.

"No." Karin shut the gate behind them, grabbed Christine by the hand, and pulled her to the front door. She knocked twice.

The door opened barely wide enough for Herr Schmitt's round face and bushy moustache to poke through. His eyes seemed to light up. "Ah, what brings you two pretty little *Frauleins* out on such a blustery day?"

Karin swallowed hard—Herr Schmitt towered above her. "We came to see if you had any post for us? I'm hoping for a letter from Pappa."

"A letter? Hmmm . . ." Herr Schmitt's plump cheeks sagged. "It's Karin Graeber, isn't it?" he asked, looking her in the eye. He glanced over. "And you're Christine?"

They each nodded.

"I'm sorry, but there're no letters here for you. There're no letters here for anyone. The post service has been shut down for weeks now."

"When will there be letters again?" Karin asked, her heart sinking low.

"I can't rightly say." Herr Schmitt scratched his chin, wiggling his long mustache with a finger. "The Americans are marching in on the west, and the Russians on the east. Any day now we could be under one or the other's rule. I don't know if the Americans or the Russian'll care a rat's whisker about the German post." The light in his eyes faded, replaced by what looked like concern. "Let's just pray it's not the Russians that march into Wittgensdorf."

"Why not? What's wrong with the Ru—"

Christine grabbed Karin by the elbow, cutting off her words. "Come on, Karin. We need to get going. Herr Schmitt's a busy man; quit bothering him."

"But I want a letter. I want to know Pappa's all right." Karin pouted.

Herr Schmitt stepped outside and shut the door behind him. He bent down eye level to Karin. "Those blue eyes of yours are too pretty to be clouded with frowns. I'm sure there'll be a letter from your Pappa soon, telling you he's okay. You get on home now. I promise I'll deliver it the moment I get it." He straightened up. Placing a hand on the doorknob, he motioned with his chin for them to leave, and then he stepped inside.

CHAPTER 7

"CHRISTINE, WHAT'S WRONG?" KARIN ASKED as they followed Mutti out the door into another cloudy day to gather firewood.

"I'm still a little skittish, you know, from the b—" Christine quit talking when Mutti turned and glared at her. "Never mind." She grabbed Karin's hand and squeezed it as they stepped onto the lane.

"Okay." Karin hadn't seen any more lights glowing through the hall window at night for a whole week now. Now that she knew they'd been bombs—not fireworks—she had no desire to walk over and look out that window again. Especially at night. But for some reason, she didn't jump at the word *bomb* like others seemed to.

"Can I carry the bag?" Karin ran up in step with Mutti and tugged on the bag's handle she had slung over her shoulder. Mutti had made it from an old quilt. They'd used it last time to gather wood, and it'd been much more fun than carrying the sticks in her arms.

"I'll bear the load." Mutti held the bag tightly. "Just enjoy being a child."

"But I want to help."

"Oh, all right. But only until we find our first piece of wood," Mutti responded. She hung the heavy bag over Karin's shoulder.

"Aww." Karin accepted the bag with a stomp of her foot.

Christine fell in step beside them. "After a log or two, it won't be fun anymore. Just watch."

"Says who?" Karin spotted a broken branch that had fallen from a tree in the yard of their neighbor, Frau Krujatz. She veered from the lane and headed toward it.

"Leave it," Mutti said. "The old woman will need that for her own fire."

They continued down the lane and headed for the grove of trees that hugged the stream at the edge of the village. Karin swung the patchwork bag forward and back with her arm as she walked. It made her feel bigger—even if the bottom of the bag swept across the patches of snow on the ground.

As soon as they stepped into the trees, Karin scanned the grove's floor for dead wood—she wanted to be the first to put some wood in the bag.

The ground was bare of wood, covered only with brown grass laid low by the melting snow. And trampling feet.

"What are all these footprints?" Christine noticed them too.

"I don't know." Mutti moved out in front, leading them farther into the trees, taking slow, careful steps.

With a shift in the breeze, the smell of a bonfire added to Karin's confusion. "Who took all the wood? And why are they burning it outside?" Her toes were cold, and she was hoping to warm them soon by a good fire in the kitchen stove.

"I don't know," repeated Mutti.

"There they are." Christine pointed off to the side and then ahead. "And there."

As Karin shuffled forward behind Mutti, clusters of people became visible, their gray coats no longer blending in with the bark of the trees. There were four, no five different groups, each huddled around a fire. Near some of the groups, tents were strung up on the trees. In the closest gathering of people, there was no tent. A shelter made from branches leaned against a row of trees. Near it, a woman stood, looking straight at Mutti. She held out an empty pan and spoke. Her words were hard to hear, but her mouth appeared to say, "Please, do you have any food?"

"The poor souls, I wish I could help them." Mutti grabbed Karin's hand and turned her around. "But there are so many," she mumbled under her breath. Christine followed. Mutti walked briskly toward the lane.

"But we haven't gathered any wood," Karin said, resisting Mutti's grasp as she tried to turn. She wanted to look for wood. She wanted to be warm tonight.

"Even if a piece or two were to be found, they need it more than we do," Mutti said.

"Who are they?" Karin tilted her head, trying to get a better look at the people.

"Never you mind." Mutti kept walking fast. "And don't stare."

Karin broke into a run in order to keep up as her mother dragged her away. Once they cleared the grove, their steps slowed a bit. "Who were those people?" Karin asked again as they neared home.

"Karin!" Christine gave her that crinkled-eyebrow look, the one that meant Karin should obey Mutti.

Karin lifted her shoulders and let them slump; why did Christine always have to be such a dutiful daughter—and then expect her to be the same? As Karin let go of the last of a prolonged sigh, she spotted some people standing on their porch. "Who's that?" she asked, pointing. They didn't look like any of the Somers.

Mutti's steps slowed. She stopped, then let go of Karin's hand and darted off. "Anna!" she cried as she ran.

Karin bounded alongside Christine until they reached Mutti at the base of the steps. Mutti had Aunt Anna locked in a hug. Karin tugged on her mother's sleeve until the arm responded and welcomed Karin and Christine into the embrace. After a minute or so, Mutti, a half head taller than Aunt Anna, let go and straightened up.

Christine took a step back. She looked like she was ready to cry. "You're okay. I was so worried . . ."

Karin kept her arms in place around her aunt while Christine moved to Mutti's side. "Aunt Anna!" She cried, her insides feeling like bathwater left on the stove longer than usual. She had her favorite aunt all to herself now, so she hugged extra hard. "I prayed to Heavenly Father that you'd be safe from all those bombs."

When Karin let go of her aunt's waist, she stepped back and noticed her hands and arms were covered with soot. "Aunt Anna, your black coat's rubbing off on me."

Aunt Anna chuckled. "Sorry, little dumpling, my coat's a bit dirty right now."

"That's okay," Karin said and then realized something was different. "Where's your suitcase? Aren't you going to stay very long?" She pointed up to the young woman on the porch. "And who is—"

Mutti pulled Karin close, forcing her arm down. "Enough questions. It's cold; let's get inside."

"But . . ." Karin noticed the young woman was holding close what appeared to be a small child huddled inside her own dirty coat. "Does she have a baby? I want to see it!" Karin dashed away, bolting up the steps to the young woman's side. A bare foot with tiny cute toes kicked out from underneath the cover of the mother's coat. The child looked to be old enough to walk, maybe even older. Karin reached out and caressed the little foot. "Mutti, look at the baby."

"Yes, dear." Mutti switched her attention to Aunt Anna. "I'm so glad you're all right. You'll be staying for some time, I gather?"

Aunt Anna rushed a hand to her messy hair. "If that's all right?"

"Of course, of course." Mutti put an arm around Aunt Anna and directed her up the steps to the front door.

"You've heard about Dresden, I presume?" Aunt Anna sniffled. Tears followed. "Oh, Ida, it was horrible, just horrible."

"What about Sophronia? And Richard? Any news?"

"Richard's fine. His house is more full than ever. I couldn't go to Sophronia's; the fire was so—"

Mutti glanced at Karin and then turned to Anna. "You can tell me all the details tonight . . . after the girls are to bed."

"Oh, sorry, of course." Aunt Anna motioned for her to move out of the shadows. The young woman hiked the child up farther on her hip and shuffled over to Aunt Anna's side.

"Could you spare just a little bit more room?" Aunt Anna asked. "This is Monika and her little boy, Dieter. I met them on the road from Dresden. Their apartment was destroyed too. I told her you would gladly take them in."

The woman named Monika gazed at Mutti, her eyes wide and pleading, her face smudged with soot. She tucked the bare foot of her son back inside her coat. "Please, Frau. It will only be until I find another place to go."

"But of course," Mutti said with a smile, though her voice sounded a little shaky. She summoned everyone to come.

As Karin stepped inside, she noticed the door to the Somers' living room crack open and an eye peer into the hall. It opened wider, and Frau Somer stuck her head out. She stared at Aunt Anna and Monika, her lip curling up. "Who are all these people? What are they doing in my house?"

"For now, it is my house too," Mutti responded the way she often spoke when putting Karin in her place. "This is my sister, Anna, and her friend. They will be staying with us for a while."

"Well," Frau Somer jerked her head back, flipping her undone hair into her face. "As long as they don't bother us." She shut the door.

That night they had soup for supper. It was thinner than usual. There was no bread for Karin to sop up the broth at the bottom of her bowl. Mutti let the fire die out as soon as the soup was gone. Karin went over to the box that held their firewood, snatched up one of the few remaining pieces of wood, and handed it to Christine. Karin would have stuffed it in the stove but knew she wasn't supposed to feed the fire. "Can't we put just this in the stove?"

Mutti grabbed the log and deposited it back in the box. "Until we find more wood, we'd better save that for cooking."

"But it's cold," Karin said.

"All the more reason for you to hurry off to bed." Mutti patted the air behind Karin's backside in the direction of the bedroom. She didn't follow Karin to the door but stopped and draped an arm around Monika's shoulder. "Sorry there wasn't more hot water so you could give your little one a bath, and I didn't have more dishtowels to spare."

"We're fine. And we're so very grateful to you for sharing what you have." Monika reached up and squeezed the hand Mutti rested on her shoulder. She pulled an old towel from the leftover dishwater, wrung it out, and hung it on a line strung across the kitchen next to the diaper she'd just washed.

Aunt Anna sat in a chair next to the dying stove, rocking the heavy-eyed toddler back and forth. In a hushed voice, she said, "Monika speaks for me too, Ida. You're a saint."

"Oh, pish-posh." Mutti wagged her hand at them. "I put my sister on the couch and a guest and her baby on the floor in a cold house with one quilt between them . . . after a supper of watered-down soup. That hardly makes a saint in my book."

"I'm warm enough. I have my good coat." Aunt Anna took the sides of the black coat she was wearing and wrapped the toddler in close to her.

"And so do I," Monika said, brushing dirt from the battered blue coat she wore.

Mutti scooted Karin and Christine into the hall. Over her shoulder she called back to Aunt Anna. "I'll be back as soon as I tuck these girls in bed. We'll talk then."

The next morning, Karin awoke to the sound of crying. She sat up in bed. "What's that?"

Christine propped herself on one elbow and leaned an ear toward the kitchen. "Little Dieter."

"Oh, yes, I forgot we have a baby in the house now." Karin jumped out of bed, hurried and put on her dress, coat, and shoes—she'd left her socks on all night to keep her toes warm since they'd slept with one less blanket. She ran into the living room. There she saw the bed Mutti had made Dieter and his mother atop the thick throw rug in front of the couch.

Their old gray blanket lay neatly folded on the arm of the couch, and all signs that Aunt Anna had slept in there were gone. Karin scampered through the hall and into the kitchen, the cries having settled down to a whimper.

Little Dieter lay on the table, wiggling. Monika was fastening one of Mutti's dishtowels around his bare bottom. Mutti stirred a pot of mush on the stove top while Aunt Anna fed its belly the last piece of wood from the box. Aunt Anna looked up at Karin and said, "Be a jewel and go fetch the blanket on the couch."

"Are you going to try and burn it?" Karin asked with concern.

Aunt Anna laughed as she straightened her back. "Not hardly, my little dumpling." She stepped over to Monika, who now held Dieter over her shoulder dressed only in a shirt and the dishtowel-diaper. Aunt Anna squeezed one of his wiggling bare feet and then warmed his toes with her breath as if they were cold fingers that had played in the snow. "It's for the baby. We need to wrap him up until his things dry out."

"Okay." Karin set out for the blanket. As she left the room, she heard Mutti speak.

"Sorry, it's just not warm enough in here to dry things out properly."

"Ida, dear, no need to apologize."

"Dieter will be just fine, Frau Graeber," Monika added. "We'll just wrap him in that blanket until the day warms up."

When Karin returned with the blanket, Aunt Anna snatched it up and quickly wrapped it around little Dieter.

"The poor boy's got the sniffles." Aunt Anna handed the bundled little boy to Monika and then focused her attention on Karin. "I'm going to go find us some firewood. Does anyone want to come with me?"

"I do. I want to help!" Karin liked how Aunt Anna had a way of making the most boring things fun. And she knew Aunt Anna would actually let her help, maybe even let her carry the bag when it held some firewood. Karin buttoned her coat, ready to run for her scarf and gloves.

"Hold on." Mutti wagged a wooden spoon at Karin. "You eat your breakfast first." She turned to Aunt Anna and Christine. "And that goes for both of you too. I don't want to have to save your portions till you get back, only to watch a perfectly good meal turn into cold, lumpy wallpaper paste."

"I wasn't planning on going." Christine lowered her head. "But if you want me to, Mutti, I'll go."

"I meant *after* breakfast, Ida." Aunt Anna rested her hand on Christine's arm. "And there's no need for you to go—if you don't want to." She grabbed some bowls from the cupboard. She set them on the table, then sat herself down at one of them and motioned for Karin and Christine to do the same.

After a small bowl of mush, Karin finally got to join Aunt Anna in search of wood. On their way out the front door, they met with Frau Somer on her way in. "Good morning," Aunt Anna said with a big smile and a slight bow. "Lovely day, isn't it?"

"Hummpph." Frau Somer looked neither at Aunt Anna nor at Karin but seemed to concentrate on her living room door. "How anyone in your situation can call this day lovely is beyond me," she said with a quick glance to Aunt Anna as she slipped past them.

Karin gazed up at the sky as she stepped onto the stone path. Pure blue delighted her eyes while the sun warmed her cheeks. All the gray clouds were gone. "I think it's a lovely day, Aunt Anna."

"And so do I, dear girl. It's sad the way some people see gray clouds all the time."

"Huh?"

"Not everyone is as sunny as you, little dumpling."

Karin hiked the bag's strap back on her shoulder, wondering why grown-ups always said things that didn't make sense. At the end of the stone path, Aunt Anna turned the opposite direction from the way they usually went. "Why you going this way?"

"Ida told me those woods are full of refugees." Aunt Anna pointed ahead. "We'll try over here. There's an orchard down this way. We can pretend we're picking apples."

"Okay!" Karin liked the idea. "But how do you know there's an orchard over here?"

"It's your Uncle Richard's. I used to come down here and help him pick apples."

"What's a ref . . . u . . . gee?"

Aunt Anna looked at Karin with a wrinkled forehead. Her face then relaxed. "Oh." She gave a little chuckle. "People fleeing to a new place because they no longer have a home of their own. Like me. Like Monika and Dieter."

"I thought you were just visiting."

"Well, I am—for a very long visit. Or at least until I can find a new place. Which might take a considerable amount of time."

"What about your old place?"

"It was destroyed in the bombing."

"Oh." Karin felt like someone had punched her in the stomach. She slowed her steps because Aunt Anna did.

A blonde woman carrying a shoulder bag similar to Karin's approached. A child, about the same age as Karin, clung to the arm of an old woman who remained off to the side.

"Excuse me, Frau," said the blonde woman. "Please, do you have a bit of food you could spare?"

"I'm sorry, I have nothing." Aunt Anna held out her empty hands, palms up.

"At least might you have a spare corner in your house we could sleep in at night?"

"I wish I could help, but I'm a refugee just as you are."

The woman hung her head and passed by them. She motioned for the old woman and child to rejoin her.

"Ref . . . u . . . gees?" Karin said the word slowly again, unsure how to say it, unsure if she wanted to say it. She didn't like what it meant. Feelings of anger grew inside her, trying to understand why one person would want to destroy another person's home. As the uncomfortable feelings churned in her chest, Karin realized something. "Am I a refugee too?" Her mind raced back to that horrible night in Berlin.

"Yes, I guess you are." Aunt Anna looked at the sky. "Your Mutti will probably chastise me for enlightening you," she mumbled under her breath. "But Lord knows she's going to be hard-pressed to preserve your innocence in this place."

Karin didn't want to be a refugee. She wanted things to be normal. She wanted the mean people to quit ruining other people's lives. Those mean people made her mad. And that made her remember losing her own home. She'd told herself then she wasn't going to let the mean people make her life miserable—because that's what they wanted. She told herself that again. "I hope we can find lots of good firewood today," she said in a more cheery voice than she felt.

Once in the orchard, Karin had to search hard to find firewood, as there wasn't much dead wood. Aunt Anna seemed to have forgotten about pretending to pick apples. Soon enough, however, the old quilt bag held some good pieces of wood, and Karin struggled to lug it from tree to tree.

"Do you want me to take that?" Aunt Anna reached for the bag.

"No, I want to do it. I *want* to help." Karin liked how she didn't have to give it up after the first scrap of wood got put in.

"Good for you." Aunt Anna hugged Karin.

Scraping snow away from bumps on the ground with their shoes, they continued to find treasures of broken branches and dead wood. When the bag became so loaded that Karin could barely drag it along, and Aunt Anna's arms were full, they headed home.

"We're going to have a fire in the living room stove tonight! I don't care what Ida says," Aunt Anna said as they approached the house, her jaw firm.

Karin liked that idea. The thought of heat seeping into the bedroom from the living room, not just the kitchen that was so far away, sounded good. She spotted the broken branch on Frau Krujatz's yard. Maybe if they had just a little bit more wood, Mutti would not keep Aunt Anna from building that extra fire. She veered from the lane and headed for the fallen branch.

"Hold on," Aunt Anna hollered. "You'd better ask first. That's not ours to take."

Karin wanted that extra fire. She headed to Frau Krujatz's front door—she'd talked to Herr Schmitt, and it hadn't been that hard. Aunt Anna remained out in the lane while Karin approached the porch. Karin reached up and knocked on the door.

The door cracked open, and the wrinkled but kind face of Frau Krujatz peered through the slit at Karin. "Well, well, if it's not the sweet little girl from next door. Karin, isn't it?"

"Yes, Frau." Karin swallowed the wad stuck in her throat and pointed to the broken branch beneath the tree. "We're gathering wood. If you don't need that, could we take it?"

"Surely." Frau Krujatz opened the door wider and swept her wrinkled hand toward a large pile of firewood stacked neatly inside. "I won't miss that twig." She glanced at Aunt Anna. "And who is that with you?"

"My Aunt Anna. She's living with us now because her home in Dresden was bombed." Somehow saying it out loud to someone made Karin's ache inside feel better.

"Oh, dear, another one?" Frau Krujatz brought her hand to her forehead. "Come in, come in. Get out of the weather." She motioned for Aunt Anna to come in and join them. As Aunt Anna stepped onto the porch, the old woman muttered, "I swear this has been the coldest winter I ever remember."

"We didn't mean to intrude," said Aunt Anna. "The child just wanted—"

"Oh, nonsense. You're not intruding—I'd love to hear your story too." Frau Krujatz made them set their wood on the porch and practically pulled them inside.

"Too?" Aunt Anna sounded confused. Then she looked around the living room. Her eyes widened as if she now understood. "Oh."

An old woman sat on the couch sandwiched between two old men. On the floor, two young women about the age of Ella or Brunhilde huddled together, perched atop a pile of folded bedding. One of the old men spoke up. "Come, share your story with these others—it helps . . . you know . . . takes away some of the pain."

"Would you like a bite to eat first?" Frau Krujatz looked at us.

Aunt Anna glanced at the five strangers filling the room and then back to Frau Krujatz. "Thank you, no. I'm not hungry."

"I am," Karin said.

Frau Krujatz smiled, slung a thin arm around Karin's shoulder, and motioned for Aunt Anna to take a seat. The old woman on the couch slid over to make a sliver of space. Frau Krujatz channeled Karin into the kitchen and onto a chair at the table. A moment later, she placed a small bowl of bread and milk before Karin. She hurried back into the living room, her voice trailing behind her. "It was just awful, what happened. Do share your story with us, Anna."

Karin listened carefully as she devoured the soggy, sweet bread. Her aunt's move, Mutti had told Karin, was because Aunt Anna wanted to be close to them. Karin wanted to know what really happened.

"There were no warning sirens." Aunt Anna's voice reached into the kitchen. It was easy to hear, and it carried with it a sense of fear. "I was completely surprised."

"So was I," came the voice of the older woman. "I was lucky to have a root cellar. What did you do? Where did you go?"

"I rushed down to the cellar of the hospital. My building was full. But the hospital quickly became hopelessly overcrowded."

"And you were safe there? For two whole days?" It was the voice of one of the old men.

"No, Pappa, she couldn't have been," said the voice of a young woman. "The hospital was burned to the ground."

"No, I didn't stay there. Thank the good Lord," Aunt Anna said. "The crush was unbearable; we were so tight you couldn't fall over if you wanted to."

Karin jerked away from the bowl of bread and milk and stared into the living room at her aunt.

"Oh, that must have been horrible." Frau Krujatz patted Aunt Anna's hand.

"Apart from the fire risk, it became harder and harder to breathe in the cellar because the air was being pulled out by the flames—they were increasing in strength. I had to get out of there."

"But how, if you were packed in there like sausages in a can?" asked the other young woman.

"I don't know how I did it, exhausted as I was. But I managed to squeeze my way through the bodies toward the door. Everyone tried to tell me it was safer in there, but I didn't care—I had to leave."

"But once outside, it wasn't any better, was it?" said the same young woman. "I remember as I ran away the wind beat at me with bits of debris, all of them blazing with fire."

"Yes, yes," Aunt Anna said with passion. "Once out the door, I didn't dare stand up. I crawled on all fours. There were charred bodies everywhere. I headed for a building that didn't appear to be burning. It was a stone shed of some sort. I curled up in a corner atop soiled burlap bags and waited out the remaining two days of the bombing."

"With nothing to eat? And knowing all your earthly possessions were gone? How dreadful," Frau Krujatz said with a trembling voice.

"That was the least of her worries," said the old woman.

"Absolutely," agreed Aunt Anna.

"It was lucky your place of refuge never caught fire," Frau Krujatz added.

"Oh, it was not luck that preserved me." Aunt Anna sighed. "I have no doubt there was a divine hand in there somewhere."

It was almost afternoon by the time they left Frau Krujatz's house. Karin normally would have liked to skip down the lane toward home, but the things she'd just heard seemed to keep her legs from doing anything but walk slowly, like Aunt Anna. As they approached their house, Karin saw Mutti out on the porch talking with Herr Somer. He must have come home early from the garage in the neighboring village. He was still dressed in his greasy overalls. There were some other people there too.

"Who are they?" Karin asked.

"I don't know. More refugees, most likely. I imagine a lot of them don't have family to go to like me." Aunt Anna squeezed Karin's shoulder.

As they approached the porch, Karin could hear Herr Somer's rough voice boom across the yard.

"I'm not takin' in any more people. It's bad enough we had to give up half our house to her lot." Herr Somer pointed his grease-stained hand in Mutti's direction. "We've got no more room."

The same two women and child Karin had seen earlier backed away from Herr Somer toward the edge of the porch. Mutti stepped forward. "You know very well we did not take half your house. We've barely got three small rooms while you still have a double room upstairs and the whole of five rooms downstairs. But no matter, these folks are welcome to stay with us!" Mutti pushed open the front door and glared at Herr Somer. She plowed inside and motioned for the blonde-haired women, the old woman, and the child to follow.

Karin ran and caught up with them on the stairs. "I'm sorry you lost your house," she said to the child. Now that she was closer, she could tell that he was a boy even though he wore a woman's scarf. He ducked his head and buried it under the blonde woman's arm as if he didn't want to talk.

That night Karin ate her soup, wondering how Mutti managed to make the pot stretch to feed three extra mouths. When Karin climbed into bed, the cold sheets gave her a chill. Her face felt the heat from the living room stove wafting into the bedroom, making it more tolerable. She was glad she'd gathered that little bit of extra wood. Not just because of the fire but because she'd made a new friend. Frau Krujatz was the nicest old lady she'd ever met. She pulled the blanket up farther. "Christine," she whispered, "Where's the other quilt?"

"Mutti had to give it to the others. Hush up and go to sleep. Be happy you have your little blue one. Be happy Mutti didn't take that away too."

"I am."

Karin snuggled next to Christine, pulling her favorite blue quilt up to her chin. She wished it was bigger so Christine could feel it too. She was glad they'd managed to save it from their house in Berlin—it was as precious as Hilda. Pappa had given it to her for Christmas, the one before he'd left for the war. It had been his when he was a child. That Christmas seemed so long ago to Karin. How she longed for a Christmas like that again. Or any day like that again, a day when Pappa was living with them, right there in the same house, not away being a soldier.

In the middle of the night, Karin woke to the sound of crying. At first she thought it was Dieter, but it sounded older. It quit. Now that she was awake, the urge to go to the toilet hit her hard. She realized she'd forgotten to go before she went to bed. She crawled out of bed, wishing she was still young enough to wake and drag Mutti with her. She put on her slippers and crept through the living room, careful not to step on Monika or little Dieter as she tip-toed through.

Once she reached the hall, the moonlight from the front window lit her way much better. She heard the crying once again. It was more like a whimper this time, and it came from the kitchen. The door was open as usual so the heat from the stove could seep into the living room and bedroom. She peered inside. Three bodies lay huddled together on the floor next to the stove, the kitchen table having been shoved to the wall. Heat no longer came from the stove. Karin could see the blanket shared among the three of them covered only part of the child. He appeared to be shivering.

The need to pee pulled Karin away from the door and down the stairs—she couldn't hold it much longer. She opened the door to the toilet and left it ajar because the room had no light bulb. Hopefully the moonlight pouring in through the front door window would help her see. She stepped inside, holding her breath from the smell like she always did. The wooden seat seemed higher than usual in the dark. Even in the daytime this place scared her, with its tall seat and round hole big enough to swallow her whole and suck her into its black, stinky pit. Now, in the dark of night, it was terrifying.

Carefully, Karin pulled down her underwear and climbed onto the wooden seat. It creaked as she maneuvered her bottom into place. What if it broke? She'd fall in. No one would hear her scream. They wouldn't find her till morning, her night spent in total darkness, breathing the stench, swimming in poop—probably with rats the size of dogs. She clung on to the front of the bench, her knuckles wanting to explode from the tightness of her grip while her exposed flesh was nipped by the cold of the deep hole. She hurried and peed. The second she was done she jumped off, pulled up her underwear, and shot to the stairs.

As she hurried past the kitchen door, the image of the shivering boy filled her thoughts. His earlier cries had sounded like ones of fear as much as of being cold. Karin thought of how terrifying that toilet had been in the dark. But that was over now; she had her warm bed next to Christine to climb into and her blue quilt to comfort her. Hearing about what her aunt had gone through in Dresden, and knowing that boy had probably gone through the same thing, and that he now he lay on a hard floor with not much to cover him, Karin felt like crying.

She tiptoed through the living room, into the bedroom, and grabbed her little blue quilt. Hugging it close to her, she scurried back into the kitchen and placed it over the boy.

CHAPTER 8

KARIN SAT AT THE KITCHEN table next to the cold stove, grateful spring was finally here and, with it, some warmth.

Christine burst into the room, making little Dieter jump in Karin's lap as she pretended to read him a story. "They're coming, Mutti!" Christine yelled. She leaned against the door frame and panted.

"Slow down, girl." Mutti rushed to Christine's side. "Take a deep breath and tell us what's going on. Who's coming?"

Aunt Anna came through the door, panting harder than Christine. "The Russians," she said. "I caught sight of them when I was coming home from Frau Krujatz's house. From a distance it looked like a huge black snake winding through the fields, but when the darkness moved up and down in rhythm, there was no question. It was an army."

"We knew it was just a matter of time." Monika pulled Dieter close and held him tight as if he was a doll lending her comfort.

The walls began to vibrate. The sound of thudding pounded through the open window. Karin rushed over to look out. Mutti was by her side in a moment. "Quick, grab something. A towel, a clean diaper, anything white."

"Why?" Karin didn't understand.

"Wave it out the window to show them we surrender. We mean them no harm." Mutti grabbed a dishtowel/diaper from the line strung across the kitchen and rushed back to the window.

Anna grabbed one too. "I'll go to the hall window."

Karin grabbed a blue towel. That was all that was left. She squeezed in between Christine and Mutti and waved her towel, wondering how that would tell the Russians they meant no harm. And why would an army—"the Russians," such a scary name—be afraid of them anyway?

Karin stood on her toes. She could barely see over the bottom of the window. Rows and rows of soldiers in uniforms, that looked nothing like Pappa's, marched down the lane. They raised their legs so high Karin swore they'd tip over backwards. They did it all at the same time so it looked like one big set of legs instead of lots of individual men. She could see Frau Krujatz waving a white cloth from her window. Everyone else down the lane was doing the same.

Finally, the army slipped out of sight, and the pounding stopped. The villagers moved away from their windows. So did Karin and her family. Mutti got back to work making soup for supper, though her hands were shaking. Monika finished packing up the dishtowel diapers Mutti had given her and a few bags of supplies.

"Why are you leaving?" Karin asked Monika. "Don't you like it here with us?"

"Of course I do." Monika looked at Karin with sad eyes. "But I can't take advantage of your Mutti forever. I have to move on, make a life of my own—me and Dieter."

"What about his Pappa?" Karin asked.

"He died in the war." Monika glanced at Mutti and twisted her mouth. "I thought you knew."

"No, I didn't." Karin felt her stomach churn, not a hungry churn but that painful kind that came when she thought about Pappa not coming home.

"I was going to leave in the morning. But maybe I'll leave right now." Monika looked out the window. The lane looked ugly now that the Russians had trampled it so.

"It's not safe traveling in the dark," Aunt Anna said.

"She's right," Mutti added. "Perhaps you should wait until the morning. There's no rush on our behalf. The other three have been gone for three days now."

Karin went to bed but couldn't sleep. Screams from outside penetrated the walls. Some sounded distant, some like they were from next door.

Monika and little Dieter and even Aunt Anna came in and stayed in the bedroom really late, until the screams quit coming.

As Monika said her last good-byes the next morning, a knock came to the kitchen door. Aunt Anna stepped over to open it. Frau Krujatz stood in the doorway; her face looked as pale as old dishwater. "Ida, Anna, I must speak to you." She glanced over at Karin and then at Christine. "Without the children if possible." She noticed Monika and added, "You should hear this too."

"But I was just leaving—I've burdened Frau Graeber too long."

"You'll want to be aware of this before you leave, before you go anywhere in Russian-occupied Germany." Frau Krujatz wagged a hand at Monika.

The four of them slipped out into the hall, shutting the door behind them. Karin rushed over and pressed her ear near the keyhole.

Christine didn't stop her but came over and leaned her ear close. "What are they saying?" she whispered.

"Shhh, I can't hear anything if you're talking." Karin moved her ear over the hole and concentrated hard.

"Is everyone here all right?" Frau Krujatz asked in a voice a lot higher than normal.

"We're fine," Mutti replied. "Why?"

"The Russians, they were breaking into houses last night . . . stealing food and . . . raping women."

Karin pulled her ear away and glanced up at Christine. "What is raping?"

"Shh." Christine brought a finger to her lips, her ear still against the door. "I'm not sure, but I know it's something really bad."

Fear fueled Karin's curiosity further, and she returned her ear to the keyhole.

"What about the Burgermeister?" Mutti asked. "Couldn't he stop them? Throw the perpetrators in jail?"

"His hands are tied." It was Frau Krujatz's voice. "He's basically a figurehead anymore. We're under the Russian government now."

"Can he do nothing?" Aunt Anna joined in.

"Just warn us," Frau Krujatz said. "He told me I was to find all the women I could and tell them to prepare every night for . . . well, you know." She gasped before letting out a sob. "Oh, this is just horrible . . . absolutely horrible."

"What about the Russian officers?" Monika asked. "Can they not control their men?"

"Burgermeister Schmitt asked the same questions." Frau Krujatz no longer sobbed but sounded angry. "The Russian officers just told him that our people should understand—that his soldiers had just crossed thousands of kilometers, through blood and fire and death, and that his men deserve to take some trifle, have a little fun with a woman."

"No!" the others said all together.

"Yes," Frau Krujatz said. "And it's more than 'some trifle' they take. You know the farmer on the south end of town, Herr Hemmer? His wife was . . . well, he had to go fetch the doctor . . ."

Karin quit listening—their words no longer made sense. But it was as if the fear stirring up Frau Krujatz reached through the closed door and grabbed hold of her. Christine too. Her sister was shivering.

Karin moved away from the door even though Frau Krujatz continued to speak to Mutti and the others. She *knew* Mutti wouldn't want her hearing this. "Christine," Karin said, staring at her sister, not knowing what else to say.

"Don't worry; Mutti will take care of things." Her voice was so shaky that Karin didn't think Christine believed it.

A moment later the doorknob turned. Karin and Christine shot to the other side of the room. Christine picked up a book as if she'd been reading it all along.

Mutti followed Monika and Aunt Anna into the room, her face wearing an expression Karin had never seen before: sad, mad, and scared all rolled up in one. "Monika, don't feel like you have to go on account of us," Mutti said. "You're welcome to stay a little longer. We'll have a garden soon, and . . ."

"No, I've stayed long enough." Monika's face looked pale. "And my Aunt Gertrude is expecting me."

Aunt Anna snatched a diaper from the line strung across the kitchen. "I'll hurry and change Dieter; then we need to get you on your way."

"Yes," Mutti said. "The more distance you can travel in the daylight, the better. How long do you figure it will take you to get to your great aunt's house?"

"About two days."

"Don't let them see you. Stay on the back roads. And you'd best find an out-of-the-way place to hide tonight."

"Then hurry on to your aunt's bright and early tomorrow morning." Aunt Anna scooped little Dieter off the floor, where he was playing with Hilda. She handed the doll to Karin and laid the toddler on the table.

While she changed his diaper, Mutti pulled the remaining diapers from the line and added them to the bundle of belongings Monika was tying up inside one of their singed blankets. A minute later Monika was on her way, walking down the stone path with Dieter in one arm and her blanket of belongings in the other.

Karin hadn't even had a chance to give little Dieter a hug. "*Auf wiedersehen,*" she said, not knowing what else to say.

As they walked back upstairs, Mutti turned to Aunt Anna and said quietly, "Well, I for one refuse to be paralyzed by fear. Life must go on. We'll just have to rely on the good Lord that much more."

"Agreed," Aunt Anna responded.

"Good," Mutti said, "Because we have a garden to plant."

Karin didn't know what paralyzed meant, but like her aunt, she was not going to be afraid. Somehow.

After a lunch of bread, they all went outside to plant their garden. Neither Mutti nor Aunt Anna spoke of Monika, wondering if she'd make it to her aunt's okay or if she'd find a safe place to hide tonight. It was as if not expressing worry would keep the bad stuff from happening. But Karin could see it in their faces. Christine's too. She wanted them all to smile, to think about something else, something pleasant— that's what she did when she had to do something hard.

"I'm excited to have a garden," Karin skipped ahead of them and turned around to wave them on toward the backyard.

That did get a smile out of Mutti.

Karin loved the way the moist soil squished between her fingers. Poking holes in the smoothed-out dirt and dropping a seed inside was such fun. "I need more seeds," Karin said when her handful of pea seeds ran out before the end of the row.

"That's all you get," Christine said.

"Mutti," Karin looked to her mother, her lower lip sticking out in protest.

"There's no more. That's all Herr Reinhart could spare." Mutti stood up, put her hands on her back, and stretched backward. She looked over the square piece of dirt behind the house with a smile on her face. "But it will be enough; we've got peas, carrots, and cabbage. In another month, we'll plant pumpkins and cucumbers."

The smile faded as Mutti looked at the sun. It sat low in the sky. "Hurry, clean up now. Anna, you return the rake to the Somers' shed. Christine, you and Karin follow me into the house, and I'll hurry and warm some water for a bath."

"Do I have to take a bath?" Karin protested as she hurried to keep up with Mutti. "I'd rather stay out here and plant some more seeds."

"There are no more seeds," Christine reminded her.

"I can pretend," Karin said, a little bit mad. Now that Christine was twelve, she wasn't as much fun as she used to be.

"You have to take a bath, Karin." Mutti grabbed her by the hand and hurried her toward the front door. "Just look at you." With a sweep of her hand, she brought Karin's attention to the soil caked to her bare knees and covering her arms. "Besides, it's church tomorrow." Mutti pulled her through the front door and headed up the staircase.

The clap of shoes on the steps below told Karin that Aunt Anna had caught up with them.

"Are you sure?" Aunt Anna said, climbing past Karin and Christine to get alongside Mutti. "It's been just over a month since the bombing. Has the branch president even found another place to meet? Are there enough members left *to* meet?"

"We've got a new place." Mutti stepped onto the hall landing. She opened the door to the kitchen and stepped aside for Aunt Anna to enter first. "Our home teacher, Brother Kraus, sent me the word about our new location," she continued as she pulled the wash tub from the closet.

"Do you think it's safe to go?" Aunt Anna raised an eyebrow. "You know, with the Russians everywhere? Poor Monika, she felt as though she had to go. But we don't have to, Ida. Loosen up a bit. You can miss a week or two of church."

Mutti's face looked as though Aunt Anna had slapped it. "I . . . uh . . . it's already been over a month . . . and he mentioned nothing about Sophronia. If we go into Dresden for church, we can find out if she and her family are safe."

"Ida, I worry about our sister too." Aunt Anna stuffed some kindling into the belly of the stove while Mutti filled the water heater on the side of the stove. "I say we stay home and worry about our safety this week." She lit the fire then turned to Karin. "Go get your nightclothes. It's time for your bath."

Karin returned from the bedroom, slipped off her clothes, and stuck a foot into the washtub that had been filled with water. The scent of the homemade soap made Karin lift it to her nose and breathe in its familiar smell. Slipping into the tub of warm water felt good. Until Mutti started scrubbing her hair. She didn't complain, having already tried Mutti's patience enough for the day.

While Christine took her bath, Mutti made Karin move into the cold living room to brush out her wet hair. The sun had set and with it went the warmth of the day. Christine brushed out her own hair while Aunt Anna took her turn in the tub of water.

While Mutti was in the tub, Aunt Anna came into the living room dressed in her regular clothes. "Where are your bed clothes?" Karin asked.

"I'm not wearing them."

Why did Aunt Anna say that? Karin could see that plain as day.

"And, Christine, change back out of yours." Aunt Anna held out a clean dress for Christine.

"What?" Christine looked as confused as Karin felt.

Mutti stepped into the room, ruffling her hair with a towel. "You, your aunt, and I need to leave as soon as possible. We probably won't be back until well after midnight, so dress warmly."

"What about me?" Karin stiffened as Mutti picked her up and plopped her on the turned-down bed.

"You're staying here." Mutti pulled the covers up to Karin's chin and then tucked the edges under the mattress. Karin felt like a mouse in a trap; she couldn't move.

"You'll be okay." Aunt Anna patted Karin's shoulder. "You're a *little* girl."

"Where are we going? Why are we going?" Christine sounded like she was going to cry.

Mutti put on her coat and scarf. "We've got to hide from the Russians." She said it as if she was speaking to a wall, no feeling in her voice. "Karin, I can't hide this from you, so you've got to be brave." She turned to Christine. "You too, Christine . . . especially you." She took a deep breath. "We are under Russian rule now. Things are going to change. But that doesn't mean we have to. If we are strong and stay close to God, He'll guide us through this. That's why we'll have to hide—every night if we have to—until their victory rampage is over. I feel it is what we must do. Hurry, Christine, and get dressed. I've been told it's usually after dark that they come looking for women."

"But, Mutti," Christine seemed to beg. "I'm only eleven."

"That's woman enough for them." Aunt Anna held Christine's coat out. Her face appeared angry.

"I want to come." Karin struggled to sit up. "Don't leave me alone."

"You might give us away." Aunt Anna stroked Karin's wet hair. "You're not good at holding still or keeping quiet."

"I can try," Karin said. "Honest I will."

Mutti sat down on the side of the bed. She gave Karin a bigger hug than usual. It made Karin feel like they'd never see each other again. She felt tears swell in her eyes. "I don't want to stay here alone."

"You'll be safer here. Really. The Russians won't bother you. I'll lock the door."

"On second thought, maybe that's not such a good idea," Aunt Anna said. She whispered something to Mutti.

Karin swore her aunt said something about making the Russians mad and breaking down the door. Her stomach felt sick.

Mutti rose slowly from the bed, looking from Christine to Aunt Anna and then at the window. The sun had just set. "Let's hurry."

Before Karin could protest further, the three of them were gone. Karin was alone. Wrapped tight like a bug in a web, Karin felt she couldn't move. She heard noises downstairs—maybe she wasn't alone. What if it wasn't the Somers?

What if it was the Russians?

She stared at the ceiling. Gray light reached from the window, making creepy shadows dance across the walls. Sleep wouldn't come.

She wiggled loose from her blanket cocoon. Kneeling on the bed underneath the covers, she prayed that she and her family would be safe.

And that no Russians would come into her room.

CHAPTER 9

AFTER TAKING A LONG TIME to fall asleep, Karin awoke reluctantly the next morning to noise sounding in her ears. As her mind cleared, she recognized it as Mutti's voice. Relief wrapped around her, warmer and sweeter than her favorite blue quilt. She felt Christine next to her in bed. More relief.

They didn't go to church. They read scriptures seated on the couch instead, like they had every Sunday since the bombing. It was Karin's turn to read the next verse. She was about to repeat the words Mutti recited for her when a knock sounded through the door. "I'll get it." Karin jumped up and ran to the door. Her excitement at seeing Frau Krujatz standing in the hall faded as fast as she'd opened the door. The lines on the old woman's face appeared to have doubled. Her wide-opened eyes had a strange look to them. They scared Karin.

"Is your mother at home, dear?" Frau Krujatz's question shook from her lips, sounding like a plea.

"I'm over here, Frau." Mutti leaned forward on the couch so the old lady could see her.

Frau Krujatz scurried inside. She glanced at Aunt Anna as she approached the couch. "You'll want to know about this too." Her eyes skirted over to the bedroom door. "Can we talk in there? I don't . . . uh . . . the girls don't need to hear this."

Mutti rose and ushered Aunt Anna into the bedroom. Frau Krujatz followed close behind, grabbing the doorknob on her way. The door *whoosed* shut. Karin jumped from the couch.

"Where are you going?" Christine latched onto Karin's arm.

"Over there." Karin pointed to the bedroom door. Maybe she didn't need to hear what Frau Krujatz had to say, but she *wanted* to hear. She pulled her arm free, crept across the floor, and positioned her ear next to the keyhole. The old lady's frantic voice carried through the small hole almost as clearly as if Karin stood inside the bedroom with Mutti and Aunt Anna. She heard Monika's name mentioned. Karin's ear pulled away when she turned her head to tell Christine. "They're talking about Monika."

"I don't care." Christine fidgeted in her seat. "Come away from that door. I don't think Frau Krujatz wants us to hear what she had to say, or she would have stayed in here."

Karin returned her ear to the keyhole. "I don't care that you don't care. I care." If they were talking about Monika, she definitely wanted to hear. She listened further.

". . . Herr Schmitt found her a few kilometers outside of the village in that grove of trees next to Fisher's Creek. It was her baby's cries that led him to her. He found the whimpering child draped over his mother's—" her voice broke and then paused—"naked body. Herr Schmitt wrapped Monika in his coat, grabbed the child, and hurried to fetch Dr. Bruin. They left the child with Frau Bruin and hurried back to Monika. But when the doctor got there, he said there wasn't much he could do for her, said she must have been raped multiple times."

There was that word again. Karin pulled her ear away from the keyhole, her insides heavy with a sick feeling she couldn't describe. She walked to sister. "Christine, what is rape? I keep hearing that word."

Christine sprang up, confirming to Karin that her sister cared after all. "Rape?" Christine gasped. "Monika was raped?"

Karin nodded. "A lot, I think. Tell me what it means."

Christine urged Karin over to the couch. "I told you before, I don't know exactly. Only that it's something bad."

The bedroom door creaked open. Mutti and the others trudged out, their faces pale and eyes glistening with tears. Mutti approached Karin and Christine. She opened her mouth, then closed it, chewed on her lower lip, and gazed at the ceiling for a moment. When she finally focused back on Karin and Christine and spoke, her voice sounded different. "Girls, I have some bad news," she said, the tone of each word ringing in Karin's ears like a warning that things would never be the same. "Monika is dead." With that, she headed toward the hall, grabbing her scarf and coat on the way. "Christine, watch Karin. Your aunt and I are going to go help Frau Krujatz prepare her for a proper burial."

"What about little Dieter?" Christine clamped onto Mutti's arm. "Who's going to take care of him now?"

"I don't know," Mutti said like she was angry.

Karin rushed over and held fast to Mutti's other arm. "Can we keep him? I'll help take care of him."

Aunt Anna pulled Karin and Christine away from Mutti. "You children hush now. Your mother can barely keep enough food in your bellies. She can't afford to take on orphans now." She slipped on her coat and stepped out of the room behind Mutti and Frau Krujatz.

Karin fell to the floor where she stood. The idea of Monika being dead and little Dieter an orphan made her burst into tears. Bad things had been happening all around her. She'd tried to keep a smile on her face through them all. She really had. But she hadn't planned on things like this when she'd come up with that stupid idea to stay happy.

Christine lowered onto her knees beside Karin. "I feel like crying too."

"Then why don't you?" Karin said between sniffles.

"I can't let myself cry." Christine bit down on her lip and wrinkled her brow like she was trying to hold back a mountain of tears. "Nearly every day Mutti asks me to be strong. I can't let her down."

"Do you plan on doing everything Mutti asks you?"

"Ja."

Karin sniffed away her tears, amazement crowding out a little of her sadness. "Really?"

"At least, I'll try." Christine rose to her feet, urging Karin to do the same. "I need to help Mutti . . . however I can. It's been so hard on her since Pappa went away to the army."

"How come Mutti doesn't ask me to be strong?" Karin said feeling a bit sad—or was it bad, or was she actually feeling mad? It had been hard on her, too, with Pappa gone.

"You're still her baby."

"I'm not a baby; I'm six! I can be strong for Mutti." And while Karin was at it, she'd stick out her tongue at the mean people and put a

smile back on her face because she knew that being happy would help
Mutti too.

The next Sunday they didn't go to church either.

By the time the following Sunday came, Mutti declared first thing
in the morning, "No more! I'm not going to miss another week." She
gave Karin and Christine each a gentle nudge as they lay in bed. "Karin,
Christine, get up. We need to get ready for church."

They had a quick breakfast of thin mush and then set out on their
three-hour journey. After one hour of walking through the countryside,
they arrived at the edge of the city. Karin knew the city of Dresden had
been bombed, but now she saw the blackened remains of buildings.
It was beyond anything she could have imagined. The once lively city
with its beautiful churches, whitewashed homes, and tall trees was now
flattened, black, and dead. It left her with an uncomfortable feeling as
she walked through the quiet streets. She continued on her way to the
new place they'd be meeting for church without a word from Mutti,
Christine, or Aunt Anna. "How much longer until there's a street car?"
Karin asked, her legs tired and her ears wanting conversation.

"I have no idea," Mutti said. "Things are definitely not the same as
before."

"Good thing we left early," Aunt Anna said. "What's that address
again?"

Mutti rattled something off about it being on the far side of town.
Karin didn't pay attention—she focused on the apartment building
they passed. It still held a hint of red while everything else around it
was black. She pulled away from Christine, skipped over, and turned
the doorknob. It opened. "Come on, everybody, let's look inside."

Karin pushed the door open wide and stepped inside. A door to
a bottom apartment hung from one hinge, close to falling off. She
peered into what was once someone's home. A couch, two arm chairs,
and a table sat in the room like in any normal living room waiting for
its family to come in, sit, and read the book that rested on the table.
There were even paintings hanging from the walls. But everything was
black. She sensed Christine, Mutti, and Aunt Anna gather around her.

"Oh," Mutti said. "Those poor people." She pulled away, headed to the main door, and slowly moved down the few steps back onto the sidewalk. As they passed the next building, it was as if the blackened bricks beckoned Karin. She scurried up to the front door. "Can we look in here too?"

"All right." Mutti trudged up its steps alongside Aunt Anna, behind Karin and Christine. They all peered inside an apartment after Karin opened the door. More blackened walls and other reminders that a happy family had once lived there.

"I wonder if these people got away." Aunt Anna mumbled.

"*Ja*," Karin responded. She turned and ran back outside, hollering over her shoulder. "Let's look at some more." She sprinted next door.

"Karin! You wait for us." Mutti lagged behind.

Karin kept going—Mutti was too slow, and Karin wanted to look some more before they had to hurry off to church. The ruins intrigued her. They felt like something out of a bad dream. The crumbling black structures didn't even seem real, yet in a creepy way, they beckoned her to come explore.

She crept up a stairwell without its railing, gazing at the singed wallpaper, wondering if it used to be green like her favorite wallpaper in Berlin. Peering through holes in the wall, she listened to the odd echo of her footsteps. She turned the knob of an unlocked door. Upon opening it, she expected to see a blackened living room like that last one. As she swung the door in, she only saw blue sky. "Look, the whole floor is gone." She pointed to the open air. The action made her sway toward the opening. She lost her balance.

"Karin!" Christine yelled.

Karin grabbed the door frame. Miraculously, she managed to keep from falling to the same fate as the apartment—a pile of rubble several meters down.

"Karin, come down from there!" Mutti looked angry. Karin climbed back down the rail-less stairs. Mutti grabbed her by the hand and pulled her outside. "No more exploring."

"I'm all right." Karin didn't want to stop exploring. She resisted, but Mutti's grasp was too strong. They kept walking, Mutti continually nudging Karin's face to look forward.

In the middle of town, they found one street car that was running. "What luck! I believe this will take us close to where we need to go," Aunt Anna said.

Mutti stared down the road at the approaching street car with a serious look on her face. "Luck is man's explanation for God's hand."

After getting off the trolley, it felt to Karin as if the church was on the other side of the world and they'd never stop walking. She was ready to give up.

Aunt Anna pointed down the street. "There it is." In the distance, a huge stone building appeared to rise out of a meadow, the trees and shrubbery stepping off to the side to make way for the uninviting structure.

"That's where we're going to church?" Christine sounded disappointed. Karin felt too tired to care.

"It was a military post," Mutti said as they made their way down the lane leading to the building.

It reminded Karin of the place she'd visited Pappa, that big stone building with soldiers everywhere. Maybe if there were extra soldiers here, they could come home with them and protect them from the Russians. "Where are all the soldiers?" Maybe Pappa was here!

"They're gone, darling." Aunt Anna took Karin by the hand. "The Russians are here now."

"I don't like the Russians," Christine said, taking hold of Aunt Anna's other hand. "I wish things were like they used to be."

"I do too, Christine." Aunt Anna squeezed her hand.

"Me too," Karin chimed in.

Mutti nodded as if in agreement. She urged them onward. "It's good to have one thing that doesn't change." She walked up to the front door, taking long steps. With a smile on her face, she opened it.

Cool air brushed Karin's face as she stepped inside, and a musty smell filled her nose. Their footsteps echoed off the stone walls of a long hallway lined with empty rooms. At the end of the hall, the walls opened up into an auditorium. People gathered at the front of the room. So small were their numbers, the room seemed to dwarf them down to the size of ants.

"Ah, here they are." Mutti brought her palms together just under her chin.

Karin followed Christine extra close, worried about getting lost—the new meeting house felt enormous. They shuffled in step behind Mutti down an aisle of three rows of folding chairs. Aunt Anna walked close behind. They sat down on the front row next to an older man and woman. A second later, both Mutti and Aunt Anna rose from their chairs. "Sophronia! Stefan!" they said at the same time. Together they rushed to a man and woman on the other side of the front row and hugged them.

"Come on." Christine motioned Karin to follow with a sweep of her hand.

The woman—who looked a lot like Mutti, only a little older, and who Karin figured was her Aunt Sophronia—gave her and Christine big hugs. "It's been way too long since I've seen these girls."

Way too long? Karin didn't remember ever seeing this aunt and uncle before—she'd only heard Mutti talk about them. Maybe it was like Uncle Johann. Karin didn't ever remember seeing Aunt Anna's husband, but Mutti said he always fussed over her when he came for a visit. Mutti had told Karin that when she was almost two, Uncle Johann was called to fight in the war and he never came back. That made her think of Pappa. Would he never come back? *No!* She refused to think of such things.

Instead, Karin concentrated on the calming sense of relief that filled her insides as she found a seat next to her aunt and uncle, knowing they had survived the bombing. She perched herself on the folding chair, swinging her legs back and forth, and tried to sit still until Sunday School started.

Mutti and Aunt Anna were chatting much louder than she was ever allowed to in church. Karin was tempted to speak up just because everyone else was. But what would she say? They wouldn't want to listen to her. They all talked about grown-up stuff.

"The war's basically over."

"The Germans have lost."

"So many have fled."

"Dresden will rebuild."

"Not a single member of our branch was killed."

The last statement caught Karin's attention. It made her feel good, almost safe in the crazy world that seemed to spin around her. She had to admit, being here at church had a comfortable, familiar feeling to it—unlike everything else as of late.

After the opening song, the branch president spoke, urging everyone to keep each other in their prayers. "Things will get better, I promise," he said. "We must have faith in God—faith that He will deliver us from these trials that have befallen us through no fault of our own. Keep the commandments. Cry unto Him every day. If the Russians forbid you to do so, cry to Him in your hearts, just as the followers of Alma did in the Book of Mormon."

Karin thought it strange that he told her she should cry—Mutti had told Christine to be strong and sniff back the tears. But if God wanted her to cry, if that would help when things got bad, she would cry. So long as Mutti didn't see her.

The branch president finished his talk and excused everyone to go to their classes. Karin and Christine got directed into one of the rooms she'd seen when they first walked in. She had to take the folding chair she'd been sitting in with her. It weighed down her arms and was hard to carry. Karin managed without any help—though it'd been offered by many an unfamiliar face. In class, it was only Christine and Karin and one other boy. She didn't know him. Christine seemed to because the two of them talked a lot—when the teacher let them.

Karin was bored. She wanted to go home. But not really. It was such a long walk. And she didn't look forward to falling asleep alone again while the others went and hid.

Finally, class was over. Karin left Christine to talk to that boy, and she ran out of the class room to go and find Mutti and Aunt Anna.

They stood by the front door with Aunt Sophronia, chattering so much they didn't even notice Karin. She leaned against the stone wall off to the side and waited, knowing Mutti would not be pleased if she interrupted them.

"I've convinced Anna to stay here in Dresden," Aunt Sophronia said to Mutti.

Aunt Anna placed a hand on Mutti's arm. "I'm sorry, Ida, but it didn't take a lot. You've got enough to worry about with your two girls."

"You're not a worry," Mutti insisted.

"Ida, I've stayed long enough. I never intended for it to be permanent. Sophronia knows of a place not too far from her and Stefan.

It's only one room, but it's still in one piece—and vacant. And if I can work for Stefan here and there in his leather shop, I'll make ends meet."

Sophronia leaned into Mutti. "The Russians seem to have an aversion to the rubble of our neighborhood. Maybe you should consider moving back too."

Mutti clasped her hand over Sophronia's. "We're all right. We'll stay in Wittgensdorf, for the same reason Russians probably choose to do so—there's food to be had. Plus, I have my job there." Mutti gave her a hug and then turned and wrapped her arms around Aunt Anna. "Well, I suppose this is auf wiedersehen then?"

Aunt Anna hugged her back. "I'll come visit. Don't worry."

"Please, do." Mutti pulled away after a hug that lasted forever and looked around. She seemed to notice Karin for the first time. "Oh, Karin, good. Where is your sister?"

Karin pointed down the hallway to the classroom where Christine continued to talk with that boy.

"Christine," Mutti said in her "listen-up" voice. "We're leaving. Hurry, we need to get back before dark."

The walk back home from church always felt longer. Though the days were getting warmer and longer now, the ground was still soggy. Karin's feet were wet. They felt cold.

Karin readied herself to complain about it, as she always did on the last leg of their journey home, but then she realized something. "I can walk farther now without getting tired," she announced.

"I'm so glad to hear that." Mutti wrapped an arm around her.

Christine moved to Mutti's other side. "Is the war really over?"

"Over?" Mutti dropped her arm from Karin and gave her attention to Christine. "Not really."

"But everyone at church today was talking like it was," Christine said.

"I guess you could say it is—for all intents and purposes." Mutti cocked her head slightly.

Karin didn't know what "intents and purposes" meant, but if it was over, she had a big question. "Mutti, if the war's over, why isn't Pappa home?"

"It's not really over—yet. Germany needs all her soldiers until the Nazi government officially surrenders."

"Then will he come home?" Karin tugged on Mutti's arm.

"How long will that be?" Christine added

"I don't know, girls."

Karin wondered why Mutti didn't act more excited about Pappa coming home. She moved her eyes from Mutti's sad face and looked into the sky. Its blue seemed to go on forever as the sun drifted off to the west.

A spot of black moved across the blue. She'd seen this before. The hum of engines followed. "Mutti," Karin screamed, pointing upward.

A plane darkened the sky directly overhead.

"But the war's over!" Christine cried.

"Not yet," Mutti yelled. "Run for cover!"

Karin ran with Mutti and Christine to a nearby ditch.

As she lay on her stomach, mud engulfed her, soaking her and sending an added chill through her body. She remembered what the branch president had told her to do. So she did it. She cried.

CHAPTER 10

"PLEASE, MUTTI, LET ME COME with you and Christine." Karin absolutely didn't want them to go. After seeing those planes a few hours ago, she didn't dare be alone for one more night.

"No, Karin, you are safer here." Mutti tucked Karin in bed.

A minute later they were gone.

Karin cried, just like she had in the ditch. That had worked then; it should work now. The tears flowed even easier than before. Then a thought came to her head: pray. "Please, Heavenly Father," she said as she cried, "protect me. Protect Mutti and Christine. Keep the mean people Mutti calls Russians from hurting us." The tears tapered off. A feeling, as sweet as honey on cake, settled over her, and she was able to lie there in the dark without crying anymore. She felt herself get sleepy.

The next thing she remembered was someone jabbing her with an elbow. She opened her eyes to see Christine turning over in bed and the morning's light streaming in through the window. The relief of seeing her sister safe beside her gave her the urge to hug Christine—and to talk and to know. "How long do you have to hide?" Karin said after she'd let go. Asking came more easily than she'd expected. Usually she avoided the subject. She ventured another question. "What time do you get home?"

"We're usually home by midnight." Christine's words came out slow and choppy, almost like they were painful. "We've found that the Russians want their sleep too; they turn in by eleven, eleven thirty."

"Where did you hide last night? Was it in Frau Krujatz's dog house again?"

"No." Christine pulled the blankets up to her chin and stared at the ceiling. "We could see some soldiers coming from that direction when we first headed out. So we went the other way, to Herr Reinhart's. Mutti said he had a bunch of hives on his farm. She figured the bees might scare off the Russians."

"Were you afraid of getting stung?"

Christine turned onto her side and faced Karin. "I'd take a million bee stings over one of those Russians anytime. But they kept away."

"The bees or the Russians?"

"The Russians," Christine said with a slight smile. "We heard someone walk by at a distance. Actually, two of them. They were talking. They sounded drunk. One of them mentioned something about hearing buzzing and bees. Then they left quickly."

"See, it worked," Karin said, excited.

"What worked? Hiding under the beehives?"

"No, I prayed really hard last night—while I cried like the branch president said—and it worked. Heavenly Father watched out for you. He protected you from the Russians."

"And I suppose you're going to say He protected us from the bees too," said Christine, "since neither Mutti nor I got stung."

"Of course," Karin said, even more pleased.

"Or maybe it was just because bees aren't as active at night," Christine said with a smug look on her face.

"I don't care what you say." Karin twisted her face into a pout to show Christine she disapproved. "I know it was my prayer."

The next night Karin cried just as hard and prayed just as hard. Going to sleep was easier that night. Christine and Mutti came home just as safe. They had hidden by the beehives again.

The following night, Christine told her they tried someplace else. "We need to keep moving around, just to be on the side of caution," Mutti had said. They came home safely again.

Not everyone else in the village was as fortunate.

Mutti talked to Frau Somer in the hall one sunny day as spring merged into summer. Karin opened the living room door to head down to the toilet. She heard Mutti's voice. Then Frau Somer's. Karin crept to the top of the stairs and hid behind the railing so they couldn't see her. What would they have to say for so long?

" . . . She's over in the hospital at Lungkwitz now." Mutti's voice carried up the stairs noticeably upset. "Practically every bone in her body was broken."

"The Fisher girl would have been a darn sight better off if she hadn't run from them. It wasn't the Russians that made her a cripple. She jumped out of that upper window of her own choice."

"Still, it was a Russian soldier who chased her up the stairs. She wouldn't have jumped if she hadn't known what was in store for her." Mutti let out a huff of air and trudged up the stairs.

Karin ran back into the living room, wanting to get there before Mutti saw her. She tried to calm the uncomfortable churning in her stomach. Maybe she shouldn't have listened in on that story.

Green leaves poked above the soil right where Karin had planted those seeds a few weeks earlier. She moved the rocks away from the tender, new sprouts so they wouldn't have to struggle to grow. Christine pulled weeds away from the cabbage she had planted. Karin sucked in a deep breath, delighting in the fresh smell of the garden and enjoying a carefree Saturday with her sister. It had been almost a week since Christine spoke about her and Mutti's hiding places. Maybe things were getting better. Maybe the Russians were being nicer. And now that the war was really over, Pappa would come home. She wished she could ask Mutti how long it would be until he got here.

Karin rose to her feet, tired of stooping over the seedlings. "Let's go visit Mutti!" she declared, thinking it was a great idea.

"At the farm?"

"Yeah!"

"But she's working."

"So? We'll just say hello. For a minute. And then go see Sonnenschein and come right back home." Karin liked that idea. She gazed out over the green that went on forever behind their house, delighted by the rows of leafy trees that bordered the patchwork of fields. "It's such a pretty day. I don't want to go back inside the house."

"Sonnenschein?" Christine perked up. "Okay, but if Mutti gets upset at us, I get to tell her you made me go."

"Fine." Karin took off running across the yard and out onto the lane. She slowed down by the time she passed Herr Schmitt's house.

Christine caught up with her. "I hear he's not the postman anymore," Christine said, pointing to the big home Herr Schmitt shared with the farmer, Herr Grun—also five Russian soldiers now—in the center of the village. "Ella says the Russians have taken over the post."

"But he's still the Burgermeister," Karin said. She liked Herr Schmitt now that she knew that under that big, bushy moustache he was just a nice old man. His promise to deliver Pappa's next letter came to mind. "The Russians won't care about Pappa's letters, will they?"

"Probably not—probably just throw away any letters from German soldiers. That's what they'll do."

"You think so?" Karin swallowed. She hoped her sister was wrong.

"No . . . They probably can't even read the addresses, so they'll just deliver them to all the wrong places."

"That wasn't very nice to say."

"Sorry. But they aren't the smartest soldiers I've seen, that's for sure," Christine said. "The other night, while we were hiding, before it got too dark, I saw a Russian soldier take a drink out of the faucet on the side of the Fishers' house. Then you know what he did next?"

Karin shook her head.

"He tore the faucet right off the side of their house and put it in his pocket. About a half hour later, I saw that same soldier searching their neighbor's yard. I don't know because it was kind of hard to see from our hiding place in the Fishers' tool shed, but it looked like that soldier held that faucet up to the other house and tried to get a drink out of it."

"He must have thought it was magic or something." Karin giggled as they walked down the lane.

They went to the packing shed first, the one they'd helped clean last winter. Christine stuck her head inside. "Anyone here?" Her voice echoed out through the opened door. No one responded.

"Let's try the barn," Karin said.

The barn held only tools, hay, and a musty, rotten smell. It made Karin hold her breath as she looked inside, scanning for Mutti, searching for Sonnenschein. "We could ask at the house." Karin started toward it.

On their way to the farmhouse, Karin spotted a small chestnut horse grazing in the field next to two large ones. It didn't look like a baby though. Could it be? She pointed to the field. "Is that Sonnenschein?"

"I think so. Come on," Christine swept her hand toward the horse that now trotted through the grass in circles like he was having fun.

"But . . . the Mutter and Pappa horses might get mad."

"Not if we walk slowly. We'll just sneak over to where Sonnenschein is. Don't give them cause to notice us. If they do happen to see us, act calm, don't let them think you're scared."

"But . . . I am scared. Now." Karin crept slowly behind Christine, poking her head around her sister now and then to catch sight of Sonnenschein. As they neared the colt, the two big ones gave her and Christine a quick glance and each returned to nibbling at the new grass with their big teeth. Karin relaxed a bit and moved out to Christine's side. Sonnenschein pulled his head up from the ground and turned it toward Karin and Christine. His eyes seemed to sparkle as if he recognized them, and he trotted toward them.

When they met up, he bent his head down. Karin patted his sun spot. He lowered his head farther, nuzzled her cheek with his soft pink nose, and then swung it over to Christine's smiling face and nuzzled it. They stroked his legs, his chest, and his tail. Karin enjoyed every minute as they basked in Sonnenschein's presence.

The colt grew tired of the attention before Karin did, for he ran away and resumed nibbling the grass next to his mother. Karin sighed and walked away from the horses. "Let's find Mutti."

Christine grabbed her arm. "No, let's go home. It's a big farm. She might be anywhere." She then gasped and nodded toward the far side of the farmhouse.

Karin looked. The dirt lane that split off the main road and led to the Reinhart farm held two men walking briskly in their direction. They each wore the mustard-brown uniform that Karin had grown to hate. "Russians! Are they coming to get you and Mutti?" She felt as though one of those big horses had just kicked her in the chest.

"I don't think so—not in broad daylight. I think they're just policing the area. But . . ." Christine grabbed Karin's arm. "I don't think we're supposed to be wandering about—what in the world was I thinking? I should have never listened to you. Let's get home." She pulled Karin in the opposite direction, craning her neck, keeping her eyes fixed on the soldiers.

Karin followed Christine, locking her gaze on the Russians. The large strides of the soldiers brought the pair closer and closer to her and Christine. "Let's run," she cried and broke into a sprint. Now Christine followed her.

"Halt!" yelled one of the Russians.

They dove into the field behind the barn, hiding among the rows of new corn. Karin crouched down next Christine, the stalks luckily towering above them by half a meter. After several minutes curled in a ball and heart pounding in her ears, Karin whispered, "What will they do if they find us wandering about, Christine?"

"I don't know; maybe nothing."

"Then why are we hiding?"

"Just to be on the safe side. Who knows, maybe they could fine Mutti lots of money—or lock us up in jail." Several more minutes passed before Christine rose slowly and peered over the tops of the corn stalks. "I think they're gone. Let's hurry home. And then stay there."

They circled around the corn field and came out in Frau Krujatz's backyard. Creeping across the yard, they tried not to wake the old woman's black dog as it slept in its dog house.

Woof, woof, woof. The dog sprung to life. He darted out of his house and headed straight at Karin. He licked her face.

Karin wrapped her arms around the big dog.

"Fritz!" Frau Krujatz's voice came from the house. The back door swung open about the same time two different Russian soldiers came around the other side of the house.

"Is there a problem here?" said one of the soldiers in a poor rendition of German.

"No, no," said Frau Krujatz. "Not at all." She hurried down the steps and ran toward Karin and Christine. "These are just my . . . my granddaughters. They're playing with my dog. Can't you see?"

"Very well, Frau," the same soldier said and turned around in sync with the other soldier.

Karin took a deep breath as she watched them slip out of sight. She didn't know why the old woman had lied and called her and Christine her granddaughters. But it made Karin feel special. And made the Russians go away. She ran over and gave Frau Krujatz a hug. "Thank you, Frau Krujatz!"

The old lady invited them in for a slice of bread. She even spread it with a layer of jam. It tasted so good. Karin wanted to ask for another piece, but Christine gave her a stern look as she stood from the table. "Thank you for the bread and jam, Frau."

"Would you like a drink of water to wash it down?" asked Frau Krujatz.

"No, thank you, we'd better get on home now."

"Your Mutter will be coming home shortly. I see her pass by every day about this time—time enough to make you supper before . . . well, you know what I mean," she mumbled. "Fine woman, your Mutter. You girls should know that."

"Oh, we do," said Christine before she slipped out the door with Karin in tow.

As they walked up the stone path to their house, Brunhilde lounged across the porch steps, practically blocking Christine and Karin's way to the front door. Ella sat cross-legged in the shadows of the far corner of the porch.

"Where have you Liebchens been?" Brunhilde asked. She took a bite out of something that looked like a sausage.

"Just taking a walk," Karin said, wishing she had a sausage to nibble on.

"The Russians might not like that." Brunhilde lifted her eyebrows and wagged her finger at Karin. "Children are supposed to be supervised at all times," she said, eyeing Christine.

"Uh . . . I didn't know that." Christine stiffened.

Karin wondered why Christine lied—earlier she seemed to know that. That wasn't like her sister.

"Well, don't tell me. It's them you'll have to explain that to . . . if they catch you." Brunhilde twisted her mouth into a scary-looking grin. "And if they catch you, they might—"

"But, but—" Christine stiffened even more.

"Stop it." Ella uncrossed her legs and let them drop to the ground. "Don't tease the poor things—at least when it comes to the Russians."

"You're just jealous that I got a box of sausages and you got nothing." Brunhilde waved her sausage.

"Don't remind me. Last night was awful. I swear he was smellier and drunker than usual."

Christine's eyes opened wide as goose eggs. "You two don't go hide every night?"

"No," Brunhilde answered. "You wouldn't have to either if you just went willingly. Or invited a handsome one to be your protector." She took a bit of her sausage. "They might even reward you with some food. Heaven knows you could use some." Brunhilde pinched Christine's arm.

"Where'd you get that sausage?" Karin asked. They looked like the kind the Fishers made and sold to the others in the village.

"From my soldier." Brunhilde took another bite and then wagged it at Karin.

"He probably stole them," Ella said. "Those soldiers get rations that'd make even these two Liebchens' supper look like a feast."

"How could you do that? Let them—" Christine hunched her shoulders and pulled a face like she'd tasted something sour. She glared at Brunhilde and then at Ella.

"Hey, don't judge me." Ella stood quickly. "I'm just doing what I have to, to survive." She headed for the door and rushed in without another word.

"Yeah, what she said." Brunhilde followed Ella into the house.

Karin watched the Somer girls leave, not knowing what to say. She kept silent, feeling the urge to cry. The day had worn her out.

She'd been wrong. Things weren't getting better. Maybe she should try "crying" to the Lord again.

CHAPTER 11

"I don't want Frau Somer to watch me." Karin stomped her foot. "Why can't Christine stay home? Or Frau Krujatz take care of me?"

"Because Frau Krujatz is visiting family," Mutti said.

Christine grabbed her ranzen and opened the door. "And I've already missed enough school. Sorry. Just wait another week, and it'll be my summer break. Auf wiedersehen," she said, giving a quick wave before she disappeared into the hall.

"Can't I just come to the farm with you?" Karin asked Mutti.

"I'll be hoeing in the fields all day. That's no place for a little girl, especially one who gets bored at the drop of a hat."

"I can play with Sonnenschein."

"The answer is no." Mutti took Karin by the arm and led her out of the kitchen.

Karin held back the urge to protest further. In silence, she trudged down the stairs. She chewed on her bottom lip as Mutti knocked on the door to the Somers' living room, and they waited. Mutti knocked again.

The door finally opened. Frau Somer poked her head out. "Yes?"

"Karin's had her breakfast. Her lunch is in here." Mutti handed Frau Somer a clean dish cloth Karin knew held a slice of bread.

"Oh." Frau Somer accepted it with reluctance.

"Have you forgotten?" Mutti's voice sounded higher than usual. "You agreed last Friday to watch Karin this week."

"I suppose I did, didn't I?" Frau Somer turned and yelled back into the room, "Ella, Brunhilde, one of you keep an eye on the Graeber girl. I told her Mutter I'd do it, but I forgot I had plans."

"I don't want to." Brunhilde's voice came through the door loud and whiny.

"Well, I can't possibly do it today," Frau Somer said.

The sound of footsteps clapped across the floor. "Oh, *all right*. I'll do it." Ella's face appeared in the door way. She snatched the towel-covered bread with one hand and extended the other to Karin. "Come on, Liebschen, I'll take you today."

Mutti smiled at Ella. "Thank you, dear." She turned to Frau Somer. "Karin will only need to stay here until her sister gets home from school. And I'll bring those radishes I promised by this evening after work."

"Sure, sure, that'll work." Frau Somer flapped a hand at Mutti. "Sorry, I can't talk longer, but I've got someplace to be." She slipped past Karin and out the front door.

Mutti's mouth tightened into a straight line. She stared at the front door as it closed and then shifted her gaze to Karin. "Mind your manners now. I'll be back in time for supper."

"Yes, Mutti." Karin stepped into the Somers' living room without Mutti. Her stomach soured, rebelling against being left here all day. She sighed and said to Ella, "I've never been in here before."

"Well, lucky you." Ella set Karin's lunch on a table that held a fancy lamp along with a dusty vase and someone's sweater. "It's not all that great."

"What do you mean?" Karin gazed around. Though clothes and newspapers cluttered the room, it was huge—and none of the chairs were singed black. "Look at this big room and all its nice furniture." She peered into the kitchen through an open door. "And look at the size of that stove. You're probably never cold down here."

Brunhilde lay across a big green couch with one of her legs draped up on its back. "Wrong there, von-Karin." She slowly swung both legs to the floor and eased up off the couch, glaring at Ella. "And what are *you* going to do to entertain the kid all day?"

Karin backed away, clinging to the security of a big stuffed chair's soft arm. She didn't need to be entertained! Mutti should have left her upstairs in their own living room. Alone. She would have been just fine. She would have stayed put—maybe. All day was a long time.

"We'll start in the garden," Ella said to Brunhilde. "There's plenty of weeds to keep her occupied."

"Leave me out of it, whatever you do." Brunhilde held her stomach and hurried to the door. A moment later, the sound of vomiting echoed through the hall and into the living room.

"Poor Brunhilde," Karin said. "Is she sick?"

"Yes," responded Ella. "Every morning, at least. Now stay put while I go change into some gardening clothes." She stepped into the hall and turned toward the stairs.

Karin sat down in the fancy chair she'd been clinging to, examining the blue and green flowers dotting its fabric. She jumped back up, turning around to remove a wadded-up towel that caused a lump in her seat. Folding it neatly, she had the urge to help tidy things up. Why didn't Frau Somer ask her girls to help tidy up? Maybe she was like Mutti—doing it all herself so her girls "wouldn't grow up before they had to." No, that couldn't be it—Brunhilde and Ella were already grown up.

I'll just tidy up for them. It'll be fun. There was something actually to clean. Mutti always kept their place so spotless that there was nothing left for Karin to do even though she wanted so much to help her mother. She picked up a pair of dirty socks and sat them next to the folded towel on the chair.

"What are you doing?" Brunhilde shuffled in and headed for the couch.

"Tidying up. It's fun."

"You're a strange little girl. Why would you help if you didn't have to?"

"Because . . . I want to."

Ella walked into the living room dressed in a pair of trousers. "Let's go out to the garden. Brunhilde is rotten company this time of the day."

Brunhilde stuck out her tongue.

Ella held out her hand for Karin to accept. Karin grabbed hold somewhat reluctantly, and they walked outside.

Sunshine wrapped Karin in warmth when she stepped off the porch. The pleasant sensation reminded her of Herr Reinhart's baby horse, and that reminded her of Mutti and how she'd rather be down at the farm helping Mutti than here with Ella. Sadness spread down to her feet. She dragged them across the grass.

"Come on, Liebschen. You're walking too slowly."

"Sorry," Karin responded. She tried to walk a little faster for her mother's sake—it would make Mutti sad if she knew Karin was unhappy while she was away at work. Karin needed to be strong.

The warble of a bird caught her ear. She looked up, scanned the leafy tree tops and then the clear blue sky. It was all so pretty. It was almost as if the summer day's beauty took Mutti's place momentarily. Karin felt the urge to skip—just a little. She skirted ahead and made it to the backyard before Ella.

Ella rounded the corner of the house. "I didn't mean you had to run." She headed to the tool shed and returned holding two hoes. "You ever used one of these?"

"No." Karin looked over to their garden in the far corner of the backyard. "Mutti does most of the weeding in our garden here."

"Don't sound so disappointed. My Mutter *saves* the weeding for Brunhilde and me. Hey, I'll gladly share some of those annoying little things with you." Ella gave her a funny grin and handed her the smallest hoe. "Don't use it yet. Just hold on to it and watch me for a while."

Ella dragged her hoe across the soil, scraping away a pile of green. "You've got to be careful and only hoe away the plants in between the rows of potatoes. Now you try."

Karin pulled her hoe between two rows of bigger plants that had crinkled leaves and looked like they were meant to be there. It was kind of fun to see the ground turn back to brown as her hoe scraped away the green weeds.

"Good job, Liebschen."

After they had cut down everything between the rows, Ella had Karin lower down onto her knees and showed her which plants to pull and which were potatoes. Karin found it kind of fun.

When they were almost finished, Karin pointed to the small patch the Somers had given Mutti. "Can we work in our garden next?" She envisioned Mutti's surprise if she and Ella removed all those weeds.

"Not on your life." Ella wiped the back of her hand across her forehead. "I've had enough weeding for one day. Haven't you?"

"I guess." Karin chewed on her lip and looked around. The sun now shone directly overhead, and the shade next to the tall trees bordering the lane looked awfully inviting. She noticed a man walk down the lane and then lean against one of the trees as if cooling-off in the shade. The way he tilted his head seemed to draw her in. Though tall, the man was as thin as a lamppost and looked as frail as an old woman. He wore a tattered uniform. Karin thought it might be a German one, but she wasn't sure, not having seen one of those for a while.

His head turned in Karin's direction. He seemed to perk up when he noticed her and Ella. Walking with a slight limp, he made his way across the yard with his eyes fixed on Karin.

It made Karin uncomfortable; she wanted to run into the house—but to whom? Brunhilde? She bit on her bottom lip even harder, trying to calm her jumpy stomach.

"Karin?" the man said, now only a few paces away. His voice sounded familiar.

Karin examined him closely. She knew those blue eyes, the way he swung his hands as he walked.

"Pappa!"

She jumped to her feet and ran into his arms. His embrace nearly broke her in two.

As he loosened his hold, a sob came from his trembling lips. He stepped back, keeping his hands on Karin's shoulders, and gazed at her like his life depended on the action. "My Little Streusel," he said wiping away a tear from his eye. "I thought I'd never see you again. My, how you've grown."

"I'm six now," Karin said, feeling her smile grow so big her cheeks ached. "I've been helping Ella in the garden." She pointed to Ella, who nodded at Pappa. "She's watching me today."

Pappa tipped his cap and smiled at Ella. He turned back to Karin. "Where's your Mutti? Where's Christine? Are they here? Are they all right?"

"Ja, Mutti's working at the farm. And Christine's at school."

Pappa let out a big sigh.

Karin grabbed hold of his hand and pulled him away from the garden. "You look like you're hungry." She turned to Ella, feeling her smile stretch wide as ever. "You don't have to watch me anymore. I've got my Pappa now. I'm going to take him inside and make him some dinner."

Christine got home shortly after Karin had washed a bowl of radishes and shared them with Pappa. "Karin, what are you doing up here all alone?" she said as she swung the kitchen door open. Christine's eyes widened and then lit up. "Pappa!" She ran over and hugged him for longer than Karin thought was good for Pappa. "My arms feel like they're going to fall off, but I don't want to stop," Christine said.

"Well, you need to." Karin put her hands on her hips. "He needs to rest. He's been walking for a week. Haven't you, Pappa?"

"Not quite. But it feels like it. Actually, it feels like I've been walking for a year—three years to be exact." Pappa stood up from the table. "I'd like to go see your Mutter. Please, take me to her." He reached out to Christine.

Christine took Pappa by the hand and glanced at the window. "I'm not always sure where to find her. But she should be home shortly. I promise. Just rest and wait here with us." She pulled him toward the living room.

"Well . . . if you're sure she'll be home soon," Pappa said with hesitation.

"Ja, wait here with us." Karin took his other hand. She skipped as they made their way through the hall.

Pappa plopped onto the couch, pulling Karin and Christine down with him. His arms went around their shoulders and squeezed them." You'll never know how much I missed you girls."

"I missed you too." Christine laid her head on his chest. "So very, very much."

"Me too, Pappa," Karin said with emphasis. She didn't want him to think her sister was the only one who missed him just because she said "so very, very much."

"Thank the good Lord I'm home now." He let go of Christine, moving his hand up to cover a big yawn.

Karin felt Pappa's arm grow limp around her shoulders. She snuggled in closer, not wanting his embrace to stop. With her ear against his side, she heard the calm thump of his heart. Moments later she felt his chest rise and fall with the slow, steady breaths of one who is sleeping. She pulled herself upright and looked into Pappa's face. His eyes were closed. *No.* She wanted him to keep hugging her.

Karin latched onto his shoulder, ready to shake it, but Christine stood and pulled her away.

"No, let Pappa sleep," Christine said. "At least until Mutti gets home."

Karin chewed down all her fingernails, waiting for him to wake up. She wanted to talk to him, hug him, play with him—leaving him alone about drove her crazy. But she never left Pappa's side. Neither did Christine.

"I wonder what Mutti will do when she sees him?" Christine whispered just as the quiet waiting grew too much for Karin to bear.

"Ja." Karin perked up. "Hey, let's surprise her, tease her a bit."

Christine's eyes radiated in favor of the idea. But after taking a moment to think about it, the mischievous glint disappeared. "Uh . . . Mutti might not be too happy with that. She's missed him something awful—almost given him up for dead."

"Aw, come on. It'll be just for a minute. We won't say anything about Pappa. We'll let her walk into the room and see him sleeping here on the couch. It'll be fun to see her face."

"Oh . . . okay."

The sun had set when Karin finally heard the hurried clomp of Mutti's shoes on the stairs. "Sorry, I'm late girls," Mutti's voice echoed in from the hall, but her footsteps sounded like they were headed for the kitchen. "It's going to have to be a quick dinner if Christine and I are going to get us a good hiding place for tonight."

Hiding place! Karin had enjoyed having Pappa home so much, she'd completely forgotten about that. Like she'd done often as of late, she quickly swept the unpleasant event out of her thoughts. She'd deal with it only when she had to. Right now she wanted to surprise Mutti.

Unable to hold back her excitement, she took off for the kitchen. "Mutti! We've got a surprise for you."

Christine followed right behind. "Ja, it's the best surprise ever. Come into the living room."

Mutti stood at the sink giving a bowl of radishes a quick wash. "I don't have time for surprises," she said, rolling her eyes up at the ceiling.

Karin tugged on her arm. "You'll really like this one."

"Oh, all right. What is it?" Mutti wiped her hands on her apron. She followed Karin and Christine into the living room at a leisurely stroll compared to Karin's sprint.

Mutti froze. Her jaw sagged and eyes widened. She stood in the doorway for a drawn-out moment as if she couldn't move or speak. Finally a word came, sounding deep, almost bottomless.

"Paul!"

Pappa blinked the sleep from his eyes and rose from the couch with arms spread wide. "My dear Ida!"

Tears flowed from Mutti's eyes as she lowered onto the couch in Pappa's arms. "I thought I'd never see you again."

"Me too, me too," Pappa murmured, his lips brushing her cheek. "But it was the only thing that kept me going, wanting to see you . . . to be with my family." His voice waivered; his eyes filled with moisture. "And now I'm finally here."

Karin sat in the big chair with her arms around her sister. Christine returned each squeeze Karin gave her. Happy feelings overflowed inside Karin, so much so that her legs wanted to jump and her arms wanted to fly up and clap. But her heart wanted to keep hugging her sister more. She remained entwined with Christine, though her legs wiggled about.

The room soon grew dim as the setting sun withdrew its light from the window. Mutti reluctantly pulled herself from Pappa's embrace. "Dear me, it's getting dark!" She straightened the front of her dress as she readied herself to stand.

"So it is," replied Pappa, pulling Mutti back into his arms. "Turn on the lights. This place does have electricity, does it not?"

"Yes, it does. If only that were the problem." Mutti held Pappa's arms down to his side as she stood; the light in her eyes dimming to a look of sorrow. "It's the Russians, Paul. Christine and I must hide from them. Every night."

"We haven't hidden under Herr Reinhart's beehives for a while." Christine released her hold on Karin. "Should we try there tonight?"

Pappa cut in. "So what I've heard is true?"

Mutti and Christine nodded at the same time.

Pappa's face paled. His fist clenched. "But I'm here now. Surely they won't bother you with a man in the house." He stood and followed Mutti. "We'll stay together tonight."

Karin hopped down off the chair at the same time as Christine, and they followed their parents to the kitchen. She hoped Mutti would listen to Pappa. It would be wonderful to have the whole family together tonight. She hated being left alone while Mutti and Christine hid.

"There's nothing I would love more. But . . ." Mutti hesitated. "No, Paul. It's not safe." Her words echoed with sadness in the hall.

Pappa grabbed her by the arm. "But I'll protect you—there's no need to hide."

Mutti slipped from his grasp and moved into the kitchen. "They'd just shoot you if you tried to stop them from getting to us," she said, her voice higher and more intense than usual. "They did that to a farmer on the other side of the village. Or they might choose to put a gun to your head and just make you watch." Mutti lowered her voice when Karin and Christine stepped into the kitchen. "You need to trust me on this, Paul."

Pappa pounded his fist on the table. "Those dirty, rotten scum." He sank into a chair and looked up at Mutti. "Is there nothing the government can do about this?"

Mutti shook her head.

"Or the townspeople?" Pappa asked.

"I pray constantly for their rampage to end." Mutti placed a bowl of washed radishes on the table. "But I need to do everything in my power as well. So far we've survived just fine." She sat down at the table next to Pappa. "Whatever you do, Paul, don't fight them. Promise me you won't."

Pappa let out a sigh and gave a slow nod of his head.

Mutti scooted out a chair for Karin to climb onto. Christine pulled out her own chair. "Paul, would you offer thanks on this food?"

Pappa nodded and bowed his head. "Dear Lord, thank you for this fine food. Please bless it for our good. And please, Lord, help me to protect my family . . ."

After Pappa's prayer, he gazed up, meeting Christine's eyes. With a touch of sadness darkening his eyes, he said, "Gray is a good color to help hide you. Do you have a gray coat?" Christine nodded as she took a bite of her bread. "Good. I think your Mutter is right; it's probably best that you hide." He glanced at Mutti. "Perhaps I should come with you."

"No, no." Mutti shook her head. "It's hard enough to hide two people, let alone a third who is a tall man."

"What?" Pappa asked. "Does Karin not go with you?"

"I get her to bed before we go. But there's no time—or need tonight. You're here. They won't bother you or her if we're not here."

"So you've left her alone all these nights?" Pappa furrowed his brow as he popped a radish in his mouth.

Mutti swallowed the bite of bread she'd been chewing. "Paul, to take her would have been even more dangerous. She's a child. Like I said, hiding the two of us is hard enough, let alone having a third body to conceal—one that is prone to become bored and whine."

Pappa's jaw jutted out as he spoke slowly. "This is not good; none of this is. I don't—"

"I know it's not good. Nothing is since the Russians took over." Mutti stuffed the remaining morsel of bread into her mouth. "But you're here now, so she won't be alone anymore. They might search the place, but they won't bother you or her . . . *if* we're not here. That's pretty much a known fact here in the village. So don't worry."

Karin had just gotten to where she could pray away the worry that lingered with her after Mutti and Christine left each night. But Mutti's words heaped it back upon her. Had the Russians searched their place while she was asleep? The thought made her skin prickle.

Mutti stood from the table and tied a scarf under her chin. "Enough talk. We must be going. Will you clean up supper?" She looked at Pappa. She then motioned for Christine to come, and together they scurried out the door.

Karin was so glad to have Pappa with her tonight. Not only would she fall asleep a little easier now, she'd have his attention all to herself. She grabbed his fingers and pulled him from the kitchen. "Let's dance." She wanted to hold his hand and dance around the living room, have him toss her into the air like he used to.

Pappa's hand slipped from her grasp. He trudged to the couch, dropped down in its cushions, and cradled his face in his hands. "What has become of Germany?"

CHAPTER 12

THE FIRST WEEK OF SUMMER seemed even sunnier with Pappa around. It was worth having to split their food four ways instead of just three. Pappa recovered slowly as a result of the rationing, and he rested a lot.

The end of June came, and so did Christine's summer break from school. The first day Christine was home, Pappa felt stronger and played tag with Karin and Christine in the yard. He helped them weed the garden and accompanied them on a walk through the village and nearby woods. Karen loved having Pappa home.

"This is lovely," Christine said as the three of them strolled through a canopy of green arching over the trail through the woods. "Is this where you and Pappa came every day while I was at school?" Her voice held a hint of envy.

"Not really." Karin grabbed hold of Christine's hand, her other hand retaining its grip on Pappa's. "But now that Pappa's feeling better, we *should* do this every day until you go back to school. And I start school," she added. She looked up at Pappa. "I won't mind. Is that okay with you?"

"There is nothing I would like more, Karin." Pappa's smile stiffened and then disappeared before he spoke again. "But I need to start working. Find a job. It should be your Mutter out here strolling the woods with you—I should be the one at work."

"But Mutti never plays tag," Karin said.

"She'd be too busy doing chores even if she didn't have to go to work on the farm," Christine added.

Pappa ran a hand down his face, resting it on his chin. "All the more reason I need to find a job."

"But Mutti says there're no jobs out there." Karin let go of Christine's hand and placed both of hers around Pappa's and pulled hard. "Stay here. You can watch me. Mutti says I'm a job to take care of."

Pappa chuckled. "That you are." His eyes skirted away from Karin's face and stared at the base of a nearby tree. "Ah, I haven't seen those for a while."

"What?" Christine asked.

"Ja, what?" Karin said as Pappa pulled her toward the tree.

Pappa let go of her hand as he approached the tree and knelt down near its trunk. He ran his fingers over a mound of gray and white bumps. "Wild mushrooms. We made many a meal out of them, my army buddies and I, last summer while out in the battlefield near Dusseldorf."

Christine pulled a face and knelt down next to Pappa. "Really? Ugh."

"Christine doesn't like them," Karin said, kneeling on the other side of Pappa.

"You've had these before?"

Karin nodded her head.

Christine's face twisted even more. "Almost every night for a while." She stood up and brushed off her knees. "That was before the farm started producing. Mutti brought us out here to hunt for mushrooms after the farmer's wife had shown her how to search for the right kind. But if you ask me, no mushroom is the right kind."

"I didn't like them either," added Karin, not wanting to be left out of the conversation, though she hadn't minded the mushrooms that much—they had taken her hunger away.

"They can be tasty enough if you cook them just right." Pappa removed his hat. He turned it upside down and began picking mushrooms, placing them within the battered brown hat. "Look at them all. We can't let food go to waste. Tell you what, I'll cook these up for you girls tonight like I did for my buddies in the army, and I bet you a game of tag that they'll taste good enough you'll ask for more."

Mutti was delighted with their find of mushrooms. She even sat at the kitchen table and put her feet up on a chair while Pappa fried them up with a little oil and salt. Mutti then served them with a slice of bread for supper. Karin liked how Mutti had cooked them last time better than Pappa's way, but she didn't say anything. She wanted that game of tag. Christine must have been just as confused because she nibbled on them without saying a word, though she did pull a face when Mutti and Pappa weren't looking. Karin ate all of hers and then remained in her chair, staring at Pappa.

"Good news, Paul," Mutti said after she'd finished her last bite of mushrooms. She stood and started clearing the table. "Herr Reinhart said he could use some more help in the fields until after the harvest. Perhaps he'd be willing to hire you—as soon as you've got your strength back."

"It's back—enough so." Pappa stood and nodded to Karin and Christine, indicating they were free to leave the table. He grabbed some dishes and followed Mutti to the sink. "I'll talk to him tomorrow. Hopefully, it could work into something permanent later on. There's not much need for a shopkeeper in Wittgensdorf, is there?"

"No, unfortunately," Mutti said. "It's just a farming village."

"So I've noticed. How far is it to the next town?"

"Lungkwitz is about two kilometers away."

"That's where I go to school," Christine spoke up. "They do have two shops there. Though one is closing down."

Pappa let out a sigh. He then glanced at Karin as she leaned against the door frame, continuing to stare at him. "What is it, Karin? You want something?"

"Are we going to play tag now? Me and Christine ate your mush-rooms." Karin didn't want to lie and say she liked them, so she left it at that.

Pappa grinned wide. "Tomorrow, sweetie. It's time for your Mutti and Christine to hide and for you to go to bed."

Karin kicked the air. "I don't want to go to bed."

"Dear me," gasped Mutti. "It *is* time for you to get to bed—and us to hide." Mutti swept Karin from the doorway and toward her and Christine's new bedroom.

Karin still thought of it as the living room, even if a beat-up white baby crib sat against one wall and Christine's pillow rested continually atop a folded quilt at the end of the couch—her sister's bed now. There was not enough room in Mutti's big bed for her, Christine, *and* Pappa.

Karin didn't like sleeping in the crib. Her head touched one end, and her feet touched the other. She was too old for a crib. But Pappa and Mutti couldn't afford another bed right now. Herr Somer had offered to let Pappa borrow it for her to sleep in, "at least until Brunhilde's baby comes," he'd said. Karin hoped Brunhilde's baby would come soon. But how? Brunhilde didn't have a big belly, and she wasn't even married. Was this just another one of those confusing things grown-ups said?

"I don't want to go to bed," Karin said.

"I don't have time to fight with you right now," Mutti said as she helped Karin out of her dress and into her nightclothes. "Just climb in here and go to sleep."

"I don't like that cri—" She cut her words short. Sleeping in a baby's bed was worth having Pappa home. She stomped her foot to ease her frustration. "Can't I sleep in your bed until you get home?"

"Let her do it just this once," Pappa said, settling onto the couch with a book in hand. "I'll wait till you get home to go to bed. I'll move her then."

"Oh, all right!" Mutti tried the doorknob to the bedroom. When it didn't open, she pulled the key from the nail on the wall and unlocked the bedroom door. "Hurry, get in here and climb into bed." She quickly tucked Karin in bed and yelled through the door. "Christine!"

"Yes, Mutti."

"Are you ready to go? We need to hurry."

Christine appeared in the doorway. Her eyes looked tired. "Can't I stay home? It'll probably be just another quiet night."

"No." Mutti grabbed Christine's arm and pulled her into the hall. The door clicked shut.

Karin knew she was supposed to go to sleep, but she wasn't sleepy. Though she snuggled amidst the quilt of her parents' bed, that familiar uncomfortable feeling appeared. But Pappa was home now. Knowing he was on the other side of the door reading a book helped calm her. She used to have to pray that feeling away.

She must have fallen asleep, because she awoke to loud voices out in the living room. Moonlight streamed through the window, all remnants of the setting sun long gone.

"There's no one in there but my baby girl." Pappa's voice sounded strained.

"Well, that is for us to decide," said a man with a Russian accent.

Russian soldiers! It must have been one of them trying the doorknob—Pappa would never shake it so violently. Karin feared the knob would be pulled out of its place.

"This door isss locked. Why?"

"Sorry. It wasn't meant to be locked." Pappa sounded nervous.

"We musssht . . . access all rooms!" The slur in the soldier's voice told Karin he'd been drinking alcohol. "Our job to search everywhere. Our priv . . . ilege . . . to take what we want."

Loud crashes brought Karin upright. She hugged her pillow, envisioning overturned furniture. Anger-filled rants in Russian pulled her back down into the security of the quilt. She pulled it over her head.

Footsteps pounded up the stairs. A third voice could be heard: Herr Somer's. "What's going on here?"

"Ah, Edward! Thank heavens," Pappa said. "Maybe you have a key to this door? I can't find our key anywhere."

"I don't," Herr Somer said. His boots clapped across the floor. The doorknob rattled. "Is there anyone inside?"

"Only my Karin. And she's asleep."

"Wake her. Maybe she's got the key in there."

Loud knocking pulled Karin's head out from beneath the covers.

"Karin, Karin, wake up." It must have been Pappa pounding on the door.

Karin sat up. "Yes, Pappa?"

"Can you unlock the door?"

"I don't know."

"If she cannot, I shooot doorknob."

"No!" Pappa screamed. A scuffle of feet. "You could hit her!"

"I dooo not care. You know the rules. I will schooot you if I have to."

"No! Wait!" Herr Somer cried out. "Hold on. There's no need to do that. Maybe we can take the door off its hinges."

"I've already thought of that," Pappa said. "They're on the other side of the door."

"I'd say to kick the door in, but the wood's too blasted thick—I know, I've tried before," Herr Somer said. "Have your girl look inside the room for the key while I go see what I can find."

"We wait for a minute," one of the soldiers said. "Hurry."

Herr Somer's footsteps pounded in quick fashion out of the living room and down the stairs.

"Karin, hurry. Turn on the light, and look for the key. It's really important, my Little Streusel. Can you do that for me?"

Karin scrambled out of the bed. "Yes, Pappa." Her legs shook as they touched the floor—she'd never heard Pappa sound that scared before. She felt her way to the wall that held the light switch. The moonlight from the window didn't reach into this corner of the room. Her fingers searched furiously for the round form that held the switch. *Found it!*

The bulb hanging from the ceiling filled the room with light. It brought a tiny measure of comfort but not enough to calm all the fear that raced inside her stomach like a swarm of enemy planes. She looked under the bed, on the end table, and in the keyhole. Maintaining her gaze in the keyhole, she peered into the living room. All she could see was the back of Pappa's trousers. He was in front of the door but was standing anything but still. "I can't find it," Karin cried.

"Try harder," Pappa said.

"Okay." Karin caught a glimpse of one of the Russian soldiers as Pappa's jittering took him away from the keyhole for a moment. The man held a gun. He had it pointed at Pappa.

Karin gasped.

"Are you okay, Karin?"

"Yes." Why had she lied? She backed away from the door.

"Hurry, keep trying to find it," Pappa said.

Karin scurried around the room searching frantically. "Please, God, help us," she whispered as she looked. Scuffling noises in the living room pulled her focus away from her search.

"Enough!" shouted one of the Russians. "Stop stalling. You are hiding something in that room. Open the door, or I shoot you."

"No!" Karin screamed.

A stampede of footsteps came up the stairs.

"Wait," called out Herr Somer. "I brought the Burgermeister."

"Sooo what? Can he open the door?"

"Hold on, sergeant," cried Herr Schmitt. He sounded short of breath. "You don't want to shoot Herr Graeber. He's a good comrade. You're a good comrade. Now, just put that gun back in its holster. Nice. And. Easy."

"It is our right to search this room. Graeber iss hiding someone. I know it."

"There's no one for you in there. It's just my baby daughter. I promise. She's only six, for goodness's sake—you don't want her." Pappa's voice sounded defiant.

Karin worried Pappa would forget Mutti's words, worried he'd fight the Russians. She couldn't lose Pappa. "Be careful Pa—"

"Maybeee I do." The Russian's words drowned out her plea. "And . . . maybe I want to shoot you too . . . for locking door."

"No, sergeant." Herr Schmitt's voice boomed with command. "There's no need to shoot Comrade Graeber. Come, we'll fetch a ladder. You can access the room through its window. And see they're not hiding any women in there."

After a shuffle and footsteps pounded down the steps, the upstairs grew quiet. Karin curled up in a ball on the bed. Though the room was warm, she rubbed her arms to calm her shivers. A loud thump sounded beneath the window and then the click of pebbles being thrown at the glass.

"Karin!" Pappa's voice called from outside. "Open the window."

Karin ran to the window. It wouldn't budge. She pushed harder, her heart beating so loud she could hear it in her ears. Amazingly, the window budged. She pushed it up and poked her head out.

Pappa was on the ladder, climbing toward her. "Hold on, Little Streusel. I'm coming up to help you find the key."

"No! We will search without you!" The biggest of the soldiers pulled Pappa from the ladder and threw him to the ground. He scrabbled onto the ladder and climbed toward Karin with the smaller soldier following right behind him. The moon lit him just enough to see a face she swore could be Satan's. She pulled her head back in and stifled a scream, crouching beneath the sill. Through the open window she heard the ladder creak. It creaked again. And again. She pictured the soldiers moving closer to her with each creak. Now she could hear their breathing, huffing and laboring—they were almost to the window. *Slap!* Fingers, large as sausages, reached around and clasped onto the window sill.

Karin bolted toward the bed, dropped to the floor, and shimmied beneath it. Peering past the dangling quilt, she watched the first soldier struggle to pull himself through the window. The smaller soldier climbed in with less effort. They immediately started searching the room, tearing through clothing in the wardrobe and tossing it on the floor, slapping the floor-length drapes and then peering behind them. They pulled away the quilt that had served as Karin's flimsy shield.

There was not anywhere else for them to look—except under the bed. She curled up tighter. It was inevitable, but still she prayed they wouldn't find her.

The stocky legs of the largest soldier lowered onto the floor. A second later, eyes, red and glassy, set deep in his pock-marked face, peered under the bed.

"AHHH!" Karin's throat burned as she screamed.

He grabbed her arm and pulled her out. The other soldier glared at her as she was held motionless by the big soldier's grasp. He said something in Russian. The smaller soldier nodded. Karin felt his other large hand scoop her off the floor. The alcohol in his breathe and the smell of sweat sickened her further, especially when he held her close to his chest.

He threw her onto the bed.

Karin immediately curled into a ball.

His lip curled. "Too young." He spat the words.

The smaller soldier moved to the window and crawled out. The bigger one stumbled after him and struggled up and over the ledge. "Whoa!" His fat fingers flew from the sill. "Uhhhh!" A sickening scream started loud but quickly trailed off. *Thud!*

Karin jumped up and looked out. And down. With the help of the moonlight, she could see that the big Russian soldier lay in a heap at the base of the ladder. Pappa, Herr Somer, and the Burgermeister gathered around him.

"He's out cold." Herr Schmitt nudged the unmoving body with the tip of his boot. "Same for the one beneath him. Drunk men should know better than to climb a ladder that high."

"How long do you figure they'll be out?" Herr Somer asked.

"If we leave them alone, they'll probably wake up in this very spot come daybreak—with more than a hangover," Herr Schmitt said, adding a "humpf!"

"And justly so," Pappa said. He looked up at the window. "Karin, are you all right?"

"Yes, Pappa."

"Good. I'm coming up to get you."

Karin refused to go to sleep until Mutti and Christine got home. Karin sat at Pappa's side on the couch when Mutti and Christine walked in the door. When he told Mutti about what happened, Mutti's face lost all color—a hard thing to do in the poor light of a single light bulb. She reached into her pocket. Fumbling around, she grabbed hold of something and pulled it out. She held out the key. "Oh, I am so very, very sorry." Mutti looked like she was sick.

At first, Karin was upset at Mutti for taking the key. And then something inside told her to let that anger go; it had been a mistake after all. That idea surfaced in her thoughts. She knew that being upset with her mother would just make everyone miserable. She was not going to let that happen. "It's okay, Mutti," Karin said, reaching up to her mother. "I'm all right, and so is Pappa. But I want to go to bed now."

Mutti swept Karin up into her arms. Hugging her tightly, she kissed Karin's forehead and muttered, "Ja, Ja, thank the good Lord."

CHAPTER 13

THE LONG DAYS OF SUMMER made it easier to remain in Dresden on Sundays. The lingering light offered sufficient safety for Mutti to feel comfortable staying for the evening sacrament meeting. Aunt Anna too. She joined them after Sunday School on what was left of the grass outside the large stone building.

"How come Aunt Sophronia doesn't come to our picnics?" Karin asked as her family and Aunt Anna nibbled on the two large sandwiches Mutti had cut into five pieces.

"She doesn't usually go to sacrament meeting, darling." Aunt Anna looked at Karin. "If she does, then she doesn't go to Sunday School."

"She told me it's too far to make the trip twice." Pappa leaned back on his hands, having finished his sandwich in three bites.

"It's not like she lives twenty kilometers away." Mutti picked a crumb from her skirt and inserted it in her mouth.

"Not everyone is as fanatical about church as you are, dear sister." Aunt Anna gave Mutti a twisted smile. "She still has to walk a far distance even with the street cars."

"But if she stayed for the picnic like you, Aunt Anna, she wouldn't have to walk as much," Karin said.

"I'm afraid that if both Sophronia and your uncle Stefan were to join us, the sandwiches wouldn't go very far," Aunt Anna said. She glanced at Mutti. "I suppose I shouldn't be taking advantage of you either."

"Oh, nonsense, Anna, we're glad to share." Mutti placed a hand on her sister's arm. "And with Sophronia and Stefan, too, if need be. I'd make more."

Karin popped the last bite of her sandwich in her mouth. "Why don't they just make their own picnic? It'd be so fun to have them join us," she said as she chewed.

"Yes, that would be nice," Mutti said. "And don't talk with your mouth full." She looked at Christine and gave her a quick nod.

Christine stood and extended her hand down to Karin. "Come on, let's go play tag."

As Karin rose to her feet, feeling like Christine was pulling her away from the conversation, she noticed Aunt Anna lean toward Pappa and Mutti. Her aunt muttered under her breath, but Karin could still hear her say, "You are truly blessed, living out there in the country, having space for a garden, working for the farmers, allowed to glean the fields. Things aren't getting any better here in the city. Even if we had the money, the food still isn't there to buy."

Karin chased Christine across the splotchy grass, tagging and being tagged, enjoying the game with her sister. Karin especially loved it when Pappa joined in for a few rounds. As the afternoon merged into evening, she and Christine rejoined the grown-ups under the tree before following them back into the big stone building for sacrament meeting.

Once inside, Karin swung her feet under her folding chair—until Mutti placed a firm hand on her knee. She tried to sit still, though her body wanted to wiggle about. Karin found it hard to listen to long boring talks of old men—at least in Sunday School they had pictures and interesting stories. Finally a young man stood and offered the closing prayer.

". . . Bless our members near Czechoslovakia—and throughout Germany. Not just the members of our church but all our fellow Germans. Protect them from the hate aimed at us . . ."

Some of his words caught Karin's attention. She had heard of asking for protection from harm and evil but never from hate. She found it peculiar but didn't dwell on it after the young man said amen. Her thoughts automatically shifted to getting out of the hot, stuffy building and going home.

On the street car ride to the edge of town, an elderly man in a well-worn suit that Karin recognized from church sat down next to Pappa. It sounded like they were discussing things that the young man had mentioned in his prayer. She couldn't hear all their words, sitting across the aisle from them as she was.

"Didn't matter; they didn't need to kill them." Pappa's words increased in volume. His face looked sad. "Their only crime was they were German."

The old man sitting next to him gave a nod.

The conversation reminded Karin of Sister Klein back in Berlin when she'd spoken of mean people hating Germans. The old lady's words rang in her head, sending a shiver down her back. *They don't care if we die. In fact, they want us to die.*

Karin wrapped her arms around herself, grateful her family was all still alive.

The beginning of August brought the beginning of school for Karin. She wanted to learn how to read like Christine, but she didn't look forward to walking two kilometers to Lungkwitz each morning and two kilometers back home again in the afternoon. But what made it even worse was that all that time she'd be stuck at school, she'd miss out on Pappa. She'd been without him long enough; she didn't want to miss out on being with him on purpose now.

"Can't I just stay home with you?" she asked Pappa the Saturday before school started as they pulled weeds together in the garden.

"No, Little Streusel, you need to go to school and learn." Pappa untangled a pair of pumpkins so they'd have room to grow. "And Monday, I'm expected to be at the farm and start working for Herr Reinhart. I can't very well do that if you stay home from school, now can I?"

"No, I guess not," Karin responded.

After the first week of school, Aunt Anna came home with them on Sunday for a visit.

"I don't want to go to school anymore. Can I stay home?" Karin asked as the five of them trod down the lane toward Wittgensdorf after church. She'd found the school teacher mean, the seats hard, and the urge to wiggle constant.

"No, Karin," Pappa said. "We've already discussed this."

"But Aunt Anna's here now. She can watch me."

Aunt Anna wrapped an arm around Karin. "Darling, I'm only going to be here till next Sunday. A week from Monday you'd have to go back to school. Then how are you going to explain to your teacher missing a whole week of school without your being the least bit sick? She'll probably make you miss recesses for a month while you catch up. You really want that?"

Karin shook her head. Recess was the only part of school she liked. And to miss it for a month, having to stay inside with her mean teacher—and do lessons—sounded almost as horrible as Pappa having to leave again for another war.

Karin went to school the next day, dragging her feet. Christine and Ingrid, a girl Christine's age who lived in the village, had to keep hurrying her along. On the way home, after they dropped Ingrid off, Karin skipped down the lane. Aunt Anna would be there awaiting her return. And Pappa would be home shortly afterward. Christine could go back to Ingrid's house without having to drag Karin along. That was the one thing Karin didn't like about Wittgensdorf—there were no children her age to play with.

Aunt Anna ambled down the lane toward them with the firewood bag draped over one shoulder and a basket in her other hand.

"Where are you going?" Karin asked, disappointed that her aunt was leaving.

"I thought I'd search for a little wood to help out."

"What's the basket for?" Christine asked as they came together on the hard-packed dirt of the lane.

"Are you going to fill it with wood too?" Karin wondered why they needed so much wood when it was hot inside at night.

"No, darling. Your Mutter is going to teach me how to hunt for mushrooms after she's finished with work. A whole week with another mouth to feed . . . well, I was hoping I could contribute something to ease the burden."

"You're no burden, Aunt Anna. We've got plenty of food."

"Ah, the eyes of a child." Aunt Anna pulled Karin into a hug.

"My eyes? What's wrong with them?" Karin asked, a bit confused. It didn't matter. She liked the hug. It was too bad she didn't like mushrooms that much.

Karin remembered the time she'd searched for mushrooms with Pappa in the shade of the woods. Birds had warbled while a breeze ruffled the leaves, making their stroll all the more pleasant. She had enjoyed looking for them. It was like a treasure hunt, finding the mushrooms in varying shades of white, gray, and dark brown; some with round tops, some with flat; some large, some small. Pappa had been careful to point out the ones that were good to eat and the ones they should leave alone.

Maybe she should go with Aunt Anna to make sure she knew which ones to pick. After all, her aunt was from the city. "Can I come with you?" Karin asked.

"Not this time, darling." Aunt Anna patted Karin's head. "I don't know how long we'll be. And your Mutter mentioned you need to practice your letters."

"But I don't—"

"Go now. Christine, you help her with her school work."

"Yes, Aunt Anna." Christine corralled Karin with her arm and led her toward the house.

That evening Aunt Anna and Mutti came through the door with a bag of wood and a basket full of mushrooms. "Oh, dear me," Mutti said, bringing her hand to her cheek. "I forgot the potatoes Herr Reinhart gave us." She handed the basket to Aunt Anna, who had just laid the firewood by the stove. "You wash these up and get them cooking. I'll run back for the potatoes." On her way out, she mumbled something about mushrooms tasting better with potatoes by their side.

After washing the dirt from the mushrooms, Aunt Anna fried them with a little fat and sprinkled on some salt and pepper. The savory aroma made Karin's stomach rumble. Mutti returned shortly. She hurried, cooked and mashed three potatoes, and placed them on the table next to the bowl of mushrooms.

After the blessing on the food, Mutti dished up potatoes and mushrooms for Karin. Christine served herself, plopping a small scoop of potatoes onto her plate. She immediately dug in her fork and began to eat.

Aunt Anna pushed the pan of mushrooms in front of her. "You forgot the mushrooms."

"No, thank you," Christine said quietly.

"Christine," Mutti said. "Take some mushrooms, or you're going to be awfully hungry."

"I'm sorry." Christine's face sagged with a frown. "I don't like them. They make me gag. Do I really have to eat them?"

Mutti placed a loving hand on Christine's shoulder. "Well . . . no, not if you really don't want to." She scooped a few more potatoes onto Christine's plate. "Have my share of potatoes then."

Karin wanted more potatoes than mushrooms. "If Christine doesn't have to eat them, I don't want to either."

"Suit yourself, but it's a long time until breakfast." Mutti scraped the mushrooms off Karin's plate onto Pappa's and some onto her own plate. She cleaned the remaining potatoes from the bowl and divided them equally between Pappa and Aunt Anna—none went onto Karin's plate. "Don't be asking your Pappa for a snack while the rest of us are out hiding tonight."

"I won't." Karin ducked her head, not wanting to be reminded of Mutti and Christine—and now Aunt Anna—having to hide from the Russians. She longed for the days when Mutti would tuck her and Christine in bed with a story and a kiss. Karin would gladly eat mushrooms every night if things could be like they used to. And how was it that Mutti seemed to know that she was just being stubborn? Karin glanced down at her small serving of mashed potatoes, thinking maybe she should have kept her mouth shut.

"Don't worry." Pappa scooped some mushrooms from the pan onto his plate, making a good-sized pile, and then passed them to Aunt Anna. "I'll get her asleep early so she won't have time to feel hungry." He patted Karin's arm.

After the others left to go hide, Karin let Pappa put her to bed earlier than usual. She hoped that would actually help her not feel hungry. She felt herself easily falling asleep as daylight faded into darkness.

It was still dark when she awoke. The sound of moaning made her sit up. It came from her parents' bedroom. "Pappa?"

She stretched her leg over the top of the bar and climbed out of the crib. As she scurried across the darkened room, her body tensed with uneasiness. She turned the knob and cracked open the bedroom door. When she peered inside, it only revealed more darkness. A quick, loud moan startled her. "Pappa," she cried out and ran toward the bed. Enough starlight filtered through the window for her to see her Pappa curled in a ball, rocking from side to side on the bed.

"I don't feel good." Pappa reached out.

Karin felt his hand latch onto her shoulder and squeeze to where it almost hurt. "Pappa," was all she could say. She wanted to help him. But she didn't know how.

"Bring me the pot." Pappa leaned over the side of the bed.

Karin ran into the kitchen, grabbed the handle of the porcelain pot they used when they were too sick to make it to the toilet, and hauled it back to the bedroom. She flipped on the light switch and rushed the bucket to Pappa's side.

He heaved, but nothing came.

Footsteps trudged up the stairs. "Paul? Are you still up?" Aunt Anna's voice reached in from the hall. "Come help me. We had to come home early. Ida's not feeling well."

"Neither is Pappa," Karin hollered into the other room.

"Karin?" Mutti's voice sounded weak.

A moment later Mutti stumbled into the room with one arm wrapped around Aunt Anna and the other one around Christine. Mutti crawled onto the other side of the bed while Christine ushered Karin out of the room and back to her crib.

"What's wrong with Mutti and Pappa?" Karin asked as she climbed up and over.

"I don't know." Christine spread her blanket across the borrowed straw mattress in the corner and crawled onto it, her usual bed on the couch left for Aunt Anna. "Try to go to sleep. Okay?" She punched her pillow before she let her head sink into its fold. Then she wrapped a corner over her face, shielding her eyes from the light shining from the bedroom.

Karin tried to go to sleep. It was no use. She was worried about Pappa. She was worried about Mutti. Bits and pieces of a labored conversation coming from the other room didn't help.

"It must be the mushrooms," Mutti said between moans.

"Nonsense!" Aunt Anna sounded defensive.

"Are you sure you didn't . . ." Mutti paused, taking a deep breath, "get a bad one in there by mistake?"

"Of course I didn't!" Aunt Anna's voice rose in pitch. "I ate a good share, and I'm fine."

Karin felt sick, and it wasn't her stomach. Could her aunt have picked the wrong mushrooms? After all, she'd never picked them before.

The next morning Karin didn't go to school. She and Christine stayed home to help Aunt Anna. Karin got the job of carrying the pot back and forth from the bedroom to the toilet. Mutti threw up over and over. Pappa tried, but nothing seemed to come. Aunt Anna tried to help Pappa throw up with some concoctions she put together in the kitchen but ended up lying down, not feeling well herself. By evening, she felt a little better and finished making her tonic for Pappa and then made potato soup for Karin and Christine—Mutti and Pappa didn't feel like eating. They kept to their bed. Aunt Anna put cool rags on their foreheads to bring down their fevers.

The following morning, Karin clung to the door frame as she peered into the bedroom. Mutti pulled herself up and lay back against the headboard as Aunt Anna offered her a glass of water. She took several sips before handing it back. "How's his fever?" She glanced at Pappa curled up, shivering on the other side of the bed.

"It hasn't broken." Aunt Anna looked worried. "He has yet to throw up. His body doesn't seem to be able to get rid of them like yours. Hopefully, he'll hurry and push them out the other end so he can start to get better."

Pappa rolled slowly over and looked at Mutti. "I'm glad . . . you're . . . doing better." It looked like he tried to smile.

"Thank you." Mutti placed a hand on his forehead and frowned. "No more talking, dear. Save your energy to get better."

Pappa nodded and curled his knees closer to his chest.

Aunt Anna set the glass on the nightstand and left the room, peeling Karin from the doorframe as she passed. "You go outside and play now." She urged Karin toward the stairs. "I'll go tell Christine to do the same. The sunshine will do you both good."

Karin clomped down the stairs and went outside. She plopped her-self in the chair on the porch, wondering what to do. Nothing sounded fun.

Christine emerged from the front door a minute later. She trudged over and sat on the edge of the porch next to Karin. "I'm worried about Pappa. What if he doesn't get better?"

"Why wouldn't he?" Karin hadn't thought about that. "People get sick and then get better all the time."

"I know." Christine kicked at the dirt with her shoe. "But Pappa is still weak from the war." She jumped off the edge of the porch onto her feet, turned, and looked straight at Karin. "*Dummkopf* mushrooms. She should have been more careful picking them."

"You mean Aunt Anna?" Karin's throat tightened, and her whole body wanted to cry. "She was just trying to help."

"I'm sure she was." Christine turned her back to Karin. "But mistakes are made." Her shoulders heaved.

"Are you crying?" Karin wasn't used to seeing her sister cry.

Christine kept her back turned. "What if I am?" she said, a little too sharply for Karin's comfort.

"I'm sorry."

"It's not your fault." Christine turned back around and gazed off at nothing. "Even if Aunt Anna picked them, she should have caught the bad ones when she cleaned them and cooked them."

That evening Aunt Anna came and went from the bedroom more than ever. Karin couldn't fall asleep in the commotion. However, she was glad for the second night in a row that everyone was home, not in hiding.

Karin's eyes fluttered open—a noise had awakened her. It wasn't quite morning. Gray light filtered through the curtains. She rolled over, wanting to go back to sleep. The noise sounded again. Crying. It came from the bedroom. She scrambled out of her crib and stepped carefully toward the bedroom, noticing that both Christine's and Aunt Anna's beds were empty. With a gentle nudge, she opened the door and peered into the room. The light was on. Aunt Anna hovered over the bed on

Pappa's side. Christine stood next to her, clinging to her waist. Mutti's head lay on Pappa's chest. All three of them were crying.

Pappa was no longer curled up in a ball. He lay still and peaceful. The pain was gone from his face.

"What's wrong?" Karin asked. But she already knew the answer.

CHAPTER 14

"THAT CAN'T BE PAPPA," KARIN said to Christine as she looked into the coffin perched in the front hall atop four kitchen chairs. She lowered down off her toes. Her eyes focused on the light brown wood of the coffin, but the image of what she just saw was etched in her mind. The stiff body lying in that wooden box must be someone else. Had to be. Any minute Pappa would walk down those stairs and lift her onto his shoulders and take her outside to play. "Anyway, doesn't look like him."

"It's because he was so sick before he died." Christine sniffled and then wiped her red eyes.

Karin rose back up on her toes and peered over the edge of the coffin again. There was no smile on his face as he lay there in his Sunday suit. He *always* wore a smile when he dressed for church—and most other times. A dark blue tie cinched the white collar close to the folds of skin on his neck. His face was the color of ashes, and not a single strand of his dark hair was out of place like usual. Karin was in her Sunday clothes too. Aunt Anna had insisted. Karin didn't feel like smiling either. Why had her aunt wanted to make her more miserable than she already was? Karin had sworn she wasn't going to let anyone make her life miserable. But being forced to wear a long-sleeved dress on a hot day, a dress she couldn't wear outside or get dirty, was more than Karin could bear. She wanted, wanted, wanted to complain, but Mutti was still sick in bed.

Instead, she reached in and touched Pappa's hand. The cold, leathery skin surprised her, and she jerked her hand away. An urge to cry swelled inside her—Pappa never felt like that. More than anything

Karin didn't want it to be him. But she was afraid that was Pappa. She felt tears trickle down her face.

"It's all right." Christine's arm went around Karin's shoulder and guided her toward the front door that had been propped open to let in a breeze. "Let's move to the side, let others take a look."

Karin resisted Christine's pull. She latched onto one of the kitchen chairs, wanting to stay close to Pappa as long as she could before they took him to the cemetery.

With his hat in his hand, Herr Reinhart glided his wife past the coffin. Both wore glum faces. They approached Karin and Christine. "We just wanted to come and pay our last respects to your Pappa," Herr Reinhart said. "He was a good man."

"We're so sorry for your loss," Frau Reinhart added before slipping outside.

A man and a woman Karin didn't recognize stepped in front of the coffin after the farmer—there had been lots of people she didn't know stop by today. As they filed out the front door, a commotion could be heard upstairs.

Mutti appeared at the top of the steps dressed in her house coat and her hair matted from being in bed for days. Aunt Anna and Frau Krujatz stood on each side of her. She batted away their arms. "Let me go! I want to see my husband before they take him away." Her voice sounded full of anger, though she cried as she struggled down the stairs. "I'll never be able to see his sweet face again." The crying took over, and sobs gushed from Mutti as she draped herself over the coffin. Karin couldn't hold back the tears when she saw her mother cry.

Everyone's tears finally dried up about the time Uncle Richard walked into the front hall. "I don't think your health is up to coming to the cemetery, Ida." He removed his hat, wiped the sweat from his brow, and gazed into the coffin a final time. "Be assured everyone understands—no one will expect you to be there. I'll make sure he has a proper burial, even offer a short memorial." As his hand latched on to the lid of the coffin, he motioned to Karin and Christine with a jerk of his chin. "You children want to say a final good-bye to your Pappa before I close this?"

Christine nodded and approached the coffin, bringing Karin with her. Christine reached in, took Pappa's hand, and squeezed it.

"Oh, Pappa, why did you have to die? You didn't need to. You made it through the war. You came home to us. You can't leave us now!" She gazed up at nothing in particular. "Senseless, senseless, senseless; this is all so *dumm*! It didn't need to happen!"

Karin tugged on Christine's arm. "Aren't we supposed to say good-bye?"

"Uh, ja." Christine refocused her gaze on Karin. "Sorry." She wiped her eyes and looked in the coffin. "Auf wiedersehen, Pappa."

Karin stood on tiptoe, braved her hand, remembering the leathery feel, and reached out for Pappa's face. She patted his cheek. "Auf wiedersehen, Pappa." As Karin lowered off her toes, a young woman walked through the door with suitcase in hand. She wore a gray traveling suit and a matching pillbox hat pinned next to her bun of black hair. Her rosy high cheeks and kind eyes made her look not only beautiful but familiar.

"Liesel!" Christine ran to her and gave their half-sister a hug. "How did you know to come?"

"Aunt Anna sent word." Liesel let go of her suitcase and Christine and hurried to the side of the coffin. "I'm glad I'm not too late." She reached in and stroked Pappa's face with the back of her hand. "He was more of a father to me than my own ever was," Liesel said to no one in particular. "I couldn't have asked for a better stepfather. Auf wiedersehen, Pappa." Liesel turned away from the coffin and, with handkerchief in hand, dabbed her nose and cried. Her eyes caught sight of Mutti clinging to Aunt Anna and Frau Krujatz for support. "Mutter!" Liesel rushed to Mutti's side. "Are you still not well?"

Mutti shook her head and wrapped her arms around Liesel.

"Help me get her back to bed." Aunt Anna draped one of Mutti's arms over her shoulder and motioned to Liesel to do the same. Frau Krujatz stepped away and let Liesel take over for her. "It's good to see you, dear," Aunt Anna said as the two of them hoisted Mutti up the stairs. "It seems it's always under the worst of circumstances."

"Ja, it is," Liesel said. "All three of us have lost our husbands now." She gazed into Mutti's glassy eyes. "I have bad news about Hans, but I'll share it later. Right now you need to get back to bed."

"Blast the infernal war. And all that has followed!" Aunt Anna's voice got harder to hear as they reached the top of the stairs.

"How long can you stay, dear?" Mutti asked weakly.

"I must leave tomorrow. I have to be back to work the following day," Liesel said before she slipped out of Karin's sight.

Karin barely remembered her oldest sister living with them. She'd been just three when Liesel got married and moved out. Liesel did visit when they'd lived in Berlin, but since their move to Wittgensdorf, the whole family had never been together. Until today. But now Pappa was gone. For good. And it sounded like Liesel's husband was gone too. Karin felt like crying again. She didn't feel like being strong.

Uncle Richard looked out the door and summoned three other men inside. He lowered the lid of the coffin. When it snapped shut, it was like something inside Karin went missing—and she'd never find it again.

Each of the four men then took a corner of the coffin and carried it outside and loaded it in the back of a horse-drawn wagon. Karin darted out of the door. "Uncle Richard, take me with you," she hollered as the wagon pulled away.

Uncle Richard turned his head toward her. "Stay here with your Mutter, little Karin. It will be easier that way." He flicked the reins. The horse broke into a trot. Karin ran after the wagon. She could never catch up. As soon as she got close, the horse would speed up. Finally, at the edge of the village, her legs gave out. She sank into the soft dust of the road, exhausted, and sobbed.

Later in the afternoon, the sadness in the house was harder to bear than the heat. Karin changed into her play dress and begged Christine, then Aunt Anna, and then Liesel to come outside with her and play. No one wanted to budge from their chairs. Karin didn't feel like being alone, so she stayed inside. She rested her elbows on the sill of the living room's opened window, cupping her chin in her palms, and stared toward the woods where Mutti and Aunt Anna had picked those mushrooms. Dummkopf mushrooms. If she never saw another mushroom as long as she lived, that was fine with her. Just as her elbows grew sore and her body begged for something different to do, Karin felt a tap on her shoulder.

"Come on," Liesel said, grabbing Karin by the hand. "I'll go outside with you. It'll do me good too." With her free hand, Liesel pulled a pin from her hair, letting it fall onto her shoulders and down her back. She tucked the pin in her pocket and massaged her scalp, like removing that pin had felt good, then dabbed her red eyes.

Karin and Liesel stepped quietly down the stairs. As they walked past the chairs in the hall that earlier had held up Pappa's coffin, Liesel let go of Karin's hand. "Hold on a minute, Karin. We need to return these chairs to your neighbors. Aunt Anna asked me to do it earlier, and I forgot." She grabbed a chair and lifted a hand to knock on the door. With a glance at Karin, she asked, "What is their name again?"

"Somer," Karin said as Liesel knocked and then hurried and slipped into the shadows of the banister.

"What do you want?" Herr Somer's voice echoed into the hall before the door was fully opened.

"Good evening, Herr Somer. We just wanted to return your chairs," Liesel said in her sweet, polite voice.

"Oh, ja, sure. Come in." Herr Somer grabbed hold of the door with his grease-stained hand and pushed it all the way open. His eyes locked on Liesel.

"Who is it, Edward?" Frau Somer asked. A second later she stood at her husband's side, surveying Liesel from head to toe. "You're that fancy stepdaughter of his from the city, aren't you?"

"Yes, Paul Graeber is my stepfather." Liesel stepped into the Somers' living room with chair in hand. She set down the chair and headed back into the hall for another one with her back straight and not a hint of bother in her face.

From behind the banister, Karin watched with awe as her sister carried the remaining chairs past Herr and Frau Somer without so much as a flinch. Karin wished she could be more like Liesel—strong and fearless around those who made her feel inferior, dry-eyed even though she'd lost Pappa and her husband. Liesel held her head high as the couple glared at her, especially Frau Somer. It was as if she didn't like Liesel. But how could that be? She didn't even know her. Plus, Liesel was the sweetest, prettiest young woman in the whole village, as far as Karin was concerned. Ja, Karin wanted to be like her oldest sister.

With her task completed, Liesel shut the Somers' door, retrieved Karin from behind the banister, and together they ventured outside. "Some might tag our little outing as unfitting," Liesel said as they neared the woods. "But I believe this is what Pappa would want us to do."

"Take a stroll in the woods?" Karin responded.

"Ja! And enjoy God's handiwork rather than sit in the stuffy house and mourn until we're miserable." Liesel slowed her steps and took in her surroundings as if the green trees, the babble of the brook, and the scent of pine were as delicious as a big Christmas dinner. Karin mimicked her sister, pausing to take a deep breath and hold it while she feasted on the sights and sounds of the woods. It did help take some of the bad feelings away, and Karin liked that.

An hour into their walk, Karin heard a branch snap like it had been stepped on. She stopped, bade Liesel to do the same, and looked around. "It's nothing," she said, realizing she must still be on edge because of all that had occurred over the last few days. After a thorough survey of the meadowed clearing and fringe of trees, she looked up at Liesel. "Thanks for coming with me. I'm feeling a little better now."

Liesel wrapped her arm around Karin, and they continued walking. "I'm so glad. I know that's what Pappa would want. I also know he'd want you to stay strong like this for Mutti. The next little while is going to be hard for her. I wish I could be here, but I can't. She's going to need your strength. Can you be strong for her?"

Liesel thought of her as strong! Maybe she was. "Ja, I can be strong. Like you. Like Christine."

"Good. That means you won't complain or cry to Mutti."

"I won't, not to Mutti," Karin said. But she knew she'd still cry to the Lord.

When the shadows lengthened beyond view and the sunlight took on its amber hue of evening, Karin grabbed Liesel's hand. "We'd better get home." She wondered if Liesel had to hide at night back in Berlin. Mutti and Christine hadn't hidden since Mutti and Pappa got sick. The Russians hadn't bothered them—but they hadn't been walking around to be seen by the soldiers either. The walk had done her good, but now she longed for the safety of home.

They walked briskly out of the woods and onto the dirt lane that ran through the village. As they turned onto the stone path that led to the front porch, something caught Karin's eye. Russian soldiers lumbered down the lane. It looked as though they were headed for the house. Even if it was still light outside, they scared her. The two soldiers swaggered a bit with each step. "Let's hurry inside," she urged Liesel.

"*Jawohl.*" Liesel opened the front door but didn't move inside as fast as Karin would have liked. Karin grabbed her hand and pulled. "I'm coming, I'm coming," Liesel said as she ran up the stairs behind Karin. As they stepped into the upper hall, the sound of the front door being thrown open made Karin jump.

"Where is she?" The words shot up the stairs very loud and heavy with a Russian accent.

"The beautiful one," said a deeper voice with even a thicker Russian flair. "She is ours!" A thunderous pounding upon the Somers' door followed.

Aunt Anna rushed into the hall from the kitchen. "What's going on?"

"The Russians!" Karin cried through the noise of the pounding downstairs. "I think they're after Liesel."

Liesel nodded her head while her whole body shook. "Where can I hide?"

"Hide?" Aunt Anna clapped her hands against her face. "From the Russians? Dear, child, I don't know, I don't know!" She backed up into the kitchen, her eyes searching frantically.

Karin pulled Liesel toward their living room door, hoping the Somers would send the Russians away somehow. "We'll find a place." The words flew from Karin's mouth in a whisper, but inside, she uttered them as a prayer.

Downstairs, the pounding stopped. Frau Somer's scratchy voice reached up the stairwell and ripped through Karin's insides. "She's upstairs."

Liesel tore open the door and ran through the living room into the bedroom. Karin followed her as far as the living room, shutting the door to the hall behind her. "Where's the key?" she cried out to Christine, who sat on the edge of the couch, helping Mutti sit up. Christine's face paled as she looked at Karin with widened red eyes and shook her head.

"No, don't lock the door." Mutti mustered those words with a surprising amount of force.

Recalling the last time the Russians had met with a locked door, Karin shuddered and left the door alone. She hurried over to Mutti and Christine. "What about you? Don't you need to hide too? And Aunt Anna?"

"Where?" Christine's arms, pale, shaking, clasped onto Mutti's.

"It'll be no use now," Mutti said, her face drained of color and her body of energy. "Sit, be still," she said to Karin and patted the couch next to her. "If we run, it'll only encourage them."

Karin dropped onto the couch next to Mutti. It was hard to sit there and not dash into the bedroom to make sure Liesel had found a good place to hide, especially because she knew there were *no* good hiding places. Sitting still became impossible when she heard the heavy clomp of boots climbing the stairs. Every part of her body tingled with fear and begged to run away. She didn't want them to find Liesel. But if they didn't find Liesel, would they take Christine instead? Or Mutti, or Aunt Anna? Or her?

The door crashed open. Two Russian soldiers lumbered in? "Where is she?" said the larger of the pair.

"Who?" Mutti's voice sounded as weak as she looked.

"The pretty girl we saw in woods," the shorter soldier said as he looked behind the overstuffed chair.

"With long, black hair." The larger soldier jabbed the curtains with his rifle. "We know she's visiting here."

"We want her," the shorter soldier added.

"She's not here," Mutti said with firmness.

"Humpf!" The short soldier opened the bedroom door and motioned to his comrade to follow.

The thump of Karin's heart pounded in her ears almost as loudly as the Russians' boots clomped on the bedroom floor as they searched. She made a daring lean to one side to peer in at their efforts. One of them knelt down and lifted the bedspread to look under the double bed. Karin prepared herself to see Liesel curled up next to the wall. *Nothing.*

"Where is she?" The large soldier stormed into the living room.

The short one followed. "We were told she was here."

"You were told wrong," Mutti said but not as firmly this time. Her whole body shook, making her appear even more sickly. Christine clung to Mutti, tears streaming down her white face and wetting her matted hair, causing her eyes to turn a more intense shade of red.

The short soldier said something in Russian while he leaned his rifle against the stuffed chair and approached Christine and Mutti. He leaned down, lifted a lock of Christine's hair, and ran his fingers through it. His breath reeked of alcohol, causing Karin's stomach to recoil while her heart thumped away like a motor.

The large soldier stepped over and clamped a hand on his comrade's shoulder. "No." A look of disgust twisted his face as he glared at Mutti and Christine. "I want the pretty one!"

The short soldier let go of Christine's hair and wiped his hand on his uniform. "*Da*. We keep searching." He let his comrade pull him away. Together they headed for the door.

"They're drunk," Christine whispered as their uneven footsteps echoed up the stairs. Her face was as pale as snow.

It wasn't until the front door slammed shut down below that Karin dared move. She jumped to her feet. "Are they gone?"

Mutti's eyes lifted to the ceiling. "I pray to God they are."

"Liesel!" Karin darted into the bedroom, filled with a curious mixture of feelings—elation, confusion, fear, and awe. What had become of her sister? "Liesel, where are you?"

"Are they gone?" whispered Liesel, her voice sounding shaky.

"Yes," Karin responded. "You can come out now."

The bed began to move, scooting away from the wall by itself. The scrape of its legs across the wood sent prickles down Karin's arms. Relief blanketed her when she saw Liesel crawl up from behind the bed.

Christine rushed into the room. "Liesel! Where were you?"

Liesel pointed to the floor in between the wall and the bed. She then patted the pink bedspread that ran from the top of the mattress all the way down to the floor. "I crawled back here and then pulled the bed frame next to the wall and lay on my side as stiff as a plank. Apparently they couldn't see me from above, and when they looked under the bed all they could see was the back of the bedspread."

"Liesel, great hiding place!" Christine hugged her big sister. "Of course, it helped that they were drunk."

"*Ja!*" Karin joined the hug, thinking it hadn't helped that the Russians were drunk—it had helped that she had prayed.

CHAPTER 15

IT WAS LIKE A BLANKET of smothering silence fell over the household after Liesel left to go back to Berlin. Mutti slowly recovered from the mushroom poisoning. Aunt Anna continued to nurse her back to health. But it was the rare occasion when anyone spoke to each other.

One day after school, Karin was relieved to find Mutti sitting in the kitchen while Aunt Anna prepared supper. Karin slipped into the chair next to Mutti at the table. "Will you help me with my lessons?" A tickle of happiness ran through her. She was so glad Mutti was finally feeling better—and she was actually glad for her homework for once. It gave her something to talk about besides Pappa.

"Of course I'll help you." Mutti reached across the table and gave Karin's hand a squeeze. It lacked her usual grip, but the intensity in Mutti's eyes gave Karin hope that her mother was on the mend.

Christine draped her ranzen strap on the hook inside the door. "I don't have homework tonight. Let me help you with supper," she said as she joined Aunt Anna at the sink.

"I'll finish cleaning up these potatoes." Aunt Anna nodded at the cupboard. "You grab the pot and fill it with water and get it boiling on the stove."

It was so nice having everyone talk again. Karin had a hard time concentrating on her lessons. She wanted to talk about Aunt Anna's bad knees, about what Mutti had read in the scriptures lately, about the boy that slipped Christine a note at lunch—anything to keep the conversation going.

"Use your fingers if you have to," Mutti said softly to Karin. "It's okay at first to help you learn to add." She looked up at Aunt Anna, leaning to the side of her chair to get a better view of the sink. "Make sure you wash them well. And cut out the bad parts before you cook them."

Aunt Anna stopped scrubbing and threw down the potato she held. "What are you trying to say?" She squared her shoulders, spun around, and glared at Mutti.

"Nothing." Mutti straighten in her chair. "Only that gleaned potatoes are usually damaged."

"Humpf." Aunt Anna untied her apron and stuffed it in the cupboard. Her face tightened, especially her lips as they puckered into a knob.

Aunt Anna went back to Dresden first thing the next morning.

Mutti returned to her bed. She had recovered from the mushrooms, but Karin feared her mother would never recover from losing Pappa. Her eyes, constantly red from crying, lacked the sparkle of determination to which Karin had grown familiar. Mutti had no interest in anything.

"Why, oh, why did Paul survive the war only to die this way?" The question constantly came from Mutti's lips.

But it was also in Karin's thoughts. The Russians were succeeding; her family was miserable. No, it hadn't been the Russians, or any other mean people, that killed Pappa. But they were the ones who had invaded Germany, ruined it, and taken away all the food. Pappa would have never had to eat wild mushrooms if there was enough food to eat. Everyone Karin talked to, it seemed, hated the Russians. She was tired of trying to keep a smile on her face—it was easier to hate the Russians too.

A few weeks after Aunt Anna left, Karin awoke to the smell of mush cooking in the kitchen. It had been so long since she'd had a hot breakfast to warm her insides and help her face the long walk to school in the cool fall weather. For the week after Aunt Anna had left, Christine had sliced her and Karin bread for breakfast. But the loaf quickly dwindled, and Mutti didn't feel up to making more. Christine could make a lousy pot of soup for supper, but she didn't know how to make bread. The previous week Karin had walked to school on an empty stomach. The aroma of food prompted Karin to climb out of her crib and head for the kitchen. As she crept past the couch, Christine stirred, pulling the blankets up to her chin.

"Christine!" Karin exclaimed.

Christine's eyes popped open. She rose up on an elbow, her eyebrows furrowed. "What are you doing?"

"I thought you were up already," Karin said, a bit confused. "I thought you were in the kitchen . . . making us breakfast."

"Why would I . . ." Christine pulled herself up all the way, her neck craning toward the kitchen, her nose breathing in a long breath. "I smell mush." She arose and herded Karin into the kitchen in front of her.

Mutti stood at the stove dressed for the day. At the sound of Karin and Christine's feet, she turned and looked at them with a gleam in her eyes that had been absent since Pappa died. "*Guten morgen*, girls."

"Guten morgen, Mutti," Christine practically sang.

"Ja, guten morgen, Mutti," Karin joined in. She rushed to Mutti's side and hugged her leg. It had felt like forever since anyone said good morning to each other. What was going on? It didn't matter. Whatever it was, Karin liked it. She gazed up into those eyes that had been red, puffy, and sad for so long and basked in their new brightness. "Mutti, you're happy again!"

"Ja," Christine said. "How? What's happened?"

"I had a dream last night." Mutti ushered them to the table with pot in hand. "Sit. Let's say the blessing, and I'll tell you about it."

Karin scrambled onto a chair in anticipation of a hot breakfast. But it dwarfed compared to hearing whatever it was that had managed to pull Mutti out of her sadness and restore her to the bright-eyed, cheerful mother Karin knew and depended on. She swung her feet during the blessing, finding it extra difficult to sit still and listen to the words. Thank goodness it was Christine offering the blessing on the food rather than Mutti.

Christine had no sooner finished her prayer when she said, "Please, tell us about your dream, Mutti. It must have been amazing, simply grand!"

"Actually, it was rather simple," Mutti said, spooning mush into Christine's bowl. "But the impression it emblazoned in my heart was profound."

"Tell us, please." Karin wanted to hear the dream, not all this unimportant stuff cluttered with big words.

"Well, the dream was not that detailed," Mutti said as she dished up Karin's mush. "I saw your Pappa dressed in white. Somehow I knew I was seeing him before we got married. He was reluctant to marry—me being seven years older than he and a divorcee with a young child. But the Lord told him that his days on earth were numbered, so he'd better make the best of them before he was called back home to heaven. And I sensed that . . . that he'd made the best of them. Also that his time to go had been prolonged for our sakes—so we could see him and say auf wiedersehen before he returned home to God."

Soothing warmth filled Karin. It had nothing to do with the steaming hot mush sitting before her.

CHAPTER 16

"Do I HAVE TO GO?" Karin asked as Mutti placed a bowl of mush in front of her. School had gotten worse and worse after missing all those days when Pappa was sick. The teacher expected Karin to do things she didn't understand. And yesterday she'd had to stand in the corner for what felt like forever—just because she had talked. Of course she had talked! How else could she ask the girl next to her what the teacher meant?

"Can't I just stay home today?" Karin said.

"Who will watch you?" Christine asked. "I'm certainly not going to miss any more school."

If Pappa was still here, Karin could have him do it. But he wasn't. The ache inside her flared up again. Mutti's dream had helped Karin heal from Pappa's passing a little bit—but not as much as it had helped her mother. She swallowed the lump in her throat and tried to be strong. "I don't need anyone to watch me," Karin said, telling herself Pappa would have been at work anyway.

"And who's going to teach you to read?" Mutti tilted her head, meeting Karin's eyes with a stern gaze. "And write? And do arithmetic?"

"Christine."

"No, not me." Christine looked up from her mush.

"You can, Mutti. You're smart."

"That's right." Mutti's mouth curved into a slight grin. "And that's why I'm making you go to school today. Now hurry and eat your breakfast. That two-kilometer walk won't get any shorter the longer you wait."

Karin knew she'd have to go to school. But at least she could let her family know she wasn't pleased about it. She folded her arms tightly across her belly and frowned.

Christine pointed to Karin's bowl with her spoon. "If you don't want that mush, I'll eat it."

"And I will give it to your sister if you don't pull that lip back in and put it to work eating your breakfast." Mutti sat down at the table. She leaned over and hugged Karin. "How about you hurry, eat your mush, and go off to school today with a smile? Things have slowed down on the farm. I'll talk to Herr Reinhart and see if I can come home early tomorrow and bring you girls down for a visit. Maybe you can help out with that horse of his you like so much."

"You mean Sonnenschein?" Karin perked up.

"I think that's his name . . . thanks to you."

Karin dug her spoon into her mush and had her breakfast eaten by the time Christine finished hers. They each grabbed their ranzens, headed down the stairs, and hurried outside.

After picking up Ingrid, the three of them ambled down the lane that led to Lungkwitz, taking turns kicking the rocks that cluttered the dirt road. As they reached the edge of the village, Karin gazed beyond golden brown fields of grain toward Herr Reinhart's farm. A lively horse trotted across a pasture speckled with milk cows.

"Look! It's Sonnenschein." Karin pointed to the faraway speck of frolicking brown moving among stationary black and white ones. Its distinctive chestnut coat and light brown mane told her it was he. But his size made her wonder. It'd been a while since she'd seen him. "He's grown a lot."

Christine turned her head and gazed at the pasture. "Ja, he's almost as tall as those cows." She returned her attention to the road. "Come on, we don't want to be late for school. We'll get to see him up close tomorrow."

Ingrid shot Christine a look, her raised eyebrows begging for an explanation. "Sonnenschein?"

"The horse over there," Christine said, walking even faster than before. "Our Mutti works for his owner. We get to play with him tomorrow. We'll probably brush him down, pull burrs from his mane. Stuff like that."

"It sounds like fun." Ingrid glanced over her shoulder at the fading view of the pasture. "Could I come too?"

"I'll have to ask my Mutter," Christine said. "But I don't think Herr Reinhart would mind. It's not like we're going to ride the horse."

"You don't think he'd let us ride Sonnenschein this time?" Karin pulled on Christine's arm. "He looks big enough now. I won't hurt him; I'm not that heavy."

"He's a work horse, Karin." Christine gave her a look that reminded her of Mutti. "The farmer told us he wasn't bred for riding."

"Even if he was," Ingrid added, "he'd have to be *brechen* first."

Karin gave Ingrid a sideways glance. Why would anyone want to break Sonnenschein? Why did people older than she make no sense? She wished she could have a friend of her own, one her age. All the children in her class lived too far away to play with after school. And during school—they all liked school more than she did—they told her to be quiet when she'd ask them questions.

She forced her feet to keep up with Christine and Ingrid. The promise of seeing Sonnenschein kept her going. It didn't matter that she couldn't ride him. He was like a spark of sunshine in her gray world.

Karin and Christine had barely gotten home from school when the talk of hiding entered the conversation. With the days getting shorter, Mutti got home sooner, and they all went out to hide earlier. There it was again—her ache for Pappa. As long as they had kept all the doors unlocked, the Russians hadn't threatened Pappa or her anymore. But now that Pappa was gone, Mutti made Karin come hide with her and Christine. Karin couldn't decide whether she liked that better or if she'd rather stay home alone.

"Where are we hiding tonight?" Christine asked.

"Well, we can't hide under the beehives anymore." Mutti hurriedly placed a bowl of steamed potatoes on the table. "Herr Reinhart told me the Russians came by today and inspected them. The way they motioned while looking under them made Herr Reinhart figure they had seen us leave there last night. We should've never left early." Mutti shook her head. "It was such a good hiding place."

"But we were all so tired." Christine looked up, her eyes full of apology. "And everybody admits the Russians are settling down."

"Still . . ." Mutti glanced at the ceiling, "until I feel prompted otherwise, we must continue to be on guard." She sat down, poked a potato, and put it on her plate. As she smashed it with her fork and sprinkled it with salt, she said, "And wrap up warm tonight. A storm's on its way."

Karin hurried and ate her potato, wishing Mutti had made it into soup instead. With her last bite still in her mouth, she got up from the table, along with Mutti and Christine, and rushed for her coat.

A blast of cold air blew on Karin's face as she stepped onto the porch. Dark gray clouds billowed across the setting sun, swallowing up its last rays of light. She grabbed hold of Mutti's hand because her own felt cold as the wind. They should have remembered their mittens. Even though hers had holes in them, they would have brought with them a small bit of warmth.

Mutti towed Karin quickly down the steps, nodding to Christine to follow. "We'd better find some place close."

"How about Fritz's dog house?" Karin pointed toward Frau Krujatz's backyard. Thoughts of snuggling up against the big warm dog sounded as good as things could get at the moment.

"Ja," Christine said. "It's not a bad hiding place."

Mutti headed toward it, urging Karin to move faster. "I hope it will fit all three of us."

Karin peered inside the rectangular doorway as they approached the dog house. "Where's Fritz?"

"I'm sure he's inside protecting Frau Krujatz." Mutti lowered to her knees and poked her head in the dark opening. "Russian's aren't too fond of big German Shepherds," she said, her voice echoing back out the doorway

"Or old women," Christine said with a note of bitterness. Or was it envy? Karin couldn't tell, just that her sister didn't want to be out here. Neither did Karin.

"Christine!" Mutti scolded as her body disappeared into the darkness. Her hand jutted back out, motioning for them to follow. "I think there'll be enough room if we squeeze together. I'll sit in the middle, where the roof is taller. Christine, you crawl in after me, then Karin."

Karin could barely make out Mutti's and Christine's faces when she stuck her head inside. An elbow poked her in the side, and her knee produced a yelp from her sister as she struggled to turn around and maneuver into the sliver of space between Mutti and the side of the dog house. Through the rectangular opening directly in front of Mutti's legs that were pulled up to her chin, Karin watched the last remnants of daylight fade away. But even with clouds cloaking the moon, the outside remained much lighter than the inside of the dog house.

Karin's hips soon felt like a smashed slice of sausage sandwiched between Mutti and the wall. Why did she have to think of a sandwich? She wished she'd had a bigger potato for supper. And while she was at it, she wished it wasn't so cold and smelly in that dog house. If she was going to have to breathe that smell, she wished she could have the dog to go with it to keep her warm. Better yet, if they had a dog like Fritz, they could stay inside like Frau Krujatz at night. And during the day, she would have a friend to play with.

"Why don't we get a dog?" Karin whispered even though she'd been told the answer many times: they didn't have the food to feed one.

"Shhh." Mutti's hand grabbed Karin's arm.

"I hear someone," Christine whispered.

"Shhh!" Mutti stiffened, squeezing Karin even tighter against the wall.

The grind of gravel responding to heavy footsteps made Karin lean closer to Mutti. Male voices followed, two of them—speaking Russian. Karin latched onto Mutti's arm, squeezing hard but trying to be still at the same time. She stared through the door, awaiting, dreading, fearing. At any moment she expected to see soldiers' boots approach and block the rectangular opening.

The footsteps faded, as did the voices.

Karin let go of Mutti.

Mutti rubbed her arm.

Christine sighed.

They sat again for a long time without speaking. Only the occasional soft sound of hands rubbing arms for warmth interrupted the silence.

Karin couldn't hold back anymore. "How much longer?" she asked as she wiggled her legs.

"The night's still young for them, dear," Mutti responded. "And remember to whisper. And be still."

"Sorry," Karin whispered. She tried again not to move or say a word. And waited.

Karin's eyelids felt heavy, and she leaned her head on Mutti's shoulder. Images of warm quilts and soup with big chunks of beef, carrots, and potatoes swirled in her mind, carrying her away to a better place. Just as she imagined sinking her teeth into a bite of meat, a man's voice swept it all away. It sounded like Herr Schmitt's, the Burgermeister. He was calling Christine's name. Was he trying to find her so he could tell her it was safe to go home now? Karin jerked upright and called out, "She's in here."

Mutti's hand clamped over Karin's mouth and pulled her close. Mutti's heart thumped like a motor in Karin's right ear while Russian voices alerted Karin through her left one. She wiggled to free both ears, dreading, but wanting to hear what approached. Mutti increased her hold, the smell of wet dog hair on her hand even stronger than her grasp. Karin struggled to breathe.

Christine leaned across Mutti and whispered to Karin, "They called 'Christian,' not Christine!"

"Shhh!" Mutti let go of Karin and pulled Christine away.

Footsteps approached. The clap of boots against gravel sent shivers down Karin's back.

The footsteps grew louder. So did the babble of Russian. One of them sounded like the soldier everyone in the village feared above the others, the one Brunhilde nicknamed *Tollwütiger Hund*. Karin could only hope a man called "mad dog" would want to stay away from dog houses. She feared there was little chance.

The clouded moonlight ceased to pour in through the dog house door. A silhouette of a stooping soldier blocked most of the rectangular opening, and the smell of alcohol made her nose and stomach sick. Enough light caught the man's eyes that Karin could tell it was *Tollwütiger Hund*, and he was staring directly at her.

She said a quick prayer, pleading in her heart they'd be all right.

A second soldier bent over and peered in, blocking the remainder of the doorway.

Karin didn't dare breathe. She swore neither Mutti nor Christine took in a breath either, and Mutti felt like a stone at her side.

"*Hnyto*," the second soldier said. He straightened up and pulled Tollwütiger Hund away.

Karin stared at the doorway, a rectangle of gray. Even though the voices faded in the distance, Mutti and Christine didn't move, they didn't say a word—not even a whisper. Karin figured she'd better do the same. But her head felt heavy, so heavy. Ever so quietly, she let it drop onto Mutti's shoulder.

"Karin, wake up." Mutti's voice interrupted Karin's dream of biting into a huge helping of apple strudel. "It's time to go home now."

Karin felt her head being nudged upright. Her eyes popped open as someone grabbed her arms. She felt herself being dragged from the dog house. A gust of cold wind awakened her fully as Mutti pulled Karin to her feet.

"Sorry, sweetie, but you'll have to walk on your own," Mutti said. "You're too big, and I'm too exhausted to carry you."

Karin pulled her coat closed to the neck and trudged across Frau Krujatz's backyard. "Have the Russians all gone to bed?"

"Yes, Karin, they've all gone to bed." Mutti took hold of Karin's hand.

Karin let Mutti's fingers comfort her with their warmth. But it wasn't enough. "They almost got us, didn't they?"

"Thanks to you." Christine walked briskly a step ahead. "Why did you—"

"Because she was half asleep," Mutti cut in. She quickened her pace to catch up to Christine, dragging Karin with her. "It's over now, and we're all right. No need to point fingers."

"Mutti?" Karin gave her both hands to hold. "What did that soldier say that made them leave us alone?"

"It sounded like he said, 'Neeshtoh,'" Christine said. "Whatever that means."

"*Hnyto*. In Russian, I believe, that means 'nothing.'" Mutti rubbed Karin's hands.

"They saw nothing?" Karin perked up.

"Apparently."

"That was because it was so dark inside they obviously couldn't see us," Christine said.

"No, it was because Heavenly Father made it so they couldn't see us." The more Karin thought about it, the more she knew it. They'd prayed before they went out to hide, and she'd prayed when Tollwütiger Hund first looked in the dog house. Karin liked her own explanation best. It made her feel better about having to hide again tomorrow night.

Karin had no problem waking up early, even though it had been well after midnight by the time she had gone to bed—she got to see Sonnenschein today. Christine still slept soundly, her back turned to Karin as she lay on the edge of the bed. Karin slipped out of the double bed on Mutti's side and tiptoed over to her play dress that hung from a hook on the wall. She glanced at the crib that had been pushed into the corner. Herr Somer was going to take it away today. Brunhilde's baby wasn't due for a few more months, but Mutti had asked for him to come get it. Karin hadn't slept in it since Mutti had her dream.

After getting dressed, Karin walked by the crib on her way to the door. She ran a finger down a white bar, remembering how she disliked sleeping in what felt like a cage. But it had been worth it to have Pappa home. She would gladly sleep in there well after she was grown if it could bring him back.

But nothing would bring Pappa back.

It hurt when she remembered losing Pappa.

Curiously, however, peaceful thoughts about other things always seemed to flow into her mind and crowd out such unpleasant memories. Right now it was a baby horse filling her thoughts, one with big brown eyes and a coat the shade of chestnuts—a ray of sunshine to brighten her day.

Mutti stood at the sink washing an apple as Karin entered the kitchen. She turned, glancing at Karin. "You're up early for a Saturday."

"I didn't want to miss going to the farm with you today," Karin said, breathing in the nutty aroma of the mush cooking on the stove.

Mutti smiled. "No need to worry on that front—I don't work Saturdays anymore." Her smile faded as she cut the apple up into little pieces. "In fact, I won't be working Monday through Friday either. The farmer told me yesterday that there's no more need for me to come back until spring."

"What?" Karin's insides sank to her toes. "What about seeing Sonnenschein?"

Mutti's smile returned. "Oh, we can still visit the farm, go see your little horse anytime we want. Especially now. There's just no work for me there." Once again, her grin disappeared. She nodded at the three burlap bags resting in the corner of the kitchen, one each of apples, onions, and potatoes. "Nor any more fields for us to glean."

Karin watched Mutti dump the small bits of apple into the pot of mush, wishing she'd cut up another and add it too. There was plenty—a whole bag full. She and Christine had helped Mutti gather them from the ground after the orchard had been harvested last week.

"We'll have to make these last, so no more apples in the mush after today. I just wanted to make today's breakfast special in keeping with our little outing." Mutti wagged a spoon at Karin. "Go wake your sister while I dish up your breakfast."

After a tasty bowl of apple-flavored mush, the three of them donned their coats and scarves and headed out the door. A cool breeze nipped at Karin's cheeks. The autumn sun managed to warm the rest of her as she strolled down the lane, kicking the occasional pile of fallen leaves that had accumulated in the potholes. She gazed over the hectares of recently harvested field, observing the beauty of the mixed shades of browns, golds, and lingering wisps of green. Her eyes came to rest on Herr Reinhart's pasture. "Where's Sonnenschein?"

"Maybe Herr Reinhart has him waiting for us at the barn." Christine looked to Mutti as if for affirmation.

"Ja, I'm sure that's the case."

Ingrid met them on the lane leading to the Reinhart farm. As the four of them approached the barn, the farmer stormed out of its big hanging door with his hands clenched. He spotted them, and his hands relaxed somewhat. "Uh, Frau Graeber—your girls. I forgot . . ." He seemed to drag his feet as he approached them. "I'm afraid I won't need their help with my colt today."

"What?" Karin held her feet still so it would be easier not to stomp them. She looked up at Mutti. "You promised!" She bit her lip so she wouldn't say more.

Christine stood on Mutti's other side in silence, but her eyes looked at Mutti as if expressing those exact same words.

"I understand if you're too busy today," Mutti said. "We can come back another day. One that would work better for you. The girls really want to see the little horse they helped name. Perhaps Monday?"

"Monday is not good." The farmer's face was like stone, his mouth a straight line. "No day is good."

Karin tried hard to hold her tongue. Did he know how much she needed to see Sonnenschein, to be lifted by the sunshine he always shared with her? "But—" Mutti shushed her.

"I'm sorry." Herr Reinhart hung his head. "He's dead."

"What?" Christine squeaked

"That's terrible." Ingrid chewed on her knuckle with eyes wide.

"But he can't be." Karin pulled on Mutti's arm and looked into her eyes. "I just saw him yesterday." She moved her attention to Herr Reinhart and pointed toward the pasture. "Out there, in that field."

The farmer motioned for them to follow him. "Last night, some Russian soldiers got it in their heads that they wanted to ride him." He walked back toward the barn. "I didn't see it, but our neighbor did. Herr Fischer tried to tell them he was just a *fohlen*, a work horse at that—he was not meant to be ridden. But those idiot Russians were too drunk, too dumb to understand. They beat the colt nearly to death, trying to make him obey them." Herr Reinhart swallowed hard, his fists still clenched. "He had the makings to be a fine plow horse— better than his Pappa."

"And you needed him." Mutti stopped him just inside the barn and took his hand in both of hers. "I know how much you looked forward to his help next spring. Oh, Herr Reinhart, I'm so sorry."

"I've been up with him all night, but I couldn't save him." Herr Reinhart motioned to a stall. "You're welcome to take one last look at him. I was headed for the butcher's when you came."

"Butcher? No!" Karin couldn't let them cut up Sonnenschein to be made into *Sauerbraten*. He should be buried in the pasture, where she could make him a headstone out of rocks, where she could place bundles of tall grass on his grave like a *Teppich* of flowers, where she could visit after she'd left flowers on Pappa's grave.

"Karin." Mutti gathered Karin into her arms and bent down to look into her eyes. "You know that's not practical now, don't you?"

Karin nodded, sniffing back the river of moisture in her nose. Herr Reinhart and his family could maybe eat sausages or sauerbraten made from Sonnenschein, but she certainly wouldn't. No matter how hungry she got.

Christmas came. And so did the cold. There never seemed to be enough wood to feed the stove or food to feed the family. Herr Reinhart gave Mutti a sausage for Christmas.

Karin ate her portion, grateful for the food, but still angry at the Russians for the source of that food.

Come January, she wished for more sausage. And again in February and in March. She found it extra hard to keep a smile on her face—especially when she thought about the Russians. They had finally quit with their "rampages," as Mutti called them, so Karin and her family no longer had to hide every night, but the awful memory of what they did to Sonnenschein—and Monika—wouldn't quit. She hated the Russians. So did everyone else in the village. Except Mutti. And Christine, for some reason.

Spring came. With its return, Mutti returned to work at Herr Reinhart's farm.

With the sun warming the spring sky to a point of delight, after school Karin strolled down the village lane with Christine and Ingrid, feeling more cheerful than she had for months. Karin and Christine waved goodbye to Ingrid when she turned down her lane. They then headed toward Herr Reinhart's farm instead of home. Karin was looking forward to helping Mutti clean out the packing shed like they'd done last year.

The road to the farm wove through a grove of trees, their tall shadows shading puddles left over from yesterday's rain and preventing them from drying out. Karin wanted so much to jump in a puddle or two, but the thought of working the entire evening in wet shoes kept her feet to the dry parts of the road.

As they turned with the bend in the road, Karin gasped, stopping so fast she lost her balance and nearly fell into a puddle. She latched on to her sister's arm and squeezed as hard as the hatred inside squeezed at her heart. "Russians!"

Christine peeled Karin's fingers from her arms and urged Karin to keep walking. "Don't let them see that you're scared. Just ignore them. I can see Herr Reinhart down the road; we'll be okay."

"I'm not scared," Karin whispered as the two soldiers approached. "I just don't, don't like them."

The soldiers kept to their side of the narrow road, passing Karin and Christine with nothing more than a long glance, scanning the girls from toe to head.

After the Russians were well behind, Christine said, "You shouldn't hate them, Karin."

"Why not?"

"Mutti says it's wrong."

"I don't care. It's hard not to."

"I used to think that too." Christine twisted her mouth in that way that meant she was thinking about difficult stuff. "Then I listened to Mutti. She told me about these poor soldiers." She jerked her fist, pointing a thumb back over her shoulder. "Their lives are worse than ours . . . by far. Imagine being just six years older than me and being forced to leave your family and move to a new country where no one wants you. You don't hardly get fed, you sleep on the hard ground, you get beaten up by your commanding officer, and you don't know when—or if—you'll ever get to go home. And then you are hated by the people you are assigned to watch over."

"But they've done such horrible things."

"Mutti said they don't know better. Remember how I used to say the Russians were so stupid?" Christine winced. "That was mean of me. I don't think they're stupid, they're . . . well . . . they've never been taught what's right and wrong. Most of them don't get to go to school. They don't know what we know. Mutti says Russia is about a hundred years behind Germany."

Karin wasn't sure what it meant to be "a hundred years behind Germany," but she did know Christine had been happier than she had lately. Her sister usually was the miserable one, the child who rarely smiled but kept her complaints to herself. But Christine always obeyed Mutti. Maybe Mutti did know best. Karin had tried to obey her mother—when it wasn't a hard thing.

Not wanting to take all the blame, Karin asked, "How come Mutti never told me it was wrong to hate the Russians?"

"She tried, but you didn't listen."

"Oh," Karin muttered, feeling bad this time rather than mad. "And so . . . you feel sorry for the Russians?"

"Ja, it helps me not hate them. And that helps me feel better about having them around." Christine took Karin by the hand to lead her down the smaller lane to the packing shed. "You should try feeling sorry for them instead. Hate doesn't help anything; it only makes you feel miserable."

"Okay, I'll try." Karin promised herself she *would* try. She did not want to be miserable.

CHAPTER 17

Lockwitz, fall 1949

KARIN CARRIED AN ARMFUL OF bedding up the stairs to their new apartment. This place Mutti had found for them to live was even smaller and more run down than the rooms they shared with the Somers back in Wittgensdorf. She placed her load on the bottom tier of the bunk bed and turned to Mutti, who sat a meter away on the twin bed against the other wall, sorting through some family pictures.

"I wish you'd have left me in Wittgensdorf," Karin said. "I'll be glad to go back. You and Christine wouldn't feel so crowded here if I did."

"And you think a ten-year-old can take care of herself, do you? Pay rent? Find food?" Mutti raised her eyebrows. "And go to school on her own—without any prodding?"

"Frau Krujatz would be more than willing to let me stay there. She'd take good care of me. And make sure I got to school. I'm sure of it."

"I don't care. And I don't care that our new place is little more than two rooms. We're staying together as a family. That's why we moved! No more going over this. You know this is the right decision."

Karin gave a reluctant nod and headed down the stairs for another load. She met Christine on the stairs with an armload and had to squeeze flat against the wall to allow her sister to pass. Christine smiled as she slid by, her face beaming with an excitement Karin certainly didn't share. But then, Karin hadn't just graduated from school. She wasn't set up for good vocational training at a prestigious business firm. No business would want to train her for a future career—even if her family were to move all the way to Berlin to find a willing company. The only thing Karin excelled in at school was poetry. Unfortunately, there weren't many careers looking for that skill.

Karin didn't care! She didn't need to worry about vocational school for three or four more years—and she enjoyed memorizing and reciting poems. As of late, she'd even started writing her own poetry. Her creations brought her smiles, whereas Christine's shorthand and typing seemed to always make her sister cross.

She trudged outside to grab another armful of belongings from the rented truck. Only a box of books and a kitchen chair remained in the bed of the rusty, blue vehicle. The driver leaned against the cab of the truck with one leg bent like the number four to support him where his back couldn't. He tipped his hat. "Nearly finished, I see. That'll be three marks." He lowered his leg and stood. "Could you tell your Mutter? I would like to be getting home shortly."

"Ja." Karin grabbed the box of books and carried them up the narrow staircase they shared with a young family who lived in the three other upper rooms. An older woman had the whole bottom floor of the old house to herself. It had a big kitchen, a living room, and a dining room, not to mention *two* bedrooms. A lot of space for *one* ornery old lady.

She set the books on the kitchen table—that had been wedged into the corner—and took one step over to the bedroom door. "Mutti, the truck's almost empty, and the man's waiting to be paid."

"I'll head right down. Thanks." Mutti slipped past Karin. Over her shoulder, she hollered, "Christine, make the beds up while I'm gone."

Karin stepped back to the table, ready to put the books away. She glanced around the living room and then back to a tiny shelf above the table. It would never hold all their books. She leaned over to the doorway to the kitchen. It was like a closet, a meter and a half square. The room held but a stove and a small sink. Its only daylight came through the clouded glass of an angled window in the roof, built after the fact. No room for books in there. That certainly wasn't because of excess food on the shelves. Or wood stacked beside the stove.

It was October; cold weather would soon be upon them. Last winter had brought many a cold, supperless night in Wittgensdorf. Karin shuddered when she contemplated what the upcoming months might be like in this community of Lockwitz on the outskirts of Dresden.

The box of books pushed their way back to the forefront of her thoughts. She backed up and went straight for them—at least for the brown school notebook mixed in somewhere with the books. She dug through stacks of Mutti's genealogy, Christine's books, and their scriptures until she found it.

Hugging it to her chest, she longed to run for the sanctuary of Frau Krujatz's covered back porch. There, her dear friend always allowed her privacy to read and write her poetry. What was she going to do without those bright spots in her days, the comfort she derived from the food and flowers Frau Krujatz gave her—comfort she used to get from thinking about Pappa before he died? And then Sonnenschein. Now it would have to be her poems. They would be much better anyway. They wouldn't go away.

She looked around for a place to read them, perhaps write a new one. The window above the couch gave her a glimpse of a storm's gray fury moving in. With the sun due to set within the hour, she knew this crowded living room was her best choice. She plopped onto their singed blue couch, the only piece of living room furniture they had brought with them.

She opened her notebook to a random page. It was a poem she'd copied and memorized last year, a serious one named "The Song of the Bell." She remembered it compared the building of a bell with the path of life. But then, most of those she'd learned in school were that way. The teacher had said she'd chosen those because she wanted her students to know life was hard.

As she glanced at the words, ready to recite them, she realized she'd not practiced it for a while and had forgotten parts of it. Determined not to let her memory abandon what she'd tried so hard to learn, she read through the first stanza, closed her eyes and recited it. The more she read and recited, the easier it became until she got to one of her favorite parts and didn't have to even read it first. She looked straight ahead and said with confidence:

"*. . . because with the festive sound of joy*
She greets the well beloved child
on his Life's first walk
Which he begins in the arms of sleep . . ."

"Who are you talking to, Karin?" Christine hollered from the bedroom.

"No one. Just reciting poems," Karin said, feeling a bit silly.

"Fine, just as long as you can keep working while you do it."

"Don't worry." Karin pulled a couple of books from the box and placed it on a built-in shelf in the corner of the room. She then returned to her notebook and flipped through the pages to one of her favorites she had written.

Lilies of the field
dressed in yellow, green, and white,
how peaceful you must lay your heads
down on your pillow every night.
Never must you spin,
nor toil the whole day through.
You put your trust in God,
that He'll take care of you.
You give me lots of hope
that I can do that too,
for God loves me as much
as He loves you.

Warmth spread out from her chest, prompting a smile as she remembered writing this one. It had been part of an assignment at school. She could tell the teacher liked its rhythm and its rhyme. Frau Schultz had even given Karin praise—the first Karin had ever received in school. But Frau Schultz also given her a warning written in red across the top of her paper along with the A. *Be careful; do not mention God in any future writing assignments.*

The teacher didn't have Karin read it in front of the class like she did others with A grades. Karin wondered if school here near Dresden would be as hush-hush about God. She had no idea, only that she knew it was something else she wasn't looking forward to: going to school tomorrow. Especially without Christine.

CHAPTER 18

"Aren't you going to have any mush?" Karin looked up at Mutti, thinking she looked thinner than usual.

Mutti scraped the last remnants of the pot into Christine's bowl after dishing up Karin's small helping. "No . . . I'm not that hungry." She scurried back into the tiny kitchen and rinsed out the pot. Over her shoulder, she asked, "Christine, could you walk Karin to school—at least part way?"

"Yes, Mutti."

Karin shoveled in the last bites of her mush and licked the remaining morsels from her shallow bowl.

"Karin!" Mutti shot her a stern look. "Manners."

Karin lowered her bowl. "Sorry, Mutti. It just tasted so good. I didn't want to waste any of it." She gathered her spoon and glass into the licked-clean bowl and carried them to the sink, reaching around Mutti to deposit them into the dishwater. She gave Mutti a hug while she was so close. "Auf wiedersehen." She would have preferred Mutti accompanying her to school on this first day but understood Mutti had to travel in the opposite direction, whereas Christine's vocational training was at the food processing plant just a block away.

Mutti returned the hug. "I'll most likely still be over at Sophronia's after school. Your Uncle Stefan is training me today to do odd jobs around his shop. Stay put here until either Christine or I get home." She glanced at Christine and cleared her throat.

Christine stood by the door, putting on her coat. "Oh, sorry, Mutti, prayer."

Mutti gathered them around the couch. They knelt, and Mutti prayed. After the usual outpouring of thanks and pleas for protection, Mutti said, ". . . and Lord, please bless Stefan's shop with business so there will be work for me to do. I know that's something within Thy power. We thank Thee in Jesus Christ's blessed name, amen."

Karin said "amen" and ran out the door after Christine. She thought about the prayer and felt good. Mutti always seemed to pray for things that blessed more than one person's life at a time. Or was it that God always managed to bless multiple people while answering a single person's prayer? In either case, Karin was glad Mutti loved to pray and had taught her and Christine to pray.

At the bottom of the stairs, Karin raised up on her toes to look through the glass of a door to the left of the one that led outside. "Where does this go?"

"To the lower apartment," Christine said. "It's Frau Drescher's back door."

The door's light blue paint didn't match the darker blue of the stairwell. Karin guessed the door hadn't always been there. Probably at one time the upstairs and downstairs were used by just one family. She pressed her nose to the glass as she peered inside. Lace curtains partially blocked her view, but she could see enough to make out a painting of a cross-looking man—probably the woman's deceased husband—hanging on the fireplace above a cluttered mantel. It appeared their downstairs neighbor wasn't as tidy as Mutti. Karin strained her feet to rise even higher so she could a better look. The kitchen looked even messier than the fireplace.

The curtains moved aside. Cold, blue eyes, framed in wrinkled skin, glared back through the glass. The old lady's puckered lips twitched as her muffled voice penetrated the door. "Insolent child!" The unsettling sound and sight made Karin jump back.

"Come on." Christine grabbed Karin's arm. "Mutti said we should leave Frau Drescher alone. Remember?"

"Ja, I remember." Karin shook off Christine's grasp as they stepped onto the porch. "But why?"

"Doesn't matter."

"I still want to know."

"Maybe it's because the old lady is ornery," Christine said, rolling her eyes.

"So was Frau Somer, but Mutti never told us to leave her alone. I just figured that out for myself."

"I really don't know." Christine turned her head and locked eyes with Karin. "And I don't care. If Mutti said to leave her alone, I'm going to do just that." She hurried down the sidewalk and urged Karin to keep up by intensifying her glare. "And I suggest you do the same. Okay?"

"Humpf." Karin twisted her face.

"We're not in Wittgensdorf anymore, Karin. Not every old lady you meet is going to be an old-fashioned German Mutti who loves children."

"I know we're not in Wittgensdorf." Karin sighed. She glanced down the street, at the number of houses packed into a single block; at their peeling paint and missing shutters; at the tiny yards without gardens. "The Russians soldiers finally leave . . . and we do too! I could have stayed, you know."

"Karin!" Christine quickened her pace. "Your stubbornness is not a good thing."

Karin hurried to catch up with Christine. She had to swerve to avoid a man walking the opposite direction on the sidewalk. He wore a tattered suit and a sour look on his face. Not only were the houses of the city rundown compared to the country village, so were the people. She didn't want to be here. "And I don't think being stubborn is such a bad thing."

"That's debatable," Christine said. "And unfortunately, I don't have time to do that right now. I've got to be to the factory by nine." She urged Karin to walk faster.

Several blocks into their trek, a street car passed them by heading in the right direction. Karin tugged on Christine's arm. "Look, it's stopping. Can't we just take it?"

"You got some extra pfennig in your pocket I don't know about?"

"No." Karin stared at her scuffed shoes clapping against the sidewalk at a fast pace. She knew what little extra change they had needed to be spent for Mutti's streetcar fare rather than hers and Christine's.

"Try and be a little more pleasant about this move. For Mutti's sake. Okay?" Christine looked Karin in the eye again, appearing even more grown-up than her fifteen years would suggest. "She did it for all of us. Not just me." Christine rechanneled her gaze at the sky. "I would have liked to stay in Wittgensdorf too. But there was no place for me to continue my schooling. They picked this factory for me. Told me what I'd be trained in—I didn't really have much choice."

"They? Who are 'they'?" Karin asked.

"They? They are . . . the people who . . . make the laws . . . tell us what to do and how to think. People who can make our lives miserable if we don't obey them."

"You mean the government?"

"Ja, the government." Christine focused on the street ahead.

"Oh." Karin had thought Christine had wanted to move, had chosen the Lockwitz factory. And a career in bookkeeping. She'd heard Mutti talk about the government. Though she'd never complained about it in front of Karin, the way her eyebrows furrowed when she spoke of all their new laws told Karin that Mutti disapproved of most of them. But Karin never imagined that the government controlled this sort of thing.

For the next several blocks, they clipped along in silence. Christine glanced up at a clock set in the stonework of a bank. "Uh, I've got to go. It's my first day too." She pointed left, down the street that intersected the one they were on. "Your school is just three blocks farther down. You've walked by it before, so you'll find it just fine." She wrapped an arm around Karin's shoulder in a quick embrace. "How about you think of me, and I'll think of you when things get tough? We'll keep a prayer in our hearts for each other. Okay?"

"Okay." Karin leaned her head in to Christine. "Thanks."

Christine let go of her and hurried away without looking back. Karin's feet felt cemented to the sidewalk next to an abandoned shop. The fall breeze blew open the front of her coat. She buttoned it up to her neck, knowing she should start walking to keep warm, but she didn't want to.

It took her a minute before she could force her feet to move in the direction of the school. She trudged by the first block with her eyes to the ground and her heart feeling just as low.

The second block brought her eyes up, at least as high as the ground floor of a row of blackened apartment buildings. The upper floors lay as rubble in what once must have been several families' homes. It brought back memories of Wittgensdorf—those nights four and a half years ago when the skies above Dresden were lit up like fireworks. She quickly brushed the unsettling image aside and let a good memory shine through. Frau Krujatz . . . and the bouquet of flowers her sweet, old friend would give her each year for her birthday.

She walked by the next block with a quicker step than the last, remembering the Sunday Mutti had walked out of the way on their journey home after church to show Karin the school. Mutti's feet had hurt; she hadn't felt good that week. But she'd insisted on the journey, offering comforting hugs, encouraging words every step of the way.

When it got right down to it, Karin couldn't have stayed in Wittgensdorf without Mutti and Christine. And Mutti would have never sent Christine to live in the city without her and Karin. They were a family. All they really had of value was each other. And with all the new laws and the changes being made in Germany, Karin valued her family more than ever. At least she could be grateful no one was trying to change her family.

The school yard came into view first. Brick fence posts and iron rods sectioned off the concrete school yard from the street. The two-story building rose up out of a square of straggly shrubs, its beige stucco flaking on nearly every corner. Karin took a deep breath and headed for the large double doors she'd seen a handful of other children enter. She'd go in there, do her best not to get sent to the corner, and learn. Things were hard enough with the move; Karin didn't need to add to Mutti's worries.

As she stepped inside, the smell of chalk and a hint of something stale did little to welcome her. The worn burgundy-and-gold checkered tile reminded her of an old shirt Ella used to wear to work in the garden. There they were: thoughts of Wittgensdorf again. She concentrated on what needed to be done and looked for the office. She spotted it and headed in that direction, grateful she'd come a little early. Other children trickled in through the front door, but the classrooms she passed were mostly empty. Karin didn't know which one was hers and had to trust that Mutti had taken care of registering her.

She clung to the door frame just outside the office, mustering the courage to go in. The woman behind the desk—the only person in there—looked like a less-wrinkled version of their new downstairs neighbor, Frau Drescher. The woman's ice blue eyes glared at the typewriter as she pecked at its keys. Her mouth puckered into a short line. Those cold eyes glanced up and pierced Karin. "What is it, child? Don't lurk in doorways. Come in and state your business, or get out."

Karin took one step into the office, hovering close to the exit. "I don't know where to go. I'm new."

"Name?" The woman asked while shuffling through a stack of papers on her desk.

"Karin Graeber."

The woman quit shuffling, extracted a sheet of paper, and held it up to read. "Yes, here it is. It appears a Sophronia Braun came in last week and registered you."

"She's my aunt," Karin said with a sigh of relief.

"So she is," the woman said slowly as if uninterested in that detail. She studied the paper for a minute and stood up from her desk. "Follow me, Fraulein Graeber. I'll show you to your classroom."

Karin followed her out the door and down the hall. She expected to hear more chatter from the children she passed, but all she heard was the clap of their shoes on the floor tiles. They entered a classroom where a small number of children already sat at their desks. A short man stood at the front, writing a list of words on the blackboard. His face looked about as friendly as that of the woman Karin had followed into the room. He didn't look like a teacher to Karin, more like a mechanic. His hands were rough and stained the color of dirty oil. Black accentuated the edges of each fingernail. They reminded her of Herr Somer's hands.

"Herr Fuchs, you have a new student." The woman slid to the side and prompted Karin with a shove to step forward. "She's transferred from a village school down south, so you might have to bring her up to speed in social studies."

"Ja. I'll be sure to do that," Herr Fuchs said in a firm voice. He nodded the woman away and turned his attention to Karin. With pen hovering over a roll book, he said, "State your name."

"Karin Graeber, sir."

"Well, Fraulein Graeber, welcome to my class. Be warned that this is no country school. I run my classroom with a strict hand. I'll expect you not to speak without permission, answer when called upon, and accept what I teach as fact. Is that clear?"

"Yes, sir."

He maneuvered his way through four railroad-straight rows of desks, stopping at one that was almost dead center in the room. He slapped the top of the desk, and it made Karin and the other children jump. "This is my only available desk. The student who sits here hasn't been here for a while. Sit here for today, and I'll work at getting another desk in here." His straight-faced glare prompted Karin to lower onto the desk's chair.

As Karin scooted her chair up to the desk, more children filed into the room. She surveyed each face, hoping to find one that offered signs of friendliness, wondering if any were as afraid of Herr Fuchs as she was. Memories of school back in Wittgensdorf filled her thoughts, reminding her of the numerous complaints she'd often voiced to Mutti and Christine. She'd give anything to be back there right now.

A tall girl trod slowly into the classroom. She had round cheeks and a tiny mouth. Her blonde hair hung in braids on each side of her face. She looked at Karin and walked toward her, a smile bringing out dimples on her face. As she slid into the desk next to Karin, she said, "Is Hanna not here again today?"

"Hanna?"

"The girl who's supposed to sit here." The girl touched Karin's desk with her finger. "I wonder if her Mutter really did it?"

"Did what?" Karin asked. "What did her Mutter do?"

"Never mind." The girl quickly shook her hand in the air as if to erase what she'd said. "You're new, aren't you? What's your name?"

"Karin Graeber." She nodded her head.

"Where did you move from?"

"Wittgensdorf."

"Where's that? Sounds familiar."

"About an hour's walk south of here."

"Oh, one of those farming villages." The girl's forehead wrinkled. "Why would you want to move into the city if you lived on a *farm*?"

"We moved so my sister could finish her schooling."

"And your Pappa gave up his farm just so your sister could be close to school?" The girl's eyes widened.

"We didn't live on a farm—just stayed in a house there. And my Pappa's dead," Karin added, that tender spot in her heart allowing her to say the words without it hurting as much as it used to.

"He die in the war?"

Karin nodded. That was easier than to try and explain about those dummkopf mushrooms—Karin had sworn she'd never eat a mushroom again as long as she lived. But last spring when the winter food they'd stored got so low . . .

"I'm so sorry." The girl's eyes radiated warmth that made Karin feel her sincerity.

"What's your name?" Karin asked as a bell rang.

"Greta." The girl brought her finger to her lip and then pointed to Herr Fuchs. In a whisper she said, "Time to stop talking, or . . ." Her eyes skirted over to a corner of the classroom that held a chair facing the wall. A paddle hung next to it. In a whisper she added, "We'll talk at lunch."

Karin focused her eyes on the teacher, sitting up straight and trying to appear the model student. Her mind, however, dwelt on Greta's words. *We'll talk at lunch.* A friend! Karin was making a friend already. *Why would you want to move into the city if you lived on a farm?* Karin hadn't wanted to move—even this girl recognized things were better out in the country. *I wonder if her Mutter really did it?* Who was Hanna? What did her mother really do?

"Fraulein Graeber . . ." Herr Fuchs's mention of her name snatched Karin's attention. She refocused on the teacher—she'd promised herself to try harder in this new school.

Herr Fuchs cleared his throat. "Fraulein Graeber! Please stand." Karin shot to her feet, her heart thumping in her chest. "This is a new member of our class. Please help make her feel welcome. Please help her to see that we here in Dresden schools, dedicated citizens of a socialist society, are interested in the well-being of all its people." He motioned to Karin with his eyes. "You may sit down now."

Karin dropped to her chair, wanting to stick up for Wittgensdorf—though she wasn't sure why—but wanting to bolt out the door at the same time.

"For the benefit of our new student, today's social studies lesson will be a review of recent current events, our country's advances toward a superior society. I expect stellar participation from all and accurate answers when called upon." Herr Fuchs glared at the class members, who in return bore various expressions of concern. Karin was unsure if that was because they didn't want to go through the material a second time or they didn't want to be called upon.

Herr Fuchs looked straight at Karin. "And you, Fraulein, would be wise to listen intently and absorb what is being taught. Though I won't require you to take the test your classmates took last week, as a good member of the new German Democratic Republic, you *must* know and follow its precepts. I fear, as has often been the case in the rural schools, that your education in the ways of socialism has been woefully inadequate.

"That brings me to my first point. Though the production of food is important, it doesn't concern you as school children in my class. Your responsibility is to concentrate on industry and to choose a career path that will benefit the republic." His eyes focused on a boy in the second row by the wall. "Harold, what is communism?"

The boy swallowed hard and responded with concentration etched on his face. "A final stage of socialism in which all class differences disappear and humankind live in harmony."

"Excellent." Herr Fuchs paced across the front of the class to the side of the room. He eyed a girl on the front row. "Liza, what significant event happened last week?"

A girl with a dark brown braid running down her back took in a deep breath and responded. "Russia," the girl made a hurried correction, "I mean, the Soviet Union withdrew from its headquarters in East Berlin."

"And what else did it do?" He glanced at Karin, then shifted his eyes to her new friend.

"Greta. Could you put that chattering tongue of yours to good use this time and give us the correct answer? And nothing more?"

Greta's eyes stared off as if in thought. After a moment, she said, "Uh . . . They gave control of the government to the New German Democratic Republic." She then raised her fingers to scratch her nose and mouthed something to Karin under her hand while a glint of stubbornness shown in her eyes.

Karin was sure only she saw Greta's mouth move. *What was Greta saying silently—that she obviously didn't want anyone else to see?* Karin liked this girl more and more. She glanced at the clock on the wall above the door. Lunch break was so far away. She couldn't wait. It would be so nice having a friend her own age, one who appeared as headstrong as she. Karin's mind wandered off to that possibility.

Herr Fuchs's words filtered into her daydreams, making her sit up straight. She really needed to focus. What if he gave her that test after all?

She listened as he rambled on.

" . . . We must rise against everyone who desires to rob us of our great political and social achievements and to threaten our peaceful future." Herr Fuchs's hands beat the air with the same jerking rhythm the words spewed from his mouth. "It's okay to hate such enemies of socialism. Remember, we only strive for a peaceful, constructive society, one with equality for all. Our way is right, not theirs."

Karin found it easy to focus on his hands, the way they were almost black compared with his arms, especially in the creases. But not his words; they made her uncomfortable—like everything else in this new city. It sounded like he was saying one thing but meant another. Was this new society supposed to be good? Or not? She squirmed in her seat.

Herr Fuchs raised his eyebrows as he looked at Karin. "In this classroom, my students sit still. If you have a question about what's been covered, please raise your hand and ask. Don't squirm."

"Yes, sir."

"So, did you have a question about the material just covered?

"I guess."

"No guessing. Yes or no?"

Karin nodded.

"Well, then raise your hand and state it. You're not in kindergarten anymore."

His words hurt. She really was trying. And yes, she did want an answer! And if her teacher was making her ask for it, she was very well going to do just that.

Karin jabbed her hand in the air. Herr Fuchs nodded for her to speak. She stumbled on her words. "So . . . this new German demo . . . re . . ."

"Democratic Republic," Herr Fuchs corrected her.

"Ja. But if it's so peaceful, why are they teaching us to hate others?"

Herr Fuchs's face reddened. "Enough! An enemy to the state; that's what comes out of such belligerence." His hand balled into a fist before releasing a stained finger to point to the corner of the room. "Fraulein Graeber. To the corner. Now. You will face the wall and stare at it until I tell you otherwise. Understand?"

"Yes, sir." Karin stood slowly and shuffled to the dreaded chair, wondering if she was feeling bad because of being punished or because more and more it seemed that nobody liked the way she thought.

CHAPTER 19

IT SEEMED AS THOUGH LUNCHTIME would never come. When the bell rang, it sounded like heavenly music to Karin's ears. Sitting in the corner had felt twice as long and ten times more humiliating as it had been at her old school in Lungkwitz—everyone practically expected it of her back there. But here? She'd wanted to change things, be a good student. That's exactly why she'd responded to the teacher and asked questions. Maybe she'd stick to daydreaming. At least then when she got disciplined she'd feel as if she'd deserved it.

"Okay, Fraulein Graeber." Herr Fuchs spoke over the noise of the exiting class. "You may return to your desk now."

Karin gratefully removed her gaze from the blank gray-green wall and turned around. Several children pulled sandwiches from their desks. Others filed out into the hallway. She caught a glimpse of Greta's green dress leaving the room and darted for the only person she knew. Mutti hadn't had time to make Karin a sandwich that morning—or to make bread since their move. Karin had no desire to sit in a room full of others eating their lunches and having them stare at her for just sitting there, especially after having stood in the corner.

Herr Fuchs held up a finger, indicating for her to stop. "Fraulein, hopefully, that will teach you that there are right and *wrong* questions to ask in this classroom."

"Yes, sir," Karin said, thinking that the only thing she'd learned was that she didn't like what was being taught in that class.

"You're free to go now." He gave her a brushing wave of his hand.

Free? That made her laugh inside. She didn't feel free to do anything. She ran for the door, hoping she could still find Greta—hoping Greta and the others weren't off to buy a lunch. Karin hadn't even a single pfennig in her pocket.

Once out in the hall, Karin spotted a line-up of children. On the end nearest her was Greta. The girl must have slipped to the back of the line to wait for Karin! Students poured from another classroom and were merging into the line-up. Karin hurried and slipped into line behind Greta.

Greta turned her head. Her eyes brightened. "Are you okay?"

"Ja." Karin wasn't going to say she was used to being sent to the corner.

"I'm glad," Greta said. "It's awful having to stand there, and everyone staring at your back."

Karin wanted so much to ask her if she knew that because she'd sat in the corner before. She stifled the urge and changed the subject. "Where are all of you going?"

"To get our lunches," Greta said.

"Can I still come with you . . . even if I'm not going to eat?"

"I imagine so. But why don't you want to eat?"

Karin looked at the ground before responding. "I didn't bring any money."

"You're a half-orphan, like me." Greta nodded. "My Pappa died in the war too. Like the rest of us." She pointed to the others in line. "We don't have to pay for our lunch. They'll give us a bowl of soup for free."

"Free? Well, it's the only thing." Karin had always brought a lunch from home back at Lungkwitz. So there was *one* benefit to going to this city school. "I certainly don't feel free to ask questions. At least the *wrong* ones."

Greta's dimples appeared when her small mouth spread into a grin. "No, it wasn't wrong. It was a great question!"

"But he never answered it," Karin said as they shuffled along with the line that ran down the hall. "Just sent me to the corner, warning me I'd become an enemy to the state if I wasn't careful." She followed Greta's example and grabbed a spoon from a table next to the wall. "I don't see that I did anything wrong. I was just doing what he asked." She bit on her lip, not wanting to admit that she'd had a feeling that it wasn't a good question—at least to ask out loud.

Greta was about to say something but then lifted a finger to her lips and let her eyes point to a middle-aged woman standing behind a second table.

Karin took that to mean they shouldn't talk anymore, at least not in front of this woman. She breathed in the savory aroma of some kind of broth instead and looked around. A large pot became visible as the line moved forward. It rested on the table in front of the woman. With her hair pulled tight into a bun, and her lips pulled almost as tightly into a straight line, she ladled soup into a bowl and handed it to Greta. Karin's insides tightened. Would this woman ask for money? For proof that Karin was a half-orphan?

The woman with the bun said nothing. Her face unmoving, she dished up a bowl of soup and held it out. Karin grabbed it and followed Greta back into their classroom.

They set their bowls on their desks and sat down. Greta immediately set to talking, leaning close to Karin and speaking in a quiet voice so no one else could hear her. "I'm so sorry you got sent to the corner. I hate going there. Herr Fuchs is the meanest teacher in the school. But then, all the new teachers are ornery. When my big sister used to go here, that was back before Russia took over, she said the teachers were better. She said that's because they were real teachers. She told me that now they don't care if you're a real teacher, only if you're loyal to the new government."

Karin took a sip of the salty broth. Though the soup was thinner and less tasty than Mutti's, it felt good in her stomach. She continued to sip and listened, amazed at how long Greta could ramble without stopping. She didn't mind that Greta did most of the talking—she had a friend and something to eat. Things were good.

When Greta took a break from talking and worked on her soup, Karin surveyed the other students sitting at their desks, eating. Most of them were dressed like her, in clean yet worn clothing. But she found it peculiar how some of them wore neck kerchiefs, all the same shade of light blue. While lined up for soup, she'd seen others wearing them too.

The desire to fit in swelled inside her. "Why is everyone wearing the same colored kerchief?" she said.

"They belong to the Young Pioneers," Greta said without even a hint of dimple showing. "Just wait until Thursday, when they have their meeting after school. All members are supposed to wear them that day."

"What about you? Are you a member?"

"No, my Mutter doesn't want me to join." Greta looked down.

Karin knew how disappointed she'd feel if Mutti didn't let her join. "That must be hard on you."

Greta looked from side to side before responding. "Ja. Especially on Thursdays, when I'm the only one in the class who's not wearing a blue kerchief."

"So why doesn't your Mutter want you to join? What exactly do the Young Pioneers do?"

"They teach you to be a good communist; at least, that's what my Mutter says."

"Communist? Oh, my Mutter will probably not want me to join either."

"Speaking of Mutter, I was going to tell you about Hanna." Greta lifted her bowl to her mouth and drained its last remnants of soup.

"Hanna?"

"The girl whose desk you're sitting in."

"Oh, ja, tell me."

"Hanna didn't have a lot of friends; her hair was messy, and sometimes she'd come to school in a dirty dress. But I didn't care; I liked her—even if she didn't talk much. A week or so ago, she told me her Mutter wasn't there when she'd woken up that morning. Only a note. She'd left Hanna some money and told her to use it to buy food . . . and take care of herself. And that she was going away for a while."

"Where did her Mutter go?"

"Hanna didn't know. That was all the note said." Greta's voice became quieter. "I bet she was trying to escape."

"To where?" Karin didn't care for Lockwitz either. "And why would she need to escape?"

"To the west." Greta rolled her eyes and then looked up at the clock. "How else would she get there but escape? She certainly couldn't say, 'I want to go to Hamburg,' and they'd let her." Greta rose to her feet. "Come on, we've got to hurry and take our bowls back."

As Karin stood from her desk, she noticed that no one else still had their bowls on their desks. She and Greta scurried into the hall, returned their dishes, and hurried back to their desks. They sat down as the bell rang.

Herr Fuchs stood before the class and held out his hands, ready to speak. The lady from the office poked her head into the room. She crooked her finger and motioned him to the door. With a puzzled look on his face, Herr Fuchs marched over to the door. They talked for a minute or two before he returned to his position in front of the class. Now his face looked even more cross than usual.

Herr Fuchs cleared his throat. "It is with great displeasure that I tell you this. But as friends and classmates of Hanna's, and dutiful members of the New German Democratic Republic, I believe you have the right to know. Hanna will no longer be attending this school. She has been taken to an orphanage in another city. You see, her Mutter has disgraced not only Hanna by leaving illegally and going to the West but has disgraced the Republic as well. There is an important lesson here. The Republic will take care of you if by chance your parents are selfish enough to leave. But in return, you must be loyal to the Republic and tell them about any plans your parents might have to leave. For our superior society to run smoothly, we must all work together for the benefit of all."

So Hanna's mother did escape. To the West. What was in the West? What did it have that would make people want to go there so badly that they had to "escape" to get there? And why would they have to escape to get there? Why did the government not want Hanna's mother to go there? And why would it put Hanna in an orphanage? Surely her mother would come back and get Hanna to return with her so they could be together in the West? The word *escape* made it sound like Hanna's mother was in prison here in the German Democratic Republic.

Thoughts of escape, orphanages, and prison churned Karin's thoughts to where she gave up listening to Herr Fuchs talk about arithmetic. Were things better in the West? If so, how? Maybe people could think and say what they wanted. Maybe over there Christine could become a seamstress like she'd always wanted rather than work in an office. Or maybe there was more food over there. Karin was tired of always feeling hungry. Was that what made Hanna's mother escape to the West? But why hadn't she taken Hanna? Were children not allowed?

Karin wanted to know about the West. Her chest felt heavy with the desire to know about it. But no matter how good it was over there—if it even was—it wouldn't be that good if her family couldn't be together.

CHAPTER 20

KARIN ROSE UP ON TIPTOE and peeked into Frau Drescher's apartment before she stepped outside. She didn't know why she liked peeking in at the messy kitchen. But every time she did, she appreciated even more how comfortable Mutti made their tiny apartment feel.

Once out on the porch, she wished she would have remembered her gloves, even if a few of her fingers poked through the holes. She wedged her hands under her armpits and trudged toward school. A rumbling in her stomach begged for more mush. She took a deep breath to try and soothe it—she should be glad for the portion she got. One day last week, she'd gone to school without anything to eat. She'd mentioned it to Frau Drescher when they'd run into each other on the front sidewalk. Later that evening, Frau Drescher had stopped Mutti and Karin on their way up the stairs.

"Not that I'm that fond of children, mind you, but I do not want to see them go hungry," Frau Drescher had said to Mutti. "I can help you. It will only take a moment." She had opened the door with the lace curtain in the window and motioned for them to step into her apartment. It was the first and only time Karin had been in there. A sickening sweet smell, like fruit, mold, and meat aged together, made her cover her nose. While Frau Drescher, in a curt manner, explained to Mutti something about the benefits of socialism, Karin gazed around the kitchen.

Piled-up dishes had made it hard to see the sink, and dark splotches on the floor had made it hard to see the blue and gray linoleum. Coffee cans, some new but most with worn labels and hints of rust, filled the cupboard countertops. It made Karin wonder if the old lady was collecting them like Frau Krujatz collected stamps. Stacks of magazines cluttered the kitchen table. Frau Drescher had shoved them to one side so Mutti could sit next to her at the table. She had then helped Mutti fill out some papers. Karin wanted to go in the living room and get a better look at all the curious things cluttering the fireplace. She had moved her feet in that direction.

"Keep your child in place." Frau Drescher had peered over the tops of her glasses at Mutti. "I don't want children wandering about the place."

"Yes, Frau." Mutti had grabbed Karin's arm and reined her in.

Karin was stuck listening to Mutti and Frau Drescher. She hadn't understood much of what they said, but somehow what they did with all those papers got her family a small amount of food from the government. And they'd be getting more next week and the next.

Karin was grateful for that food . . . and for the old lady's help. Lowering her head, Karin plowed through the late fall wind that seemed determined to chill her to the bone. She wondered if the government would hand out new coats too. Was there a form Mutti could fill out for that? Maybe this new government was truly as good as Frau Drescher and Herr Fuchs said it was going to be. Karin anticipated the day everyone would have plenty of food for their bellies, coats for their bodies, and wood for their stoves. She hoped it would come soon.

As the school came into view, so did swarms of children. They materialized from all directions and moved toward the two-story beige building like ants gravitating to an abandoned piece of sweet bread. Poking out from beneath their coats, many a blue neck kerchief caught Karin's eye, reminding her it was Thursday. She was tired of feeling left out. The rude words she'd had to shrug off now and again made it even worse. This would be her fourth Thursday since she'd come to Lockwitz. She still hadn't joined the Young Pioneers. With what Frau Drescher had said, and the food they'd received from the government, how could Mutti be against the Young Pioneers? It irked Karin how Mutti wouldn't give a good reason why she shouldn't join—just like Greta's mother. Mutti had simply told her, "I said no, and that should be reason enough."

But it wasn't enough.

Upon entering the schoolyard, Karin scanned the playground, look-ing for Greta. Maybe they should both go to the meeting after school today—at least to check it out. She dragged her feet as she stepped inside the school, walking slower than usual, seaching the hallway, hoping to meet up with Greta before going to their class. The hands of the clock, hanging just inside the door of her classroom, pointed a minute away from Karin being sent to the corner if she wasn't in her seat. Karin scurried inside to her desk. A few seconds later, Greta ran into the classroom and dropped into her seat a blink or two before the bell rang.

"I need to talk to you," Karin mouthed the words to Greta while Herr Fuchs had his back turned to them as he wrote on the board.

"At recess," Greta mouthed back.

Herr Fuchs pivoted on his heel to face the class, and Karin straightened up in her seat. "Picking up where we left off yesterday, we'll finish our discussion on communism." He pointed to the sentence he'd written on the blackboard: *The more modern a society is, the more secular it will be.* "We discussed the term *secular* yesterday, and be assured that word will be on your vocabulary test."

Karin chewed on her bottom lip. She didn't remember hearing that definition—it was so hard not to daydream during social studies. Concentrating hard, she tried to listen to Herr Fuchs, all the time wondering what *secular* meant. The way the teacher talked, it must mean something good.

"Communism is the most advanced form of socialism," he continued. "It promises to bring about an earthly paradise by means of a communist society where everyone works together for the greater good of all. When the 'perfect society' evolves, there will be no state, no family, no religious morality, and man will thus have no unhappiness. There will be lasting peace." He stepped over to his desk and picked up a book from off its corner. "Doesn't that sound wonderful? Who would not like to have lasting peace?" He scanned the classroom as if expecting some sort of response.

All the other students sat at their desks as quiet and straight-backed as Karin. She didn't like how this teacher used such big words, and she wondered if her classmates were as confused as she. Some of what Herr Fuchs said sounded really good. But some sounded bad—like the part about no family.

Flipping through the pages of the book, he said, "Of course, it will take commitment from every person to obtain such a society. I'm going to read to you a story about a white rabbit who didn't work with the greater good of his fellow rabbits in mind. Of course, this is just a fictional story, but much can be learned from it about the danger of selfishness."

Karin relaxed a bit as Herr Fuchs opened the book. Stories were a lot easier to remember than all that communism stuff.

"Four young rabbits sing happily on their way to gather mushrooms," Herr Fuchs read from the first page. He lifted it high so the class could see the picture of a white, a black, a brown, and a gray rabbit skipping through the woods. He turned the page and continued reading.

"'A lot of mushrooms here!' Little Brown says. 'Big Black and Little White gather them here. Little Grey and I will go over there. Let's have a competition!'

"'All right!' Little White says.

"While Big Black and Little White are busy picking mushrooms, two butterflies fly about them.

"'How beautiful!' Little White dashes over to catch them.

"Big Black calls out, 'Little White, how can you fool around when you are supposed to be working?' But naughty Little White goes on chasing the butterflies as if he hasn't heard.

"Little White runs after them all the way to a cliff, and there he discovers a big mushroom below. He climbs down as Big Black looks on from atop the cliff. 'I've got it! I've got it!' Little White exclaims with happiness. He holds the big mushroom up and is about to take a bite when Big Black stops him.

"'Little White, the mushrooms we've gathered belong to everyone. You mustn't eat it first.' Little White doesn't care and insists on having his way. Big Black advises him, 'Little White, you mustn't only think of yourself.'

"Grumbling, Little White walks away toward the woods with the big mushroom on his shoulder.

"Big Black is worried and quickly warns him, 'Don't go! There're wolves in there!'"

As Herr Fuchs continued reading the story, Karin's mind wandered. She thought about the time she'd gone for a walk in the woods with Liesel. There was no one around to warn her and her sister about wolves—or Russians; same thing. Liesel was amazing with her quick thinking. Then Karin thought about gathering mushrooms, the time Aunt Anna had picked that fateful batch. She shook her head in an attempt to refocus. Herr Fuchs's story of the white rabbit would probably be on a test.

As she listened intently, she found she kind of liked the hard-headed personality of the white rabbit. He didn't want to listen to the advice of a squirrel when she warned him to worry about wolves. And when it started to rain and the mushroom was too big to fit into a hole in the tree where he sought shelter, he wouldn't give up trying to make it fit inside. But Karin felt a lump form in her throat when the white rabbit crossed a bridge and was freezing, lonely, and longing to be with Big Black. She gripped the edge of her desk when a big wolf appeared and tried to capture and eat the white rabbit. Relief spread through her when Big Black found Little White and, with the help of the other rabbits, tricked the wolf and pushed him off a bridge.

"Little Grey claps his hands, and Little White dances," Herr Fuchs read after the rabbits had defeated the wolf. "'Together we are strong. No enemy can knock us down,' Big Black and Little Brown sing joyfully," he continued. "Standing together with his friends, Little White bows his head shamefully. 'Big Black, I was wrong.'

"Big Black tells him, 'Don't be sad. Everything will be fine if you correct your mistakes.' Then he asks, 'Where is your big mushroom?'

"'I lost it,' Little White says, shaking his head.

"They search around and find the big mushroom behind a stone. 'It belongs to all of us!'" Little White says happily.

"Great little story." Herr Fuchs closed the book. "Could you see the problems the white rabbit brought upon his comrades because of his selfishness? Also, how strong the rabbits were when they worked together? You can learn much from the white rabbit." He sat the book down and walked to the chalkboard. "Enough of that. Time to move on to arithmetic."

As he jotted down a handful of number problems, Karin's mind begged to wander, but she wouldn't let it. After working on multiplication, Herr Fuchs moved on to writing. To practice their penmanship, he let them do some creative writing. Karin perked up and decided to write a poem about clouds. She remembered the warning from her teacher back in Wittgensdorf and was careful not to mention God.

She finished her poem quickly and then pretended to still work on it so as to look busy. A quick glimpse around the classroom at all the blue kerchiefs made her certain she wanted to talk to Greta. They were the only two in the room not wearing one—except for Herr Fuchs, but he didn't count. Her first Thursday here she'd been told the Young Pioneers membership was totally voluntary and that it didn't matter if she joined or not. But when she hadn't joined by the following Thursday, she'd felt as though the other children never talked to her. Even Herr Fuchs, it seemed, treated her differently. She couldn't put her finger on how, but she swore he didn't like her even though she'd been working hard and hadn't been sent to the corner since that first day.

As soon as Herr Fuchs excused them for recess, she jumped out of her seat and motioned for Greta to follow her. They put on their coats, hurried down the hall, and slipped outside into the cold air.

"Okay, *was gibts*?" Greta asked.

"Can you stay after school with me today?"

"You want to go to Young Pioneers?" Greta lifted both eyebrows.

"Ja, I think we should. At least to see what they're all about."

"That's wonderful! I've wanted to go for several weeks now, but I didn't want to go alone. My Mutter doesn't get home from her job until after dark, so she won't even know that I came." Greta scrunched her forehead. "But what about your Mutter? I thought she didn't want you to join either?"

"She'll be gone too . . . and remember, we're not necessarily joining. We're just checking it out. Okay?"

"Okay!"

After school, Karin and Greta followed the blue-kerchiefed children into the school's large common room. They fell in step next to a boy named Hans from their class.

"You girls finally joining the Young Pioneers?" Hans asked with a hint of taunting in his voice.

"Maybe," Karin responded.

"We thought we'd at least see what it's all about . . . before we decide to join or not," Greta said.

"What's to decide?" Hans curled his lip.

"Then tell us about it . . . and why we should join." Karin was about to say she needed some good reasons so she could convince her mother to let her join, but she didn't want to get Mutti in trouble.

"Well . . . we take socialism to heart." Hans patted his chest. "We are prepared to help others whenever, however we can." He motioned for them to take a seat on the floor among the children forming a semicircle around Frau Heinz, the other fourth grade teacher. This teacher wore a blue kerchief too. "Our slogan is: For peace and socialism be ready—always ready."

Karin elbowed Greta. "That doesn't sound bad."

"No, it doesn't." Greta sat down cross-legged on the floor and pulled Karin down with her.

"See, it doesn't make sense not to—" Hans cut his words short and looked straight ahead the minute the teacher with the blue kerchief began speaking.

"Listen carefully, children." Frau Heinz brought her finger to her lips. A hush fell over the large room. Karin liked how this teacher could demand obedience from the children without being terrifying like Herr Fuchs. "This week marks the beginning of our recycling competition. I will review the rules one more time. Then I'll answer your questions and split you into teams. I will excuse you early this afternoon so you can go out and get to work immediately.

"The contest will run for two weeks. But that doesn't mean you can't continue to bring in goods to recycle thereafter. Remember your duty to society. Young Pioneers are always ready to help their country. And reclaiming that much-needed metal shows that even the society's youngest members can contribute.

"The rules are simple: scour your neighborhoods—in the trash, on the roadsides, or in your homes—for discarded cans or unused pieces of metal of any kind. Ask your neighbors to participate; tell them it's for the Young Pioneers. Remind them it's their duty to contribute. The team that collects the most kilos of scrap metal wins. Are there any questions?" Frau Heinz smiled as she scanned the audience of students, all in the first through fourth grades.

No hands went up. Were the children afraid to speak, or did they really have no questions? Karin had one. Despite feeling as though she stuck out like a plain brown tile in a wall of fancy blue ones, she raised her hand.

Frau Heinz's smile relaxed into a blank expression as she looked at Karin. "Yes?"

"What do you win?" Karin asked. "Those on the winning team, I mean."

"Aren't you that new girl who just moved in?" Frau Heinz tilted her head, her eyes remaining fixed on Karin.

Karin nodded.

"Who hasn't yet joined our ranks?" Frau Heinz's eyebrows furrowed as if she was puzzled.

Karin nodded again and said, "I just haven't decided yet whether or not I'm going to join. But I was told I could still come to the meetings anyway."

"I—that is true." Frau Heinz looked out over the other children. "Would someone like to answer our guest's question?"

A girl in the front row raised her hand, and Frau Heinz motioned for her to speak. She turned around to face Karin. "We, in the Young Pioneers, seek to promote socialism and so will not raise one person or group above another." She said it like she was reciting a memorized verse. "The winning team will receive the satisfaction of a job well done," she concluded and then smirked at Karin before turning back around.

"Thank you, Hilda."

Greta leaned toward Karin and whispered, "Satisfaction of a job well done? Horse feathers!"

Karin brought her hand up to cover her mouth and snickered. It did sound like a worthless made-up reward an adult would come up with.

Frau Heinz's smile returned. "Any more questions before I divide you into teams?"

Before anyone had a chance to raise their hands, the teacher drew imaginary lines, sectioned the students off into nine groups. She then spoke to Karin and Greta. "You girls will be with group number five." She indicated two girls who looked almost identical except for their heights—obviously sisters—and three boys who looked as different as night and day and evening. Frau Heinz focused on the oldest of the sisters, a girl Karin recognized from her class. "Maria, you're the leader." Her attention switched to Karin. "I think this activity will be really fun. Hopefully you'll convince your friend to join along with you after this competition," she said with a jerk of her head toward Greta. She then wove her way back to the front of the commons room.

"Children." Frau Heinz gathered everyone's attention again. "Bring the scrap metal you collect to school next Thursday. At our meeting we'll compare the progress of each group." She brought her palms together, pointing her fingers up at her chin like she was going to pray. "I'll dismiss you early today so you can get to work."

Karin laughed inside at the idea. She would have liked it if Frau Heinz would have prayed—it would have been a nice conclusion to the meeting. But she knew that would never happen. Nobody mentioned God in school. Why would it be any different after school with the Young Pioneers? As her mind wandered along those thoughts, she felt someone grab her elbow. It was a boy in her group.

He towered above Karin even though he was in third grade. His hair was the color of the blackboard. To one side stood another boy, much shorter and with eyes that matched the kerchief around his neck. On the other side was a boy the same height as Karin. The boys stood close together, as if supporting each other in what the tall one was about to say.

"It's not fair we got stuck with you two." The dark-haired boy shoved a finger at Greta and then Karin.

Karin's knees shook.

The sisters stood close, nodding their heads at what the dark-haired boy said. Maria spoke up. "Why don't you just join up right now? Frau Heinz will give you a kerchief and everything. It'll be easier on everybody if you do."

"We don't have the time right now." Karin grabbed Greta's elbow and tugged toward the door. "Later," she said as she and Greta slipped through the crowd of children. Once out in the hall, she turned on Greta. "Okay, now we're stuck. What are going to do?"

"What do you mean, stuck?" Greta said as they marched toward the front door.

"We were just going to check out the Young Pioneers. Or at least I was—I wasn't going to come back."

"But now if we don't come next week—"

"I know, I know, it wouldn't be fair to the team we got put on." Karin couldn't do that to them.

"We should at least participate in the contest. What they're doing is a good thing. Maybe the other stuff they do is just as good. We don't have to decide right now. After it's over, if we still don't want to join, we'll come up with a good excuse to get out of it."

"You're right," Karin said, a bit relieved. Something else that needed to be taken care of came to Karin's mind. "Hey, what does *secular* mean?"

"Weren't you listening today?" Greta smiled as she opened the door for them to leave.

"Uh . . . maybe not all the time." Karin chewed on her finger.

"It means something that has nothing to do with religion or God," Greta said as a cold wind whipped Karin in the face.

"Oh," Karin responded. She had her definition for Herr Fuchs's test. But she didn't like what it meant.

CHAPTER 21

THE NEXT THURSDAY, KARIN STAYED after school for the Young Pioneers. As she sat cross-legged on the floor next to Greta, waiting for the meeting to start, Karin's insides churned. Greta, with an empty, washed-clean can in each hand, leaned close and spoke in Karin's ear. "Didn't you collect anything?"

Karin shook her head.

When it came to the part of the meeting where they split into their recycling groups, Karin's stomach grew more uncomfortable.

"So . . . you brought nothing?" said Fritz, the dark-haired boy. He towered above her several centimeters and made her feel small in more ways than just height.

"My Mutter doesn't cook much from cans," Karin squeaked, backing against the wall in the corner of the commons room.

"It doesn't have to be cans," said Maria. "Any kind of metal will work."

"We've got nothing to throw away either." Karin felt like a stray dog surrounded by five mean dogs ready to pounce.

Greta stepped in front of Fritz, holding up her two cans. "Come on, the contest isn't over. Let's hand in what we've all brought today and see where our team sits."

Fritz grabbed Greta's cans and backed off. He stuffed them into a half-full box he'd brought and then held it out for the others to add their collections. With the box now almost full, he strutted to the front of the commons room, where Frau Heinz and another teacher weighed each group's metal. As he made his way back, his feet seemed to drag.

"Some of those groups really have a lot." He glared at Karin and then Greta.

"Shh." The short blue-eyed boy, Karl, pointed to the front of the large room. "She's going tell us who is winning so far." The group turned and faced Frau Heinz.

"Children, may I have your attention?" Frau Heinz stepped to the side of the blackboard to reveal a quickly made chart. "Here are this week's results."

Karin didn't need to hear Frau Heinz announce the results. She could see them just fine. And feel them. The knot in her stomach cinched tighter. Almost to the point of making her want to throw up.

"Those groups at the bottom should not be discouraged," said Frau Heinz. "There is still plenty of time and opportunity to show your loyalty to the Republic. Now let's go out and make the next week's results even better."

"Don't be discouraged?" Karl laughed. "Huh! We're at the very bottom."

"That's because group five is only *five* people." Fritz furrowed his eyebrows and glared at Karin and Greta. "You two are going to make us lose. And why aren't you wearing your blue kerchiefs?"

Maria stepped forward. "Stop being so bossy, Fritz. Frau Heinz assigned me as leader of this group. I say we all need to try harder."

"We promise we will," Greta said. "The contest still has another week. Maybe we need to make a plan or something."

"Good idea." Maria nodded. "Everyone think of some new ways to find junk and promise to bring at least twice as much as we each brought this week."

"That won't work for her." Fritz pointed to Karin. "Two times zero is zero."

"I promise I'll do better." Karin really meant it, but she wasn't sure how she could.

"That's not good enough." Fritz pushed his face toward Karin. "A plan of action! That's what you've got to give us!"

Karin took a step backward, away from Fritz. Her mind raced, grappling for ideas—she was not going to let her group down. Maybe the factory Christine worked for had damaged applesauce cans they would donate. *No good*; that would require getting Christine involved, and then Mutti would find out. And she wasn't sure they had bad cans. An image of Frau Drescher's cluttered cupboard popped in her head.

"My neighbor! She's got lots of junk. Her kitchen is full of old coffee cans. I've seen them. She loves the Republic. I know she'll contribute."

"Good," Maria said. "We'll all plan on you getting those old cans."

"And bringing in the most scrap next week." Fritz looked to the others in the group, nodding his head, getting them to agree.

"Ja." They all nodded their heads.

"She won't let us down." Greta pulled Karin to her side. "I'll make sure. I'll go with her to help get them." She urged Karin toward the door. "Come on, we'll go right now."

"Okay," Karin said. But it wasn't okay. She didn't know if Frau Drescher would part with her coffee cans, even if they looked like junk. Karin didn't even know if the old lady would let her in the door. Why had she said those things?

What Karin did know was that she didn't want to talk to Frau Drescher.

"This is where you live?" Greta's eyes widened as they opened the gate at the street and approached Karin's house. "It's big."

"We just have two of the rooms on the top floor. Three, if you count the closet-sized kitchen." Karin pointed to the top story of the white stucco house that the clouded sky made appear more dingy than usual. She had hoped the gray clouds would have produced rain rather than just threatening to do so. Then Greta might have decided against coming home with her, and she wouldn't have to face Frau Drescher right now.

The two large elm trees in the front yard welcomed the girls with their vibrant display of falling yellow leaves. Greta snatched a handful of yellow from the ground and tossed them in the air. "So pretty. I like this place."

At the moment Karin didn't think it was pretty or likeable. Not with Frau Drescher there, clinging to those coffee cans like they were treasures. What was she going to say to the old woman? Greta would figure out Karin was a liar. Then nobody would be her friend.

Greta grabbed Karin by the elbow after her second handful of leaves splayed into the air. "Come on, let's go get those cans." She pulled Karin onto the front porch. "Go ahead, knock."

Karin raised her hand reluctantly, made a fist, and rapped her knuckles against the smooth door, creating a hollow-sounding knock.

Greta tapped her toes on the wood porch as she waited for the door to open. "So about how much stuff would you say your neighbor's got? From what you said, she's bound to have a whole lot more than old cans we can recycle. We've got to collect a lot this week, Karin. Okay? If I'm going to go, I don't want a repeat of the last meeting."

"I know, I know."

Greta took a step over to the window and peered in. "I wish I could see in. The curtains are in the way."

"It looks like she's not home." Karin headed back down the steps. "Let's just go look in the garbage cans in the alley."

"You give up too easy." Greta hopped down the steps alongside Karin.

"No, I don't." Karin didn't like hearing that.

"Didn't you say the old lady had a back door? That leads to her kitchen? Let's try that. Maybe she's hard of hearing and is sitting at her kitchen table sipping a cup of coffee—hopefully emptying another can for us." Greta's dimple next to her small mouth became very pronounced.

Karin doubted knocking at the back door would do any good. Rather, it made her a bit uneasy since she'd rarely seen Frau Drescher use that door. But Greta's enthusiasm pulled Karin along, and she ran ahead of Greta to show her the way to the side door.

They raced up the porch steps. As she turned the doorknob, Karin said, "This is the door to our home too . . . and to the other upstairs apartment."

They stepped into the small landing at the base of the stairs and squeezed together next to the steps so Karin could shut the door against the breeze. Clouded daylight seeped in through the window of the exterior door, creating more eerie shadows than light leading up the stairwell. But it looked a whole lot more inviting than trying to visit Frau Drescher. "The old lady doesn't really use this door," Karin pointed at the lace-covered window, "so I don't know if it's a good idea to knock at it."

"You worry too much. What's she going to do?"

"Nothing. Probably." Prickles ran down her back as Karin remembered Frau Drescher's expression that first time she'd peeked in that lace-covered window.

Greta raised her knuckles and knocked. She waited a few seconds. "Ja, I don't think she's home." She peered through the lace curtains, being tall enough to do so without standing on tiptoe. "You're right; the place is full of junk."

"What if she doesn't want to give them to us?" Karin thought about Frau Krujatz and her treasured stamp collection. Coffee cans weren't exactly stamps and neither were those piles of magazines on Frau Drescher's table or the menagerie of knickknacks on the mantel, but who knew what odd things the ornery old lady liked to collect?

"Is she a good citizen?"

"Oh, ja. Mutti says she's about as loyal of a communist as they come."

"Just tell her it's for the 'greater good.' Remember the story of the white rabbit?"

"You can tell her." Karin's insides soured at the thought. "I'm not going to. You haven't met Frau Drescher."

"Well, unfortunately, I can't. She's not here, and I need to get home before my Mutter does." Greta headed up the stairs. "Show me your place before I go."

Karin let out a deep breath as her muscles relaxed. She hurried and caught up to Greta on the stairs.

She gave Greta a quick tour of their living room, furnished with only the old blue couch, kitchen table, and an end table holding a lamp. Then the bedroom and then the cooking kitchen. All the while Greta chattered away, telling Karin about her own apartment and how it wasn't much bigger than Karin's, but her mother didn't care because they were moving some place much better the first chance they got. Karin then walked Greta to the end of the block, and they said their good-byes.

As Karin returned to her house, she saw Frau Drescher on the sidewalk, coming from the other direction. The sting from Greta's words was still fresh. *I do not give up too easily!* She ran to catch up with Frau Drescher before the woman made it to the front steps. "Frau

Drescher," she hollered, determined not to be humiliated at next week's Young Pioneer meeting. "Can I ask you something?"

Frau Drescher stopped at gate to their yard, her wrinkled hand on the handle, gripping it with seeming impatience. "What is it, child?"

Karin was at her side a moment later. A minute ago it'd sounded easy. Now the thought of asking tangled her tongue. "The Young Pioneers . . . at school . . ."

"Spit it out, child. I don't have all day. I've got my own meeting I've got to worry about—I'm hosting a FDJ meeting tonight. I've got to prepare."

"FDJ?"

"*Freie Deutsche Jugend,* the young adult version of the Young Pioneers." Frau Drescher pushed the gate open. "Don't you know anything, child?"

Of course Karin knew—or at least had heard about the Free German Youth. She'd just not realized that they and FDJ were one in the same. And she didn't like how the old lady made her feel. She forced her request out. "The Young Pioneers are collecting metal to recycle. I thought maybe you'd like to donate something." Thinking about the story of the white rabbit, she added, "It's for the greater good."

"The Young Pioneers?" Frau Drescher walked toward the front steps, her back still to Karin. "I'm glad your Mutter is seeing things as she should. Metal, you say?"

"Ja." Karin mustered the courage. "Like those old coffee cans you have on your cupboard."

Frau Drescher spun around with the energy of a woman half her age. "Those are mine! Herr Drescher bought each and every one of those cans of coffee for me during the war. He loved me. Adored me! Tried to make life good for me—despite losing our darling Olga to typhus. Nobody touches them!"

"I didn't mean—"

"I imagine you didn't, child." Frau Drescher turned her back again to Karin and hobbled up the steps. "I'll try and find something to contribute. I'll have it for you by tomorrow. But not now." She shooed Karin away with the flap of a hand and slipped into her house.

The sun warmed the air, and Frau Drescher had promised to give Karin some things to recycle, making the walk home from school much more delightful than yesterday's.

"How much stuff do you think she'll give us?" Greta skipped as she chattered. "I hope it's a lot. I'm not having much luck in my neighborhood. It should be a lot. If she just gave us half the junk I saw through that window, our team could win."

"She didn't say how much, just that she'd have some things ready for me." Karin opened the gate and then kicked her feet through the leaves littering the cobblestones that led up to their house. Greta copied her. Together they ran up the front steps. Greta knocked loudly on the door.

"Is she gone again?" Karin muttered when the front door remained closed after a minute or so of waiting.

Greta tried the doorknob. "It's locked," she said with disappointment obvious in her voice. "I can't keep coming over here after school."

"Sorry." Karin felt horrible, not wanting to let Greta and her group down again. "How about we go upstairs and rest for a minute?" She hopped down the steps. "Maybe I can find us some sort of snack before you go." She thought about the loaf of bread Mutti had baked two days earlier, telling Karin she could have a thin slice every day after school. It was almost as if Mutti was trying to make up for not being there when Karin got home from school. But Karin didn't mind. She understood. However, that slice of plain bread always gave her something to look forward to each morning when she left for school.

The girls traipsed around to the side of the house and dragged their feet up the steps. Out of desperation, Karin rose up on tiptoe and glanced through the lace curtains into Frau Drescher's kitchen to see if the old lady was possibly home. As Greta stood next to her and peered in, she reached around Karin and grabbed the doorknob.

The sound of a doorknob turning didn't quite register with Karin until the glass in front of her nose moved forward and she toppled off her tiptoes and into Frau Drescher's kitchen. "What in the—" she cried out and fell to the dirty floor.

"Sorry." Greta held out her hands, palms up. "I just had to try the doorknob. I didn't expect it to open." She reached down and gave Karin a hand up.

Back on her feet, Karin brushed off her knees. She took a quick, deep breath. That unpleasant sweet smell still lingered in the kitchen. "Let's get out of here."

Greta gravitated to the coffee cans, running her fingers down the tarnished stacks of blues, reds, and greens. "Wow, imagine what Fritz and the others will say when we bring these in."

"Those aren't for us."

"How do you know?"

"I just know."

"Well, then which pile of stuff is she going to give to us?" Greta headed toward the living room without waiting for an answer.

"Greta, get back here." Karin rushed after her, hesitating at the doorway. She remained in the kitchen and poked her head into the living room. "Hurry, she might come back any minute."

"What's all this about?" Greta pointed at a collection of kitchen and mismatched chairs set in three rows, all facing a folding table placed in front of the fire place.

"That must be from the meeting she had last night." Karin noticed the living room was tidier than the last time she'd been in there.

"What kind of meeting?"

"FDJ." Karin darted into the room and grabbed Greta by the elbow. "Let's get out of here."

Greta stood firm, staring at some papers atop the folding table. "She must be a FDJ leader or something." She picked up a sheet of paper with notes scribed in neat handwriting and held it out for Karin to see.

Karin glanced at the page that read *FDJ Meeting, October 20, 1949* at the top and *Items to Discuss* just beneath it.

Greta pulled the paper away and held it in front of her face. "New law lowering age from 21 to 18 at which a person is not bound by parental supervision," she read. "What does that mean?"

"I don't know." Karin reached for the paper.

Greta turned away and kept reading. "Role of parents is to bear children; role of society is to raise, educate, and train them. Marxism, not religion, will aid and strengthen citizens." She lowered the paper, turned back, and handed it to Karin. "Sounds boring; you can have it."

Karin grabbed it and slapped it onto the card table. The click of a key turning in the front door made her jump. "She's coming!"

She and Greta bolted for the back door. The front door creaked open just as they made it to the kitchen. Footsteps clapped across the wooden floor behind them. Karin opened the back door—as quietly and quickly as possible—anxious for the sanctuary of the stairwell.

The girls rushed out, Greta grabbing the doorknob. Karin peered over Greta's shoulder at the narrowing view of the kitchen through the closing door. Frau Drescher's cold eyes opened wide as her gaze connected with Karin's.

"Frauleins!" Frau Drescher snapped. "What are you doing?"

Karin froze. Except for a twitch of the head and a few jitters in her hands, she felt unable to move.

Greta pushed the door open wider, poking her head back into the kitchen. "Uh . . . we were coming to visit you."

"Who are you, child? I don't know you."

Greta pulled Karin forward, causing the door to open further. "I'm Karin's friend from school." Karin nodded her head as Greta rambled on faster than usual. "We're collecting metal scrap to recycle. It's for the Young Pioneers. She said you loved the Young Pioneers. She said you told her you'd have something ready to donate today. That's why we were, uh . . . knocking on your door. But then it opened. We were just looking in to see if you were home, when you, uh—"

"Ja, ja." Frau Drescher flapped a hand at Greta as if to shut her up. "That still gives you no call to open my door." She glided over to the chairless kitchen table. From behind a pile of newspapers, she extracted a metal handle that appeared to have broken off some sort of crank and three empty tin cans. "I'm not sure you frauleins deserve these. I will, however, make sure they get donated to the scrap drive through some other child who has more respect for my property." She shooed Karin and Greta out the back door with the flick of her wrist.

The door clicked shut. Greta turned to Karin. Her forehead wrinkled up, and her round face flushed pink. "I can't believe she wasn't going to give us all those coffee cans. Three measly cans! And we didn't even get those. We're worse off than last week."

"She'd never give those coffee cans away. They remind her of her husband and daughter, who . . . are both dead." Karin could understand what Frau Drescher was feeling. She, herself, cherished everything that reminded her of Pappa.

"So now what are we going to do?"

"I don't know," Karin muttered.

CHAPTER 22

AFTER KARIN SHARED A SLICE of bread with Greta and then said good-bye to her, she searched the tiny kitchen. On her knees, sifting through the pots and pans in the cupboard under the sink, she found a bent-up lid that had fallen under the truck and been run over when they'd moved here. She turned it over and over in her hands. Surely Mutti would be glad to get rid of it since it sat like a crippled hen on a nest of rocks each time she used that pot.

"What are you doing?" Christine stood in the doorframe of the kitchen.

Karin startled, looked up at Christine, and spoke without thinking. "I'm trying to find some metal for our scrap drive at school."

"Well, don't take this." Christine picked up the misshapen lid. "We still use it. And I doubt you'll find anything else in this kitchen we can spare." She placed the lid back in the cupboard and pulled Karin to her feet.

"I know." Karin stared at her feet on the floor, her heart feeling like it was ready to sink down to them. It would help so much if she could share her pain with her sister.

She gave in—she'd already blabbed about the scrap drive. "I've already looked in here a hundred times. I was just hoping that some-thing new—I mean old, like junk—would just magically show up or something." She let out a weak laugh. "For sure, nobody will want to be friends with me now. Especially not my team."

"So . . . you're trying to collect scrap metal?" Christine guided Karin out of the kitchen and onto a chair at the table.

"Ja. Recycling is a good thing."

"It is." Christine put her arm around Karin. "How much metal do you think you'll need to help your team win?"

"I don't really know. And I don't really care if our team wins. It's not like we get a real prize or anything. I just don't want to make us lose." Karin took courage from Christine's kindness. "Does your factory ever have extra cans . . . you know . . . that they might donate?"

"I've been told there's usually a can or two every hour that doesn't go through the machines properly. The applesauce is reclaimed, but the cans get tossed in a pile. Of course, they recycle them. But I think I can convince my boss to donate some cans to your school scrap drive since your school, my factory . . . everything, is run by the same people."

Karin didn't feel good stretching the truth any longer. "Well . . . it's not really the school doing the scrap drive."

"Then who?" Christine raised an eyebrow.

"It's something we're doing after school, kind of like a club. Don't tell Mutti about it."

"You mean the Young Pioneers?" Christine gave Karin a piercing look like Mutti did when Karin was misbehaving.

"Ja." Karin stared at her hands. She jerked her head back up, feeling defiant. "I don't see why Mutti doesn't want me to join. They do good things. Like this scrap drive. You, yourself, said recycling was good."

The click of a closing door made Karin turn around. Mutti stood by the door to the stairwell, her hand resting on the knob. "Apparently, my say-so alone was not enough to satisfy you." She walked over to the table and gathered Karin's hands into hers. "I'd hoped your desire to obey your Mutter would be enough reason not to join the Young Pioneers. But I guess I was wrong."

"But Mutti, they do good things there. Like recycle and teach us to put others first. And I want a blue kerchief . . . and friends!"

"You have Greta," Christine said.

"She won't always be here. Her Mutter wants to move."

"Do you really want the kind of friends that like you only because you wear a blue kerchief?" Mutti asked, squeezing Karin's hands. "Karin, I'm sure the Young Pioneers do have some good activities, teach some worthwhile ideas. But the government doesn't place the same value on families as we do. I know you want more friends, but you have to trust me on this."

"But . . ." Karin thought Mutti was talking nonsense. They'd survived the war and then the Russians. The government was trying to help families through tough times—of course they valued them.

"Karin," Mutti said with water gathering in her eyes, "you have to go to school . . . to learn arithmetic, to read and write. And because it's the law. But you don't have to go to Young Pioneers. God gave us families to help us become what He wants us to be. He's given me, not the government, the duty to teach you what is best. But if you think joining up will be the best thing for you despite what I've told you, I won't interfere with your choice. And I won't stop Christine from donating those cans from her factory if she chooses." Mutti offered a weak smile and a nod of the head. "Ja, I heard you two discussing it when I came in."

The following Thursday, Karin hefted the burlap bag filled with damaged applesauce cans over her shoulder and plunged into the chilly October morning. Halfway to school, her body ached despite switching the burden of the bag from shoulder to shoulder every other minute. If only Greta could have come over yesterday after school to help, but her mother was beginning to suspect Greta was up to something. Karin hadn't thought about wearing gloves. But then, her pockets had always been there to keep her hands warm.

When Karin finally dragged herself and her load into the school, she had hoped there'd be more children around to see her deposit her large bag of cans in the commons room alongside the other donations awaiting the end of the scrap drive after school. With little more than numb hands and sore shoulders to acknowledge her efforts, she trudged down the hall to her classroom.

Herr Fuchs stood in front of the class as soon as the bell rang. "Today in social studies I want to talk about your big family. Some of you might be thinking, 'It's just me and my Mutti and Pappa. That's not big.' But I'm talking about your other family—the one that really takes care of you, knows what's best for you, and to which you owe a deep devotion. I'm talking about society. Most you have already shown your devotion to this big family." Herr Fuchs sent a scowling glance in Karin's direction. "I applaud you in the Young Pioneers for all the scrap metal you have collected."

Karin fumed. If only he'd seen her haul in that bag of cans a few minutes ago, he'd be applauding her, not scowling at her. Especially when she officially joined up after school today and got her blue kerchief.

She didn't want to listen to what Herr Fuchs had to say. Unfortunately, some of his words stuck in her head like a cocklebur latching on to her stockings, uncomfortable and annoying. *Your other family . . . the one that knows what's best for you.* That didn't sound right. It didn't feel right. She felt the urge to correct her teacher, but that would only get her sent to the corner. As her feelings churned, Mutti's words sneaked into her thoughts. *God gave us families. He's given me the duty to teach you what is best.* Karin would trust her mother over Herr Fuchs any day to teach her what was best.

The churning stopped.

After school at Young Pioneers, when Karin hefted her bag of metal onto the scales, the excitement she'd anticipated when Christine had given her the cans wasn't there. She walked slowly back to her group.

Greta's eyes sparkled with approval. "Karin, you've put us in second place!" She turned Karin around to face the blackboard. "Look."

"It's a good thing you did," Fritz said. "Or I would have complained about having you on my team."

Maria glided over to Karin's side and patted her on the back. "Thanks. So when are you two going to get your blue kerchief?" She then glanced at Greta.

"Not right now." Karin couldn't believe she was saying this. But it felt right.

"What?" Greta glared at Karin.

"Sorry. I need more time to think about it," Karin said, even though she doubted time would make a difference.

"Well, I'm going to get mine," Greta said to Maria. She glanced at the others in the group before walking up to Frau Heinz at the front of the room.

When Greta returned, she wore a blue kerchief. Though it was around Greta's neck, it felt as if it was choking Karin. An overwhelming desire to cry swelled in Karin's throat. Had she made a mistake?

Greta pulled Karin to the side. "Frau Heinz has yours waiting for you." She pointed to her new kerchief and smiled. "Don't you want to wear it next week?"

Karin's mind sped through a collection of memories, ones involving her ever-obedient sister. At times Christine's blind obedience annoyed Karin. She thought her sister didn't know how to think for herself—something Karin prided herself on. Then Karin remembered the Russians, how she hated them to the point of being miserable. Christine had just as much reason to hate them as Karin did. But she didn't. And Christine remained happy despite the unhappy place the Russians had created. She'd listened to Mutti and tried feeling sorry for those soldiers instead despising them. Tired of being unhappy, Karin had followed Christine's example, and then her miserable feelings went away. But whereas Christine always obeyed Mutti because it was the proper thing to do, Karin had followed Mutti's advice that time because she had decided for herself that it was a good thing to do.

A few weeks ago, Karin had thought for herself once again, had thought that the Young Pioneers was the best thing to do. But now she realized that this after-school program was just an extension of school. It had turned her to lying. The friends she'd made were not true friends. And if Young Pioneers grew up to go to meetings like the one Frau Drescher had . . .? The idea sent shivers down her arms.

Mutti did know best.

Karin chewed on her lip, thinking, and then said, "I'm not coming next week. I'm not joining. I've decided to obey my Mutter."

CHAPTER 23

Lockwitz, February 1953

Four years ago, Karin had not regretted her decision to heed Mutti. Though Greta joined the Young Pioneers, she and Karin had remained good friends for the short time Greta had stayed. Karin found it ironic that Greta hadn't much chance to participate in the Young Pioneers past the scrap drive. Greta and her mother had moved shortly afterward. At least, that was the story Herr Fuchs had told the class.

Karin remained at the kitchen table, still turning the salt shaker over in her hands. Aunt Anna had retired to the couch early in Karin's musing of the past. Mutti had followed, fussing over Aunt Anna, propping pillows behind her head and laying a blanket over her feet. They now chatted in soft voices, each wearing a strained face. Karin knew they must be discussing the subject that had prompted her memories: escape.

She hoped so. Half an hour ago, Mutti had planted the idea of leaving East Germany in Karin's head. Now it had sunk roots down into her heart. It felt right. It felt right despite all the unknown elements—possibilities that terrified her worse than bombs. In whispers during recess, many times she and Greta had shared rumors, tales of imprisonment and gruesome deaths inflicted upon citizens who tried to escape. Karin forced her uneasy feelings into that spot where she'd learned to push bad memories. Escaping felt right.

She thought again of Greta. Greta had taken on that happy spot for a while—the one Pappa, Sonnenschein, and Frau Krujatz had once filled. But it wasn't an old happy spot she was reaching for at the moment; it was another memory. It was that coincidental meeting a year ago with one of Greta's aunts. The one where she'd learned that Greta and her mother did not move to a neighboring city as Herr Fuchs had said. They had actually escaped to the West.

If Greta and her mother could do it, Karin knew her family could. After all, they had Mutti. Karin knew of no one whose prayers could reach into heaven and call down God's hand better than her mother's.

Karin rose from her chair at the table and stepped over to the couch, driven, almost excited, to continue with their plans. "So, are we going to do it? Escape?" She froze. Gazing down at Mutti, sitting at Aunt Anna's feet, immersed in a quiet discussion, she could see that her mother's eyes revealed more than fear. "What's wrong?" Karin's plea sounded like a siren next to Mutti's whispers.

It was Aunt Anna who looked up. "We have a problem."

Karin couldn't imagine what could be worse than possible torturous imprisonment and/or death.

Mutti cleared her throat and raised her eyes to Karin. "You forget. I don't think Christine will be as willing as you to leave."

"But—" Karin wasn't worried. She knew her sister would come if Mutti insisted.

Aunt Anna reached up, squeezing Karin's hand and looking her in the eye. "Your Mutti's right. Our Christine is not very adventuresome, to say the least."

"And I think she's got a new boyfriend," Mutti added.

Karin reached out with hope in what she knew to be Christine's strongest point. "I still think Christine will come with us, Mutti, if you ask her."

"You could be right," Mutti said. She sat silent for a moment, wringing the corner of Aunt Anna's blanket like it was laundry. Her eyes appeared lost in thought, staring at her hands, but not really looking at them. She placed the blanket down slowly, as if it was fragile.

"And why do you say that?" Aunt Anna raised an eyebrow.

"Because Christine has always been so obedient," Mutti said. "Perhaps we might leave after all."

"Speaking of leaving." Aunt Anna struggled her way up off the couch. "I need to head to the streetcar before it gets dark and the side-walks freeze over."

As Aunt Anna put on her coat, Mutti doted over her, giving her hugs and tightening the scarf around her neck. "Are you sure about this now?" she said softy as Aunt Anna slipped out the door.

Karin felt a jab of guilt. Maybe she shouldn't have been so quick to encourage them. She swore she could feel Mutti's fear filling the air of their small apartment. It enveloped her. A rumor from when she was in fourth grade surfaced in her mind: Hanna's mother. What if Hanna's mother never sent for her because she was caught fleeing across the border? The rumors, that she'd never sent for Hanna because she was only looking out for herself, had always bothered Karin. She doubted any mother's ability to be so uncaring of a daughter. Karin knew it was more likely that she'd been caught and was sent to prison. Or worse.

Suddenly the repercussions of a failed escape took on a sharper edge. Having this small connection to someone who actually got caught made it real. What started out sounding like an adventure to Karin now took on the true colors of what Mutti and Aunt Anna obviously saw it as—what it really was—a possible nightmare.

But Karin couldn't let go of the idea. Life was getting worse in East Germany, and she was determined now not to let the German Democratic Republic destroy her happiness.

The following day Karin chose to take the long way home from school in hopes of seeing Christine at the factory. If she hurried, and Christine chose to step outside for a breath of fresh air, she might catch her sister while on break. As her legs clipped along as fast as they could without running, Karin watched her breath form puffs of white against a backdrop of winter trees. Their bare branches looked like faded brown lace, and the color of the sky blended almost seamlessly into the gray of an old warehouse. Added to the smell of apples from the cannery around the bend, she found it beautiful and poem-worthy. She forced her thoughts away from poetry and ran through ways to present Christine the idea of fleeing to the West—she'd avoid the word escape. Christine had come home late last night, and from the way she chattered on at breakfast about work and weather, Karin doubted Mutti had told her of their possible plans. Karin figured she'd better take matters into her own hands.

Karin rounded the corner. The chain-link fence of the factory came into view. She breathed a sigh of relief as she spotted a number of people walking around inside the enclosure. A blue coat caught her eye right away. It had to be Christine; Karin recognized her sister's worn green skirt that hung a little bit below the hem of the coat. She walked faster—her sister's break didn't last long. "Christine," Karin hollered as she drew within hearing range.

Christine turned. As she did so, a brown coat and the striking face of a young woman became visible. It must be Christine's friend. Karin couldn't remember her name, only that Christine had mentioned the girl's father was high up in the government.

Christine's eyes lit up. "Karin! What are you doing here?" She stepped away from the girl and walked toward the portion of the fence that ran alongside the road. The girl followed close behind, her square jaw sporting a charming smile. She wore a crisp tweed coat over a vivid red skirt, and both appeared relatively new.

"I'm just walking home from school." Karin wished now she hadn't come this way. She didn't dare talk to her sister about leaving East Germany with that girl there.

Christine reached the fence at the same time as Karin. She looked back over her shoulder to the girl. "This is my sister, Karin."

"Pleased to meet you." The other girl nodded at Karin.

Christine reached two fingers through the chain link and beckoned for Karin to grab them. "What made you decide to come this way?"

Karin reached up and gave Christine's fingers a squeeze. "I was going to ask you something. But it can wait."

"Well, I'm glad you came." Christine withdrew her fingers. "Now I can introduce you to my friend, Helga. She's scheduled to complete her schooling this April, the same time as I."

Helga's eyes met Karin's. "Christine tells me what a cheerful child you are despite your family's hardships. What an admirable quality. I imagine you will be quite an asset to society when you grow up."

"Thank you," Karin said out of courtesy but didn't really feel it. She didn't want to be an asset to *this* society.

"Oh, Karin," Christine jumped in. "And I've got good news." There was a sparkle in Christine's eyes as she looked at her friend. "Helga's Pappa might be able to get me a permanent position as a secretary with a big company in Dresden after I graduate." Christine brought her hand up to her cheek. "Isn't that wonderful? Mutti would be able to stop working for Uncle Stefan."

Karin offered a weak nod.

A bell sounded, pulling both Helga and Christine's heads in the direction of the factory. "Thank you for stopping by." Christine waved.

"We've got to get back to work," Helga said, nudging Christine away from the fence. Together they walked toward the factory.

Karin headed toward home. Her feet felt like dragging. Maybe leaving here wasn't the best thing for Christine. But how could Karin and Mutti leave without her?

That night, as Karin lay in her top bunk waiting for Christine to finish up her chores and come to bed, she tried to think of a way to talk to Christine about leaving East Germany. Mutti still hadn't done it.

The bedroom door creaked open. A slice of yellow light cut through the darkness.

"Christine?" Karin asked, not sure what she'd say next.

"Karin, are you still awake?"

"Ja, I wanted to ask you something."

"That's right." Christine's shoes crept quietly across the floor. "That's why you took the long way home from school today. I'm sorry; I was so excited about Helga's good news. Ask me anything you want."

Karin listened to the *swoosh* of her sister's nightgown as Christine changed her clothes, grasping for ideas of how to say this just right. "What do you think it's like over there?" Karin asked. The bed jiggled beneath her, and she could hear her sister snuggle beneath the bed covers.

"Over where?"

"In West Germany?"

"Why do you ask?" Christine's voice stiffened.

"I've heard it's better . . . they have more food . . . and I doubt that old people just disappear when they get sick."

"What are you talking about? You're not making any sense, Karin."

"Sorry. I was just wondering how my old friend Greta's doing. She always told me how her Mutter wanted to leave East Germany and go over there . . . to the West. And they did it; they escaped."

"You make it sound like they were in prison here," Christine snapped her response.

"I'm just repeating what Greta said. Her Mutter seemed to think things were better in the West. Wouldn't you want to live someplace that was better?"

"Things are just fine right where I am." As Christine said that, Karin knew her sister had a vision of that secretary job in Dresden running through her mind. "And your old friend and her Mutter were foolish if they indeed went across the border into the west. It's against the law, you understand, Karin. Greta is probably in an orphanage up north right now because her Mutter is dead. That's what they do, you realize, to people who cross the border without permission—they are sent to prison. For life. If they're my age or older, that is. So why would I want to even consider such a foolhardy idea?"

"What if Mutti asked you to go . . . because . . . the government wouldn't let us go to church anymore or something?" Karin knew this was a possibility. "Would you obey her?" Maybe she should tell Christine about Aunt Anna.

"Mutti would never do anything that was against the law—or involved such danger." Christine shook the bed once more as she tossed and turned below. "It would be wise if you forgot about your old friend and her mother's dangerous ideas and go to sleep."

Karin laid there—not daring to say any more—her mind churning, pushing all sleepiness away, worried that Christine wouldn't want to leave. Her sister wasn't a child anymore. She was nineteen—old enough to make her own choices. And it didn't help that this new government downplayed the role of families, telling youth that if they were eighteen, they didn't need to obey their parents anymore.

A vicious snow storm kept Karin home from school and Christine from going to work. Mutti had planned on staying home before the storm even blew in. The work at Uncle Stefan's leather repair business had tapered off dramatically. Each planted themselves close to the warmth of the coal, Christine on the couch reading a book, Mutti doing some mending next to her, and Karin in the stuffed chair working on her poems.

The clap of footsteps up the stairwell pulled Karin's attention to the door. "Who could that be?" she said, looking from Mutti to Christine.

After a hurried knock, the door swung open, and Aunt Anna hobbled in. "Oh, it's freezing out there. I swear this is the coldest February I can remember."

"Well, what kind of person comes for a visit on a day like this?" Mutti set down her mending and rose to give her sister a hug.

"It wasn't that bad when I started out." Aunt Anna returned the embrace. "I hope you won't mind if I stay the night though."

"Of course not," Mutti said. "But I still don't understand why you'd brave that weather. Especially since it's been barely a week since you last visited."

"This couldn't wait," Anna said, huffing as she removed her coat and hung it on the hook next to the door. "I had a dream. About our leaving. I knew I must tell you about it."

"Leaving?" Christine sat down her book. "What are you talking about?" She stood from the couch and moved over to a kitchen chair, indicating for Aunt Anna to take her place on the couch.

Mutti ducked her head. "Oh, yes, Christine, I've been meaning to tell you about this. I was just waiting for the right time."

"This might be a good time." Christine's usually calm face appeared upset. "Please . . . don't tell me you're considering leaving Germany?" She shot a tense glance in Karin's direction, and Karin's heart sank.

"Not Germany, dear. Just East Germany. And it wouldn't be only me; it would be all of us, including Aunt Anna." Mutti nodded toward Aunt Anna.

"But what about my schooling?"

"Don't worry. It probably won't be for a while. At least not until spring. Or better weather," Mutti said.

"I don't care if it's next year. We can't go!" Christine stood from the chair and paced across the small room and back, bringing to life Karin's fear.

Aunt Anna shook her head and motioned to Mutti to sit down beside her. "We need to start preparing. Now," she emphasized as Mutti lowered herself down onto the couch.

"But the weather?" Karin shivered at the thought of going outside, let alone abandoning their home in this unseasonably cold winter.

"And why the hurry?" Mutti added with an edge of scolding to her voice.

Aunt Anna's face hardened like stone. "We need to leave by February 28."

"That's impossible," Christine interrupted. "I'm not going. I'm staying here. I am, after all, an adult."

Karin felt as though her sister may as well have kicked her in the stomach.

"Christine," Mutti said in that stern tone she had used on Karin as a small child when she challenged Mutti. As long as Karin remembered, she'd never recalled Mutti using it on Christine. "If one of us escapes, we all escape. Remember: family—we all stick together."

"Yes, stick together. Here!"

"Christine!" Mutti stared at Christine.

"I'm sorry." Christine hung her head and lumbered back to the table.

Even though Christine had apologized, Karin sensed from her sister's tight mouth that Christine absolutely did not want to go. And if Christine wouldn't go, none of them would go. And Mutti and Aunt Anna would have to grow old here . . . and just "disappear" when they got sick.

Why hadn't Mutti mentioned that? If her sister understood that, it might help. "You've got to come with us, Christine," Karin spoke up. "If you don't, then Mutti and Aunt Anna will stay here."

"What's wrong with that?" Christine dropped onto a kitchen chair and perked up. "It's the safe thing to do."

"No, it's not." Karin glanced at Aunt Anna. "Tell her what your doctor told you."

As Aunt Anna spoke of her recent visit to the doctor and his advice for her to leave because he feared she was becoming too old and sickly to be of use to the society, Christine's shoulders slumped. They slumped farther as Mutti reminded her of how going to church was becoming more difficult each week.

Christine peered up at Aunt Anna, shaking her head. "Why February 28? Why such a random date? Couldn't we at least wait for two more months—until I finish school and earn my diploma?"

"Ja, why that date?" Mutti picked up the stocking she was mending but wrung it in her hands rather than working on it.

"I don't really know," Aunt Anna admitted. "I just know that's when we need to leave by. I had a dream last night. The details were fuzzy, but I knew we were escaping to the West. The date on the calendar was the only thing that stuck out in the dream. It was February 28. When I awoke, there it was, the memory of that calendar pounding at my brain. When I let go of my hesitancy and committed to escape by the 28, I felt this sweet peace fill my insides." She patted her chest.

"That's so close." Mutti's eyes grew large.

Karin felt the grip of fear coming back. Her doubts resurfaced, especially as she considered the danger of putting all their trust in a dream that might not mean a thing. "Ja, that's only two weeks away."

"Exactly. That's why I didn't want to wait another day to tell you. Storm or no storm, I was coming over here."

"So, what do we do now?" Mutti looked to Aunt Anna. "Do you have a plan?"

"Ja," Aunt Anna said. "It came to me right after I told the Lord I'd be willing to leave on that day." She motioned for Christine to pull her chair closer and Karin to lean over the arm of the stuffed chair. "We're all going to a wedding. In Berlin."

"Whose?" Mutti's brow wrinkled.

"Liesel's."

Karin grabbled with her excitement. "Liesel's getting married?" Why hadn't she heard anything about this good news earlier? And what did a wedding have to do with escaping to the West?

"No, she's not," Mutti said. She turned to Aunt Anna. "But I think I can see where you're going with this. It's documented that I have a widowed daughter in Berlin. We are considered close family, so we can get traveling papers to attend her wedding."

"What good will that do us?" asked Christine. "She lives in *East* Berlin."

"Ja." Aunt Anna smiled. "We'll get off the train in East Berlin. We'll take the subway through the city as if heading for the wedding, but we'll stay in the car. We won't get off at Liesel's stop in Frierichshain but continue to ride the subway into West Berlin."

"And then what will we do once we're in West Berlin?" Christine asked in a skeptical tone. "And what if we're forced to get off at our stop—which is more than likely? Have you considered the repercussions if we get caught?"

Aunt Anna bit her fingernail. "I can't answer any of those questions."

CHAPTER 24

Karin hurried home after school, grateful for the sunshine and glad it wasn't snowing like yesterday. She stopped short of their house and approached her neighbor's house to the north. Once on their porch, she offered a timid knock. As she waited for an answer, she kept telling herself this was part of the adventure, a crucial part of their escape. But she'd have to be a good actress. No one, especially not Frau Drescher, could suspect what they were up to.

The front door cracked open. A kind-looking older gentleman opened the door. Karin hadn't really gotten to know him in the four years they'd lived in Lockwitz, but she'd spoken to him on occasion in the summertime while she was out playing and he worked in his garden. She'd seen him use the wooden wagon then.

"What is it? May I help you?" asked the old man.

"Ja." Karin's voice came out a little unsteady. What if he was a hard-core communist like Frau Drescher? Karin tried to not think about that, concentrated, and continued. "Could I possibly borrow your small *leiterwagen*?"

"What for?

She swallowed a wad of spit that had lodged in her throat. "I need to take some things over to my Aunt Sophronia. She lives a few kilometers from here, and it's such a long way to carry them." Karin held out her hands, palms up as if to demonstrate.

"Ja, ja, you can take it." He pointed to a weathered shed to the side of his house. "It's in there. Just return it and shut the door when you're done."

Karin mustered some more courage. "I might need to use it again . . . tomorrow."

"You know where it is. Just make sure you secure the door when you use it next. The wind blows it open if you don't, and the snow will ruin my tools."

"*Danke!* I promise I will." Karin turned and ran down the steps, trying hard to keep her smile from growing any larger. The old man had just made her job easier. She wouldn't have to knock on his door when she used his wagon again. And according to Mutti, that might be several times.

She scurried over to the shed, undid the latch, and pulled out the wagon, careful to shut the door behind her. When she reached the edge of the old man's yard, she stopped, keeping herself hidden behind a hedge of shrubbery. Carefully, she peered around the bushes, focusing on the main floor of her own house. A light was on in the front room, but all of the curtains were drawn. She hurried down the sidewalk to the gate. Once through, she headed toward the side porch, grateful for Frau Drescher's oddity of not liking to let in the sunlight. The wagon resisted being pulled over the threshold of the side door. Karin fought with it as quietly as possible. A silent prayer moved her lips ever so slightly. "Please, Lord, keep the old lady in the living room and away from that lace-covered window in the kitchen." If Frau Drescher were to figure out that Karin's family was preparing to leave, she'd not only stop them but alert the authorities. Mutti would be sent to prison.

Karin considered loading the wagon outside on the porch. It would be easier. But it might also draw attention. Sticking to her original plan, she finally managed to move the wagon inside onto the bottom stairwell landing. She left it just inside the door, glanced at the window in Frau Drescher's kitchen door to make sure the lace curtain wasn't moving, and bounded up the stairs.

Mutti sorted through papers as Karin stepped inside the apartment. "Where's the stuff you want me to take?" Karin said.

Mutti handed her a bundle of papers bound neatly with string tied off in a bow as if Mutti had just tied a shoe. It reminded Karin of a Christmas gift but with none of the excitement. A second bundle rested on the couch, also tied up with string. "These will go first," Mutti said. "Do be careful. They're our family photos and most of our genealogy."

Her hands shook as she shuffled through the papers again. "I'll send the rest of it with your next trip . . . after I find it all. Dear, dear, I worry about you taking this all by yourself."

"I still don't understand why you can't go over to Aunt Sophronia's like you were just going to work for Uncle Stephen. Then you could take these things by street car."

"First of all, that wagon of Herr Bruker's carries a lot more than my arms ever could. Secondly, I would attract too much attention getting on the street car carrying such loads. Especially two or three days in a row." Mutti tightened the scarf around Karin's neck a little too tightly. "But a young girl pulling a wagon appears less suspicious. Hurry, now, so you can get back before it gets dark. And don't talk to anyone if you don't have to."

Karin trudged down the stairs, plopped the heavy bundle of paper in the wagon and ran upstairs for the other one. Once she had that loaded, she poked her head out the door to make sure Frau Drescher was nowhere to be seen. She wrestled the wagon out the door and down the three steps. Karin didn't look forward to the hour's walk over to her aunt's. What if someone asked her what was in the wagon? She wished Christine could come with her; it would make the long, cold walk easier, less scary.

But Christine was at work. And her sister might draw suspicion, being too old to play with a wagon. Plus, Christine didn't seem too fond of Mutti and Aunt Anna's plan.

Karin thought back to a week ago when Christine had told her about the possibility of getting that good job. She worried that when February 28 came, Christine might not leave with them. Or Mutti wouldn't go because Christine wouldn't. Karin clung to the hope that her sister hadn't outgrown her obedient nature and pulled the wagon across the cobblestones to the gate. The latch clicked shut behind her. She breathed out a big sigh, feeling somewhat hidden now from the eyes of Frau Drescher. Ducking, she headed into the cold February breeze. She only hoped she wouldn't have to bring all their belongings back from Aunt Sophronia next week.

Their preparations for sneaking away to the West filled her thoughts as she lumbered down the sidewalk, pulling the wagon behind her. Mutti hoped Aunt Sophronia could send their genealogy and the family photos to her sometime in the future—if things got better with the government. After today the wagon would be filled with bedding and anything else of value that could be smuggled over to Aunt Sophronia's under the guise of a girl pulling her little wagon down the street. For once Karin was glad she looked younger than her almost fourteen years of age. She would have liked to take more of their belongings with them to the West. But she understood when Mutti had explained that it was important that they didn't take anything more than one suitcase to the pretend wedding, or it would draw suspicion.

And Karin would much rather give what they could to Aunt Sophronia's family than leave it in their apartment for the authorities to seize once they discovered they were gone. *We're going to go through with this!* That hope sent strength down to her legs. She plowed onward, pulling the wagon with more speed.

Karin pushed aside the barren branches of the large shrub where she'd parked the wagon on the side of the house while loading it. After her struggles with the wagon in the stairwell that first time, she'd come up with a better place to load it without drawing notice. She loaded the leiterwagen for the last time. The mattresses upstairs in their apartment had been stripped bare. Tomorrow was February 27. Tonight they'd sleep with their coats for blankets and their change of clothes as pillows. Even Christine. Yesterday, Christine had finally agreed to leave with them. But she'd been very quiet ever since. Karin hoped her sister wouldn't change her mind at the last minute.

Karin checked first if the way looked clear and then carefully pulled the wagon across the brown lawn. The noonday sun warmed her back. She was so glad it was Saturday and there was no school. The past few days she'd had to return from Aunt Sophronia's as the sun set, taking its feeble warmth with it. As Karin pulled the wagon through the gate and onto the sidewalk, she froze. Frau Drescher walked down the street, headed toward her. Karin hurried and changed directions. She'd just circle around the block before heading to her aunt's.

"Fraulein Graeber!" Frau Drescher's grating voice sounded even worse when she yelled. "Stop. What are you doing with Herr Bruker's leiterwagen?"

Karin stopped, fearing if she gave in to the urge to run it would only draw attention and make things worse. Over her shoulder, she muttered, "He said I could use it."

Frau Drescher caught up with Karin. Her brow furrowed as she looked in the wagon. She reached down and picked up the blue quilt Pappa had given to Karin so long ago; her favorite. How she hated to let it go—and watch Frau Drescher examine it.

"What's this all about?" Frau Drescher's lip curled.

"Nothing."

"Where are you taking these . . . these blankets?"

"Over to my aunt's house."

"And why would you do that? Your Mutter can barely take care of you and your sister. She can least afford to part with good bedding."

"Uh . . . it's only for a little while," Karin said. "Uh . . . until my other aunt finds a new place to live. Right now she's sleeping on the couch, and my Aunt Sophronia can use the extra bedding."

"Humpf. There's something unsettling about this." Frau Drescher let the blue blanket drop back into the wagon as if it was diseased. "You'd better be telling the truth, or I'll have to report this." She turned on her heel and proceeded through the gate to the house.

Karin let out the breath she'd been holding and lurched forward, wagon in tow. Halfway into the next block, she let a quiet laugh escape her lips. Her obsession with the Young Pioneers years ago wasn't such a bad thing after all. If she hadn't tried to join, she might never have learned the skill of stretching the truth while holding a straight face.

The following morning, Mutti cooked up the last bit of oatmeal in the pot with the misshapen lid, the only pot left in the house. All the other pots and pans had ridden in the wagon under a pile of bedding over to Aunt Sophronia's. The same with the dishes—except for the three bowls and spoons awaiting their last breakfast in Lockwitz.

As they knelt on the bare floor for family prayer, Karin noticed Christine sniffled a lot—like Mutti. If more of them got sick, Mutti might postpone their leaving. But they couldn't. Aunt Anna had been so certain about her dream. "Have you got a cold too?" Karin whispered before Mutti started praying.

"No." Christine attempted a smile. "It's nothing like that."

After the prayer, each of them grabbed a suitcase and headed for the stairs. Karin paused and took one last look around the tiny apartment she'd called home for the last four years. Stripped clean of everything except the larger pieces of furniture, it held nothing that beckoned her to stay. Without the family photos, Mutti's crocheted doilies, and Christine's books, the place felt hollow, and the singed spots on the furniture stood out with an eerie ugliness.

"Come on, Karin." Christine motioned to the door but didn't make eye contact with Karin.

"We need to hurry," Mutti added. "With these suitcases, it will take us longer than usual to get to church this morning."

Karin followed them out to the landing. Huddled together at the top of the stairs, Mutti and Christine at her side, a swell of gratitude filled her chest. They were leaving, finally leaving this place—and all together, as a family.

"Now remember," Mutti warned as they treaded down the stairs, "if anyone inquires about your suitcase, we are on our way to your sister's wedding."

"Even at church?" Karin thought for sure that wouldn't be necessary.

"Ja, even at church." Mutti paused at the base of the stairs. With her hand on the doorknob, she said, "Remember, you've brought your suitcases today because we're not going home after church. We're setting out on our trip tonight. That part is true." She opened the door, and the three of them stepped outside into the cold.

They'd barely turned the corner of the house, merging onto the cobblestone path that led to the street, when Frau Drescher opened her front door. With her coat held snug at her throat and her gray hair unpinned, dangling in wisps around her face, she poked her upper body out the door. "What are doing? Where are you going? You're always going somewhere Sunday morning. Church, maybe?" Her lip curled. "But you have suitcases today. How strange."

Mutti and Christine stopped. Karin followed their lead. She sensed her sister's and Mutti's bodies stiffen. Mutti stepped forward. Karin froze, though she felt like running. Her mother never lied. Surely Frau Drescher would see right through Mutti's answer.

"We're going to my oldest daughter's wedding. In Berlin," Mutti said with amazing calm. She lifted her suitcase to show it to Frau Drescher. "So we're going to be gone for some time." She resumed walking, her back now to Frau Drescher. "Sorry, but we need to get going." Her voice shook.

Karin followed Mutti and Christine through the gate. From behind, she heard Frau Drescher offer a "Humpf!" Out of the corner of her eye, Karin noticed Frau Drescher continue down the cobblestone toward the street. *Was she following them?* Karin let out a penned-up breath when the old lady turned the opposite direction after she passed through the gate.

When Karin turned the corner at the end of their street, she looked back at their old home for one last glimpse. A sudden lump scratched at her throat. Though it was quite a distance, she could see Frau Drescher standing under the big elm tree at the opposite end of their street talking to a man—she could tell by the ugly purple coat. She could also tell he was from the GDR military, having seen enough of those drab brown uniforms to recognize it right off. Karin elbowed Mutti and bade her to look back.

Mutti turned her head slowly. Her eyes widened. She snapped her head back in place. "Keep going. We've done nothing wrong. There's no need to worry. I'm sure it doesn't mean anything."

Karin forced her legs to walk faster to keep up with Mutti and Christine. Her grip on her suitcase tightened. She hoped Mutti was right.

Half an hour later, about ten blocks from their street car stop, Karin's arm started to ache. She switched her suitcase to the other hand, knowing it would have been worse if she'd been allowed to pack the suitcase as full as she'd wanted. "We can only take as much as if going to a wedding," Mutti's words replayed in her mind. Karin had complied, knowing the threat of an official inspecting her suitcase was real. With the image of that GDR official still fresh in her mind, she envisioned being stopped even before they boarded the streetcar, compliments of Frau Drescher. Karin chewed on her lip, trying to reassure her pounding heart that she had nothing to hide if her suitcase was searched; that if they found her notebook full of poetry, the official would not think that out of the ordinary to take to a wedding. Or suspicious. She wanted that notebook, and the pencil she'd packed with it, to be with her.

When they stopped at the all-too-familiar corner to wait for their streetcar, Karin scanned the intersecting streets as far as she could see. Apartment buildings rose four floors above the closed shops that lined the near-empty Sunday sidewalks. Curtains were drawn on most of the windows, telling Karin that those tenants chose to sleep late on their only day off rather than go to church. Mutti had said very few people went to church anymore. Karin focused on the pedestrians. None were dressed in a brown government uniform.

Karin took a deep breath. As she let her body relax a bit, she felt cold settle on her feet. She sat her suitcase on the sidewalk and stepped quickly from foot to foot to keep them warm. Despite the extra dress and two pair of stockings she wore, cold clung to her.

A middle-aged man waited with them at the stop. He wore thick boots and long trousers. With his knee-length coat, hat, and hand-knit scarf, he appeared warm. He also appeared to be staring at Karin's suitcase. And Christine's. And Mutti's. A flush of warmth spread across Karin's face despite the cold air. Would he notice the guilt in her face? Would it make him suspicious? Maybe he was a friend of Frau Drescher's. What if she'd discovered they'd left their apartment empty?

The streetcar rumbled to a stop. Karin grabbed her suitcase. She ran out to the middle of the road where the streetcar awaited them, not wanting to give the man a chance to ask her any questions. "Karin, stop!" Mutti yelled after her.

Karin scrabbled up the streetcar's steps. She hurried to the back, claimed the entire wide bench with her suitcase, and dropped onto one end. The man in the hand-knit scarf stepped into the street car, taking a seat at the front without even so much as a glance back at her. She blew out a breath, feeling a bit foolish as Mutti huffed down the aisle, her face creased with worry.

"Karin," Mutti whispered after she and Christine settled in next to Karin. "You've got to be more careful. Just because we prayed for protection this morning doesn't mean we can be careless now, does it?"

"No." Karin looked away from Mutti and stared out the window. "Sorry."

After seeing her fill of gray skies and run-down apartment buildings, she turned her attention away from the window and focused on her sister, who seemed extra quiet. Karin had noticed Christine hadn't said much since she'd told Mutti she was coming with them. That was two days ago.

"Why are you folding your arms and bowing your head?" Karin whispered loudly enough so Christine could hear her over the clack of the streetcar wheels. "We're not even in church yet," she added with a little jab of her elbow and a grin.

Christine lifted her head and looked at Karin. "Sorry."

"You don't have to be sorry." Karin connected with Christine's eyes, which looked a bit red. "I just wanted to see you smile." The corners of Christine's mouth turned up ever so slightly. Karin could tell it wasn't real. A mountain-sized ache hurt inside Karin for her sister. "I know this was hard for you—giving up your diploma—but I'm so glad you came with us, Christine. I would have been miserable if you hadn't come." It made the ache worse to see moisture swell up in Christine's eyes. "I'm afraid too," Karin continued, more softly this time so no one could possibly hear over the noise of the street car. "But we'll be okay. I can feel it."

"*Danke*." Christine gathered Karin's hands into hers. "I am scared, I admit it. But that's not what's upset me."

Karin leaned close. "Then what's wrong?"

"I shouldn't let it bother me." Christine wiped her eye with her coat sleeve. "I just wish I could say auf wiedersehen to someone . . . before we leave."

"Who?" Karin couldn't imagine who. It certainly wouldn't be Christine's girlfriend, Helga, not with her pappa working for the GDR.

"Sigmund."

"From our branch?" Karin remembered seeing Christine talking to the tall boy with blond curly hair and a pronounced Adam's apple at church several times.

"Ja." Christine gazed up at the ceiling of the street car. "I think things could have worked out for us. He's a good Mormon boy . . . with a bright future. Those are hard to find around here. What if it becomes even harder where we're going?"

"You'll find someone, Christine. I know you will." Karin squeezed her sister's hand. "And maybe you'll see Sigmund at church. You can tell him auf wiedersehen then."

"You forget," Christine said. "We can't let anyone know we are leaving."

CHAPTER 25

AFTER A TRANSFER AND ANOTHER half an hour on the street car, they arrived at church. They each left their suitcases by the door. Karin hung her coat upon one of the hooks in the foyer of the old office building they rented for a meeting house. When she turned to head to the room they used as a chapel, she noticed Mutti chatting with a man and a woman Karin didn't know that well. She walked by slowly so she could hear what they were saying.

"Why the suitcases?" the woman asked Mutti.

"Oh . . . we're going to my sister's house right after church because tomorrow we're headed to my oldest daughter's wedding."

"Congratulations," the man said. "Best wishes to the happy couple."

"Is he a nice man?" the woman asked. "Do you like him?"

"Who?"

"The fellow she's marrying," the woman said, wrinkling her forehead. "You're soon-to-be son-in-law."

"Oh, ja, him." Mutti straightened her sleeve, her eyes focusing on it. "Well . . . uh . . . I'd rather not talk about it."

"I'm so sorry." The woman patted Mutti's hand. "I understand; there's no need to speak more of it."

"Do have a safe trip, though," the man added.

"Thank you." Mutti gave them a nod and caught up with Karin and Christine. "The sooner we're done with this charade, the better," she whispered.

Charade or no charade, Karin just wanted this to be over with, to be already in the West, where she'd be free to say what she wanted.

After opening exercises, Mutti and Christine stayed in the makeshift chapel, and Karin filed into the windowless room where all the youth met for their Sunday School class. Taking a seat next to a fourteen-year-old girl named Anne, the only girl close to her age, she settled in for Sister Snyder's lesson. This would be her last one. For the previous year, she'd enjoyed this kind sister's lessons. The scriptures had come alive for her. Karin cleared her throat, trying to dislodge the lump forming behind her tongue.

"Hope you're not coming down with something," Anne said, leaning toward Karin.

"No, I'm fine," Karin said, a little surprised that Anne had made the effort to strike up a conversation. Since Karin had moved into the youth class nearly two years ago when she'd turned twelve, the girl had rarely spoken to her. Anne was nice, but she was also dreadfully shy. "Thanks for your concern though."

"You're welcome." Anne smiled, her eyes seeming to beg to continue the conversation.

"I like your dress," Karin said, trying to think of something to say that wouldn't reveal what was actually on her mind. "It's pretty."

"Thank you." Anne straightened the dress's green and gray fabric around her knees. "I—never mind." She pointed to Sister Snyder, who stood up front ready to start the lesson.

"Oh," Karin said. She wondered if a friendship could grow with this girl if Karin and her family were to stay. Emotions swelled within her: homesickness, regret, excitement, and uncertainty. Did she want to do this?

Yes!

Was she afraid?

Yes.

Did she regret leaving?

No! The word Greta had used to describe what they were doing fit perfectly: escape.

A strong feeling deep inside strengthened her resolve.

That evening Aunt Anna met up with them for sacrament meeting. She deposited her suitcase by the door next to Karin's and filed into the chapel behind Karin, Christine, and Mutti. Karin liked how they huddled together on the same row of folding chairs, scrunching in tightly as if they were seated on a crowded bench. Mutti wrung her hands constantly during the meeting. Aunt Anna bit at her nails. Karin chewed on her lip more than usual, so much so that she tasted blood. She doubted any of them listened to a thing the speakers said—she certainly didn't. Even Aunt Sophronia seemed tense.

After the meeting, Aunt Sophronia drove them to her home in Uncle Stefan's car. With five people and four suitcases, Karin felt as though the car's doors would pop open. No wonder her uncle had stayed home.

The four of them sat in the living room and waited for time to pass, their four suitcases stacked by the front door. Aunt Sophronia and Uncle Stefan waited with them. All conversation felt stiff, not much of substance being said after Uncle Stefan's initial greeting, the rundown of the plan, and a family prayer. Mutti blew her nose a few times, which broke up the silence. Karin's eyes skirted often to the clock on the mantel. When both hands pointed straight up to midnight, she expected to doze off soon. When the clock read one o'clock, she was still awake.

When the hands approached the two o'clock position, Uncle Stefan shook off his sleepiness and stood. "It's time. The streets are as dead as they're going get, and the Russians, or the GDR—or whoever is in charge anymore—are as drunk as they're going to get. Let's go."

The night air sliced through Karin's coat like blades of ice. Uncle Stefan hurried ahead of them, turning on the engine and then opening the trunk. Only three suitcases fit. "Yours is the smallest, Karin." Uncle Stefan handed her suitcase back. "You'll have to sit it on your lap. You sit up front."

Karin hurried to the semi-warmth of the car, squeezing herself and her suitcase into the front seat. Mutti, Christine, and Aunt Anna were already huddled together in the back. All the doors shut, making it feel warmer immediately. "Thank you for taking us in your car, Uncle Stefan," Karin said. The thought of having to walk all the way to the other side of Dresden to the train station in the dark, in that cold, gave her the urge to reach out and hug her uncle. He was taking a risk just doing this much. Her suitcase was in the way. She touched his arm.

"You're welcome." Uncle Stefan pulled the car onto the road.

Only the hum of the engine could be heard. No one spoke. Everything that needed to be said had already been discussed. A tense feeling filled the car, so heavy it seemed it would crush Karin like a boulder. She offered a silent prayer. The weight lifted slightly, and the lights of the train station came into view.

Uncle Stefan maneuvered his car to the curb next to the unloading area. Not a single car was around to compete with him for parking. So far, things were going as planned; they'd have no problem catching an early train out. He unloaded the other suitcases and gave Karin and then Christine, Mutti, and Aunt Anna a hug. "This is as far as I go. You're on your own now. God be with you."

With that, he was off, out of Karin's life for who knew how long. She clenched the handle of her suitcase and followed Mutti and the others into the station. As they approached the ticket booth, Karin tried to make sense of the huge sign overhead. It listed arrivals and departures and cities she'd never heard of. She gave up and followed Mutti.

Mutti approached a counter with a sliding window that separated a small room from the cavernous station. A man stood behind the counter dressed in an official-looking brown uniform that told Karin he worked for the government. "May I help you?" he said to Mutti.

From her bag, Mutti pulled out almost every last pfennig they had, which included a little she'd borrowed from Uncle Stefan, and placed it on the counter. "I'd like to purchase two adult and one child's ticket to Berlin."

"East Berlin," the official corrected her.

"Ja, of course." Mutti's hand shook as she pushed the money toward him. "That's what I meant, East Berlin."

Aunt Anna stepped to the counter beside Mutti. "And I'd like to buy one adult ticket." She slid her money across the counter. "I'm traveling with them. I'm her sister. We're going to a wedding," she said, a little too mechanically for Karin's comfort.

"May I see your traveling papers, please?" The official stuck his hand from the booth and pointed to Karin and Christine, who stood off to the side. "And theirs too."

Mutti pulled the papers from her bag and unfolded them for the man to see. Anna placed hers next to them. Several minutes passed while he scanned their documents. Karin swore he read each and every word on each sheet of paper. "Friedrichshain?" he said, looking at Aunt Anna. "Is that where your daughter lives?"

"She's my niece," Aunt Anna corrected. She pointed to Mutti. "It's her daughter."

"So is the wedding in Friedrichshain as well?" The man kept his eyes on one of the papers.

"Ja, it is in Friedrichshain," Mutti blurted out.

After several minutes the official looked up, pulled the papers into a single pile, and handed them to Mutti. "Everything looks in order. You may purchase your tickets."

"We'd like tickets for the first train to the *Hauptbahnhof*." Mutti glanced at the giant clock that hung above the ticket counter in the middle of the schedules. It showed the time as 3:14 a.m. "I believe it leaves at six o'clock, is that not correct?"

"Ja, but you'll want the Lichtenberg Station, the *Ostbahnhof*." He lifted an eyebrow. "It's closer to Friedrichshain."

Karin glanced up at the board and noticed that train didn't leave until ten.

"Give us tickets on the first train out—to the *Hauptbahnhof*," Mutti insisted.

"But—" the man said.

Mutti cut him off. "I used to live in Berlin. I know that city like the back of my hand. Just get the tickets. I know where I'm going."

Mutti's command of the situation infused Karin with courage. This was the Mutti she knew, the woman who managed to put food on their table when other families—*with* fathers—went hungry. It was the Mutti she wanted taking charge of this venture.

"Very well." The official slid three tickets across the counter to Mutti and one to Aunt Anna.

Mutti grabbed them and motioned for Karin and Christine to follow her. She led them through the nearly empty station to a pair of benches in a far corner.

"Let's try and get some rest. I don't know how long it will be until we get another chance to sleep. The only thing I know is that it won't be until we're in . . ." Mutti looked from side to side. "Well, you know where." She deposited her suitcase on the ground and dropped onto a bench.

"*If* we even make it to West Berlin," Christine whispered. It was the most she'd said all night.

"Christine!" Aunt Anna's mouth became a straight line. "We don't need comments like that."

"Anna's right." Mutti frowned.

"Sorry, Mutti." Christine curled up on the other bench and closed her eyes. Karin sat down next to Christine and placed a hand on her sister's arm and gave it a squeeze. Christine cracked open one eye at Karin and muttered softly, "Danke."

Two and a half hours later, they boarded the train. Karin dozed in and out for most of the trip, losing track of time. Her stomach rumbled along the way, making it hard to sleep. She recited poems in her head to help her not think about food. When the train came to a stop and Mutti announced it was time to disembark, nervous excitement replaced the gnaw of hunger.

When Karin stepped off the train onto the platform, the cavernous station seemed to engulf her. The high arching ceiling above and smooth tile beneath her feet felt overwhelmingly unfamiliar and uncomfortable. She took in a deep breath. What did she expect? She'd been very young when she'd last lived in Berlin—and she'd never been to this particular train station. The discomposed feeling worsened, its true source becoming clear in her mind. So far they'd done nothing wrong. But leaving that train had marked the beginning of the treacherous part of their journey: the subway.

A wave of panic hit her. She struggled to walk straight, taking even steps as she followed Mutti toward the exit, steps like a person who had nothing to hide would take.

Across the street from the train station and down about half a block, they found the entrance to the subway. As a very young child, Karin had viewed the stairs to the subway as a giant mouth opening up in the middle of the sidewalk like it was ready to swallow her. Today felt no different. They descended into the darkness using the monster's teeth. The damp air, slimy handrails, and foul stench make Karin feel like she indeed was climbing down the throat of some unseemly creature.

People dressed for work scurried about like ants in an ant hill, passing Karin and her family on the right and on the left, paying them little notice. Mutti corralled Karin and Christine as they approached the loading platform. Aunt Anna followed. "This is the line we need. Stay close. And follow my lead," Mutti said as she stuffed her well-used handkerchief into her coat pocket.

Of course Karin would follow Mutti's lead. And concentrate on keeping a straight face, appearing like it was the most natural thing in the world for her to be traveling into the restricted section of the city.

"But we've got suitcases," Christine said. "We don't look like we're going to work."

"I know, I know." Mutti held out her hands like she was going to cup Christine's face with a caress, like when she was a little girl. "That's where our faith has got to be strong. I know the good Lord can touch the minds of the conductor—make him forget to check our traveling papers or our subway tickets, or something like that. Anna was told that this was the day we must escape. Who knows but today is the day that the right man will be on the job for us—and the wrong one for the GDR." A subway train rumbled to a stop in front of them. The doors slid open. "Let's go," Mutti said.

The four of them hurried inside. There were no seats. Mutti grabbed a looped strap hanging from the ceiling. Karin held onto Mutti. The subway train sped forward, tipping them off balance.

At the next stop, a long bench near the door emptied. Mutti scurried to it. Karin followed and squeezed in between Christine and Aunt Anna, placing her suitcase on the floor between her legs. Karin split her focus on the forward and rear doors of the car, watching for the conductor. She let her gaze wander for a bit, moving it from face to face, scrutinizing each person who shared the car. None looked her way, only stared ahead at nothing. Each face was different, but all held one thing in common: they all looked worn out. Karin ached for them. She wished she could take them all with her to the West. Better yet, that the East and West could be the same. One Germany. But the good Germany.

The dark uniform of a conductor caught Karin off guard. She straightened her back. He strolled down the aisle toward her merely a meter away. She clenched her ticket, ready to give it to him, praying all the while he wouldn't ask for it.

With a long glance down at their suitcases, he approached their bench. "May I see your tickets?" he asked in a deep voice. He examined each ticket as the four of them extended them separately for him to punch. "Going to Friedrichshain, I see." His eyes lingered on their suitcases.

"For my older sister's wedding," Christine said to him as if he'd asked for an explanation.

"It'll be the stop after this next one," he stated in a deep, authoritative voice. Nodding at Christine, he moved on down the aisle.

On either side of Karin, both Christine and Aunt Anna relaxed slightly when the conductor slipped out of view into the next car. Karin leaned forward to ask Mutti if they were getting off at the third stop. And what should they do if the conductor saw them still on the train— in West Berlin? She decided against it. Who knew who was listening? And somehow she doubted Mutti had an answer. Karin slumped down in her seat, wanting more than anything for this subway ride to be over with. And for them to be there, in West Berlin, safe and sound.

"One more stop." Mutti mouthed the words as the subway train slowed the second time. It stopped. The majority of the people got off. Only two men and a woman remained. Each sat in a different bench. Karin and her family stuck out. It felt worse than when she didn't have a blue kerchief back in fourth grade. She prayed the conductor would not come back through. He couldn't; he just couldn't! He would know they weren't supposed to be there. It would only take a matter of seconds to figure out what they were doing. Aunt Anna would never survive prison. Mutti might not either. Christine was young and pretty—and smart. Who knew what would happen to her? Karin knew what would happen to her: an orphanage. *Stop thinking such things! We're going to make it.*

The doors closed.

The trained sped onward. Into West Berlin.

They were there! Karin had actually made it to the West.

But she wasn't off the train.

She wasn't safe yet. The moment was nothing like she'd dreamed of.

CHAPTER 26

THE TRAIN SLOWED. KARIN SPOTTED a dark uniform in the car behind them. It was headed their way. "Mutti," Karin whispered, her heart racing much faster than the subway car. She pointed to the approaching figure of the conductor.

Mutti grabbed onto Karin's outstretched hand, pulled it in, and clenched her eyes shut. Karin noticed her mother's lips moving ever so slightly. Her eyes then rushed back to the conductor. His hand reached down to open the door that led to their car. He stopped and turned around. Someone was talking to him. Their conversation drew the conductor away from the door.

The train stopped.

Mutti jumped up from her seat. "Let's go!"

Less than a meter away, the door opened up. They bolted through it.

The terminal appeared nearly empty. They darted toward the stairs. Their feet clapped against the cement platform, announcing their illegal arrival to the world. Karin tried to run softly. It didn't work; she fell behind, glancing over her shoulder. Aunt Anna lagged behind her.

Her sister zipped back past Karin and grabbed her aunt's suitcase. "You can make it, Aunt Anna." Christine nudged Karin forward too.

Halfway up the stairs, a man passed them going down on the adjacent set of steps. "Are you ladies refugees?" He held out his hand, drawing attention to their suitcases.

"No, no," Mutti huffed, her eyes wide open. "We're not refugees!" She hurried up the remainder of the steps.

Karin felt an urge to laugh. *No, we run up the stairs every day carrying our suitcases.* She wanted to go back and stop the man—ask for his help. They were in West Berlin now. She caught up to Mutti near the top of the stairs. "Maybe that man could have helped us. Do you want me to go back and find him?"

"No, we've got to keep going," Mutti said. She took the last two stairs in one step. Strands of gray hair that had escaped Mutti's scarf lapped at her eyes in response to the wind. She tucked them in place as she paused at the top of the stairs to catch her breath. She turned around and, with a sweep of her free arm, motioned for Aunt Anna and Christine to hurry and catch up.

Karin emerged from the shelter of the subway, excited to finally be here. In West Berlin! A rush of cold air penetrated her coat. She huddled next to Mutti, turned, and watched Aunt Anna hobble up the stairs. *Keep going*, Mutti had said. But Aunt Anna needed help. The veins in her aunt's hand stood out even more as she gripped the grimy handrail and pulled her slight, hunched body up each step. Christine needed help too. Breathing hard, she trudged up the cement stairs, carrying Aunt Anna's suitcase along with her own.

"Are you sure you don't want me to go see if that man could help us?" Karin asked

"No." Mutti's lips tightened, and her eyes bored into Karin's with a reminder that she was treading where she shouldn't.

"Sorry, Mutti," Karin said, realizing her idea had not been well thought out. What if the GDR possibly had some amount of power here? Or, at least, influence. West Berlin, after all, was not really a city. It was half a city. She'd seen the map in school. It was more like an island of streets, buildings, and people that belonged to West Germany, surrounded on four sides by the GDR. It reminded her of those times in school where she felt alone, surrounded by children who weren't friends.

Aunt Anna and Christine emerged onto the sidewalk next to Karin and Mutti. Aunt Anna tightened her scarf in response to wind.

"Let's keep moving." Mutti swept her hand into the wind and pointed down the street.

"But to where?" Christine set both suitcases next to Mutti's. Turning her head from side to side, she murmured, "And what are we supposed to do next?"

Karin looked at the tall buildings, too, and the streets bustling with people who knew nothing of their family's plight. "Ja, I don't remember that part of the plan." Karin looked to Aunt Anna for an answer.

"Ida, you tell her." Aunt Anna pulled her suitcase away from the others. She sat on it, rubbing her hands together to warm them while huffing for air.

"This is as far as we'd planned. We, your aunt and I, didn't really know what to expect after this point. We were hoping to make our way somehow to Hamburg, where your cousin, Sarah lives. But . . ." Mutti looked to Aunt Anna.

"I haven't heard back from my daughter. I sent her a letter as soon as I had my dream, hinting about our coming. I couldn't come right out and write about our plans—nothing's private anymore. But . . . I doubt she got the letter. I've only received one correspondence from her in all these years our country has been divided."

Mutti looked from Karin to Christine. "Sorry, I wish I had a better answer. No one has returned to the GDR after leaving—that we are aware of. So how could we really know what to expect?"

"But I imagine they get other refugees here, other than us," Aunt Anna said. "Someone was bound to have helped them."

Karin looked back at the subway entrance a half block behind them. "You're right. Or why would that man have said that? I don't think he was going to arrest us," she said with a confidence she hadn't felt a moment ago. It was as if a feeling of trust materialized out of nowhere. "He looked like a clerk or something, not someone from the government."

"Even if he could have helped, he's long gone now." Christine pulled her suitcase aside and joined Aunt Anna by sitting on it.

Mutti gazed down the street. Her eyes appeared unfocused. Karin knew that look: she was either thinking or praying. Or both. After a moment she turned to face the others. "Anna's right. I'm sure there have been others who have come before us. We'll need to find whoever helped them. They're likely to help us too."

They wandered through the streets for almost an hour. Karin longed to lie down, to at least find an empty corner in a warm building to take a nap. Or have a bit of something to eat. Mutti and Aunt Anna seemed to be looking for something specific; Karin wasn't sure. Her mind kept wandering off to thoughts of all things warm, including fresh baked bread. She could, however, tell that Mutti was frustrated. Apparently, this part of the city wasn't the same as Mutti had remembered. And Aunt Anna was constantly questioning Mutti whether or not they should trust "them" once they found "them."

Whoever "them" was, Karin didn't know. She only knew she wanted to go to sleep. She wanted to be warm. She wanted to eat.

Mutti pointed to a brown stone building at the end of the block. "There." A red sign above its door read Police Station. "I don't know what other option we have at this point but to go to the *Polizei*," she said to Aunt Anna.

Karin switched hands with her suitcase, blinked to chase the sleep away, and headed toward it. She put on a smile as she passed Christine, hoping it would be contagious—her sister looked so glum. Halfway down the block, exhaustion wiped away all remnants of her smile.

Once they all reached the corner, Mutti led them inside the police station. She approached a bald-headed man in an unfamiliar blue uniform. He sat behind a high counter and looked down at them.

"Excuse me, sir. I wondered if you could help us. My girls and sister and I have just escaped from East Germany. We have no money. But we were hoping—"

"Ja, we can help." He grabbed some kind of form from the corner of his high desk and readied a pen. "I figured you as refugees the moment you walked in. We can help, but I need to get a little information from you first."

"Thank you so very much." Mutti's eyes brightened.

As she gave the bald officer the information he requested, Karin noticed a younger officer with broad shoulders approach them from an adjoining hallway. "You ladies follow me." The young officer spoke in German laced heavily with an American accent. "There's a place to wait back here until a truck can come to fetch you."

"Do we dare trust this fellow?" Christine whispered to Karin and Aunt Anna. She clung to the wall as if wanting to wait for Mutti.

"We don't have much choice," Aunt Anna whispered. She motioned for them to follow the husky officer alongside her. He led them down a hall and into a good-sized room with a few benches sitting against its far wall.

Karin shuffled over to a bench and sat between Christine and Aunt Anna. She kept glancing back to the way they came. Her whole body ached. When Mutti finally emerged from the hallway, she felt her shoulders relax. The moment Mutti joined them on the bench, Karin had a pile of questions. *What do we do now? Where will they take us? Will they feed us? When . . .* She held them back—Mutti looked exhausted. Instead, she leaned against Aunt Anna, who in turn leaned against her, and tried to think of pleasant things. The trunk of an enormous tree filled her view out of one of four windows that lined an adjacent wall. Its furrowed bark faded from brown to deepening shades of gray as the sunlight slipped away. It reminded her of the one in Frau Krujatz's yard she used to climb back in Wittgensdorf. The memory brought a momentary smile to her lips, soon vanishing as a sense of sadness overcame her. Everything she knew was behind her now.

Several hours later, a different man in uniform led them outside to a covered truck parked behind the building. It reminded Karin of ones she'd seen during the war carrying soldiers. With the sun having set long ago, the air had grown colder still. She dreaded the ride with only a canvas roof to ward off the wind. But it led to a place to go.

The only place they had to go.

Karin climbed into the back of the truck. The officers who assisted them seemed to move as if they'd done this many times.

The truck barreled through the streets of West Berlin, whipping the night air at Karin's face with a bite as cold as she had feared. The windy opening in the canvas offered her a bouncy view of the city's side streets. Lit windows speckled rows of apartment buildings. The people inside were most likely cozy and warm, ready to climb into a soft bed, maybe even with bellies full, clueless about Karin and her family.

There's bound to be other refugees where they're taking us. They'll understand how I'm feeling. Karin latched on to those thoughts, squeezing out and savoring every drop of comfort they could offer.

When the truck came to a stop, the driver rushed back to help them out before they'd even had time to stand and gather their suitcases.

As he lifted Karin down from the back of the truck, she gazed at the massive two-story building that stood before them. Light emanated from a small patch of windows on the bottom story. It appeared to Karin as some sort of factory. Were they going to put them to work right away? Exhaustion prompted tears at the very idea.

"Excuse me, young man," Aunt Anna said when he helped her out of the truck. "Could you give me the time?"

"Ten thirty, Frau."

It had been a day and a half since they'd eaten that last bowl of mush in their apartment. "Are there beds in there?" Karin asked him as he helped her down.

"Should be. But it's kind of late. Maybe they're full."

"So there have been others like us?" Karin said as he helped Christine and Mutti down. "You know, refugees from the East?"

"Oh, ja. You are not the first." He grabbed Aunt Anna's and Mutti's suitcases and walked the four of them up a long ramp. He set the suitcases down in front of a double door. "Go in here. There are a number of people in there who'll take care of you. Auf wiedersehen." He tipped his hat and ran down the ramp to his truck.

"We've made it." Mutti picked up her suitcase.

"Let's get inside," Aunt Anna said. "I'm exhausted."

"Me too." Christine's shoulder slouched toward her suitcase as if it was filled with stones.

Karin, too tired to say anything, followed them in, anxious to meet the other refugees—in the morning.

A sour, musty smell, like a dirty old coat, overwhelmed Karin the moment she stepped inside. In the dimly lit room she could see a number of desks emptied of people but cluttered with paper. A young woman in a white dress, with a red cross embroidered on the sleeve, lumbered in from an adjoining room. "Oh, more?" Blonde wisps of hair escaped her white hat and hung down into her tired-looking eyes. She held out her hand. "Give me your documentation." Mutti handed her the papers she'd been given at the police station. The young woman glanced at them as she walked over to a desk and grabbed something. When she returned, she handed them each a tag and a pen to share. "Write your name on this, and attach it to your suitcase. They'll be stored for you until more room opens up." She waited for them to complete the task and then said, "Come this way."

They followed her down a tight hallway more dimly lit than the front office. At the end of the hall was a door with a window. A small measure of light shone in from what appeared to be a large room. The woman in white opened the windowed door and bid them to enter.

Karin stepped inside. *Huge* was her first thought. She swore the room could fit the entire train station she'd seen earlier that day within its walls. Her second thought: they definitely weren't the first to escape from East Germany. There had to be several thousand people filling the cavernous space, all lying on the floor upon what appeared to be bags stuffed with straw.

An older woman entered the room. She, too, wore a white dress with a red cross. She approached the younger woman who'd led them here and spoke softly into her ear.

"What about on the second floor?" the young woman responded loud enough for Karin to hear. The older woman shook her head. The younger woman turned and faced Karin and the others. "I'm sorry, but it appears we're out of beds. There's no room for you here."

Karin felt the life drain from her entire body. She lacked the energy to hold back the rush of tears that pushed at the backs of her eyes.

CHAPTER 27

EVEN IN THE DIM LIGHT of the cavernous room, Karin could read her family's disappointment in their faces and feel it radiate from them.

"Please," Mutti begged the women. "We don't need mattresses. Is there not a spot on the floor where you can find a little room for us to lie down?"

The two women in white spoke together at length. The older one sidled over and stood close to Karin and Christine. The younger one turned to Mutti. "There might be a few spots left where we can squeeze you in. But you'll have no mattresses. And you'll have to be separated."

Mutti simply nodded at her.

"Come." The young woman reached out to Mutti and Aunt Anna. "You two follow me. Mary will take the others."

Karin watched the young woman in white lead Mutti and Aunt Anna away. Tired, hungry, and now filled with a stronger-than-usual desire to be next to her mother, she followed the older woman up a flight of stairs. She grabbed Christine's hand.

"Don't worry, we'll see Mutti and Aunt Anna again in the morning." Christine squeezed Karin's hand.

The second floor appeared just as full as the first. The old woman in white took Karin's hand from Christine's. "Watch your step," she said as she led Karin down a narrow path through rows of bodies. "Lie down right here." Her hand pointed to a slice of cement floor visible between the mattresses of two sleeping women. "Sorry, you'll have to use your coat. We've no more blankets." With that she left Karin's side and returned to Christine.

Karin tried to see where Christine bedded down, but she and the old woman soon blended into the shadows, and her eyelids grew heavy. Karin reclined, not caring that her back lay against a hard cement floor. At least the room was somewhat warm. She could feel the cushion of straw on each side of her. Her shoulders and outsides of her legs enjoyed that bit of comfort as she fell asleep.

Karin could sense the people around her stirring. She tried to ignore the noise and sleep a little longer. A hand grabbed her shoulder and shook it.

"Wake up, child," a woman's voice said. It didn't sound harsh nor was it kind but more flat and informative. "You'll miss the breakfast line if you don't."

Karin sat up and rubbed the sleep from her eyes. She took in her surroundings, searching for Christine as she scanned the room. Straw mattresses covered the vast floor. Most were empty of sleeping bodies but were covered with coats, suitcases, and other personal items. A mass of people congregated against one of the walls. Lined up in single file, they appeared to be moving slowly toward a door marked "Stairs."

"Better grab your meal tin and get in line," the woman said.

"But I don't have one." Karin didn't want to fall in line until she found her sister.

"Ah, you got here late last night, didn't you?"

"Ja."

"Stand in line anyway. I'm sure they'll issue you one when you get to the kitchen." The woman turned away and wove through the straw mattresses toward the end of the line.

"Wait!" Karin said, but the woman didn't respond. She gave up on the woman and continued to scan her surroundings. The lack of windows, and thus daylight, made her wonder what time it was. Since rows and rows of rectangular lights now illuminated the large room, she assumed it was morning. A swell of relief energized Karin when she spotted what looked like Christine's blue coat and light brown hair—she turned around. *Christine!* Their eyes met. Christine waved her hands. Karin hurried across the floor, leaping over the straw beds, her feet landing in the narrow spaces in between.

When she reached Christine, she felt weak. They embraced. "Have you seen Mutti?" Karin asked immediately.

"No." Christine sighed. She nudged Karin toward the mass of people.

The slow-moving line gave them time to discuss their night's sleep, speculate on the whereabouts of Mutti and Aunt Anna, and wonder about what came next.

As they came to the bottom floor, a heavenly scent teased Karin's stomach: the smell of oatmeal. The line moved into a kitchen of sorts. A row of tables had been set up along one wall. Each held a burner on which stood a large pot. Women stood behind the tables, ladling oatmeal into the people's outheld dishes. Once a person received a portion, he or she moved away. Some remained in the room, standing to eat. Most slipped through a far door into another room. Through the crowd, Karin thought she saw a hand waving over the heads of all the people. She felt a jab in the arm as she tried to determine if the hand was waving at her or not.

"Karin, take your plate," Christine said.

"Oh." Karin switched her attention to the tin plate being handed to her. "Thanks," she said to the man issuing them and then focused on Christine. "I think I saw Mutti."

"Where?"

Karin turned and pointed. "There."

Mutti and Anna approached, squeezing through the groups of people. "Thank heavens!" Mutti gave them each a hug. "They said to wait for you here. That you'd surely show up. Are you all right? We were beginning to not believe them, weren't we?" She looked to Aunt Anna, who nodded.

Christine held out her tin dish for some oatmeal. "We're both fine, Mutti."

"Don't you want to get in line for breakfast?" Karin asked as a ladle filled her dish with mush. She locked her eyes on Mutti, her heart filling with much, much more gratitude than she'd ever be filled by her portion of oatmeal.

"We've had ours, dear." Aunt Anna held up a tin dish that had been rinsed clean. "We've just been waiting here for you girls."

The four of them moved to a somewhat empty space in the middle of the room while Karin and Christine ate their breakfast. It tasted so good and felt wonderful going down. "Do you think they give out second helpings?" Karin asked but really didn't expect anything.

"I doubt it," Christine responded.

"How did you girls sleep?" Mutti asked.

"Okay," Christine said.

"Fine." Karin noticed the circles under her mother's eyes looked darker than usual and her back slouched. "How about you, Mutti?"

Mutti yawned. "It wasn't my best night's sleep. The woman next to me coughed all night."

Karin motioned for them to follow with a wave of her hand. "Let's go look around."

They walked around the windowless old factory all morning, exploring and meeting people, finding that some folks had been here for several weeks but most had arrived here yesterday like them. After a bowl of soup for supper, Mutti went to the office to try and determine how long they were to stay in that place and what came next.

When Mutti came back, Aunt Anna tipped her suitcase that had just been returned to her and sat on its end. "What did you determine?"

"Ja, what did you find out?" Karin did the same with her suitcase and sat down to hear what Mutti had to say.

"They're moving people out of here every day. That's why we'll have our own mattresses tonight—thank the good Lord. Just like we figured, it could take anywhere from a few days to a few weeks before we can get shipped out. But what I did find out was that it all depends on if we have a place to go."

"A place to go?" Christine said. "What do they mean by a place to go? Of course we don't have one. Why else are we here?"

"They mean if we have a close family member in West Germany, or Europe, or even America who will take us until we can get on our feet. We can't stay here in West Berlin. They made that clear."

"Why not?" asked Christine.

"There's simply not enough room," Mutti said. "The city is already bulging with refugees. And they expect more to come. They mentioned that yesterday they saw a record number of refugees. Over two thousand people."

"Sarah!" Aunt Anna eyes lit up. "Maybe they can help me get in touch with her."

"Even if they did, how would we get there?" Karin thought about that map of West Berlin from school and how the entire city was surrounded by the GDR.

"They have to airlift us out." Mutti sat on her suitcase. "Regardless if we have a place to go or not, this will take time."

"But we do have someone to take us in," Karin insisted. She glanced at Aunt Anna for reassurance.

"We have no one," Mutti said.

"Sarah will welcome you with open arms." Aunt Anna nodded.

"No, we'd be too much on her," Mutti said. "Besides, they told me the family member has to be financially able to support us until we get on our feet. Sarah's got a young family. She'll be hard pressed just taking her mother in, let alone an aunt and two cousins."

Karin shifted her thoughts to the bed she'd been promised. It sounded like it would only bring her disappointment if she placed any hope in this cousin she didn't know.

That night Karin nestled into her own straw mattress and curled up under her coat. She found it hard to sleep. Her mind kept running through the events of the last two days, over and over again. Mutti's continual coughing didn't help matters.

The next morning, as the four of them went to get in line for breakfast, Mutti insisted on sitting back down on her mattress. "Oatmeal doesn't sound that good right now. You all go on without me. I think I'll just lie down for a while longer."

Christine placed a hand on Mutti's forehead. "You're burning with fever."

Aunt Anna moved her hand into place on Mutti after Christine took hers away. "You've caught something from that woman you lay by last night, I'm sure of it." Aunt Anna appeared as angry as she was concerned.

Mutti had pneumonia. The women in white quarantined her to a section of the old factory that had been converted into an infirmary. For two days, neither Karin, nor Christine, nor Aunt Anna was allowed to visit her. Karin clung to Aunt Anna. In a small way, it helped fill the emptiness.

On the third day of Mutti's quarantine, after Karin, Christine, and Aunt Anna had just received their helping of potato and lung soup— the same as they'd been served for each supper since they'd arrived—a young man in a military uniform walked into the kitchen area. "I'm looking for the following people," he hollered. He then rattled off a few names in a very loud voice. The large room and chatter of people seemed to swallow up his voice, even though the crowd had quieted down when he'd first started to talk. Karin barely heard what he said. Except when he uttered the final name, "Anna Schmitt." He turned toward the exit. "Follow me."

"Aunt Anna," Karin gasped. "That's you."

"Yes, dear, it is." Aunt Anna hurried and swallowed several gulps of her soup before handing her tin to Christine.

"Do you think they're going to let Mutti out of the infirmary today? Is that why they've come to get you?" Karin looked at her tin of soup and then to Aunt Anna.

"I hope so." Christine responded.

Aunt Anna gazed at the young military man as the clear-cut movement of his boots carried him though the doorway. She followed him. Glancing back at Karin and Christine, she said, "Hurry and eat. I'll meet you back by our beds and tell you what I find out."

Karin liked that idea. She and Christine slurped down their soup, rinsed their tins in the trough-like sink, and rushed back to their mattresses. When they got there, Aunt Anna had her suitcase opened on top of her straw mattress, rearranging its contents.

"What are you doing, Aunt Anna?" Karin felt uncomfortable at what she saw.

"What did you find out about Mutti?" Christine added.

"They told me nothing about Ida." Aunt Anna hurriedly snapped the latches shut on her suitcase. "Only that I needed to be down by the front loading dock with my personal belongings within the next twenty minutes." She gazed into Karin's eyes as if she were saying auf wiedersehen. "Sorry."

"Are you getting shipped out?" Christine's wide eyes expressed a mixture of hope and fear.

Aunt Anna spread her arms wide and with a wag of her fingers beckoned Karin and Christine to come closer. She pulled them into an embrace. "I don't know, I don't know. But let me hug you both, just in case." She released them and grabbed her suitcase. "I'd better go." With noticeable hesitation, she turned and headed away.

"What about us?" Karin seized her aunt's arm, grabbling with things she'd never faced before. "Are we going with you? What about Mutti? What if she's not better?"

"We're coming with you, Aunt Anna." Christine hurried and stepped in sync with Aunt Anna and Karin. She leaned forward and looked over to Karin. "At least until the loading dock. I'll try to find out about us and Mutti."

"I might have a minute to stop by the office with you girls before I need to be there. If we make it quick."

They hurried down the stairwell, across the suitcase-covered mattresses of the first floor's cavernous room, and toward the front door.

Christine approached a new lady in white behind a desk in the office. "Excuse me, Frau. It appears our aunt here has received notice of her departure, but we've heard nothing concerning ours."

Aunt Anna stepped forward. "Ja. We came here together, and we'd like to leave together. I would be willing to wait . . . a little longer."

"What is your name?" The woman moved a pile of papers in position.

"Anna Schmitt."

The woman sorted through the papers. "Here it is." She read over one of the papers and looked up. "No. That would only complicate things. You are scheduled to leave in the next truck." She peered over the top of her glasses with a scolding glare. "It leaves in ten minutes."

"What about us?" Karin exclaimed.

"What are your names?" the woman asked, sorting through more papers.

"Christine and Karin Graeber," Christine said. "And our Mutter's name is Ida Graeber."

"She's in the infirmary," Karin said. "Is that why we're still here?"

"No." The woman examined one of the papers further. "It appears Frau Schmitt," she glanced up at Aunt Anna, "has a daughter in Hamburg. That's why she is being taken to our other holding facility.

Within a day or so, she'll be airlifted out." She raised a different paper to read. "Your Mutter . . . and you, her daughters . . . have no one listed. With no place to go, it will take much longer."

"How much longer?" Christine asked in a quiet voice as she rubbed the back of her neck.

"It will be at least three weeks." The woman peered over her glasses again. "Maybe longer." She turned to Aunt Anna. "And you had better hurry."

Karin turned reluctantly away from the woman's desk. Shuffling her feet across the polished concrete floor, she hurried out the door at her aunt's side. Once through the door, a pair of uniformed men whisked Aunt Anna away, one grabbing her suitcase and the other helping her into the back of the idling truck.

"Auf wiedersehen," Aunt Anna's lips appeared to say as the truck pulled away.

Karin waved, holding back tears, dazed. This couldn't be happening. They were supposed to stick together. That's why they hadn't tried to leave without Christine. Now Aunt Anna was gone.

She didn't want to contain her tears any longer. They flowed.

CHAPTER 28

THE LINES ON MUTTI'S FACE appeared deeper as she left the infirmary. But to Karin, Mutti was a most beautiful sight. She held out her arms in response to her mother's outstretched arms. "Mutti," she murmured.

Mutti hugged and released Karin, embraced Christine, and then pulled them both away from the infirmary door as if anxious to be away from the place. Halfway down the hall, after a brief description of her recovery, Mutti asked, "Where's Anna?"

"She got shipped out," Karin responded, continuing to support Mutti's elbow.

"To Sarah's," Christine added. "Two days ago."

"And left you girls alone?" Mutti gasped.

"Mutti, we were fine," Karin said, remembering how the pain of losing Aunt Anna had faded to bearable after only an hour or so. She and Christine had soothed each other. Karin was sure that a prayer, or two, or three, had also helped.

Mutti turned the opposite direction they needed to go at the end of the hall. "Well, I'm going to find out when it's our turn to leave." She took a single step toward the office and leaned against the wall. "Maybe I'll lie down for a minute or two before I do that. Where are our beds? Are they still in the same place as when Anna was here?" Her voice wavered. Was that because Mutti was weak? Or because she missed Aunt Anna?

"They are still in the same place," Karin responded to her mother concerning their beds. But nothing else in their lives felt the same.

Karin peered over the bowl of soup she was sipping, gazing at her mother. It tasted salty and good but not as good as having Mutti well again. She'd been out of the infirmary for two weeks now, and finally she seemed back to the good old Mutti Karin was used to. "What do you want to do today?" Karin asked Mutti and Christine, knowing they'd just sit on their straw mattresses if she didn't intervene. Karin couldn't understand why they'd want to sit when there were still places to explore in the old factory and its grounds, and thousands of people to talk to. Karin had never had so many other children to do things with.

Christine opened her mouth to speak but closed it when the now-familiar young man in uniform marched into the kitchen area. Every day, Karin—and every refugee around her—listened carefully to what he had to say. He rattled off name after name in a voice that attempted to project across a large area but came out rather hoarse. No doubt the result of repeating this same action several times a day in numerous locations within the massive building.

"Harold Bamberger, Maria Bamberger, Fritz Bamberger, Hilda Reinhold." The young man interrupted his list, brought a hand to his mouth and coughed. Karin didn't move, hoping he had more names to recite because he hadn't moved either. "Gretchen Reinhold, Ida Graeber, Christine Graeber, Karin Graeber . . ." Their names sounded like music. Karin's heart beat faster as she listened for the announcement that came at the end of every list. She squeezed Mutti's hand when the young man said, "Collect your belongings and proceed to the loading area in twenty minutes."

Karin, Christine, and Mutti gulped down their soup and hurried to their spot. They knelt on one of the straw mattresses so Mutti could offer a prayer of thanks. After rising, they each grabbed their suitcases, having packed them up that morning like they did every morning, at Mutti's insistence. Karin said a quick good-riddance to her straw mattress and followed Mutti and Christine to the stairs.

The sun shone warm on Karin's face as she stepped outside. Three trucks, like the one they had arrived in, stood in line at the loading area, quickly filling up with people. Mutti checked in with a man holding a clipboard. They crawled into one of the trucks, and minutes later the wind blew through Karin's hair as the truck barreled down the road.

Reaching up, she tried in vain to keep the hair out of her eyes. She leaned toward Mutti. "I forgot to keep my scarf out of my suitcase," she hollered in order to be heard over the roar of the engine and the rush of air.

The woman wedged into the bench next to Karin ventured to speak above the noise. "You'll be okay, Fraulein. It's not that far to the airport."

"Airport? Oh, ja." Karin had nearly forgotten that detail in the rush. She'd never flown before. This was new. Exciting.

The woman patted Karin's arm. "But make sure you have your scarf after you get off the plane. From what I understand, there are refugee camps scattered throughout West Germany, so the truck ride to your final destination could be short, or it could be long."

Refugee camp? What else did Karin expect? They had no one to take them in.

It didn't matter. They were free of East Germany. Things had to be better! Excitement danced inside her.

A gasp shot from her mouth when she saw a huge airplane take off from the ground and rise into the air as if it was made of paper instead of kilos upon kilos of metal. She wondered why it was white and had the letters PAN AM emblazoned in a blue circle on its tail fin. "That doesn't look like a military plane," Karin yelled so the woman could hear her.

The man next to the woman leaned forward and cupped his hand to one side of his mouth, directing his words to Karin. "I've heard there's too many of us for the military to handle, so they've called on the private sector to help lift us out."

Private sector? Obviously the government didn't control everything. Already Karin liked the West better.

Soon the truck transported them past a large, bustling building that reminded her of a train station. The vehicle came to a stop on a massive field of concrete dotted with planes—some parked, some moving slowly along the ground like a car, one speeding down the concrete. Its nose tipped up, and the plane lifted off the ground like a feather in a breeze. Karin gazed at its ascent, feeling her mouth open with awe.

The tailgate of the truck dropped with a clank. Everyone around her scurried toward the opening. Karin grabbed her suitcase and squeezed into the clump of exiting bodies next to Mutti and Christine. Once she was on the ground, several young men, dressed head to foot in dark blue, converged upon Karin's group with tags and pens in hand.

"Write your name on a tag, and put it on your suitcase," hollered one of the men. At least, that's what Karin thought he said—it was hard to hear. There were so many planes, so many engines, so much noise. The moment she attached the tag, she felt her suitcase snatched from her hands. One of the men in dark blue had taken it and was now tossing it on a long cart. The now empty-handed mass of refugees thinned out into a straight line.

At the head of the line, a young woman, wearing white gloves and a light blue suit with matching cap, yelled above the sound of engines, "Come with me." She motioned for everyone to follow. Karin fell in step. A minute later she climbed a set of steps wheeled next to an enormous white and blue plane as tall as Frau Drescher's house.

The noise diminished as Karin ventured inside. Rows of blue upholstered seats filled the interior. Men, women, and a few children filled over half of the blue seats. The young woman pointed her gloved hand at the various empty spots. "Find a vacant seat, and sit down."

By the time Karin, Christine, and Mutti made it to the back of the plane, where most of the empty seats were, no rows with three vacancies together remained. Mutti pointed to a pair of seats next to a window. "You girls take those two. I'll sit here." She then squeezed into a middle seat and sat down between two old men three rows in front of the seats she'd pointed to.

Karin settled into the seat next to the window. With her heart thumping rapid, happy beats, she buckled the belt as the lady with the white gloves had instructed and leaned toward Christine. "We're finally doing it. We're getting out of here!"

"Ja, we are, aren't we?" Christine smile appeared bigger than it had been in a long while.

"Everything's going to be okay now." Karin felt her lips turn up even more than Christine's.

An uncomfortable feeling sucked her against the back of the seat as the plane lifted off the runway. She breathed a sigh of relief as the strange pressure faded. *What a fitting comparison for a poem.* Karin wished she had a paper and a pencil. She made note of the pressure's intensity and the equal feeling of relief that had come when the plane had risen, comparing it to when they had escaped. Storing it in her thoughts for later, she peered through the window. The city of Berlin shrank below as if Karin was a bird rising above the split city, flying off to a more happy place—because she was free to do so.

CHAPTER 29

Somewhere in West Germany, 1954

CHRISTINE LEANED TOWARD KARIN. "I'M tired of doing this," she said in a quiet voice laced with sorrow.

"Maybe this will be our last time," Karin whispered, wanting to comfort her sister but not wanting her mother to hear their conversation. Together, with suitcases in tow, they shuffled in line with other refugees in the hot afternoon sun toward the awaiting military trucks. She sensed that Mutti was having a hard time, too, with being transferred to yet another refugee camp. The few complaints that had escaped Christine's lips since their escape from East Germany last year seemed to carry much more power to sadden Mutti than all of Karin's past complaints combined.

"We should have stayed in Lockwitz," Christine continued like she hadn't heard Karin. "We're worse off now than we've ever been. There are so many refugees . . . so little . . . food . . . jobs . . . everything," She sniffled. "At least we should have waited until I graduated, got my diploma. I could have a better chance at the pitiful few jobs that *are* out there."

Karin thought about Aunt Anna's dream and then of the talk she'd heard in their last camp. Apparently, there had been an onslaught of people slipping through the cracks just like Karin's family had. But no more. The GDR had tightened security on the subways. "We might not have made it out if we'd waited," Karin said.

"Would that have been so bad? I mean if we'd just stayed?" Christine's brow furrowed, her eyes held a faraway look. "I would have had a good job . . . and Sigmund . . . and a bed . . . and Aunt Anna to soothe Mutti, keep her company."

"But we wouldn't have had Aunt Anna for long. That's why we left." Karin gazed up into Christine's eyes. "And then there was Aunt Anna's dream. Remember?"

Grimacing, Christine skirted her gaze toward the ground. "Ja," she muttered before handing her suitcase to a man in uniform and climbing into the back of the old military truck.

Karin handed off her suitcase and followed her sister. She slid next to Christine on the wooden bench to make room for Mutti. In no time, the truck backed up and then headed down the road. To where? Karin didn't know. But they were together. There would be food there, and beds of some kind. And maybe, just maybe, this next camp would be better than the last one. And have more food. She leaned her head on Mutti's shoulder and closed her eyes; that always helped make these transfers go by faster.

Karin sensed a lack of movement. Rousing herself from sleep, she opened her eyes. Darkness masked everyone's faces.

Mutti leaned Karin upright. "Wake up, Karin. We're here, in a town named Weislet."

In a daze, Karin scrambled out of the back of the truck. When she felt her suitcase forced into her hand, it seemed heavier than usual. Mutti grabbed her by the elbow and guided her into a building, and then to a new straw mattress on the floor. Karin released her suitcase onto the ground as she dropped herself onto the bed. The feel of clean fabric against her face and the aroma of fresh straw, instead of mildew or someone else's sweat, lulled her easily to sleep.

Karin held back slurping down her breakfast as she sat at one of the long tables in the new camp's kitchen. She was in no hurry.

Christine leaned toward to her and whispered, "What's wrong?"

With the clank of a hundred dishes, and just as many people talking, there was little chance Mutti would hear their close conversation.

Without trying to tone down her voice, Karin leaned in and said, "It's my turn to say nothing."

Mutti sat on the other side of Christine, her eyes meeting Karin's. "What are you two talking about?"

"Nothing," Karin responded again. "Nothing important." School wasn't important, and she didn't want to talk about it.

Mutti finished her last spoonful of mush and gazed at Karin and Christine. "We've only been here three days, but don't you think this place is nicer than the last camp?"

"I suppose," Christine said without emotion.

"I like that we have tables to eat at." Karin ran her hand along the painted white tabletop.

"And isn't it wonderful," Mutti nodded at Karin, "that the camp has arranged for you to start attending school again?"

"Oh, ja," Karin muttered through a mouthful of mush. She hated being the "new girl" at school. And she hated being behind from missing so many days of school. It made going even worse. "Wonderful," she said with as much passion as a dead person. An elbow jabbed her. She turned to see who filled the empty spot next to her at the table.

A girl from her class that she'd met yesterday, Millicent, sat on the bench, empty hands fidgeting in her lap. "Are you ready to go to school?"

Karin wasn't. She'd never be. But if she had to go back to school, having a new friend to share the awkward first few days would help. "Just let me finish off my mush first." She spooned the last few bites of oatmeal into her mouth and rose from the table. "I'll see you this afternoon," she said, giving Mutti and Christine a hug.

Millicent stood, pushing herself up by placing her hand on the table. Her fingers met with a spot of spilled mush.

Mutti grabbed her bowl, readying to stand. "Are you sure you don't need me to walk—"

"I'm fifteen, Mutti," Karin said, clenching her jaw. She should have been graduated by now. "I'll be fine." She thought about all the times she'd walked to school alone in the past. Her mother had too much time on her hands.

"The school's only a few blocks from here, Frau." Millicent wiped her hands on the faded dress she wore, a dress so worn that it made both of Karin's old dresses appear not so bad.

As Karin followed Millicent to the door that led outside, she noticed other school-aged children migrating to the same opening. Then all the children, including Millicent, stopped in their tracks. Karin followed their gaze and noticed a camp official enter the dining facility from an interior door. He was accompanied by three nuns in long black dresses and white scarfs. "What's going on?" Karin asked.

"It's the Lutheran nuns," Millicent said. "They've come here two times before since I've been here."

Karin knew from yesterday, when they'd met, Millicent had been here for three months and seemed to know everything about the camp. "Why?" Karin couldn't figure why nuns would make all the children take notice.

"Each time they come, they pick out the two skinniest, unhealthiest children and take them back to their convent, where they feed them and fatten them up."

"Then what do they do with them?"

"They bring them back here and pick two more children." Millicent scanned the large room as if she was trying to guess who the nuns would pick this time. After circling the room, her eyes focused on Karin. "Are you sure you're fifteen? You don't look like it."

"My Mutter tells me I'm small boned," Karin responded, looking around too. She picked out one or two and girls who looked horribly skinny, confident they would be the ones to go.

The camp official summoned all the children to line up at one end of the room, and nuns strolled by each child, scrutinizing them from head to toe. When the first nun walked past Karin, she paused, taking longer than usual to look at her. A second nun joined the first, whispering and nodding. They summoned the last nun, who took one look at Karin, nodded her head, and announced, "This girl. She needs to come with us."

An hour later, Karin and a girl several years younger than she boarded the nuns' beat-up old bus and headed to their church.

After six weeks of having her belly full but being told to lie down and take it easy, Karin was ready to go back to the refugee camp where she could run around and explore all she wanted—and see her mother and sister. Even go to school. The day she was scheduled to return, she and some of the other children snuck into the woods behind the convent to explore. Karin fell and broke her leg.

The nuns insisted she stay another six weeks to recover.

Finally, after three months, the nuns returned Karin to the camp. Upon her arrival, Karin immediately sought out Mutti. With the help of a camp assistant, Karin found her mother soaking in the autumn sunshine on a bench outside the building they were assigned to when they'd first arrived. Two other women shared the bench, chatting with Mutti.

Karin ran to her mother and embraced her. "Where's Christine?" Karin asked as she let go of Mutti.

Mutti stood, dismissed herself from the women's conversation, and motioned for Karin to walk with her. After a few paces, Mutti said, "Christine's gone."

"What?" Karin felt as though she'd broken her leg again—but with the pain in her heart.

"No, no, it's not like that," Mutti said in soothing tones. "It's a good thing."

"Ja?"

"Ja. She's found a job." Mutti smiled wide. "Actually, it's not a job. She won't get any pay for it—except for blessings from heaven. She's been called on a mission."

"But she's only twenty," Karin said, still trying to process this upsetting, yet good news.

"I guess the mission president really needed someone with her skills. She's working in the mission office as a secretary."

"That's great, Mutti," Karin said, feeling a smile surface on her face. She really meant it. But that didn't soothe the empty feeling aching inside her. It would have been nice to have seen her sister before she left. Now it would be nearly two years before she saw Christine again. Her smile started to sag. She forced the corners of her lips back up for Mutti's sake.

Karin's heart thumped in her ears as she watched Christine step off the bus. It had been more than two years since she'd seen her, and the excitement of having her sister home from her mission set Karin's whole body to tingle. She rushed toward her, Mutti a step behind.

"Mutti! Karin!" Christine embraced them both at the same time.

After Christine let go, Karin picked up her sister's suitcase. "How does it feel to be coming home to a *home*, not a refugee camp?"

"Wonderful."

After another round of hugs and well-wishing, the three of them climbed into the back of the pickup truck that had brought them to town. The warm summer air and the offer of a free ride from a local farmer convinced Mutti that the short, windy ride would be worth it.

The farmer stuck his head out the window "You ladies ready to go?"

Mutti nodded, and the truck took off.

It was hard to talk over the rush of air. Karin's thoughts turned to her new home and life. It hadn't been too long ago that Mutti had secured the two upper rooms of a house near the Black Forest and the fabric mill where Karin worked. It was not the job Karin would have chosen. However, having missed so much school, the vocational training at the mill was the only thing available to her at the time she finished her regular schooling. When the mill had offered her a permanent position after she'd finished her training, Karin, of course, accepted it. Fabric production was all she knew. She was seventeen now, and her wages were needed to support her and Mutti.

But now that Christine was home, there would be two incomes. That made this reunion even sweeter.

A month after Christine arrived, so did a visitor: a fellow missionary from the Frankfurt, Germany Mission. He was from America. After two weeks, he asked for Christine's hand in marriage. Together they flew to Salt Lake City and were married in the temple.

Solberg, Germany, 1957

Karin gazed out the window at the Black Forest in the distance and then looked at the calendar hanging on the wall of their two-room apartment. Christine had been married for almost a year now. She imagined again her sister's white dress and happy face as she said "I do" to Tom, Karin's new brother-in-law—a good man she'd probably never get to know very well. Feelings of happiness for Christine flowed from Karin's eyes. Her sister had a wonderful husband, a job at a big bank, and she no longer had to scrape by for her next meal here in post-war Germany. *America, where jobs practically grew on trees like apples.* What Karin wouldn't give to go there.

"Quit your daydreaming," Mutti said. She scraped the last of the morning mush into Karin's bowl. "Hurry and eat your breakfast, or you'll be late for work."

"Thanks, Mutti." Karin accepted the offering of extra oatmeal with gratitude. Working at the mill took a lot out of her, and she always came home hungry at the end of the day. She relished her remaining bites of mush, washed them down with a drink of water, and stood from the small table. After giving Mutti a quick hug, she rushed out the door to begin her fifteen-minute walk to work.

The morning production went smoothly, boring but smoothly. Karin had the process down: load the spools of thread on the looms; turn them on; watch them weave the solid greens, grays, and white into solid colored fabrics. If only she was able work at the other end of the factory, where they printed them with flowers. Or, better yet, if only she could be the person who got to design the patterns for printing. Karin thought about her schooling. Why had she even bothered? She didn't need an education to do her job.

After her short break and devouring the slice of bread and cheese she'd brought from home, she returned to her station. She'd just begun the process of replacing some spools of spent thread when she noticed her boss approaching.

The large woman, with an even larger, more intimidating voice, looked at Karin. "Come here, girl."

Karin set down the empty spools she held and stepped into the open space where her boss stood. "Yes, Frau?"

"Tomorrow an inspector from company headquarters will be coming. After you finish your allotment today, you'll need to stay and help the other girls clean this entire production room until it shines."

"Yes, Frau. Is that everything?" Karin had expected much worse. The woman always seemed to be reprimanding her for one reason or another.

"Do you want more, Frauline Graeber?"

"Oh, no . . . no, I just meant—"

The woman wagged a limp hand at the loom Karin had been reloading. "Just get back to work," she said with a snippy edge to her voice and then turned to leave.

Karin hurried back and finished reloading the new spools of thread. She flipped the switch on the machine, expecting the smooth rhythmic sound of the loom in motion. A grinding sound and then a *snap* and a *clink* disturbed her ears and soured her stomach. She hurried and turned the machine off. It was too late. An empty spool blared her carelessness as it dangled from the loom along with a mass of thread and a broken piece of metal.

Her boss stormed toward her, obviously having heard the unsettling sound of the loom's demise. "Fraulein Graeber!"

Karin dragged her feet as she walked home. How could she tell Mutti she'd lost her job? How would she find another one? Who would even hire her, an eighteen-year-old with a bad reference—the terrible reference her boss had promised everyone in the manufacturing industry would hear about?

As Karin approached the white two-story house she and Mutti shared with two other families, she felt an increased appreciation for the little garden plot at its side. Hemmed in on the north by a grove of trees, the tiny rows of emerging potatoes, beans, and cabbage looked beautiful. But beauty did her little good at the moment. Those plants wouldn't feed her and Mutti for at least another month or so. She trudged up the steps, trying to look for something else to lift her spirits.

The front door swung open. Mutti stepped out on the porch with a rug in hand. She cocked her head to one side as she shook the woven rag mat and looked at Karin. "What's wrong, sweetie?"

Karin took in a deep breath and held onto the railing, allowing it to steady her. "I lost my job, Mutti," she said quietly, though her heart pounded loud in her ears. She then proceeded to report all the unpleasant details of her day.

With the rug rolled up and long since tucked under her arm, Mutti's other arm wrapped around Karin and ushered her inside. "Don't you worry. We'll manage somehow."

"What about this position?" Mutti asked as she scanned the day-old newspaper they'd borrowed from a neighbor.

Karin got up from the couch and walked over to her mother at the table. It had been almost two weeks since the incident at the mill. She appreciated Mutti's gentle handling of the uncomfortable situation. Never once had there been mention of Karin's mistakes. Instead, Mutti spent more time on her knees and reading the paper than usual. Karin moved so as to peer over Mutti's shoulder and view the ad by her finger. "That's for a seamstress. I'd never qualify for that," Karin said.

"I was thinking I could apply."

"But Mutti, you're too—" Karin sucked her lip in between her teeth.

"Too old?" Mutti lifted an eyebrow. "So I'm sixty-four. I can still work circles around most young folks."

"I'm sure you could, Mutti," Karin said, knowing her mother would try. And would make herself sick in the process. Mutti tired so easily as of late. "But let's exhaust our search for me before you apply."

Mutti nodded and stood from the table, patting the newspaper as she rose. "Here, you look for a while. I'm going to retrieve the post."

Karin read over the job advertisements. She looked again. There was nothing new. The clap of Mutti's footsteps coming up the stairs prompted Karin to mask her discouragement with a smile to greet Mutti's return. Then it dawned on Karin that her mother's footsteps sounded faster than usual. Was something wrong?

Mutti burst into their front room/kitchen with an opened letter waving in her hand and a big smile on her face. "Christine wants us to come to America. Her in-laws said they would sponsor us."

"Really?" Karin jumped to her feet and rushed to Mutti's side, reaching for the letter. "When?"

"Christine said it can happen whenever we are ready." Mutti handed Karin the letter. "As far as I'm concerned, I'm ready right now. There's nothing for us here, and the sooner we leave the better."

Karin knew Mutti must be thinking of the money they didn't have for the next month's rent. "I'm ready too," Karin said. She'd been ready for years.

"I'll write Christine back right now." Mutti went to the cupboard, pulled out a pen and paper, and sat down at the table.

America! Karin could hardly believe it.

CHAPTER 30

KARIN TREADED UP THE GANGPLANK with a stir of anxiety dampening her excitement. The red dual smoke stacks and the crisp white deck atop the black hull of the *USS United States* presented themselves with an air of elegance. The state-of-the-art ship could transport her and Mutti to America in three days' time. But was she really in a hurry to get there? Yes and no.

She took a deep breath, grasped the suitcase holding the sum of her possessions, and stepped onto the massive deck of the ship with Mutti at her side.

"What if we can't find our berth? Or it's taken?" Mutti clenched the suitcase handle with both hands. "Or they charge extra for the food?"

"If we could survive the Russians, we can do this," Karin said to Mutti above the clamor of voices and blare of the shipyard. She said it again silently to herself.

A uniformed woman dressed in red, black, and white to match the ship, stood smiling near a stairwell, directing the bustling throngs of passengers. Karin wove her way toward the woman, pulling Mutti along with her free hand. They may as well be walking on top of the Great Wall of China—everything felt so foreign: the salty smell of the ocean, spotless white deck chairs with vibrant red cushions, unfamiliar words uttered by masses of well-dressed people. Karin extracted their tickets from her pocket and held the gray stubs for the woman to view.

"Where do we go?" Karin spoke carefully in English. Nerves prompted her hand to shoot up to the braids of her hair, wrapped around her head and pinned in place—a style no one else seemed to have. She glanced down at the dress hanging from her thin body. Its yellow flowers had long since faded to beige. Mutti's pink Sunday suit appeared several sizes too large, lacking the color and crispness of its prime. But it still complimented Mutti's gray hair. Karin wished she could say the same for her own dress; it was practically the same color as her hair. And it made her look like a young girl even though more and more she was taking on the role of guardian, and Mutti was in *her* care.

The woman's eyes made a quick survey of Karin and Mutti. "Economy class . . . is—" Many of her words were hard to understand, but it was clear their tickets took her by surprise. "Oh, stateroom B31. My apologies." She gestured to the stairs and said something Karin was unsure of but gathered their cabin was down two decks. The woman's eyes fell on them with more scrutiny. "Or you can use the elevator." She gestured to a sign with arrows pointing around the corner. "If you or your mother are not up to the stairs."

"Thank you," Karin responded but only to be polite.

At the bottom of the second set of stairs, they funneled into the hallway. A plump-faced man in white shorts and an ocean-blue sweater vest blocked the narrow passage with multiple suitcases. "Excuse me." He pressed himself and his luggage against the wall the best he could so Karin and Mutti could pass.

"Thank you," Karin said, adding a nod of her head.

He opened his cabin door and mumbled something about his wife bringing the kitchen sink.

Karin wished her understanding of English was better—that surely couldn't have been what he said. The moment they'd decided to come to America, she'd started studying English, but her efforts, she feared, were too little too late. This just confirmed her anxiety. She nodded again as she passed.

Once beyond him, she found the hallway filled with individuals similar to the plump-faced man, all fleshed out with healthy constitutions and dressed like people out of a magazine. She and Mutti maneuvered their way down the hall with their single suitcases in hand, searching the crisp white doors for cabin B31. She felt like a black beetle in a boatload of beautiful butterflies. Traveling economy class would have been preferred—for many reasons. But this was all they had available when Karin had purchased their tickets last week.

Karin pulled the key from her pocket, having made all the earlier transactions in case they required English. Her pitiful command of the language would have to get them by in this new country. Mutti had learned about five words of English. And, if Karin knew her mother, it would probably remain as five words for the next five years.

Mutti took the key and inserted it in the lock. "Oh, bother these fancy locks. I can't seem to do anything right." Her hands fumbled, shaking as she tried again. It wouldn't turn.

Karin's stomach seemed to be the only thing turning. "Keep trying," she said, hoping it wouldn't cost them extra if they needed a new key.

Karin refused to let worry overshadow the excitement of finally going to America. But she couldn't get excited about living with Christine's in-laws without Christine being there. She thought back on the letter she'd received from their sponsor, Sister Smith. The woman's words had sounded cordial, willing to help, a true sister in the gospel. But they had lacked warmth. The last thing Karin wanted was for her and her mother to be a service project.

She tried to ignore the fluttering feelings inside her and followed her mother into their cabin.

A few steps into the room, Mutti stopped, gazing from wall to wall. She reached out, touching the metal trim around the mirror that hung above a small vanity table. Her fingers moved over to the plush blue towels draped over an ornate towel holder next to a miniature sink.

The room was not overly sized, but its efficient use of space made it feel roomy. It was definitely nicer than anything Karin had lived in for the last thirteen years. Two double beds rested their heads against the far wall to the right. Under the porthole of the outside wall sat a lounge chair, which was nearly buried by the contents of an opened suitcase at its side. Another opened suitcase consumed the bed next to the chair.

"I guess this is our bed." Mutti deposited her suitcase and herself on the bed closest to the door.

"Looks like it." Karin plopped down next to Mutti, wondering what their cabin mates would be like—not that it mattered. She was just glad they had found some women willing to share a cabin. It had helped to keep the cost down.

Mutti lowered her suitcase onto the floor and sank into the bed. "I think I'll lie—"

The cabin's door swung open. A woman with shiny blonde hair waltzed in wearing tight pants that reached only to midcalf. "Oh . . . our cabin mates," she said with a smile. Behind her, a dark-haired woman wearing tan shorts and a sleeveless red blouse stepped into the room. "Hello. I'm Mary." She swept a hand toward the lady with dark hair, "and this is Abigail. And you are?" Her hand beckoned to Karin.

"I am Karin Graeber." She pointed to Mutti. "My mother, Ida."

"Ah, from Germany." Mary lifted an eyebrow. "So . . . are you going to the states for business or pleasure?"

"Pardon me?" Karin didn't quite understand the question. "Sorry, my English is not good."

"Why are you going to America?" Mary spoke slowly.

No matter how deliberately this woman spoke, a decent conversation would be near impossible. "Immigrating." Karin kept it simple.

Mary said a number of things before uttering some familiar words. "*Wo kommen sie her?*"

"Dresden," Karin said, not wanting to state the million different places they'd lived.

"I thought that *Stadt* was destroyed in the war," the other woman, Abigail, spoke up, throwing in a German word as if it would help.

"It was not all destroyed," Karin said, hoping she'd responded correctly.

"But isn't Dresden in East Germany?" Mary's words were easily understood—but not her expression. Her brows lifted, and her eyes opened full in amazement as she lowered into the lounge chair, her focus remaining on Karin.

Abigail appeared just as taken back. She moved a misplaced blouse with the toe of her shoe and made her way over to the corner of her bed. "Yes, it is." She rambled off several unfamiliar words. ". . . and the East German government is letting you come to America?"

"No. We escaped," Karin said, glancing at Mutti, who nodded her head, *escape* being one of the few English words she knew.

"Oh my! I can only imagine how horrible it must have been for you in East Germany." Mary sat forward, begging with her eyes. "I'd love to hear your story."

Karin hesitated. She didn't have much to tell. "I do not know . . ." It had been a long day—a long thirteen years. She wasn't sure if she was ready to share her and Mutti's story. Especially not with an unfamiliar language and people. "I do not think I can talk about it."

Mary rose from the lounge chair, took Karin's hand in hers, and squeezed it. "I understand, sweetie. Sorry for being so insensitive." She looked to Abigail. They each grabbed their jackets and stepped to the door. "I do hope all goes well for you ladies in America," Mary said before slipping into the hallway.

The three-day voyage across the Atlantic had gone by quickly. Karin reorganized her suitcase so she could get everything back in.

"One suitcase?" Mary snapped the latches down on her third one, having finished her packing. Abigail was just starting to fill hers.

"Yes." Karin shut her suitcase and secured it.

"Leaving? Now?" Mary pointed to a clock resting on the bed table. A good hour remained before the ship docked. "Sit, relax while you wait."

"Thank you, no," Karin said, hoping she wasn't rude. "We wish to see the Statue of Liberty." She figured her roommates had seen it plenty of times—probably even forgotten what it symbolized. As for her and Mutti, they were anxious to see it. She stepped to Mary and Abigail's side to give them a farewell hug. "Good-bye." She turned and followed Mutti out the cabin's door, offering a final wave.

Each toting a suitcase, they climbed the stairs to the deck. As the green shoreline of New York came into view with its tall buildings jutting into the sky, a sense of excitement and security filled Karin. Also that niggling of anxiety she'd felt when she first stepped onto the ship. They had a daunting debt to repay Christine's in-laws. Responsibility weighed heavy on her shoulders now. She found it odd that it scared her more than all the bombs in her past.

The gentle jostling of the train car as it traveled across the rail and across kilometers and kilometers of the American countryside, relaxed Karin as it lulled Mutti asleep. It had been a long day dutifully filling out paperwork, taking multiple cabs, finding the train station, having to speak more English than ever before. Mutti's head rested on Karin's shoulder, her gray hair short and curly, blending in with the high-backed seat. The sun had slipped behind the rolling hills several minutes earlier, the same hills the train now headed toward. It felt like they were fruitlessly chasing the sun.

Karin pushed a button, and a light turned on above them. She never tired of experiencing the plethora of conveniences this new land seemed to offer. Even the comfort of the seat cradling her tired body felt superior to the many places she'd had to bed down in past years. Yet the attendant had apologized that their tickets did not include a sleeping berth—as though it was his fault. She and Mutti didn't need such luxuries. The USS *United States* had been the only available ship given the hurried nature with which they'd left Germany. But this train ride was another matter. No need to spend any more borrowed money than was necessary.

She reached into the pocket of her coat draped across the front of her body that at the moment took on the role of her blanket. The letter, well-worn by now, was the last they'd received in Germany. She unfolded it carefully and began to read:

Dear Mutti and Karin,

I am so happy that you're finally doing it; you are finally coming to America. I'm so sorry that I won't be able to meet you at the train station when you arrive, but Tom and I have just moved from Salt Lake City. The army has relocated us in a place called Tacoma, Washington. There are so many details we've got to take care of as we get settled, but I promise I'll be there as soon as I can get away.

And don't worry about my in-laws. They told me to tell you that you don't need to pay them back for the boat and train tickets for a while. I promise they are happy to have you live with them while you get settled. Once you get jobs and some money saved up, I'll help you find a darling little apartment, and you can move out on your own. Mutti, we can decorate it up to feel like you're back home in Germany if you'd like.

One more thing. Karin, I have someone I'd like you to meet. His name is Max. He lives in our old ward there in Salt Lake City. When I told him about you, he insisted that I introduce you to him when you arrive. I hope you don't mind. He's from Germany and experienced lots of hardships too. He came here a few years after the war. He's had a hard time finding someone, as he puts it, "who understands what he's been through." I thought you two would be perfect for each other.

Sorry for the short letter this time, but I've got so much to do before I return to Salt Lake City. I'm so excited to see you both!

Love, Christine

Karin refolded the letter. *Christine!* What was she thinking? Karin had a million and one things to deal with once she got to Utah. The last thing she needed was a boy who was "perfect" for her. She was eighteen. She had plenty of time to worry about that facet of her life. Right now she needed to find a job, pay back the Smiths, and take care of Mutti. Those things loomed much larger and more urgent than finding a suitor.

As she slipped the letter back into her pocket, her fingers met with the cool metal of coins, all that was left of their traveling funds. Supper had consisted of a small bowl of soup in the dining car. Breakfast tomorrow would probably be a slice of toast, maybe a single fried egg to split between her and Mutti. The food served on the train tasted divine. Tonight's soup, and most likely tomorrow's breakfast, was like a banquet compared to their meals in Germany. The savory flavor of the chunks of beef, sweet carrots, and hearty potatoes replayed in her thoughts. She could almost taste it again.

Her mind wandered back to the meals she was used to, and how they were better than most children's because Mutti went without, giving her portion to Karin and Christine. That led her to think of the many other things Mutti did in effort to shield Karin from the grim reality of life in Germany. She leaned over and kissed Mutti's forehead.

Mutti stirred. She raised her head from off Karin's shoulder, turned it, and looked into Karin's eyes. "What, you can't sleep?"

Karin nodded.

"Nervous? Still worrying about paying back the Smiths?"

"No. Just thinking about Germany."

"It's hard. I know. But Karin, dear, you've got to let go."

Karin smiled and clasped hold of Mutti's hand. "I know; I'll try." She'd let go of Germany long before they'd even left. It was what lay ahead that weighed on her. Of course she'd never admit that to Mutti. "Don't worry. I'm fine," Karin added. She felt her smile fade. Now *she* was the one shielding things from *Mutti*.

What an odd feeling it was, having the tables turned.

The feeling continued to turn and churn as she mulled over her dependence on the Smiths. All of a sudden, she felt like one of those poor Dresden refugees after the bombing. Would she and Mutti be a similar burden on the Smiths?

Mutti laid her head back on Karin's shoulder. The moonlight filtering through the window lit Mutti's face, casting shadows under her eyes and around her mouth.

It reminded Karin of the times Mutti rubbed soot on her face to look older and less appealing to the Russians. Mutti had done all she could to survive—thus helping Karin and Christine to do so. However, her faith had guided them to take different measures than the Somer sisters. To have had to "survive" like Ella and Brunhilde had done made shivers run down Karin's back.

Thinking of all Mutti had done for her brought Karin comfort and helped soften her worries of tomorrow. Her eyelids finally began to droop.

CHAPTER 31

KARIN CLOSED THE DOOR TO the toilet behind her, or "restroom," as Americans called it. Then again, it was kind of restful in there despite the noise of the train rolling down the track. She much preferred these toilets without huge gaping holes beneath the seat. It was certainly more restful than the one she'd had to share with the Somers as a young child. She couldn't hold back a smile as she remembered again of how she hated that toilet. How every time she sat on it, she'd feared she'd fall in.

She grasped the backs of each aisle seat as she made her way back to her seat. Mutti now occupied it and was gazing out the window.

The smile must have lingered on her face, for Mutti looked up as she approached and said, "It's good to see you so cheerful this morning." Karin sat down, and Mutti patted her hand. "Excited to meet that boy Christine has arranged for you?"

Karin's smile faded. "First thing: he's not a boy. He's finished college. I don't know how old he is." She let out a big breath and rolled her eyes. "And second: Christine hasn't *arranged* him for me. You make it sound like you two are conspiring to marry me off the minute I get to Utah. He just wants to meet me. That's all."

"But he is from Germany," Mutti said like that was a fact Karin could have forgotten. "And it sounds like he's looking for a German girl."

"Mutti!" Karin hushed her mother. She rolled her eyes again, stood, and stepped out into the aisle. "Let's go get our breakfast." She led the way to the dining car, grabbing on to the back of a seat now and again to maintain her balance in the jiggling train.

A middle-aged lady with bright red lips and a wide smile seated Karin and Mutti near the front of the dining car. She handed them a menu. "Take your time. We're a might short staffed this mornin'. And your waitress doesn't know when to stop yakkin' and start workin'." She motioned with a nod of her head toward a young woman in a black dress and white apron with a booklet in one hand and a wagging pencil in the other. The young woman did more talking with the two men at the table she stood at than she did writing. "It might be a coon's age before she gets to you," said the lady with the red lips as she filled their glasses with water.

"Excuse me?" Karin felt like she'd stepped into yet another country. "Sorry, our English is not good."

"No, honey, I'm sorry." The woman squeezed her lips together as she shifted her mouth to one side. "I'll try to talk more plain-like." She tapped the top of the menu Karin was scanning. "Tell you what. It's best I take your order. Suzie over there can't talk slower than a hundred miles an hour." She hurried away.

It hadn't been this difficult last night at supper. Karin felt her fear returning. Did she have what it took to take care of both her and Mutti in this new country if she couldn't even order breakfast? Maybe they should go back to their seats and forget about eating. They had such little money. It's not like they hadn't gone without breakfast before.

The red-lipped lady returned with a booklet in hand. She flipped a few pages back. "So, what can I get for you two gals?"

Karin felt trapped. Getting up and leaving the table now would be awkward. She pulled the change from her pocket and placed it on the table. "What," she pointed at the menu, "with this much?"

The lady glanced at the money and then scanned the menu. "Honey, about all's you can get is a muffin and a glass of milk."

"Okay, that," Karin responded.

The lady looked to Mutti. "And for you?"

"We will share." Karin leaned forward to divert the lady's attention off Mutti and back to her.

"That there's not enough to feed a bird, let alone—" The lady rushed her fingers to her mouth. "Excuse my ramblin'." She surveyed Karin and Mutti, her eyes seeming to scan every centimeter of their worn clothing. "Say, where you gals from?"

"Germany," Karin said.

"Yes," the lady nodded, "I thought so—from your accent. My brother's stationed in Germany—part of the war recovery effort. Tells me things are still a might tough over there. His base is in Hamburg. Is that anywhere close to where you lived?"

Karin kept her response simple like she had with the ladies on the ship. "No. We are from Dresden."

"But . . ." The woman's eyes opened wide. "That's in East Germany, isn't it?"

"Yes."

"What was it like?" The lady's jaw dropped as a look of concern filled her eyes. "You know, living under communist rule?"

"Okay."

"*Okay?*" The lady stared at Karin. "Wait a minute. I didn't think they let anyone leave. How'd you get out?"

"We had to sneak away."

"You mean you escaped? Oh my." The lady rested a hand on Mutti's shoulder. "You poor souls. I'll bring you a muffin, too, and don't worry, it's on me." With that, she was off to the kitchen.

After the lady slipped out of sight, Karin leaned across the table toward Mutti. "Why does the mention of having lived in East Germany seem to unsettle people?"

"They've obviously heard what things are like back there." Mutti reached across the table and took Karin's hand, giving it a squeeze. "But don't let their words upset you, dear. I don't think Americans will treat you poorly because of your heritage. I think they're past that now."

Karin hadn't even thought of that. Would there still be Americans who'd associate her with Hitler? Or the Russians? She grappled for something to reassure her that this wouldn't be yet another hurdle to jump. She pulled Christine's letter from her pocket. Her sister had lived in America for over a year now. Surely Christine would have mentioned this being a problem if it was, but she hadn't, not in this letter or in any previous correspondence. Karin opened the letter to reread it.

Her stomach tightened when she came to that part—the part that had bothered her before.

. . . One more thing. Karin, I have someone I'd like you to meet. His name is Max. He lives in our old ward there in Salt Lake City. When

I told him about you, he insisted that I introduce you to him when you arrive. I hope you don't mind. He's from Germany and experienced lots of hardships too. He came here a few years after the war. He's had a hard time finding someone, as he puts it, "who understands what he's been through." I thought you two would be perfect for each other.

Would Karin "understand" what this fellow had been through when she'd considered the last thirteen years of her life more as an adventure than anything? What if he asked her about her most terrifying memory? Would she be honest? Could she really say, *"Oh, I was afraid of falling into the Somers' toilet"*? She didn't want to meet this fellow. She didn't want to meet any fellows. Not right now. Why couldn't Christine just stay out of her personal matters?

They finished their breakfast and exited the dining car, returning to their seats in the adjoining car. As they chatted about the weather, about Christine, and about the thrill of being in America, Karin observed the changing landscapes through the window. After kilometers of flat prairie, the ground now rose and dipped low, forming hills and valleys barren of trees. Jagged mountains topped with snow loomed in the distance in shades of purple-blue.

The train snaked through the mountain valleys for some time before the conductor announced, "Next stop, Salt Lake City."

Karin's insides fluttered. "This is our stop, Mutti." She stood to retrieve her suitcase from the overhead bin. She set it on her seat and then grabbed Mutti's. They each held their belongings on their laps until the train came to a stop.

Once out on the platform, Karin attempted to read the signs overhead, but none seemed to offer even a hint of what she needed. "We need to find the ticket booth," she said in Mutti's ear to be heard over the hubbub of people scurrying to and fro. "Sister Smith should be meeting us there."

"Do you know where that is?" Mutti asked, concern obvious in her widened eyes.

"Maybe over there." Karin pointed to a brick structure at the far end of the platform but still under the awning that shielded them from the summer sun. Several people stood in lines in front of the building.

She urged Mutti toward it, scanning the crowd for the face she'd memorized from the photograph Christine had sent. Her eyes skirted through scores of people, none matching the piercing eyes, wavy hair, and high-cheek-boned image in her mind of Christine's mother-in-law. Everything felt so foreign: the train station; the clothes and speech of the people; the hot, dry air. Panic crept down her back and then down into her fingers.

"Excuse me, ladies?" someone addressed them in English. Karin turned around to face a tall woman wearing an orange hat that matched her straight knee-length skirt. "Are you Ida and Karin Graeber?"

"Yes," Karin said in English. She studied the woman's face. The generous amount of green shadow and red lipstick threw her off for a moment. The black-and-white photo, of course, wouldn't have revealed that. But the similarities were definite. "Are you . . . Sister Smith?"

"Please, call me Sylvia." The woman wrapped an arm around Karin's shoulder and pulled her into a hug. A pleasant floral fragrance emanated from her. The woman released Karin, embraced Mutti, and stepped back, surveying them both from head to toe. "We have some serious shopping to do once we get you settled."

Karin understood the word *shopping* but didn't understand how it could go with the word *serious*. "Excuse me, my English . . . not so good. Could you repeat?"

Sylvia wagged a limp hand at her. "Never mind. It wasn't important. Now, let's get you ladies home. I've got dinner in the oven. You both look like you could use a bite to eat. More like several bites." She reached for the suitcase in Mutti's hand and motioned to Karin's with her chin. "Is this all you have?"

Karin again felt woefully unprepared to start a new life here. She gave a timid nod of her head.

"Can you handle it by yourself?"

Karin nodded.

"That's good." Sylvia hefted Mutti's suitcase to her side, turned, and plunged into the crowd. She looked over her shoulder to Karin and Mutti. With a jerk of her head, she bade them to follow. "I wasn't able to bring my husband, George, to help." She returned her gaze to look straight ahead. "But I think we've got this. Now, if I could just remember where I parked."

"We do not take *bus*, as you call it?"

"Heavens no." Sylvia flicked her wrist and kept walking.

"Your family has a car?" Karin had rarely ridden in a car. She knew very few people who even owned one. That trip to the train station in Uncle Stephan's was the last she really remembered.

"Of course we have a car. How else do you think I got here? Lucky for me, George can take the bus to work so I can have the car the days I need one."

As Karin followed Sylvia away from the train terminal, amazement struck her as she observed the plethora of multi-colored vehicles lined up in tidy rows over an expanse of asphalt. Additional cars added to the ranks as quickly as others filed out into a street busy with even more cars. How did these people afford all these automobiles? And where did they find enough gasoline to fuel them?

Sylvia set down Mutti's suitcase behind the trunk of a shiny, white car with tail lights at the ends of fin-like appendages. "Here we are." She inserted a key and popped open the huge trunk. Mutti's suitcase went in first, and then Sylvia reached for Karin's. "Christine mentioned you'd be traveling light, but . . ." She raised her eyebrows as she closed the trunk. "Just these two suitcases?"

"Ja," Karin responded.

"Will you have more things coming?"

"No," Karin responded. Christine had alluded in her letter to the abundance in America. Karin hadn't really grasped what Christine was talking about. It was beginning to make sense. She hadn't thought much about her lack of possessions—until now.

"Come on, let's get you settled." Sylvia shut the trunk and guided Mutti to the front of the car. "Things are bound to be a little different for the two of you here."

Karin climbed into the back seat as Sylvia helped Mutti into the front seat. The beige leather was hot to the touch. Its heat penetrated her dress, warming her legs to a point of discomfort. She wanted to roll the window down but didn't dare ask for permission. Besides, she wasn't sure how to do it—there was no crank.

"It'll cool down in here once we get moving," Sylvia said as if reading Karin's action of wiping the sweat from her brow. She pushed some buttons and then patted the dashboard. "This girl has air conditioning."

They drove by a park that filled an entire city block. "This is Pioneer Park," Sylvia said. "It's where the pioneers camped when they first came into the valley one hundred ten years ago next week." She pointed toward what Karin assumed to be the center of town because of the numerous tall buildings. "And over that way is the Salt Lake Temple. Sorry, we can't drive by it right now to get a better look; we need to hurry."

A quick glimpse of a granite spire caught Karin's eye. After that, her mind wandered as Sylvia continued to point out the window and ramble much faster than Karin had the energy to try to interpret. She thought about Sylvia's meal back at her house, cooking in the oven. Who was there watching the fire, making sure the food was cooking— or didn't get burnt? Perhaps it was a daughter. Christine had briefly mentioned the Smiths' other children, but Karin couldn't remember their names now, or their ages. Would she and Mutti be able to help with the cooking once they moved in, help repay the Smiths' kindness? And the food? Would the Smiths be able to procure enough to feed two extra mouths? Especially if Karin wasn't able to find a job right off? How would they manage such things? Karin was determined to help out as much as she could and, if need be, give her portion of food to Mutti.

The car soon ambled into a neighborhood filled with individual homes in pristine condition. Built of various colors of brick and surrounded by young, well-groomed shrubbery, every house appeared large enough to fit several families. Sylvia pulled her car into the driveway of one of the biggest on the street, a red brick home trimmed with white windows and shutters. At least Karin and Mutti wouldn't be crowding the Smiths out of this house. Unless they already had another family living with them.

"What a beautiful home," Karin commented as they climbed out of the car.

"Thanks. It's home. We've raised four children here." Sylvia inserted her key in the trunk and popped it open. "But don't worry. Only two of them still live here. Our oldest, Tom, you already know. He and Christine just moved to Tacoma, unfortunately. We have another married daughter. She also lives out of state, in California, so we don't get to see her and our new little granddaughter as much as we'd like."

She hefted a suitcase from the trunk, handed it to Karin, and took the other one for herself. "Bill is eighteen. He just graduated from high school but will be moving away to college this September. And we have our daughter, Jane. She's fifteen. She'll start high school this fall. Her bedroom is upstairs. I'm afraid you and your mother," she smiled at Mutti, "will have to share a room until Bill moves out. You'll also have to share the downstairs bathroom with him for a while too," Sylvia said with a note of apology. "I hope you won't mind?"

"Oh, we will not mind." Karin followed Sylvia up the stairs, amazed that this woman would even consider the need to apologize for such a supposed inconvenience.

As they stepped inside the house, savory smells aroused Karin's stomach with anticipation. Hopefully, at least for their first meal here, there would be enough for everyone.

Sylvia set down Mutti's suitcase on the honey-colored hardwood floor of a spacious living room. "Can you wait a minute before I show you to your room? I need to check on supper." She scurried through an arched doorway into a room with gray and yellow linoleum on the floor.

Karin and Mutti followed her as far as the archway, remaining in the living room and peering into what was obviously a kitchen but unlike any kitchen Karin had used.

Sylvia opened the door to the oven and pulled out a shelf full of tin trays covered with silver foil. "Sorry about the TV dinners tonight, but with all I had going—and I figured you two would be hungry as soon as you got in—well, I needed something Jane could take out of the freezer already made and just pop in the oven for me."

"*Teevee?*" Karin said. "I am not familiar with that word." Did it mean tin? She desperately wanted to improve on her English.

"TV," Sylvia mumbled. "Oh, that's short for television. You did have television over there, did you not?"

"Yes." Karin had known of it, had seen a television set in West German shops.

"I guess they call them TV dinners because . . . well, maybe it's because the trays are shaped like a television . . . or that most people sit in front of one to eat them . . . I'm not sure. But we eat ours at the table. I don't believe in eating in the front room." Sylvia nodded through the doorway at the television sitting against the far wall of the living room. Lifting the foil from one of the trays, she added, "And it appears we won't be eating these for another five or ten minutes."

A teenage girl poked her head into the kitchen through another door. "Oh, are they here?"

"They are." Sylvia shut the oven. "Jane, could you be a dear for me and show them their room while I set the table? Dad will be home from work any minute now. Oh, and thanks for putting the dinners in the oven for me."

"Sure, Mom." Jane motioned to Karin and Mutti to walk through the kitchen. Though a few years younger than Karin, Jane stood a few inches taller and filled out the short-sleeved sweater she wore much better than Karin would have. "You guys, grab your suitcases and follow me downstairs." Jane's skirt, with a dog embroidered just above its hem, twirled as she turned toward the stairs.

Karin walked through the kitchen with suitcase in hand. Her eyes skirted from stove to icebox to a rectangular appliance next to the sink she didn't even know of the purpose of—all shiny and white, all electric, she supposed. Sylvia opened a closet as Karin slipped by her and caught a glimpse of shelves full of canned goods and bags of flour and sugar. Their own bedrooms and bathroom, pre-made dinners, a pantry full of food, a warm oven with the turn of a knob—Karin felt more out of place than she'd ever expected.

As their first Sunday in the States approached, Karin met it with anticipation. On the five-minute ride to church, she looked forward to the break from all the new stimuli bombarding her on all sides: job interviews, fancy kitchen, TV, movie theaters, shopping, food, riding everywhere. Going to church was familiar. Even if she could only understand a fraction of what she'd hear, the Spirit there would be the same.

If only Christine was here. She'd be able to translate. Karin couldn't wait to be with Christine again. It'd been almost a year and a half since she'd seen her sister. Karin contemplated the joyful reunion as she followed the Smiths into the chapel.

She slid into the pew next to Jane, and Mutti slid in next to her. She ran her fingers along the top of the bench in front of her, enjoying the smoothness of the varnished hardwood, and then reached down to extract the untattered hymnal from its wooden pocket. As she placed it on her lap, she gazed around the spacious chapel *filled* with people. Her eyes moved up to the podium, where the pulpit was actually permanent and raised above the congregation a meter.

Three men in crisp suits sat on the front row of the podium: the bishop and his counselors, most likely. Behind the bishopric, several rows of seats rose up, filling the stand but holding only two people. One was an old lady holding a hymn book and sitting next to the organ. On the other side, a sharp-looking young man sat on the edge of his seat. His dark, neatly combed hair complimented his fair skin. Though Karin couldn't determine the color of his eyes, maybe blue, she found them inviting—even though they appeared to be intent on scanning every person in the congregation before the meeting started.

The oldest of the three men on the front row of the podium approached the pulpit. The whispers filling the chapel faded into silence as the man began speaking. Karin gathered that he was the bishop and the opening hymn was number 210 but not much more. She closed her eyes in frustration. Reopening them, she saw the young man on the stand staring at her.

Karin focused on the hymnal in her lap. Through the corner of her eye, she saw the old lady with the hymnal stand and lead the congregation in a hymn. Karin could read very few of the words, but she recognized the tune and began singing in German. She glanced up and noticed a smile spread across the face of the young man on the stand, his eyes still locked on her. *Who is this person?*

Was he some kind of assistant to the bishop? A speaker? Or . . . could it possibly be him? *No. Why would he be sitting up there?*

She moved her focus to the stained-glass windows several seats over from the young man. Light streamed through the panes of lavender, blue, and green accentuating the blue upholstery of the chairs on the stand. Her singing tapered off to a mere whisper as she continued to take in her surroundings and marvel at their contrast to the rented buildings where she'd attended church back in Germany.

After the opening exercises, Karin stood with the Smiths and prepared to go to Sunday School class. Before she even moved from the pew, the young man left his seat on the stand and wove his way through the throng toward her.

He reached Karin and extended his hand as she stepped into the aisle. "Hello, I'm Max Adam. And you must be Karin Graeber?"

Flustered, Karin spoke up without thinking. "So you *are* Max. Why . . . were you sitting there?" She pointed to the stand.

"I was looking for you."

"Oh." Karin diverted her eyes to the floor, not knowing whether to be flattered or bothered. The carpet held an interesting pattern of blues and greens. It showed very little sign of wear despite the multitude of feet walking around her.

"And is this your Mutter?"

His question brought Karin's head up. "Oh, ja." She turned around and motioned to Mutti and then to Max. "Uh, Mutti . . . this is the young man from Germany Christine wrote about," she said in German.

Mutti took Max's outstretched hand and shook it.

Max turned his attention back to Karin. "So . . . what part of Germany did you come from?

Everyone over here asked that. "Dresden," Karin said, tired of the question. She'd considered that area as where she was from. All those refugee camps in West Germany were never really home.

"Oh, East Germany. *Da haben sie vicles mitgebacht!*"

What a delight to hear her own language. A thrill surged through her—until his words sunk in. Why would she come bringing many riches? "No, no," Karin responded with some confusion.

Max's smile faded, and his eyebrows scrunched upward. "You didn't?"

"*Wir haben nichts mitgebracht.* No, we're very poor," she reemphasized in English. She wasn't sure if she wanted to get to know this fellow. Was he expecting her to bring him a gift? Like she already had a connection to him . . . or something?"

Max's face reddened. "Oh, did I say *mitgebracht*? I meant to say *mitgemacht*. I'm so sorry for the misunderstanding." The flush in his face faded slightly, but his eyes held a look of seriousness. "Having lived in East Germany it's a more fitting question, as you must have had many bad experiences. And suffered much."

There it was again, that expectation of suffering. Should she respond truthfully or give the answer everyone seemed to expect—including Max.

"Ja, well, I do not know about that. But I do think we had better head to class before it starts." Karin hurried toward Sylvia, who appeared to be waiting for her and Mutti at the back of the chapel.

Max accompanied Karin down the hallway and into a large classroom filled with rows of chairs with padded seats. Karin contemplated the niceties of the church building as she took a seat. The trivial thoughts got bumped aside as Karin tried to listen to the teacher. It took a concerted effort to concentrate on all those English words.

She gave in and let her mind wander to the young man sitting next to her. He was a fellow German, a member of the Church, and handsome. Definitely an enticing combination. But finding a man was not her focus right now.

CHAPTER 32

KARIN WISHED SHE HADN'T AGREED to meet with Max tonight. Last Sunday she hadn't known Christine and Tom would be able to get here this quickly. But here they stood in the Smiths' living room, extracting myriad emotions from everyone there.

"You're here; you are really here," Christine said in German. "I feared I'd never see you again." Christine squeezed so tightly, Karin could barely breathe. "Has the last year been as long for you as it has for me?"

"Perhaps longer," Karin responded, soaking in the joy of reunion despite Christine's vice-like hug.

Christine let go of Karin and hugged Mutti again. "How have you managed?" Christine released Mutti, took a step back, and stared at Mutti and Karin, scanning them from head to toe. She shook her head. "Not as well as I'd hoped."

Christine's husband, Tom, stepped forward. He'd stayed pretty much in the background until now. "I'll make sure we rectify that," he said in German laced with an American accent.

"We're fine," Karin said and meant it. "We'll manage!" She then bit her lip, realizing she had spoken with a little too much boldness to this brother-in-law she hardly knew.

Christine's raised eyebrow expressed doubt. She turned to Tom and spoke softly in English and then turned her attention back to Mutti and Karin. "Go change your clothes. Tom and I would like to take you out to dinner tonight."

"Yes, we would," Tom said. "It's my favorite chuck wagon restaurant. You'll never believe all the food there is to choose from, all in one restaurant. And you can eat all you want."

Karin felt conflicted. The last thing she wanted to do was to tell her sister, the person she'd been dying to see for the past year, that she had a previous commitment, that he'd be here in thirty minutes.

Christine gazed at Karin, wrinkling her brow. "What is it?"

"Oh, Christine, believe me there's nothing I'd rather do tonight, but . . ."

"She's got a date," Mutti said.

"Already?" Christine's smile stretched wider than usual. "With the fellow I told you about? Max Adam?"

"That's right," Mutti said. "He seems to be a nice fellow."

"It's not a date," Karin insisted. "He's coming over to give me an English lesson. He is nice, so I think if there was some way I could contact him, tell him I can't make it tonight, he'd understand." Hoping, she turned and looked to the kitchen, where Sylvia and Julie busied themselves with the dishes. "Would Sylvia maybe have a phone number where we could reach him?"

"Don't crush the poor fellow's heart," Tom said, slurring his Rs like a typical American. "I know he's been anxious to meet you for some time." He turned to Christine. "I think it might be best, anyway, if we postpone this celebration dinner until tomorrow night. If I'm exhausted from driving all day, I'm sure you must be twice as tired." He gently placed his hand on Christine's belly.

Karin hadn't noticed until now that her sister's stomach was a little rounder than she would have expected. Happy emotions she couldn't describe swelled inside her. She reached out to Christine.

"Oh, Christine!" Mutti's hands covered her mouth. "You're going to be a Mutter."

"Yes. And you're going to be a *Grossmutter*." Christine's eyes brimmed with moisture. "I just found out a few weeks ago. I didn't tell you sooner . . . well, I knew you were coming, and . . . I wanted to tell you in person." She gathered Karin's hands into hers. Squeezing them, she said, "Tom's right. I am tired. I think if we went tomorrow it would be best for everyone. This way you can tell me about your date . . . along with everything else." She tilted her head and scanned Karin up and down. "Is this what you're wearing . . . to meet Max?"

"Ja."

Christine stepped back. "This dress," she said, flinching, "takes what little figure you've got and makes it totally disappear."

"Christine!" Karin felt her face flush. Her sister had changed. "He's simply coming over to help me with my English. That's all."

"Still . . . it looks like a dress one would wear if they were going to clean the house . . . not meet a young man."

Karin knew it was a little worn, but it was her favorite dress. She pinched a fold of its faded yellow fabric. Its softness soothed her hurt feelings as it reminded her of attending church back in Germany. "I like this dress. It's not that bad."

"Let me help you choose something more suitable." Christine gave a "wait here" glance to Tom and grabbed Karin by the elbow. "Show me what else you've got."

Karin planted her feet firmly upon the hardwood floor and resisted her sister's pull. "Christine, I'm wearing this." In response to Christine's scrunched forehead and questioning gaze, she added, "My other two dresses are no better. Actually worse."

"Oh." Christine's cheeks reddened. "Of course." She paused as if to think. "Come. I think I might have something that will work."

Karin followed Christine downstairs to Bill's room, where Tom had carried their luggage earlier. Christine pulled something pink from one of the suitcases. With a quick alteration of the waistline with a handful of safety pins, Christine soon had Karin fitted with one of her dresses.

Karin gazed in the bathroom mirror at herself, something she'd rarely done for the past five years in Germany. Was that because she'd never worn anything that warranted a stare at her reflection, or was it because they rarely had a real bathroom as refugees, let alone one with a mirror? The pink dress with white polka dots and collar gave her a confidence she hadn't felt earlier. With the chime of the doorbell, she clung to that confidence, telling herself not to be nervous.

"Karin!" Sylvia's voice echoed down the stairs. "Your young man's here."

He's not my young man!

"You look great." Christine pulled Karin away from the mirror. "Hurry, he's waiting." She led the way up the stairs and then hugged Karin at the top of the steps.

When Christine walked into the living room, Max's voice made Karin stop in her tracks. "Christine! It's so good to see you again. How is Tacoma?" he said.

"I must say it's beautiful up there." Christine offered a quick summary of their move and their hurried trip back to Utah. As Christine chatted with Max, Karin crept closer to the living room. "It's been good talking to you, Max." Christine's voice continued to carry into the kitchen. "Karin should be out shortly. Maybe I should go and see what's keeping her."

"Oh, I forgot a book for Karin's lesson in my car," Max said. "Let me go grab it. Tell Karin I'll be right back."

Karin flattened herself against the ice box, hoping Max wouldn't look in the kitchen and see her on his way out. Part of her was anxious to see Max tonight. A bigger part of her was scared. Why was this simple meeting feeling so difficult? She'd tackled much harder things in Germany. The confidence she'd felt moments earlier was melting away, kind of like the ice inside the white door she leaned against. She let out a weak laugh. This was a new-fangled ice box—one that plugged in and froze its own ice. Everything was so different over here. Like a fellow Max's age owning his own car. How old was he? He was obviously much older than she, having already graduated from university. Was that what made her uncomfortable?

No, age made no difference to her. Mutti was several years older than Pappa. It was she. What could she possibly offer Max? She'd barely even completed her basic schooling.

Why am I thinking about this? He's just helping me learn English. Nothing more.

"What are you doing in here?" Christine nudged Karin toward the living room. "And put a smile on your face."

"Ja, Karin," Mutti said from the living room. "Come in here. I want to see your dress."

"I don't know what any of you are saying," Sylvia said, "but hurry in here."

"Yeah, Karin," Jane said. "I can hear him coming back up the steps."

Karin pressed her lips together and ventured into the living room, wishing she didn't have an audience for Max's arrival. As she glanced at Mutti's, Jane's, and Sylvia's eyes, and even Christine's as her sister clung to the kitchen doorway obviously waiting for Karin to greet Max before going to bed, she saw that they all held a common expression: excitement. That made Karin even more uncomfortable.

The chime of the doorbell jolted Sylvia into action. "Hurry and sit down and loosen up a bit," she said to Karin. "You look like you're expecting the tax man."

Karin didn't know what Sylvia meant, but she sank onto the couch and took a deep breath as Sylvia opened the door.

"Come in, come in," Sylvia said with a sweep of her hand. Max strode inside with a book in hand and side-stepped over to the bookshelf so Sylvia could close the door. He stood there in a crisp pair of dark slacks and a well-pressed short-sleeved shirt that matched the blue of his eyes, stiff as the numerous figurines that decorated two of the shelves behind him.

Christine gave Karin an exaggerated smile. Karin responded back with a timid one. She felt like just another decoration in Sylvia's fancy living room, sitting there silent and stiffer than Max.

Christine turned to Max. "It's been a pleasure talking with you."

"You too." Max inclined his head.

Christine motioned to Mutti to get up out of the wingback chair. "Come downstairs with me."

Mutti rose slowly and followed Christine. "What do you need? I wanted to stay . . ." Her German words faded with her down the stairs.

Karin felt her heart beat faster when Sylvia herded Max to the long couch and sat him down next to her. "We'll be downstairs doing laundry if you should need anything," Sylvia said as she pulled Jane with her into the kitchen.

Max glanced at Karin and back at Sylvia. "Thanks, we'll be fine. Perhaps later we'll go for a drive if Karin agrees." He looked again at Karin, this time with a twist to his smile. "She might need a break from instruction—I hope to have her speaking like an American in record time."

"Good, then she can give *you* lessons." Sylvia smiled.

Max chuckled. "I know, I know, my accent is strong. The fellows at work are always giving me a hard time about it."

As Sylvia and Julie left, Karin realized she could no longer play a room ornament. He'd expect conversation. She shifted her weight on the couch, moving slightly farther away from Max. She turned to face him. "*Eine fahrt auf's land?*"

"Yes, but I insist you say it in English . . ."

About half an hour into her lesson, Karin was surprised when she found herself feeling at ease. Max's calm manner, paired with his patience, made it easy for her to learn. "You are a good teacher," she said in her English, barely louder than a whisper.

"Danke," Max responded, his chin dipping down.

Karin sighed. "Okay, what should I say next?"

"Anything that comes to mind." Max rubbed his hands together. "I don't want to be a mean teacher. Heaven knows I had my fill of them as a child in Germany. I imagine you did too."

"Ja." Memories flooded Karin's mind. "Maybe that is why I did not like school."

"You didn't?"

"No, I struggled." Karin remembered how she longed for a good friend after Greta moved, never really fitting in after her decision to not join the Young Pioneers. "Maybe it was because of a lack of friends. Or maybe because I missed so much school after we escaped. We were constantly moving from place to place. I had little training after I graduated, like Christine . . . and I am sure you did." She thought about the car out front, the job he must have to pay for such a luxury, and was positive he had lots of schooling. Feelings of inadequacy crept back. She didn't like it—she wasn't used to such feelings.

"I was fortunate to be able to continue on to engineering school," Max said. "One of the rare good things that I can attribute to Hitler. Because of it, I was able to attend university here in the States—after my mission."

"Oh, you served a mission?" Karin wanted to hear more. "In Germany, I presume—because you knew the language?"

"No." Max let out a half-hearted laugh. "I was originally called to Germany. Unfortunately, because I wasn't officially an American citizen yet, I couldn't get back in the country if I left. So they sent me to Minnesota."

"Oh." Karin still found that interesting. But then, everything he said was interesting. She hoped he found her end of the conversation at least somewhat engaging. "Christine trained in office work," she said, thinking that might make a good topic for conversation. "She would have never met Tom if she hadn't."

"Telling stories will be good," Max said. "Tell me more. But in English."

Karin switched her brain to English mode. "Would you like to hear how Christine met Tom?"

"I'm sure it's an interesting tale. Maybe later." Max stood. "I'd rather hear your story of how you escaped and ended up coming to America." His eyes moved from her face momentarily to the front window. A blue car sat at the curb reflecting the evening sun off its polished curves. "It's so delightful outside. How about we continue our English lessons while taking our 'drive in the country'? You can tell me all about it while we enjoy the forest. Around here people usually take rides up the canyon rather than out in the country. Would that be okay?" He extended his hand.

Karin took it and let him help her to her feet. "I would like that," she said. The lure of a car ride made her determined to push away her fears of inadequacy. She wanted nothing more at the moment than to enjoy such a treat, especially with Max. If only it was merely a drive in a car—no stories attached. She was certain her story was not nearly as exciting as the anticipation his eyes held. And to tell it in English would only make it worse.

Together, they walked to the front door. He opened it and motioned for her to walk out first. Max's car caught her eye and extracted an inaudible gasp from her. The evening sun kissed the foliage of the neighbor's trees, presenting vivid and varied shades of green as a backdrop to the polished dark blue and shiny chrome of the car. A flood of emotions caught her off guard. Moisture blurred her vision. They were such simple little things—a blue car, a pretty street, going for a drive with a young man who appeared to like her—silly things, when she thought about it, to get emotional about. She took in a deep breath and kept her feet in pace with Max's.

Upon reaching the curb, Max opened the car's passenger door, closing it for her once she settled into her seat. While Max walked around to the other side of the car, Karin's mind scanned her memories, grappling to extract the more exciting parts of her life so she could share them.

When Max hopped into the car, Karin found her ideas of what to talk about smothered by a sense of awkwardness. The narrow front seat had her sitting closer to him than she'd expected. She scooted as close to the door as possible.

Max started the engine and drove down the street. He pointed out a few landmarks, describing the difficulties he'd had adjusting to a country seemingly untouched by the war. His openness helped set her at ease, and she relaxed and enjoyed the ride.

They reached the mouth of a canyon within minutes. The warm summer air blew through the windows, brushing against Karin's face, teasing her nose with a musty scent mixed with pine. "May I roll down the window more?" she asked, a bit sheepish.

"Of course."

She rolled it down all the way and stuck her head out to enjoy the experience. "I rarely rode in a car in Germany," she said as she pulled her head back in.

"Yes, life was very different over there." Max had slipped back into speaking German. He leaned his elbow in the opened window, holding the upper portion of the door. He looked relaxed. "I love hearing of the difficulties my countrymen went through—rather their triumph over their adversities." He looked over to her. "So now, tell me about your escape. I really want to hear it. When did you first decide to go through with it? Were you scared?"

"Well," Karin said in German, thinking if he could speak it so could she. "I'd actually thought about escaping when I heard that my best friend and her mother had escaped. I was only ten then—there wasn't much I could do about it. I never even told Mutti about my ideas. I was afraid to. So I kept them to myself and then forgot about them. That was until my Aunt Anna went to the doctor for some ailment." Karin stuck her hand back out the window. She let the rush of air lift it up and down as she gave Max a simplified version of their escape and years in the refugee camps.

"Amazing," Max responded after she'd finished. "What strength that must have taken."

Karin ducked her head. "Things really were not that bad." She lifted her head and looked at Max. "Enough about me. What about you? Christine mentioned you served in the war." Her eyes stared at the road ahead as she did some calculations. "How old *are* you?" She clapped a hand over her mouth. "Sorry, that was not very polite."

Max chuckled. "It's okay. I was quite young when I was drafted in '44—sixteen. And I was fortunate. Many of my comrades were fourteen. It was near the end of war, and Hitler was desperate for men, so he stooped to using boys." He stared at the road ahead with a faraway look in his eyes. "I recognized Hitler early on for the evil man he was. I was eleven. That's when Hitler's people took my little brother, Harold, away."

"Why would they take your brother away?" Karin imagined how she would have felt if the Russians had taken Christine.

"He was mentally handicapped. They said they could make him better. I liked Harold the way he was. He didn't talk. But he hummed lots of songs. Beethoven was his favorite. He could recreate an entire score just from listening to it once on the radio. And he loved me. I had no doubt about that." Max's eyes watered up. "But they didn't make him better. They killed him. They used him as a guinea pig for experiments."

Karin's heart felt as though it had broken into pieces. "Oh, I am so sorry for you and your family. That's just awful."

"Awful? Ja, that's a fitting description of life in Germany under Hitler's rule." He glanced at her and nodded. "And life for you under Russian and communist rule after the war." He diverted his eyes back to the road. "It's so nice to finally meet a girl from Germany. The American girls I've courted couldn't seem to relate with the horrors I lived through. I did date a German girl when I first arrived here in the States. But she'd immigrated to America when she was three, before the war got bad. She was no different than the American girls."

"Enough about that." Max's face reddened. "Where were we before I got off track?"

"You were telling me about your brother, the one who died," she said while thinking about all the girls Max had dated.

Max continued on, telling of his brother, of being sent away from his family at age fourteen to work on a farm, of his numerous brushes with death, and of his dilemma with having to join the army and serve a man he knew was evil. His stories fascinated Karin, touched her, and made her ache for him. Sure, her story might be "interesting," but her life in Germany didn't compare to his. Hers had been relatively easy.

She realized she liked Max. The more she was with him, the more she wanted to be with him. Did he feel the same about her?

CHAPTER 34

THE LAST THREE WEEKS HAD flown by for Karin. She'd started a job as a nanny a week after moving in with the Smiths. Monday through Friday she spent her days with two delightful little girls, ages two and four, while their mother went to work. She could walk to their family's house in ten minutes. Practically every other evening she spent with Max. Plus, she saw him at church on Sundays. Her English improved daily, she never felt hungry, and today she'd make her first payment toward what she and Mutti owed the Smiths. And Max was taking her to an amusement park tonight—something she'd never done before.

And yet her shoulders felt weighed down more than they ever had before. What was wrong with her?

She tried to brush the uncomfortable feelings to the side, turning quickly in front of the full-length mirror in the basement bathroom. Her new plaid twirl skirt lived up to its name, fanning out into a circle. It looked sharp with the matching blue sweater Christine had insisted she purchase to go with the skirt. Karin hoped Max would like how she looked in her new outfit. She quit twirling so she could finish her hair. He would be ringing the doorbell in a matter of minutes.

Mutti met Karin in the hall at the bottom of the stairs. "Oh, Karin, you look lovely," she said in German. "Is Max coming over for another English lesson tonight?"

"No lesson tonight. But my next one, you really should come. You need to learn English, Mutti, you really do."

"Oh, I'm doing fine." Mutti wagged her hand at Karin. "I'm learning a little bit of English here and there. Besides, you don't need me there, getting in the way." Mutti smiled wider than usual. "So if no lesson tonight, where are you going?"

The doorbell rang. Karin knew the Smiths weren't home. She raced up the stairs, answering Mutti over her shoulder as she ascended. "To a place where you go on rides. It's called an amusement park."

"Rides?" Mutti paused and then added, "Well, have fun."

"We will," Karin said as she turned the doorknob.

Max greeted Karin with his usual bright-eyed grin. As he accompanied her down the front steps, he said, "You look very nice tonight. Is that a new outfit?"

"Yes, I am glad you like it. Christine helped me pick it out. I cannot believe how many things there are to choose from at the stores here."

"It appears you're adjusting to the American way of life a lot easier than I did," Max said with what sounded like a little questioning in his voice.

"Oh." Karin chewed on her lip, unsure what he meant by that. She let him open the door to his car, and she slid into the passenger seat without saying anything.

The warm summer air blew through the open windows, causing Max to speak up once they sped down the road. "I don't imagine you've been on an *Achterbahn* before, have you? Over here they call them 'roller coasters.'"

"Roller coasters," Karin repeated the words. "No, I have not," she responded. Embarrassment from his first comment kept her from saying more—she *was* adjusting to the American way of life quite easily, she had to admit. Did that bother him?

Max rambled on in English. Distracted by her thoughts, Karin didn't follow much of what he was saying. He paused, snatching her out of her musings. "Lagoon, that's the name of the park. It has a nice big one," he said, more slowly than usual.

"Big one?" Karin glanced at him.

"Roller coaster. I've ridden it once or twice." Max hesitated. "It's lots of fun." He looked over at her. "I hope you'll enjoy it."

After a lengthy silence, he said, "Karin, have I done something wrong?"

"No."

"So . . . then . . . why are you so quiet?" Max looked puzzled.

"Oh." Karin brought her fingers to her mouth. "Sorry." She switched back to German so she could better explain her feelings. "My mind is elsewhere, thinking about what you've said."

"What have I said?" Max responded in German and with a note of apology.

"That I'm adjusting easily to America." Karin winced. "Does that . . . bother you?"

Max let out a short laugh. His grin returned, wider than ever. "No, of course not. You had me worried there for a moment. I really thought I'd done something horribly wrong."

"So you don't care that I'm just like all those other girls you've dated?"

"If that were the case, no, I wouldn't care." Max looked her in the eye as he took her hand. "But, Karin, you are nothing like those other girls. You are strong, you are resilient, you are close to God. Those wonderful traits didn't just happen—you earned them surviving in East Germany."

Karin gulped from the tingle that moved through her hand. "You make it sound like my life has been hard," she said, forcing her composure to return. "I didn't go through a fraction of what you did. Life was not necessarily pleasant back there, but it was *not* that difficult."

Max rolled his eyes. "Sometimes we're so close to something we don't see it for what it really is."

Karin paused momentarily, mulling his words over, and then let out a weak laugh. "Ja, maybe so." Her mind raced back. "That must have been the case in Wieslet," she said without thinking as the pieces fit together.

"And . . ." Max gave her hand a tug as if to pull more information out of her.

She glanced at Max and then stared out the front window as she recalled more of the story. "Wieslet was one of the refugee camps in West Germany. I thought I was just fine. Obviously others didn't think so."

"Really? Tell me more."

"It's not all that exciting of a story," Karin responded, still in German.

Max inclined his head in her direction and raised an eyebrow.

"I'm sorry," she said. "I'll let you decide for yourself."

"That's better."

"After we were airlifted out of Berlin, as I mentioned before, we had no place to go, so we were placed in a refugee camp. For the next couple of years, we moved about ten times, from one refugee camp to another. Apparently, there were many of them scattered throughout West Germany."

"I imagine there'd have to be. How else would they be able to take care of everyone fleeing from the East?" Max let go of her hand and turned the car from the highway onto a side road. In the distance, the white wooden lattice of a huge roller coaster loomed above a parking lot of cars. "We're almost there." He pointed ahead. "Sorry. Continue. And try speaking English again. You were doing so well."

"Really?" Karin would have preferred German but continued in English, glad he thought she was doing so well. "Ja . . . so, the refugee camp in Wieslet was close to a large Lutheran church. The church had a hospital run by nuns. No, not a hospital, more like a place to heal from illness. They went around in an old bus and picked the most sickly and skinny children from each camp, took them back to their church, and fattened them up. From our camp, they picked me and this other girl. I remember thinking, 'Why did they pick me?' At first I did not want to go. But I went anyway and was gone for almost twelve weeks. I guess things must not have been that good there—and at the other camps—if I was skinny enough to be picked. I just do not remember it being that bad. The only thing I remember being bad was that Christine left for her mission while I was gone and I never got to say good-bye. That upset me."

Karin rubbed her forehead and then covered her face with her hand. "I am sorry. I am not making much sense, am I?"

Max pulled the car into a parking stall. The big white roller coaster filled the view out the front window. "No, actually you are making perfect sense." He turned off the key and reached over his seat into the back of the car.

As Max shuffled through items on the back seat, Karin rambled on, as if grasping for sense in what she'd said, determined to see what Max saw.

"I guess it was a good thing Christine got called on a mission. She was just twenty, by the way. But they needed her office skills in the mission home there in Germany. That is where she met Tom. He was a missionary, assistant to the president. If she had never met Tom, we would not have had a place to go after I lost my job in the fabric mill. Even though I had dreamed of it ever since we fled East Germany, America was a bit of a move for us. And it was a hurried, unplanned move. But all in all, I know this is what is best for Mutti and me." Karin gazed out the window at white wooden slats, not really looking at them but focusing on the low points of her past that usually led to high points. "It is interesting how the Lord works."

"Yes, it is," Max said as he retrieved a book and settled back into his seat. "He doesn't usually save us from the storm, but He does provide the comfort to weather its fury." He flipped through the pages of what Karin recognized to be the Book of Mormon. "Here, let me show you a perfect example."

Having obviously obtained his destination, he smoothed the book open, revealing a chapter in the book of Mosiah. He looked Karin in the eye. "Are you familiar with the story of Alma? How, after hearing and believing the words of the prophet Abinadi, he repents and tells others of Abinadi's message and gains a host of followers?"

"Ja, kind of."

"Remember how Alma and his followers were a righteous, God-fearing society, who, by no fault of their own, were taken captive by the Lamanites? Heavy taxes were forced upon them and guards set around their city so they couldn't leave. When they cried out to God for help, the Lamanites punished them and forbade them to pray. And what did Alma's people do?"

"They prayed anyway—silently, in their hearts," Karin responded, biting down on a smile as the story came back to her.

"Correct. Of course, the Lord heard their pleas. Let me read that part." Max placed his finger on the page. ". . . *the voice of the Lord came to them in their afflictions, saying: Lift up your heads and be of good comfort, for I know of the covenant which ye have made unto me; and I will covenant with my people and deliver them out of bondage. And I will also ease the burdens which are put upon your shoulders, that even you cannot feel them upon your backs, even while you are in bondage; and this will I do that ye may stand as witnesses for me hereafter, and that ye may know of a surety that I, the Lord God, do visit my people in their afflictions.*

And now it came to pass that the burdens which were laid upon Alma and his brethren were made light; yea, the Lord did strengthen them that they could bear up their burdens with ease."

"Don't you see it, Karin?" Max said with an extra gleam in his eyes. "This is exactly what happened to you."

It was like curtains parted from her eyes and she could see clearly through a window into her life back in Germany. She remembered that night in the cellar with vivid detail, bombs exploding closer than ever before, and then having to move to Uncle Richard's house in the country because they had nowhere else to go. But Wittgensdorf had been a blessing—no bombs, only fields to glean and woods nearby for fuel. Then the Russians came with their reign of brutality. Mutti and Christine managed to remain safe without having to do what Ella and Brunhilde had done. When Liesel came to Pappa's funeral, the Russians had gone after her. It was nothing but a miracle that kept them from finding her—or when they looked into the dog house when Karin went hiding with Mutti and Christine after Pappa died. Pappa's death. That had been horrible, so senseless. But Mutti's dream helped them all through it—also knowing Pappa died with his family around him, not out in the trenches of the war. That's how he would have wanted it. And she couldn't forget their escape from East Germany. It could have turned out disastrously. Or they could have remained in East Germany. Karin knew things had only gotten worse over there. Aunt Anna's dream had truly been a tender mercy from God.

For moments at a time, the memories tightened her stomach with their vividness. Then that familiar warmth flooded through her, washing the uncomfortable feelings away. She held on to the good feelings, as she had so many times before. Cradling them to her bosom, she basked in their comfort like she'd done when hugging her doll Hilda no longer soothed her.

Without a doubt, she knew God had strengthened her, enabled her to bear the burdens of East Germany—and West Germany—with ease, just as He had done with the people of Alma. And now that she was here, in a land free of those kinds of struggles, the Lord didn't need to lift the burdens from her back. Just help her wade through them.

Pressure filled her chest. It felt as though her chest was expanding to make room for the flood of gratitude inundating her. "You are right," she responded. "That must have been what happened to me." The realization left her with a strength all its own. The trials that lay ahead for her in this new country paled in comparison to what she'd already experienced. A deep desire, to forge ahead and take on whatever her new life in this new country presented, filled her. Of course there would be ups and downs, but she could handle them. She knew where to go for help.

Max closed the book and set it on the seat between him and Karin. "Wonderful! With that settled, are you ready to take on the roller coaster with me?" He pointed to the massive structure that filled the front window of the car with its white lattice of wooden hills and valleys.

"Ja, I am."

ABOUT THE AUTHOR

CAROLYN TWEDE FRANK IS A fan of history, with its wealth of inspiring heros and pernicious villians. Somehow, a touch or a ton of history seems to weave its way into each novel she writes.

When Carolyn is not working on a novel, she fills her spare time with grandchildren, gardening, and renovating houses. She currently lives in Kaysville, Utah, where she runs a small business out of her home, which affords her the luxury of being an author.